# The Common Thread

## By the Author

Agnes

The Common Thread

# The Common Thread

*by*

Jaime Maddox

2014

**THE COMMON THREAD**



**ISBN 13: 978-1-62639-190-1**

This Trade Paperback Original Is Published By
Bold Strokes Books, Inc.
P.O. Box 249
Valley Falls, NY 12185

First Edition: September 2014



---

**Credits**
Editor: Shelley Thrasher
Production Design: Stacia Seaman
Cover Design by Sheri (graphicartist2020@hotmail.com)

Acknowledgments

So much of who I am and who we all are is completely out of our control. It's fate, or luck, or destiny, but it has nothing to do with us and everything to do with the environment into which we were born. So, I would first like to express my eternal gratitude to the God or Goddess who sent me to the right place, at the right time, and to the right family. I feel rather fortunate that it's all turned out okay.

It's been a while since I've called Philadelphia home, and although I can still find my way to Dalessandro's for a cheesesteak, I needed a little help with navigating the landscape of today's Philly. Thanks to my BFF, Jim Renna, for all his help in that regard. My alpha readers are two dear friends, Nancy McLain and Margaret Pawling, so not only do they help me with my writing, they do it over lunch. My notes have been, on occasion, written on cocktail napkins. Thanks to them for their encouraging critiques. Much thanks and appreciation also to Carsen Taite for reviewing the courtroom scene to make it more realistic.

The staff at BSB is professional and make this easy, and I would like to thank them all—Rad, Sandy Lowe, Cindy Cresap, Stacia Seaman, and everyone else for the their work on getting the design and printed pages ready to go. I had no idea in my mind about this cover, so thanks to Sheri for her vision. Most especially, thanks to Shelley Thrasher for her editing prowess. She's like a shot of lidocaine to ease the pain.

Finally, all my love and gratitude go to the three people who share my house and continue to tolerate me while I write and travel to faraway places in my mind. Carolyn, Jamison, and Max really rock.

Yankee: A dedication to you could be longer than the book itself, so I'll get to the point. Thanks for keeping it interesting. I love you.

# Chapter One
# Shots in the Dark

Billy Wallace rolled off Katie Finan and let out a loud groan. A well-placed knee to the groin had him reconsidering the direction his hands had been taking. They were now off Katie's breasts and hanging before him, a belated attempt to protect his manhood.

"What the fuck are you doing?" Katie screamed at him, as the adrenaline coursing through her veins roused her from sleep. In the span of a single breath she was transformed from unconscious to wide-awake, an ability developed during her old days on the streets. She'd spent enough time in bad places to learn self-preservation skills like sleeping lightly and groin kicks. Predators often struck in the dark of night, coming for her money or her food, or something else. Like Billy, she often sent them away moaning in pain. Often, but not always.

Pulling her knees to her chest, Katie flipped her head and threw her mane of black hair over her shoulder. As she leaned against the bedroom wall she studied Billy. What was she going to do about him? Placing the fifth finger of her right hand into her mouth, she began to gnaw at the nail.

He'd knocked on her door a few nights earlier, fresh out of jail and with no place to spend the night. A year had passed since she'd last seen him, almost five since they'd last shared a bed, but how could she refuse him a place to sleep? Billy had taken her in when she was homeless, fed her and clothed her and kept her safe. He'd really asked nothing from her then, not even sex, and rarely asked for anything over the years. He usually had an ample supply of cash, every dollar illegally earned from selling drugs, and when things were going exceptionally well, he showered unwanted gifts on her and their children, trying to atone for all his inadequacies as a father and partner.

He propped himself against the dresser, breathing deep. Even doubled over, he was a big man, almost twice her size, and his presence seemed to fill the small room. Other than the dresser supporting him, the only other piece of furniture was the double bed, its blankets now on the narrow strip of floor separating them. She understood why people feared him. If he peeked up, his face would be handsome, but his good looks hid a lot of ugliness inside. His temper was well known, and in an instant his smile could turn menacing. No one crossed Billy, except for Katie. She'd never accepted attitude from him, had demanded to be treated with respect, and to her, he'd never been anything but kind.

Suddenly, she felt a twinge of guilt for the plans she'd been making. She'd found another apartment here in Philadelphia, more modern, in a better neighborhood, with a bigger yard for the kids and a cozy porch overlooking it. In a few days she'd sign the lease, making a move that was as spiritual as it was physical. She was leaving this life, and all she'd been here in this neighborhood, and moving on. She'd never look back. If Billy had been released from jail any later, he'd have come here looking for her and found the apartment vacant, or with new tenants who'd have turned him away into the night.

Was that so wrong? They weren't together as a couple, and he'd never been a great boyfriend or father. In fact, she'd already really left him five years earlier, when she moved out of his place. Tired of drug deals and parties, infidelity and broken promises, and wanting a better life for her children, she'd found her own apartment. It had been a big blow to his ego, but he'd been man enough to allow her to walk away without a fight, admitting to her that she was doing the right thing for their kids.

Katie had spent the years since then gaining a confidence and independence she didn't have when she first met him. A job as a nursing assistant at the clinic gave her an income and helped her to develop self-esteem. Her coworkers were intelligent people—physicians, nurses, x-ray technicians, business women—and they spoke and dressed and acted in a manner Katie had forgotten existed. It came back to her, though—proper English, respectful interactions, manners, and dress—and after a few months at the clinic she felt as if she'd never left home.

Over the course of their time apart, Katie had slowly come to understand that she wasn't in love with Billy. Now that she was beginning to understand what real love could be like, she was beginning to wonder if she'd ever really loved him at all. Billy had been good to her when she needed someone to protect and shelter her. He'd taken care of her, and she cared for him, but she now questioned whether she'd mistaken much-needed affection and attention for love.

After leaving home and hitting the streets, Katie had never really been close to anyone. Her school friends were living lives far different from hers and couldn't begin to understand the world beyond their clean homes and high-ranked schools, the world of violence and crime, drugs and alcohol that had become Katie's. After Katie's first brushes with the law, the parents of her friends had cut off the contact that had for years sustained her. At the age of fifteen, she'd found she was truly on her own.

With her support structure gone, Katie developed new relationships. These new friends didn't play music on the piano or field hockey after school. They didn't study and work on school projects. They drank and did drugs together, and when she was intoxicated with one drug or another, that camaraderie was all Katie needed.

She couldn't even remember her first sexual encounter. She recalled getting high with a bunch of people at a party and, upon awakening the next morning, felt the telltale pain and bleeding that told her she was no longer a virgin. She'd probably been raped, and she really didn't even care. All she wanted was to get high again.

Over the years before she met Billy, she'd slept with a parade of men. If they shared their drugs, she'd share her body. Only after she became pregnant with her daughter did she clean up her act, realizing the responsibility growing daily within her. Wanting to become the kind of mother she'd had, she gathered all her courage and pulled herself together. Still, she remained isolated. She'd learned not to trust, and in the world in which she lived, that meant keeping to herself. Sure, she knew the parents of her children's friends, and people at church, and her neighbors. At work, she liked everyone, and they all liked her, but none of them had ever really gotten to know her. Not until a few months ago, when Jet Fox began working at the clinic.

Just the thought of Jet brought a smile to her face and filled her heart with happiness. Katie felt she could talk about anything and laugh about nothing with her. Jet was the first friend she'd made in fifteen years, and now Katie was beginning to develop feelings of a deeper nature, feelings that both thrilled and terrified her.

Katie thought back to that first date with Jet. Was it only two months earlier? After an April shower caused a power outage, closing their clinic for the day, she and Jet had decided to share lunch. They talked for three hours, and Katie found her spirits flying as she rushed to the kids' school to pick them up that day. Where had the time gone? Katie didn't know, she only knew it was the most delightful lunch she'd ever shared, the most pleasant time she'd spent since childhood.

Since then, Katie and her children had spent some part of every weekend with Jet, picnicking in the park and exploring Penn's Landing, driving to Rehoboth, walking and playing Frisbee on the beach, hiking in the mountains, cooking out at Jet's apartment, and watching movies on her television. Katie's children, Chloe and Andre, adored Jet as much as Katie did, but lately she'd begun to understand that there was something more stirring within her than the attraction of friendship, and as she looked at Billy, she knew that something was called love.

Katie knew that Jet was a lesbian, and Jet's sexuality was causing Katie to reconsider everything she'd ever thought of herself. Sex had never been important to her before; it was just something she did to make other people happy. She didn't need feelings or attraction. She'd never felt desire, until she began to lie in bed at night and imagine Jet next to her, with her mouth and hands on her body. Then, Katie lost her senses, and when she slipped her hands into her panties she found herself wet and ready. Thinking of Jet she could make herself come. She was beginning to seriously believe she might be a lesbian, too.

"It's fuckin' hot!" Billy complained as he stood. Not surprisingly he'd decided to forget she'd assaulted him.

It wasn't really that hot, but it had rained and the humidity was high, making it seem much worse than it was. And the small apartment had no ventilation, sandwiched as it was between two others on the street, where no wayward breeze ever blew through.

"Baby, when we get your inheritance, we should buy an air conditioner and a whole house to go with it." He was standing in the doorway of the twelve-by-twelve-foot room, his large frame taking up an enormous amount of Katie's personal space, and even though the lights in the room were off, the glow of the streetlight through the front window allowed her to see his smiling face.

His comment made her uneasy, and she shifted her position to look at him, challenging him. He was smiling, attempting to charm her, but that tactic had ceased working years earlier. Katie was moving because of the inheritance. It would give her the means, for one thing. But even if she did nothing with it, just kept the money saved for her children, she couldn't trust Billy with it. He'd stolen from her before—not actually taking her money, but borrowing it with promises to return it when things turned his way. Yet they never did turn, and she knew if she allowed him he'd spend every last penny she had.

"Billy, you're not getting any money from me." It suddenly occurred to her that his release from jail might have something to do with the fact that her thirtieth birthday was just days away. That was the day Katie would receive the balance of the trust established for her when her mother died. Could he have somehow arranged to get out of jail so he could swindle her, spend this last installment like he'd spent the others? That money had been for Katie's expenses while she was in college: enough for an apartment, food, clothing, as well as books and tuition. She'd seen little of it, though—Billy had used it for payments on a sports car that the police later confiscated.

The judge had arranged the trust to be distributed in small amounts when she was a teen, then in larger allotments when she was in college, with the balance issued on her thirtieth birthday. Katie was never quite sure how much money was there—it was all so confusing. There was no life-insurance policy, no retirement plan, no savings. Her parents had been a struggling middle-class couple when her mom was killed, trying to pay the mortgage and Katie's tuition at a Catholic school, car payments and cable bills and still save enough for a few days of vacation each summer at Wildwood, New Jersey. No, there was no savings. The money came from the lawsuit her father had filed against the delivery company whose truck had killed her mother. The judge, in his wisdom, had mandated the award be put into the trust, for he had concerns about her dad's ability to keep the money safe for Katie. He had received a small award, too, but the majority of the money went to Katie. When all the deductions were added up—attorney and trust-fund fees and prior payments—she no longer had any idea what was left of the three hundred thousand dollars she'd been paid to make up for the loss of the only person in the world who mattered to her. Her lawyer managed the trust for her, but she didn't feel comfortable talking to him. Bruce Smick had been a friend of her mother, and Katie was ashamed for him to know how she'd screwed up her life. Although he obviously had her best interests in mind, it would have been far better to deal with an anonymous and uncaring stranger who had no ruler with which to measure how far she'd fallen.

For years she'd dreamed of buying a house with her birthday money, the kind she grew up in, in a working-class neighborhood where gardens with flowers bordered every finely manicured lawn. It wouldn't be a big house, but it would have a big kitchen, where she and her children could hover over school projects and homework. It would have three bedrooms—one for her, one for Chloe, and one for Andre. Her children needed their own rooms. They were getting too old to share such intimate space. And just maybe her friend Jet would sleep over on occasion. She hated when Jet came to this house, seeing the weathered houses and littered lawns that surrounded hers, and the people in the streets who monitored her movements as she came and went. So they spent most of their time at Jet's apartment, in a neighborhood just a few miles and a whole world away.

When she got her money, she'd pay a first and last month's rent, and a security deposit. If she had the money for those fees, she would have already left this place. Soon, though, she would. Just a few more days.

Once she was settled in her new apartment, she'd take her time and look around for the house she wanted, and then, in a few months or a year, she'd be a homeowner. Surely she had enough money left in the trust for a down payment. Her job at the clinic was solid, and she could get a loan for the rest. She'd gotten a car loan and paid it off promptly, and she paid her single credit-card balance monthly. Her credit scores were excellent.

If she had enough money after she purchased her house, she

planned to buy furniture, too. If not, that was okay. Her apartment's furnishings were fine, though not luxurious. She just never seemed to have enough money left over to splurge on items like a new bed, when her kids needed jackets and fresh fruit and piano lessons. The quality and quantity of her furniture didn't bother her. She managed to make the house a home, even without much to work with. She'd painted the secondhand beds herself, stenciling butterflies on her bed and the alphabet on the kids'. The interior of the house was exceptional, and she painted that as well, accenting the house's fine woodwork, bringing the walls alive with sponging and layers of paint. The children's room was a jungle, literally. She'd painted an elephant, giraffes, lions, and a zebra. The kids loved it.

The cosmetic changes were easy for her. With a little patience and time, Katie could make anything look more attractive. But the structural problems in the house gave her fits. She couldn't replace the drafty windows or the buckling floors, install a toilet that didn't constantly run, or rewire the structure that had barely enough outlets to run the major appliances.

The biggest problem with the house, though, was its location. The neighborhood hadn't been high class when she moved in, but it had been nice. Since then, it had deteriorated. Businesses that closed during the recession were boarded up and prime squatting grounds for the homeless. The drug dealers found shelter in their dark recesses. The same for the prostitutes.

Good people moved out, and less reputable people moved in. Who would move in when she left? In less than a decade, a clean and quiet neighborhood had changed from a respectable place to raise a family to one she'd avoid if she could.

Billy's voice brought her out of her reverie. "I don't need a new place for me, Baby. It's for you and the kids."

Katie fought to find her courage. She had to tell him her plans. She was leaving, and he wasn't coming with her. It would be Jet sharing the couch for movies and the seat at the dinner table, not Billy. "Billy, I want to talk to you about that. I really do want to move…it's just that—"

"How much you think your house is goin' to cost?" he asked the darkness.

"I don't know. I guess it depends on how big and how nice."

"You think a hundred grand?"

"More, probably. Maybe a hundred and fifty." Why was she having this conversation with him? She was tired, and she just wanted to go back to sleep. Yet her guilt forced from her a cordiality that wasn't genuine.

"How much you got comin'?"

"I really don't know. Maybe a hundred."

"That don't seem like enough for the kinda house you want."

Finally, she'd had enough. It was one thing to make conversation and another altogether to fight the negativity she'd battled for two decades. "It's none of your fucking business!" Besides, she didn't want to tell him her plans, let him know she had good enough credit to get a loan. Then he'd start borrowing off her, and she just couldn't afford that. Her priority was her children, not their father.

"Easy, baby." Unlike her, he didn't raise his voice. He usually didn't. "Don't you worry! Simon's comin' over and we're goin' to talk business. All I need is twenty-five grand, and I'll be set up. In six months, I'll have all the money you need for that house, and enough left over so I can buy a little corner store. Those places rake in cash. Then we'll be on Easy Street."

That was it! The last straw finally broke her resolve to show kindness. Katie leapt forward, on attack, all five feet of her on the offensive, pointing her finger into his bare chest, glaring at him. Even though he towered over her, she wasn't afraid of him. He'd never hit her. "You're out of your mind if you think I'm giving you any more of my money. That's for my house! You and Simon can go rob a bank if you need money, but you're not getting it from me."

As if on cue, the doorbell rang.

"Oh, shush, now. Settle down. Let me go talk to Simon," Billy announced as he turned and disappeared from view.

"Not one penny, Billy," she shouted to his retreating form, but he was already down the hall and heading toward the stairs. If he heard her, he didn't acknowledge it.

She stood and watched until his head disappeared. Grabbing her cigarettes from the dresser, she climbed through the open window and onto the roof that covered the porch. She and Jet were both trying to quit, and they'd been doing well with each other for support. Jet wasn't here now, though, and her frustration with Billy was suddenly too much to bear.

The rough texture of the roof against her feet was familiar, a feeling she'd come to associate with lighting a cigarette. She often came out to smoke, to keep the smell out of the house. It stained the ceilings and made Andre sneeze. Pulling one from the pack, she flicked her lighter and pulled a long, satisfying drag from the filtered end. She held the smoke in her lungs for a moment before exhaling, feeling a fraction of her anger dissipate.

She longed for a joint. When she was as stressed as she felt now, just a puff or two of marijuana would cure her angst. But she couldn't. Because of Billy's prior arrests, she was already a target of the Children and Youth Services caseworker who periodically stopped in to monitor her parenting. If they caught her with drugs, they'd take Chloe and Andre from her. And she could never allow that to happen. Besides, Jet didn't use any. Jet didn't judge her for her past, but she also wouldn't tolerate that kind of behavior in the present. One more reason Katie liked her.

She didn't really need the marijuana, just as she hadn't needed the heroin or cocaine she'd once abused. They'd offered an escape for her, a much needed safe place to get away from the misery of her life. What she needed now was to escape her stress. She needed to manage it, to control it before it controlled her.

Katie was tired. Exhausted, actually. She loved her job and couldn't live without her paycheck, but the forty hours she put in at the clinic didn't leave many for other things. Homework, laundry, shopping, cooking, and just hanging out with her kids all took time. In the end, she sacrificed her sleep, but when she did crawl into bed at night—after cleaning the house and folding the laundry and packing the lunches for the next day—she slept soundly.

Having Billy back in the house was disrupting her routine, and she hadn't slept well in days. She'd retired early tonight, and now she feared falling back to sleep would be difficult. She'd learned the universal truth of motherhood very quickly, when Chloe was a newborn and Billy invited friends over to party late into the night. *No matter what time the mom goes to bed, the kids will still be up early.*

Leaning against the clapboard siding of her north Philadelphia apartment, she pulled her knees up close and studied the street below. Too much activity for ten at night. Girls looking for men, boys looking for men, dealers looking for customers, kids looking for trouble. They were walking, standing, cruising slowly on bikes and in cars, unconcerned about anything but satisfying their own needs. The pedestrian traffic always increased on nights like this, when it was too humid to stay comfortably indoors. No one in this neighborhood had air-conditioned homes. Some of them probably didn't even have homes.

In other neighborhoods people were in bed, their windows closed, soothed by the gentle humming of those cooling machines. Their kids were asleep, too, not running in the dangerous streets. And no drug dealer named Simon Simms had just parked his car next to their house. As she looked down, she could see the roof of his oversized SUV. The car was parked illegally in the alley beside the house, and Katie wished someone in the neighborhood cared.

Tapping the ash off her cigarette, she thought about Simon for a moment. He'd been a part of Billy's life since before she came along, a shadowy figure who always seemed to lead Billy into the fire, then pull him back out before he was too badly burned. Katie knew Simon since she'd been with Billy—almost fifteen years—but she didn't quite understand the scene she'd witnessed—

Suddenly, the unmistakable sound of gunfire interrupted her thoughts. She'd heard it enough in her lifetime to recognize it. Bang! Bang! Two shots rang out in rapid succession, not from the street below her, where a shooting wouldn't have surprised her, but from behind her. In her house.

She jumped to her feet, dropping the lit cigarette, and crouched in the window, preparing to hop through. Her kids were in there, asleep in their room, and she had to get to them to make sure they were safe, to protect them.

As she looked up, about to ease her head through the opening, she screamed at the sight before her. Simon stood at the top of the stairs, a gun in his hand. He looked toward her still form in the window, and before she could scream again, he raised his arm and pointed the gun at her. The shot hit the window frame just above her head, and she jumped back as the wood splintered. She didn't have to look to know he was coming for her. She could hear his heavy footsteps on the wooden floor of the hallway, perhaps fifteen feet from where she stood. She didn't have time to think, just to act, and her survival instinct guided her.

She'd learned in the streets to trust her instincts, and they told her to run. She might have stayed and pleaded with Simon, or tried to rationalize with him. In the past, she'd done that when men with guns came looking for Billy. This time, though, something was different.

Giving no thought to her bare feet or nearly naked body, she ran to the edge of the roof and jumped, landing on her hands and knees about five feet down on the roof of Simon's car. If he didn't kill her, she'd have to thank him for parking there. Another bullet whizzed by her, but it wasn't even close. Turning, she saw he was shooting from the bedroom window, standing inside and leaning out, and from that angle he didn't have much chance of hitting her. She leapt from the car's roof to the hood as glass shattered in the car parked at the edge of the alley.

Like Billy, Simon was a big man, but it wouldn't take him long to negotiate the window, and then she'd make an easy target. She winced as she landed on the broken macadam, the sharp edges cutting the tender flesh of her feet. But she willed her legs to move, pushing them, ignoring the pain, trying to keep close to the wall of the house, in the shadows. She could hear him behind her, and from the sounds she guessed he was now on the roof of his car, but she didn't dare turn to look. A fraction of a second could be the difference between life and death, and she didn't intend to die in this dark alley on this night.

She had to keep moving, to get out of that alley. With her feet bare, she couldn't compete with Simon in a foot race. If she could reach her backyard, though, she could disappear into the shadows, out of sight, out of his line of fire. She knew the alley like the back of her hand. It was where Chloe roller-skated and Andre rode his bicycle, where they kicked a soccer ball and shot baskets. When they were in this alley—or out of the house anywhere—she was with them. Children couldn't be left alone on the streets.

In the dim light of a clouded moon she could make out the lines of each fence, each hedge, and the few garages and storage sheds that lined the route. She could see them even with her eyes closed, though, from all the times she'd chased a ball or child down the path she now ran. She reached the rear of her house, and the light from her kitchen reached out to caress her, briefly exposing her. A loud bang pierced the night, and the bullet lodged in the railing guarding her back-porch steps. She reached the bottom step and another shot rang out, hitting an unseen target in the distance.

*How many bullets in his gun?* She mentally counted the shots. Seven! He had to be running out. If she kept running and he kept missing, maybe she'd be safe.

Making a sharp left turn into the blackness, she zigzagged into her backyard, scraping her arm on the shrubs that formed the border. She trimmed them herself and knew the landscape well enough to negotiate in the dark. Grateful for the cool, soft grass she suddenly found beneath her feet, she picked up speed, hurdling the low brick wall that marked the rear edge of her modest-sized yard.

The bullets had stopped flying. She landed with a thud, but the noise was muted by the unmistakable sound of Simon's SUV screeching behind her. She could see the car's headlights scanning the alley. There was no hedge here, just the low brick wall that marked the property's edge. If he positioned the car in just the right spot, he would have a direct line of sight to her hiding place. The car stopped well before that place though, and she fought to catch her breath as she flattened herself against the wall, counting on the darkness to conceal her position.

His footsteps were heavy, even in the soft grass, and Katie could hear them growing ever closer. Then she heard his voice, chilling, taunting. "Katie! Come out, come out, wherever you are! I know you're out here somewhere. I'm goin' to find you!"

Now she forced herself to be still, afraid that even the noise of breathing might be enough to alert him to her presence. In the silence that followed his threat, she heard a sound. Then a light came on to her left, at the home of her elderly neighbor, Nanette Arlington, and the old woman walked out into the night.

Eighty years old and weighing not much more than a hundred pounds, she was an easy target standing there, illuminated by the bulb above her head. Katie knew that Nan couldn't see into the darkness, but the aging process hadn't affected the woman's hearing.

"Go on," Nan yelled into the dark. "Don't be making any more trouble! I called the police and they're coming, so you just better get goin' before they get here." As if on cue, Katie heard a sound she'd feared most of her life—police sirens. On this night, though, they were like a song to her ears. Simon wasn't stupid enough to stick around and let the police see him.

After a second, Simon's deep laughter broke the quiet. "Katie, I gotta be goin' now. But I'll be back for you. Don't you go talkin' to the cops, or I'll get those kids of yours when I come back." Katie heard him running, and then the car door slammed and his tires squealed as he sped away.

It took a few seconds to control her breathing and will her muscles to stop shaking. As she lay there in the grass, hidden in the shadows, the sirens grew louder as they drew nearer. In another minute, police would flood the area and she'd be safe.

She hadn't had time to think, but now as she sat there, she did. What the hell was going on? Why would Simon shoot at her? Had he shot Billy? Those first two shots had rung out from the first floor, and she hadn't heard a peep out of Billy since Simon's arrival. Either he was incapacitated or dead, but Katie feared it was the latter. Simon had been on a mission tonight, and it wasn't to maim. It was to kill.

At least her children were safe. Simon hadn't lingered on the second floor long enough to find them asleep in their beds, and other than the two shots on the first floor, he hadn't fired except when he'd aimed at her.

She needed to see them, though. She needed to hug them and reassure them that they were fine. She needed their hugs to confirm that she was fine. Jumping up, she was pleased to see that her legs still worked. She turned and ran back through her yard, back to her children. All the gunfire would have awakened them, and they'd be frightened. She'd discussed many safety tactics with them, but never what to do under these circumstances. Hopefully, they were hiding under their bed and not exploring the house. If her suspicions about Billy were correct, she didn't want Chloe and Andre to see him.

As a single parent raising children in a poor neighborhood, Katie faced many challenges. Teaching them was easy, for they were both bright and sweet kids, still at an age where pleasing their mother was a priority. Loving them was as natural as breathing to Katie. If her love could only protect them from the violence and pain the world served as a main course, Katie could rest and sleep at night. But it couldn't.

She didn't trust anyone to care for them. In her time on the streets she'd heard stories of young girls and boys abused by coaches and priests and scout leaders, and she saw the results. Self-esteem shattered, spirits deflated, lives destroyed. That wouldn't happen to Chloe and Andre. She'd spent eight years protecting them, exhausting her body and her mind and her bank account, but it didn't matter. They mattered. She'd do whatever she needed to in order to keep them safe.

As she reached the stairs, sweating, heart pounding, knees shaking, the first police car arrived in the alley, pulling to a stop just where Simon's SUV had been parked toward the front of her house. She could already see the flashing lights of another car, approaching in the alley from the opposite direction.

As she stared into the eerie glare of the police lights, another thought occurred to her. What if the police thought she'd shot Billy? If he was wounded, or dead, would they believe her when she told them Simon had shot him? Or would they look at her criminal record and arrest her, so they could pronounce the case closed?

In thirty seconds, the police would surround her. She didn't have time to get in and out again while dragging two small children. If they caught her, she'd most likely be arrested. Even if the charges were thrown out later, the police would handcuff her now, drag her away while her children cried. Then they'd take them away to foster homes, where evil people might harm them. Or where Simon Simms might find them and make good on his threat.

No, she decided. She couldn't go back in the house, even if it meant abandoning Chloe and Andre. If she was free, she'd find a way to get to them. She'd protect them and keep them safe. But if the police threw her into a jail cell, she'd be powerless. Jumping from the porch, she retraced her steps as the lights from the approaching police vehicle came closer. Running at full speed again, she raced toward the protection of the shadows. After that, she wasn't sure what she'd do, but she'd figure out how to survive. She always did.

If the police had looked they would have seen her racing through the yard, but instead, they pulled directly to the back porch and stopped there. Nan's clothesline, filled with the day's laundry, provided an excellent cover and an excellent opportunity. Katie would need a change of clothing. A woman wandering the streets in a shirt and underwear was bound to draw attention, even in Philadelphia, and she didn't want any attention right now.

How an eighty-year-old woman who lived alone could fill the entire clothesline was a mystery to her, but Katie was happy for the cotton shorts and shirt she borrowed, and most grateful for the socks. The short adventure in the alley had ripped up her feet. Sitting in the grass, she pulled the shorts up over her legs and sucked in her gut. Even though Katie was petite, the shorts were about two sizes too small. She was able to pull and stretch the elastic waist up over her hips. She'd look trashy, but that was better than the alternative—crazy. The top fit a little better. It was still a size smaller than Katie would have liked but a huge improvement on the paper-thin one she'd been wearing. The socks, though, were just right, and as she pulled them onto her tender feet, she wished for a pair of shoes. Then a thought occurred to her. Nan was a fanatically clean housekeeper, and she often kept her Crocs on the porch to prevent tracking dirt into her kitchen. Looking over her shoulder, she crept up the stairs. Sure enough, just next to the door, Nan's shoes sat waiting for her.

She grabbed them and turned, but before she could take a step she was startled by the sound of the door opening behind her. Nan poked her nose through. "Katie, what kind of trouble are you in?" she demanded, her voice a barely audible whisper.

Katie wished like hell she knew the answer.

## CHAPTER TWO
## LOVE AT FIRST SIGHT

A few miles south in center-city, where the buildings were taller and their windows intact, and most of their lobbies patrolled by uniformed doormen, Dr. Nicole Coussart stared angrily at *her* best friend, Dr. Louis Perro. He was sitting across the room, sharing Nic's sofa with *his* apparent new best friend, Rachael Rhodes.

Few people were in possession of the skills needed to detect Nic's mood, for she hid it well. Her well-bred parents had trained her to rein in her emotions, to hide them, to never, ever embarrass herself or others by publicly discussing or displaying the ugly truths meant to be kept hidden. Louis had the ability to read her—that was one of the reasons she loved him—but for the past few hours he'd been too preoccupied with Rae to even notice her.

She'd taken a break from them, making the excuse to prepare drinks in the kitchen, where she wouldn't have to participate in their conversation or laugh at their jokes. The move had done little to improve her mood, and she found herself taking her frustrations out on a bottle of Ketel One vodka. First, she strangled it with her hands in an effort to remove the cap, then slammed it to the counter. When it failed to shatter, she accepted that her consolation would have to wait until later, when they were alone. Then she'd enjoy the pleasure of murdering her former roommate.

As she busied herself preparing drinks in the kitchen, she could hear his laughter drifting in from the next room. It nauseated her. Because both Nic and Rae were gay, Louis had decided to introduce them. After all, weren't all lesbians destined to be great friends? On her best of days, Nic wouldn't have welcomed Rae to share the intimate evening she'd planned with Louis. On this one, which could arguably be considered one of her worst days, she was ready to explode with the rage growing steadily within.

After pouring a generous portion of vodka over the tonic and ice in her glass, Nic vigorously stirred the combination. She added a twist of lime and took a sip and, after assuring herself it was to her liking, an even bigger sip. It immediately calmed her, and she breathed deeply before starting the other two drinks.

Nic wasn't even sure what she was so angry about. Was it that Louis didn't ask before inviting Rae? Or was it just Rae? She was attractive, intelligent, witty, and successful. Perfect, to hear Louis describe her. Fucking perfect. Yet Nic immediately despised her. She couldn't pinpoint one thing about Rae she didn't like—she vaguely disliked everything about her.

From the kitchen counter, Nic could see the two of them sitting close together on her couch, their thighs intimately touching. They were leafing through a photo book Louis had put together from his humanitarian trip to Central America. The trip had been months earlier; hadn't Rae already seen the book? Why was she sitting so close to him, anyway? Was she a lesbian or not?

Pouring two glasses from a previously uncorked bottle of a Jordanian Shiraz, Nic scowled. It had been a totally rotten day, and she just wanted to crawl into bed and pull the blankets over her head. But first she'd suffer through drinks, watching the two of them act like teenagers in love and feeling like the proverbial third wheel. All he seemed to care about was Rae. Did he have some sort of abnormal attraction to lesbians?

She felt a sudden urge to run out of the apartment, but she wouldn't do that—she had to keep up appearances. She'd have a cigarette, instead.

Back in the living room, she handed them their drinks and then escaped to the balcony, cigarettes in hand, and promptly inhaled her first puff. Studying her cuticles, she enjoyed the smoke's calming effect. Her nails were looking better since she'd begun to apply a new chemical to help her stop biting. She detected a hint of growth on the left fifth finger. Progress.

She inhaled again, resting her forearms on the balcony railing, thinking about her rotten day. Her ER shift had started miserably. She hadn't even finished taking report when the first ambulance called. The paramedic unit was bringing in a teenager with a traumatic cardiac arrest. Texting while driving had claimed another victim. The girl's neck was broken and she'd probably died instantly. But the medics had tried, because how could you not try to save a sixteen-year-old? Nic had suspended resuscitation efforts and signed the death certificate just as the girl's frantic parents arrived. She'd had to tell them their daughter was dead.

Later, she'd had to write an incident report admonishing one of the nursing staff for incompetence. By the time she'd finished her shift, everyone had heard the news and none of the nurses were speaking to her. That didn't bother her too much, though. She wasn't in the ER to make friends. She had a job to do, and being nice to her coworkers didn't get it done. She was the doctor, the one ultimately responsible for the patient's care—and the one who would be sued if something went wrong.

After the nursing incident, she'd had a verbal sparring match with the oral surgeon on call. Nic had to threaten to report him to the state medical board to convince him to come in to evaluate a patient with Ludwig's angina. The patient had nearly died of throat swelling while he waited.

Then, it had taken two hours to get the report on a STAT CT scan on a patient with a potentially catastrophic headache. She was surrounded by incompetent idiots! The laziness and poor performance were inexcusable, and she hated that she had to go to war so often just to get her job done. And the girl's death was unforgettable. It had set the tone for the day, and Nicole had never quite recovered. No matter how many times she had to deliver that news, she never found it any easier.

The first anniversary of her first job was still weeks away, and she was already burnt out. It was too late to make a career change now, though. While she was highly qualified to practice in the ER, she was unprepared for any other field.

In spite of it all, though, Nic had smiled as she climbed into her SUV for the two-hour drive from Wilkes-Barre to Philadelphia. She was anxious to see Louis, her best friend from college, happy to be presenting a case report at a conference the next day, and looking forward to dinner with her godmother, Dr. Jeannie Bennett. The trip had passed quickly as her iPod played the Elton John version of *Aida*, and her mood had begun to improve as she descended from the mountains, through the tunnel and into the Lehigh Valley, where the landscape changed from tree-studded mountain peaks to flat farm land. How could the beauty of the mountains and that tragic tale of love fail to soothe her? She effortlessly negotiated the curves of the Schuylkill Expressway as it followed the river, smiling when the Philadelphia skyline appeared. Magically, her mood had turned.

Her joy had been short-lived. Instead of the quiet evening she'd envisioned, Louis had another plan—Rae.

Nicole shared little in common with most people, and making small talk wasn't her forte. She didn't like to share details about herself, and she really wasn't interested in hearing about the lives of people she'd never see again. It was a waste of her valuable time, and her evening with Rae was no exception.

They were all from the Wilkes-Barre area, all alumni of the University of Scranton, but Rae was five years older than Nic and Louis and had moved to Philly before they arrived on campus. Their paths hadn't crossed until the previous summer, when Rae moved into the apartment next to Louis. Although Louis and Rae seemed to have an endless supply of conversational topics, their hometown seemed to be the only thing she and Rae had in common.

Though Louis had touted Rae as witty, friendly, and intelligent, Nic considered her obnoxious and overbearing. She was physically quite attractive, there was no doubting that—but the attraction ended there. She wore her short, black hair spiked, and her eyes were bright green and seemed to dance in step with her abundance of energy. Her lips were full and inviting, and when she smiled, her entire face lit up. But then she spoke, and her voice was too loud, and her convictions too firm, making her sound a bit angry. She reeked of cologne and Nic feared just a whiff of Rae could trigger a migraine. And her hands were like things possessed, touching everything—the salt and pepper shakers on the dinner table, the linens, Louis, and worst of all, Nic. The woman should have been confined to a straightjacket. It was maddening. And, sadly, it wasn't over yet.

Tossing the cigarette remnant into an ashtray, Nic gazed into the night, summoning her courage. This building boasted a great view of the Ben Franklin Bridge. Both the bridge and the Delaware River below were twinkling, the blue and red lights reflecting beautifully across the water, daring her to be happy, but the sight didn't improve her miserable mood. Her nerves were a bit calmer after the nicotine and alcohol infusion, though, and she was ready to go face the enemy. Or was it enemies?

Louis was the first friend she'd made at the University of Scranton, on the very first day of chemistry lab. He'd helped her through that brutal freshman year, translating chemistry into English, so that she could understand the complexities that were so apparent to him. She'd sailed through the next three years, but couldn't deny or forget that debt she owed him. Without Louis, she wouldn't be who she was or where she was, and even though she was totally pissed off at him at the moment, she loved him.

Nic turned and headed back inside. Their friendship had withstood the tests of time and temperament and the trials of MCATs, then medical school, board exams, and residency. It would surely survive Rae.

Louis and Rae were laughing about something Nic had missed, and she tried to be happy for him. It looked like he really had a good friend in Rae, and he deserved that. He was a good, kind person, and she had no right to be jealous. Jealous? Yep, that's what this was.

Nic had left Philly a year earlier, when she finished her three-year ER residency. Louis's surgery program was a four-year ordeal. They'd been together for more than a decade, lived together, studied together, worked together, and then she'd left. While she was waiting for him back home, waiting for her friend to watch old movies and eat dinner, to play tennis and do crossword puzzles, he'd gone and found a replacement.

Nic hadn't spent the year socializing. She'd been working hard. Yes, she'd caught up with old friends, and even gone on a date or two. Nothing serious. She wasn't in the market for romance. She'd always been married to her career, dedicating the bulk of her time to studying and later practicing medicine. Women and relationships—and even friends—had taken a backseat to the career path she'd chosen. Except for Louis. He wasn't an addition to the life she'd lived, he was a part of it, the flavor of it. Unlike with other people, being with him wasn't a stress and took no effort. It was simple and easy and wonderful, and if she had a single ounce of heterosexual potential she would be Mrs. Perro by now. But she didn't, and she suddenly had to face the fact that one day, her dear, sweet, best friend would stop focusing so much on his own career, and find his true soul mate.

If he was right and Rae liked girls, then she wasn't the one. But, Nic realized, one day there would be someone, a special someone who'd take him away from her. Louis was different from her, she knew. He was social and liked people, and wanted a marriage and family. She saw herself with great potential for many one-night stands, but she didn't think she could ever tolerate anyone enough for more than that. So he would fall in love, and get married, and the friendship as she knew it would be over. She'd be alone. It was inevitable.

As Nic found a seat across from them, Rae caught her attention with a little wave and smiled. "The wine is nice. What is it?" she asked, raising her glass to the light and swirling.

Nic noted the small hands delicately cradling the glass and thought she must know a bit about wine. "It's a Shiraz. From Jordan."

"It's very good, and thank you for this." She motioned toward the cheese plate Nic had placed on the coffee table.

"Have you been to Jordan?" Louis asked, smiling at Rae, once again ignoring her as he focused on his new friend. Nic took a moment to look around the large living room, every open space filled with works of art they'd collected together, cheap originals from unknown artists and beautifully framed prints of some of their favorite masterpieces. And there were pictures, too, mostly of the two of them, a virtual documentary of their decade-old friendship. The furniture was an eclectic mix of fine pieces and cool junk, all blended to lend the room a feeling of casual elegance.

Nic watched as Rae wiped her mouth, and turned to answer Louis. It was as if Nic wasn't even in the room, and she was tired of it. Maybe she and Louis weren't destined for marriage, but Louis was her friend first, and it was time she let her feelings be known. The hell with manners, she thought as she listened to Rae's reply.

"That's one place I haven't been."

Nic raised a carefully shaped eyebrow. "*One* place?" she asked. "Does that mean you've been to all the other places?" The question might have been teasing, but she didn't inject any humor into her tone and gazed at Rae with a challenge in her eyes.

Rae met them and didn't back down an inch. She was silent a moment as she seemed to contemplate her reply. "There are about fifty, actually."

"Fifty?"

"Yes, give or take."

"Fifty what?" The woman was confusing her, and Nic no longer tried to contain her irritation. She'd had a tiring day and was exhausted by this woman.

"Fifty countries."

"What are you talking about?"

"There are fifty countries I haven't been to."

Nic nearly choked on her wine. "Oh, I see," she replied, but she didn't see at all, and she didn't intend to ask Rae to explain. Instead, she changed the subject. "Speaking of geography, exactly where are you from?" Nic hadn't been paying close attention at dinner; she was too busy being furious, but she seemed to remember something about the lower Wyoming Valley.

"West Nanticoke."

That was interesting, Nic though. Not the most exclusive town in the valley. Probably not even in the top twenty. "And *why* do you live there?" Nic asked.

The look on Rae's face was worth the cost of the bottle of wine she was wasting on her, and Nic tried hard not to smile.

"Excuse me?"

"Why do you live there? I mean, isn't it sort of…I don't know what the word is…perhaps the wrong side of the tracks?"

Rae burst into a laugh that rattled the windows, leaning full into the sofa and throwing her head back against the cushions. She stopped, started again, and then sat up and shook her head at Nic. "You are so fucking full of yourself. I don't know how you don't explode!"

"Oh, my." Nic shook her head at Louis. "I think I've angered your new friend."

"Oh, no," Rae interjected. "I'm not angry. I'm amused. And

curious to know how such a nice guy like Louis ended up with a jerk like you for a friend."

"Well," Nic said, "I think we're just destined for each other, because we've been friends for a long, long time. And no one's ever going to come between us."

"So, how about that movie we saw the other night?" Louis asked, attempting to change the subject.

Nic recognized his ploy and decided to back off. "Oh, what movie was that?"

"We saw a film at the Ritz," Rae replied. "A foreign film with subtitles."

Nic was speechless and was certain her mouth dropped. For effect, she dramatically opened it, then used the back of her left hand beneath her chin to close it again. Her gaze shifted from Rae to Louis, who slumped in his chair with a guilty expression. Reaching for a piece of cheese, he avoided her gaze. And how could he not?

She'd always been his date for foreign films. At least twice a month during their time in Philly they'd seen an independent film or documentary at the Ritz. They loved the exotic scenery of far-away lands, the romanticism of words spoken in foreign tongues, the cultures of different societies. These movies provided such a fresh, different taste compared to the canned products of most Hollywood studios. Before she visited Philly, she'd asked Louis if they could take in a film, and he'd vaguely dismissed her.

"You've gotta be kidding me." Nic looked to him for an explanation. As far as she was concerned, this was akin to having an affair.

When he didn't reply, Nic did, glaring at him as she spoke. "I guess I can cross the Ritz off my birthday wish list. But, at least, we'll be going to the Barnes. Or did you forget the tickets?" Her tone was sarcastic, but she knew that Louis wouldn't have forgotten the tickets. It was all she'd asked of him for her birthday. But the sheepish look on her face told her he had indeed failed to procure the required admission passes.

"This is un-fucking-believable, Lou," she said, her voice rising well above conversational level.

"Nic, I'm sorry. I just forgot. I've been so busy—"

"Not too busy for movies with Rae, though," she screamed. And then she remembered her manners, and rose from her seat. “Please excuse me,” she said in a much calmer voice. As she turned and stalked to her bedroom, she couldn’t resist the temptation of one last parting shot. “Feel free to spend the night, Rae. It seems you two can’t get enough of each other.”

# Chapter Three
# Nothing Ventured, Nothing Gained

Rae and Louis gazed at each other. "Give me a moment," Louis said with a sweet smile as he started to rise from the couch. Rae grabbed his arm, stopping him.

"It's late," Rae said. "I think I'll make the long walk next door."

"I would say she's not usually like this, but I'd be lying." He laughed.

"You did warn me she's a bit difficult."

Rae had met Louis at his front door a year earlier as she was moving into the apartment beside his. They'd both been wearing University of Scranton shirts and bonded instantly as they talked about their common hometown and alma mater. A few hours later, Louis had rescued her from her unpacking when he knocked on her door, bearing food and wine. They'd sat at her brand-new dining room table eating and talking away the evening.

As Rae had bid him good night she knew that a wonderful friendship had been born. She visited his apartment soon after and couldn't help but notice pictures of the striking, dark-haired woman scattered about.

Over the next few months, Rae had learned quite a bit about the woman in the pictures. She was Louis's best friend, a fellow physician named Nicole Coussart. Nic had finished her residency training and moved back to Wilkes-Barre just before Rae moved in. Nic hated Philadelphia but loved the mountains, Louis's cooking, old movies, and women.

Without ever meeting her, Rae was hooked on the idea of Nicole. Or perhaps it was the possibility of Nicole, conceived during her many hours in the easy company of their mutual friend Louis. She'd practically begged him to arrange the introduction, and he'd resisted, finally giving in and setting up the disastrous night that had thankfully ended without bloodshed.

So much for meeting people, Rae told herself as she keyed the lock and entered the apartment next door.

During the speech she'd recited as she ended their two-year relationship the year before, Rae's ex-lover, Paula, had suggested that Rae cared more about her job than anything else. She'd then kindly reminded Rae that life was too short to spend it working.

Instead of becoming defensive or sheltering in a comfortable state of denial, Rae had reflected on Paula's parting words. Paula was right. She'd spent nine years with the DEA, and all she had to show for it was a nice investment portfolio.

She'd devoted her first years after law school traveling for the job, saving most of her generous salary. Giving up her small apartment hadn't been much of a sacrifice. She'd lived in hotels on the road, staying with friends or family during the rare times she was home. She'd spent three years living in Europe and then two in South America before finally deciding she'd walked enough foreign soil. A position in the Philadelphia office became available, and for three years she'd been there, working long hours in her own little war on drugs.

Admitting Paula was right was easy compared to actually changing her life. Rae was passionate about her profession and had a hard time backing off. Her team was investigating the illegal distribution of prescription drugs—controlled substances that were resold on the streets. She spent her time researching case law and preparing for trial to convict the people responsible for the record-breaking number of deaths related to the abuse of prescription drugs. The victims of this epidemic spanned the spectrum of race and intelligence, wealth and poverty. Most of them fraudulently obtained prescriptions from doctors by faking pain, some of them visiting different doctors daily to get their fix.

Rae was also tracking the illegal sale of those same drugs. Just as some people obtained numerous prescriptions for their own use, others acquired them solely to resell them. Some stole prescriptions from family members. And some health-care workers stole the medications of unsuspecting patients in order to make a quick buck.

On the streets, Vicodin and Percocet were sold beside heroin and cocaine. Some drug addicts were now hooked on painkillers, without ever having seen a doctor for a prescription. Scarier still, these pills had become the drug of choice for experimenting teenagers. They somehow seemed safer than injecting or smoking, and those pills were *prescription*, so how bad could they be? Kids in high school and college were overdosing on these drugs and ending up just as dead as the ones who used the hard-core drugs. People were now dying more from prescription-drug overdoses than from any other source.

It all started innocently, with pills gifted from friends, who'd stolen them from home or bought them, and soon they were stealing and buying their own. Like most mind-altering drugs, though, these narcotics enslaved them, changing the shape of brain receptors so that higher and higher doses were required to achieve the same effects. Then boom! A kid ingested a few extra tabs and stopped breathing.

Finding the proof to prosecute in these overdose cases was often difficult. Friends and parents destroyed or consumed the evidence, wanting to protect their loved one or get high themselves. In a few cases over the past six months, though, Rae's office had uncovered some alarming information. Someone had illegally manufactured the pills recovered at death scenes, pills that resembled the trade-name samples on the market but contained differing quantities of narcotic and fillers.

Since that discovery, her office had been working hard to discover the source of these pills. They were used all over the region, but if one marked the areas on a map, it formed a near-perfect circle, Philadelphia at its center. These illegally manufactured pills were being distributed out of Philly, and she intended to find out the who and the what and the where, and shut it down. Too many lives had been lost, and Rae wouldn't rest until she changed things.

She hadn't always felt this way about drug users. She'd had no exposure to the kind of people who abused drugs, and she'd always assumed they were shadowy criminals who chose their dark path. She'd thought users were much to blame for their plight. After all, without buyers, no one would be selling drugs, right?

Since she began working for the DEA she'd learned how wrong she'd been. Dealers preyed on the innocent, indoctrinating them into the drug culture when they were most vulnerable. Their targets were children of single parents, recruited to deliver the product, kids without much guidance or money in their pockets. Most eventually became users. They were the mentally ill, failed by social systems and modern medicine, who turned to street drugs to control depression and anxiety and hallucinations of all varieties. They were veterans, unable to cope with the horrific memories of war, turning to drugs and overdosing at alarming rates. They were teens who were bullied, or pressured by parents to perform, or didn't fit in, turning to drugs to help them cope. They were all sucked into the vortex of prescription-drug use, which caused about a hundred of their deaths every day across the country. The ones who didn't lose their lives lost their homes and their families and their jobs instead.

Rae knew there were exceptions to these rules: bored kids who took drugs for fun, and adults who did as well, experimenting out of curiosity or because of the monotony of their lives. Their deaths were even more tragic in her mind, because she saw absolutely no reason for them.

Rae also knew that people who had less access to drugs were less likely to use them. If she could get these pills off the streets, fewer people would die. Fewer kids, and fewer fathers, and fewer veterans. Fewer human beings.

With her passion for her job, it had been difficult to back down, but after reflecting, she'd realized Paula was right. Life consisted of more than work. At least, other people's did, but she made it her goal to be more like them. She saw others with nice homes and happy relationships, and she could see herself in those kinds of pictures, snuggling beside the fire with a good book and a beautiful woman.

First she would buy the house, then spend time in it, and finally show it off to the ladies. The first two steps had gone surprisingly well. The third, not so much. She'd had about a dozen dates in the past year. First dates. Only two second dates, and no third dates. And Rae couldn't bring a girl home before the third date. What if her new friend turned out to be a psychopath? Then she'd know where Rae lived, and that situation could end in disaster. Even the fierce-looking security guard in the lobby would be defenseless against a psychopath, and Rae just didn't need that kind of aggravation.

Rae had knocked on Louis and Nic's door this evening feeling optimistic that her luck might change. After all, she adored Louis, and reasoned she'd like his friend as well. She'd hoped Nic might be different from the other dozen girls, who had a variety of disqualifying features. Her dates didn't have to be models, but she refused to go out with anyone who appeared to be wearing a Halloween costume. They didn't have to be witty, but they did have to laugh at her jokes, at least once in a while. Intelligence was non-negotiable. And so was one other, *little* factor. Height.

At five-feet-not-quite-three inches tall, Rae found herself looking up to most of the women she met, but never her dates. She was a tough butch, with a sense of pride, and under no circumstances would she ever stretch onto her tiptoes to kiss a date good night. That height requirement eliminated most of the female population.

To Rae's delight, Nic was just as short as she appeared in her photos. She was gorgeous and intelligent. But she hadn't laughed at a single joke. And she was a bitch. So, in spite of Rae's hopes, Nic would never make it to the requisite third date and find herself in Rae's apartment. She wouldn't even make it to a second.

After depositing her key in a drawer, Rae made her way across the apartment. Hers was a much smaller version of the adjacent one, with only one bedroom and a smaller combined kitchen and dining area. Just as in Louis and Nic's, the builder had done a good job, choosing fine granite and quality oak, and the prior tenant's taste was superb, so Rae had done little other than hire a moving company. She looked forward to coming home to her bright, cheerful apartment at the end of her workday.

Smiling at herself in the mirror after brushing her teeth, Rae tried not to be too disappointed. She'd had a great dinner. She'd tasted a new wine. And with her friend Louis planning to move in a few weeks, chances were good she'd never have to see Nicole Coussart again.

# CHAPTER FOUR
# WHAT ARE FRIENDS FOR?

Katie turned around to face her neighbor. She hadn't considered that Nan would still be peeking through the window when she opted to steal her shoes. Tempted to run, she once again trusted her instincts and instead asked a favor. "Can I come inside?"

Nan pushed open the door and, as quickly as Katie slipped through, closed it again behind her. She was shaking from the effects of adrenaline, but for the moment she was safe. The light was off, but enough filtered in from the living room beyond, allowing them to see. Katie reached out and pulled the woman toward her. In Nan's arms she felt herself tremble, her knees buckling, and the woman guided her gently backward and into a chair.

"I think Billy's been shot…I don't know for sure…I heard two shots, then Simon came after me…I had to run…I didn't even have any clothes on…I don't know about the kids, they were asleep in their room…I tried to go back, but the police came…I have to find out if they're okay…" It all poured out of Katie as one pressured, run-on sentence. She swallowed and tried to slow the breaths that were coming too fast again.

Walking to her cupboard, Nan turned and looked at Katie. The whites of her eyes jumped off her dark skin, even in the dim light of the kitchen, and they seemed to penetrate Katie. "You can't go back there," she said simply. She retrieved a cup and filled it with water, then handed it to Katie.

Nan was an old woman, losing her vision and her mobility, but not her senses. Nan knew how things worked. If Katie went back, the police would question her, and even if she told them nothing, Simon would think the worst and come after her. Even though she'd been living and honest life for nearly a decade, she had a criminal record. A convicted drug dealer, who happened to be the father of her children, was dead or wounded in her house. If they didn't have cause to arrest her for assault or murder or possession, they at least had enough suspicion to haul her in for questioning. It might take days, or weeks, to sort out all the evidence. She'd go to jail, and her children would go into foster care. It wasn't just or fair, but it was reality, and Nan understood.

"What do I do, Nan? I can't just leave the kids there. But you're right. If I go over there now, I'll end up in jail."

The trauma didn't faze Nan. "You stay right here. You can watch from the window if you like, but don't you leave the house. If anybody comes around, don't answer the door."

"Where are you going?"

"Over to your house, to gawk, just like all the other busybodies. And I'm going to get you some answers."

Katie bit her lip as she contemplated Nan's idea. It was risky, but even if she didn't learn anything, it was worth a try. Katie needed to know what had happened, and she needed to know that her children were safe.

"You would do that for me?" Katie was bewildered.

"Young lady," she said, "you've never been anything but good to me since you moved in over there. You do for me, and you never ask for a dime in return, although the Good Lord knows you could use one. If I can't help you when you need it, what kind of a Christian woman am I?"

Katie chewed her fifth fingernail, suddenly afraid. Nan's intentions were good, but what if she inadvertently let it slip to the police that Katie was hiding in her kitchen? What if she told them on purpose? "You won't tell them I'm here?"

"I believe in a little fib here and there. Like telling Gerald Senior he was good looking. Never hurt Gerald none. Made him feel good, I think. God didn't make a man homelier than Gerald, but he felt like a movie star when I told him that. So, sometimes you can use a little stretcher for a good purpose, and the Lord wants us to do good. If I have to tell those police officers a little fib, I think He'll forgive me."

Katie couldn't help but smile. Nan's husband Gerald had passed away many years before Katie and her children moved into the neighborhood, but Katie had seen the pictures throughout the house and he *was* homely. In every picture, though, he wore a big smile and looked happy.

Nan removed the Crocs from Katie's feet and placed them on her own, then gave her arm a squeeze of support before opening the back door. Wearing a pair of shorts pulled up to her sagging boobs, her shirt tucked in, and the bright-yellow shoes on her feet, she was quite a sight.

Off she went into the darkness, carrying her flashlight. From the kitchen door, Katie followed the light marking her neighbor's journey down the porch stairs and through the yard and into the alley. It moved along at a brutally slow pace, and each second seemed to push Katie closer to the edge of the cliff on which she was standing.

Fear squeezed the breath from her lungs and rattled the cup in her hand. Would Nan betray her? What would she find? Katie hardly had time to ponder the answers to her questions when the light reappeared in its full brightness at the end of the shrubs, and then, to Katie's surprise, Nan emerged and walked directly into the yard. Katie had assumed Nan was going to learn the gossip on the street, but apparently she had other plans. Nan held the rail as she navigated the stairs, and then she reached the porch and disappeared through Katie's kitchen door.

Leaning against the doorframe, Katie held her breath, her eyes glued to the door at the back of her house. Time seemed to stand still as she waited, and the blackness that filled the space between the porch lights seemed to grow. It was only fifty yards away, but to Katie it seemed like miles. Not knowing what Nan would find was hard, but not being with her children, to protect or comfort them, was killing her. In her mind's eye, she saw the path Nan was following across the kitchen and through a doorway into the living room. It was a small house, and even at Nan's pace, it wouldn't take long to get where she needed to go.

Before Katie finished her thought, the back door opened and Nan reappeared, flanked by two police officers, who escorted her to the bottom of the stairs and watched as she retraced her steps back home.

What had she seen? What had she learned? Katie couldn't swallow the lump in her throat, and tears were stinging her cheeks as she followed Nan with her eyes, spying through the window. When Nan finally opened the door and came into the kitchen, Katie was weeping uncontrollably. The entire adventure had taken only ten minutes—eight of which was the walk itself—yet to Katie, it had seemed an eternity.

"First of all, Katie, keep still. The police are looking for you, and I wouldn't put it past them to come and see for themselves that I'm not harboring a fugitive."

Katie didn't care. She was out of her mind with worry and no longer thinking straight. "What's going on? What happened?"

Nan was clearheaded, though. Taking her by the elbow, she guided her toward the front of her house. "Come, dear. We have to go into the living room and sit down."

"No!" Katie sobbed, bringing her hands to her face to wipe away tears, then to her side, to steady herself against the table. Bad news wouldn't be any easier to bear in the living room. "Tell me," she commanded through her sobs.

"He's dead. Billy's dead."

Another sob wracked her body and she sucked in a breath. "Chloe? Andre?" she whispered, barely able to get their names past her lips.

"Slept through the whole thing."

Nan shuffled toward the living room and Katie somehow managed to follow. Collapsing into a chair, she suddenly appreciated the wisdom of Nan's advice to sit down. Relief and grief, both in large doses, overwhelmed her. Nan sat on the couch beside her and stroked her arm.

She cried and cried, the tears springing from wells of grief over Billy, relief about her children, and a bit of fear that Simon was still out there in the darkness, looking for her. "Thank you," Katie managed after a few minutes.

All the while Katie cried, Nan remained silent. Finally, when Katie seemed calmed, she spoke. "I know this isn't what you want to hear—and Lord forgive me for speakin' ill of the dead—but he was trouble. You're much too good a woman to be with a man like him. You'll get through this. You take those kids and find a decent place to raise them, and you find a decent man to love you, and you'll be fine."

Whether Nan's words were true didn't matter to Katie at the moment. Chloe and Andre did.

"My kids? What will they do with them?"

"I asked if I could bring them over here, told the police I'm the babysitter, but they wouldn't let me have 'em. They told me they're taking them to the ER for an evaluation, and then the social worker's going to find a place for them."

Katie jumped to her feet. "No! I can't believe this! We have to get to them, Nan! They'll be scared without me. And what if Simon finds them? He's already killed once. What would stop him from murdering them to hurt me? Or kidnapping them to flush me out?"

"Calm down, now. A fit of hysterics won't solve nothin'."

"Where are they? Did they see Billy's body?" The thought horrified Katie. She paced Nan's living room, massaging away the pain that had taken root between her eyes.

"That carpet is very expensive, Katie, and I'm going to hold you accountable if you wear a hole in it." Nan stared at her until she stopped, then continued speaking. "They're fine. They're right there in the kitchen, having juice and cookies with the police. They seemed happy as could be, so I think—no—they didn't see him."

"Did they ask for me?"

"Yep. I told them you got called into the clinic to work and you'd see them soon."

Katie nodded. That was good. She sometimes did get called in—though never in the middle of the night—and her kids would believe that story. They'd stay calm for a while, at least, placated with cookies and the hope she'd soon be with them.

"You didn't happen to find out which ER they're going to, did you?"

Nan's eyes were twinkling. "Well, of course I did!"

Katie marveled at this grandmother who, despite the half-century age gap, really was her friend. They came from different backgrounds, different generations, were of different races, and had lived vastly different lives, but somehow they'd found each other and connected in a wonderful way. They needed each other. Nan helped Katie care for her kids, and Katie did things Nan could no longer manage, like change storm windows and run the lawnmower in the warm months, and shovel snow in the winter.

A smile formed as she remembered how much Nan had annoyed her when she first moved into her apartment. Somehow, she'd come to enjoy Nan's stories and her company, and it felt good to spend time with her. Katie knew that what Nan had told her about Billy were the tough words of a true friend. While Billy's death would make them all a bit sad, it wouldn't change their lives much.

"I have to get them, Nan."

"Well, then, let's get going."

# CHAPTER FIVE
# PLOTTING

They needed a plan, and while Katie showered away the sweat from her body and dirt from her feet, one came to her. She could find everything she needed at the clinic, with the exception of something to wear. Maybe Nan could help with that.

"Of course," Nan said, a twinkle in her eye. "I've saved some nice things for special occasions."

The stairs at the center of Nan's front hall marked a century of footsteps, the finish worn down to the bare wood. Like everything in Nan's home, and the neighborhood for that matter, the appointments were well done. The ends of each plank still hinted at an oak varnish that must have made them a beautiful sight. Each groaned as it bore their weight. Babbling as she slowly made her way to the top, Nan was winded when they reached the landing. Katie tried to hide her impatience. She took some deep breaths and closed her eyes, letting calmness seep into her pores. She'd need it if this octogenarian was going to serve as her partner in crime. She'd need it no matter what.

The closet in the front spare bedroom (which would be known as Gerald's room as long as his mother lived in the house) proved to be a proverbial pot of gold. Nan had worn a petite size six in the days she'd amassed her wardrobe, which by the styles on display seemed to be the 1950s. Katie could fit easily into that size with a little room to spare. She pushed hanger after hanger, discarding bold flowery prints and pulling out a few more somber suits and dresses.

"This is unbelievable," Katie said as she looked at all the clothing Nan had stored in clear plastic garment bags. She chose a conservative black funeral dress.

"And I have hats to match." Nan indicated neatly stacked hatboxes on the upper shelf of the closet.

"I think I'll pass on the hats."

"I'd think again," Nan said, and Katie searched her face, confused.

She sat on the edge of her son's bed, looking quite sure of herself, and Katie wished she could borrow some of Nan's confidence. How brave she'd been to go out onto that porch and ward off Katie's would-be assassin, to confront the police. How brave she was to embark on this mission. Katie realized she might do well to listen to her.

"Tell me your idea," Katie suggested. Nan did, and Katie smiled as she listened. Suddenly another piece fit into the puzzle. "That just might work." And with Nan's suggestion in mind, Katie returned the wardrobe selections to the closet, including the dress she'd chosen, and pulled out a totally different style. It was something she'd never wear under normal circumstances, and that made it a perfect costume for the scheme they'd concocted.

Turning her attention to the hat boxes, she climbed onto a bench and handed them down to Nan. With so many options, choosing the perfect one proved to be a bigger challenge than the dress had, but after she tried them all, Katie selected the smallest of the lot. She chose it not because it was her favorite but because it would be easiest to pack in the small, light-blue suitcase Nan had pulled out of Georgia's room. Like her brother Gerald, Georgia had left home fifty years earlier, but her childhood bedroom was still waiting for her in case she decided to move back in with her mother.

With the suitcase in hand, Katie descended the stairs just behind Nan. At the bottom, Nan turned and offered her a smile. "Are you ready?"

Katie was terrified. If this mission failed she'd end in a cold jail cell and her kids in a foster home. After not having slept for several nights, she was exhausted, her body burning adrenaline to keep the engine running. And she had a headache, a migraine that had started sometime after she was shot at earlier in the evening. But she was as ready as she was going to get, and the more time she wasted, the more likely her plan would fail. They had to move quickly. As quickly as

Nan could move, anyway. "I am. Are you sure you want to do this? You might get arrested, you know."

"As far as I know, Katie, you're just a law-abiding citizen who's picking up her kids from the hospital. What are the police going to charge me with? Aiding and abetting a mother?"

"Okay, then. Let's do this."

"First, I need a potty break."

Placing the suitcase beside her, Katie stood next to the piano in Nan's living room and studied the keys, waiting. How many times had her fingers danced across all eighty-eight of them? Without thinking, she stood before the bench, and her fingers formed the chord of C. The first few notes of Beethoven's *Ode to Joy* filled the room before she thought to quiet her hands. It was one of the earliest songs she'd mastered as a young student, and if she closed her eyes, she could still see the delight on her mother's face as she stood beside the piano in the living room in their home on Rhawn Avenue.

She'd spent her childhood there, and her mother had given piano lessons to neighborhood children after school. Katie had often heard words of praise in her mother's voice as she encouraged her students and motivated them to practice. But only Katie could put that expression of true joy on her mother's face. And that had motivated Katie more than anything else.

Katie had been shocked when she first came into Nan's home years before and realized she could still play. Apparently, the endless hours of practice had effectively chiseled the finger patterns into memory, because much of what she'd learned for recitals and Christmas pageants easily came back to her.

She didn't have much time to play now, but both her children were taking piano lessons, and she always sat beside them on the bench as they practiced, showing them the fingering and correcting their mistakes. At eight, Chloe was already very good, but Andre seemed to have inherited Katie's mom's extraordinary musical skills. Marge could play at the master level, and Andre shared her passion and ability. Katie had to pull him away from the piano just to allow Chloe equal practice time. And every once in a while, she'd play something herself.

Another memory came back to her, and Katie shuddered.

*"What are they doing with your piano?" Hope Bevan, her best friend, asked as they walked home from the school-bus stop one sunny fall afternoon. Katie was thirteen. A long, hard year had passed since her mother was killed in a car accident, and so much had changed in that time that Katie's head was spinning.*

*Katie had gotten her first period, an utterly terrifying and mortifying experience. She was humiliated as she asked her father for money to buy the necessary products, reduced to tears when he made a big deal out of the expense. As if it were her fault. Her father was angry because the judge had awarded most of the money in their lawsuit to Katie and not him. Katie would have gladly given him every penny, though, just to make him happy. She'd even visited her lawyer to discuss that option. Unfortunately, the judge had issued strict instructions, and Katie could have only a modest amount for monthly living expenses until she turned eighteen. That wouldn't buy her dad the new car he wanted, though, and he was taking his frustrations out on her.*

*She'd had to change schools, because her father didn't want to pay the tuition at Christ the King, the Catholic school she'd attended from kindergarten through sixth grade. She wouldn't be attending Archbishop Ryan High School as planned, either. She missed her friends and her teachers at CTK. They were like family to her. She still waited at the bus stop every day, though, and walked the half mile home with Hope, who was still her best friend.*

*The worst thing Katie had to deal with was the unexpected change in her household. It had increased by one when her father's new girlfriend, April, moved in. Although they hadn't officially made an announcement yet, from the look of April's ever-growing abdomen, there would soon be four of them living in the modest-sized duplex in the quiet residential area of Northeast Philly. Her father was fifty-four years old that year, and his new girlfriend hadn't even reached thirty.*

*Since she'd moved in, April had made it clear that she was now running their house. The thermostat was set at a temperature way too cold for Katie's taste. The refrigerator was filled with take-out food and diet soda. The interior of the house had been repainted, from the calm pastels that matched her mother's personality to vivid, screaming bright colors that were all April. She'd changed and rearranged so much that it hardly seemed like the same house. Katie was homesick in her own home.*

*She lifted her eyes, looking ahead to the end of her block, where April and three men were gathered on her front lawn. Her mother's piano was sitting on the small porch, and several men were positioning planks on the steps, preparing to roll the piano down and into the moving van that had backed into the driveway.*

*Katie broke into a run, dropping her backpack in the grass of a neighbor's yard, screaming as she approached the group of men set at their task. "Stop! Stop! You can't take my mother's piano! It's mine! Stop it!" Tears were running down her face, and she was sobbing so hysterically her words were barely intelligible.*

*April met her on the edge of the lawn and promptly slapped her. "Since you stole all of your mother's money, your father and I can't afford piano lessons any more. The money we got for the piano won't even keep you in Tastykakes for a month, so shut your trap, you little spoiled brat."*

*What was she talking about? Katie had never taken piano lessons; she'd learned from her mother. And her father sold Tastykakes. They got them free.*

*"What are you talking about? I don't need lessons!"*

*Another slap knocked Katie off balance, and she landed on her butt. She sat there in the grass, pleading, as April looked down at her with an inexplicable hatred in her eyes. "Shut your trap."*

*"But it's my piano! It was my mother's and she left it to me! You can't sell it. It's not fair!"*

*"There's a lot that ain't fair in this world, and the sooner you learn that, the better."*

"Okey dokey, I'm all ready now!" Nan announced, bringing Katie back to the present. She squeezed Katie's shoulder and marched right past her to the front door, as calmly as if they were headed to church.

Katie looked down at the keys once more, going back in time again, hearing April's voice in her mind. *There's a lot that ain't fair in this world.* In the years since that confrontation on her front lawn, Katie had come to know that no truer words were ever spoken.

# CHAPTER SIX
# SIMON SAYS

Simon says turn on the television!" Simon instructed Angelica as he hurried through the front door and began stripping off his clothing. This modest, single-family home in the Andorra section of Northwest Philly was the perfect hiding place for him. This was a quiet, residential area with no violence or drug trafficking, and his neighbors here had other things, like careers and children to think about. They'd pay no attention to the shooting in the Northeast, and never link their quiet neighbor to the crime.

More than an hour had passed since he'd fired two bullets into Billy Wallace, and Simon Simms was hopeful for some news about the shooting. He wanted to be sure Billy was dead. He also wanted to know if his name had been brought to the attention of the police and if the police had caught up with Katie.

Simon had never liked Katie, and on more than one occasion he'd tried to derail her relationship with Billy by leading Billy astray. Simon fixed Billy up with women and made sure Katie knew about it. He arranged for Katie's car to be stolen while Billy was driving it. He planted drugs in her apartment before his last arrest and then tipped off the police. Somehow, though, the drugs were never found and Simon was out five thousand dollars. And it was all because of that bitch. She was too smart, and he couldn't manipulate her the way he could the other girls in their circle, and she was too feisty to control. She'd always been a threat to Billy, he'd just been too blind to see it, and now she'd become a threat to Simon, too.

What if she decided to ignore his warning and talk to the police? She might not have seen him shoot Billy, but she could certainly testify that he'd shot at her. The bullets from the gun he'd used in the attack on her were scattered all over, and it would be a pretty strong case that he'd shot Billy once the ballistics experts examined all of the evidence. And while Simon could always disappear if the police got too close to him, he wasn't quite ready to go yet.

He'd already ditched the gun in the Delaware River and returned the SUV to the parking garage where he'd borrowed it. The guy working the lot was one of his dealers and had given him a vehicle that was parked for the night. Unless the owner was highly observant and checked the mileage, he'd never know Simon had used it as transportation to and from a crime scene. The vehicle wasn't damaged in any way—there were no dents and no bloodstains. He'd need to shower and toss his clothing, but since no one knew where he was staying he wasn't in a hurry. Even the car he was now driving was a difficult trace. Angelica had purchased it in her name, using his money, and it wasn't on the police radar.

Angelica, who often sheltered him, looked up from the laptop she'd been working on, then stood and closed the sliding-glass door behind her. During the daylight hours, the backyard of their property overlooking Fairmont Park would have been deserted, but at this time of night, someone with sharp hearing was bound to be sitting out on their deck enjoying the warm night. Reaching for the remote, she asked, "What channel would you like to watch?"

"Any fuckin' channel. I just want to see the news."

"What's going on?" She crossed her arms across her chest and stared at him.

"I blew away Billy Wallace. I wanna see if he's dead and if they know it was me."

Showing no reaction to his confession, she calmly pointed the remote toward the television. Her cable service offered access to local channels, and she began searching them, working her way up from the low numbers. There was no report of the shooting in North Philly. "Why don't you try the computer? Or call the hospitals?"

Simon smiled. Angelica was smart, and he couldn't help admiring her beauty. She was tall and slim, with wavy brown hair and eyes to match, and he loved how she looked at him. Even during a stressful time like this, she could bring his blood to a boil in seconds. Those were just two of the reasons he'd fallen for her. She was also cunning and ruthless and blindly ambitious, traits he greatly admired. "Great idea! Get me some phone numbers."

Simon melted into the buttery soft couch and continued to channel surf, but the television was filled with movies and reruns, and no news at all. After a few minutes, Angelica handed him a list of phone numbers for the closest hospitals and then turned her attention back to her laptop while Billy studied the paper before him.

"Where have you been for four days?" she casually asked, her eyes never leaving the screen in front of her.

Aiming the remote at the giant television, Simon pressed a button and the house grew silent. He knew it would remain that way until he spoke. Angelica would wait him out, make him squirm and sweat, waiting to find out if he was forgiven. He wished he could tell her the truth, but he didn't want to hurt her, and he knew it would. And never was he sorrier that he hadn't been here with Angelica than he was now. If he had, none of this shit with Billy would have happened. "I'm sorry. There's nothing else I can say."

"Did you have an obligation?" she asked.

"I did."

"You should have told me."

"Soon, baby. This is all going to change."

She didn't acknowledge the unspoken promise in his words. "Why'd you shoot Billy?" she asked as she looked up from the computer a minute later.

Angelica had never met Billy; she was part of Simon's other life. His dealers, his couriers, his friends on the streets—they were his tough life. He had other people, too—family, coworkers, and associates—in what he considered the good life. Angelica, she was real life. She knew she was the only woman, the only person with whom he'd ever connected. With her, Simon felt truly alive, truly real, and he considered this place, with her, to be his home. They'd bought this house together, and he spent much of his time there, eating at the glass table they'd picked out together, cuddling on this couch, wearing out the mattress in the bedroom.

"He's a fuckin' snitch. He got out of jail early for givin' up names." This was a lie, but Angelica didn't need to know that. The truth would have pissed her off. Simon hadn't planned to kill Billy, but when he met him at the bar, something he said had caught Simon's attention.

"Katie told me she ran into you down at the beach. You workin' on your suntan?" he'd asked. Simon had known at that moment he had to kill Katie. And to diminish suspicion, he'd make it look like Billy was the target. Normally, he was patient and calculating. He took his time and decided the best course of action only after weighing all his options. Tonight, he hadn't done that, and he hoped he wouldn't live to regret it.

Billy had also told Simon that Katie had just received the last of her inheritance. He knew Katie had gotten money in the past, and Billy had squandered every penny of it. Simon figured he'd take the money while he was there, as a sort of bonus for his troubles. All that money would be a nice addition to the nest egg he'd been accumulating, the money that would keep Angelica and him living in style for the rest of their lives. For the past two years, they'd been quietly smuggling money into the islands, using a chartered boat to haul the loot and taking along her young niece and nephew to lend the appearance of family and help avoid suspicion. It'd been Angelica's idea to move the money—which he'd been stockpiling in a bank safe in his home—to an account where it could earn interest. In a few years, he'd have enough money transferred so he could live comfortably forever. He'd disappear to the islands and live a good life with the woman he loved.

He didn't really need Katie's money, but he wanted it anyway. Years earlier he'd heard Billy bragging about all the money Katie had coming, and Simon figured that was the only reason Billy kept her around. He'd never given much thought to stealing it, though, because with the drugs she was doing back then, Simon didn't think she'd live long enough to see it.

But Katie had surprised him, cleaning up and getting a respectable job. And Billy had, too. He seemed to be like the proverbial cat with nine lives, avoiding shootings and police raids, often escaping out the back door as the police were coming in the front. And then it occurred to Simon that perhaps Billy really was a snitch. Simon wondered now about the many near misses Billy had over the years, thinking perhaps his luck had more to do with police information than the hands of fate. It all made sense when he looked at it from that perspective. He'd have to be more careful and review his staff of distributors, start looking for problems.

"Well, you don't have to worry about him anymore, Si. KYW says a man's dead in a North Philadelphia shooting. Police are looking for Kathleen Finan. Ha! They think she'd have the guts to shoot somebody?" Angelica laughed.

Simon didn't share her lighthearted attitude. "She might have the guts to talk to the police. I need to silence her. Do they know where she is? Where are they looking for her?"

Scanning the article again before looking at him, she raised her blue eyes to meet his dark ones. "It doesn't say specifically, just that they're looking for her. But I can tell you where she is, without question." Her eyes held many emotions—passion, hatred, anger—as she waited for him to ask.

"Oh, yeah? How would you know?"

He studied her beautiful face and she finally offered a teasing smile, just one corner of her mouth lifting. "I just do."

"Okay, so where the fuck is she?" Simon was tired, he was stressed, and he was in no mood to play games, no matter how beautiful she was.

"Si, don't go getting' pissy with me. I'm only trying to help you."

He looked at her again, but her eyes were now on the computer screen. He really liked her courage. She didn't take any of his attitude and didn't back down from him. Angelica had bigger balls than most men.

"You're right. I'm sorry."

Angelica met his gaze. Staring at him silently for a moment to prove her continued dissatisfaction, she finally shared her thoughts. "If you find Katie's kids, you'll find Katie. Children and Youth Services will take them to the ER for a check-up. Once they see everything's okay, they'll send them to some foster home. Katie doesn't have any family to take care of them, does she?"

"No, she was an orphan. That's how she got all the money—from a car crash, I think. She didn't have any family to take her in, so she ended up with Billy."

"Well, then, let's find the kids."

Leaning back in his chair, Simon began to laugh. Once again, she amazed him. He'd been sitting there, thinking of all the friends she might have run to, frustrated that he didn't know as much about Katie as he should have. Since she was the significant other of a man who worked for him, he should have been keeping a closer eye on her. But Katie was just plain boring. She didn't do anything illegal anymore, and her pathetic little life revolved around those two brats she was raising. "I knew there was a reason I stay with you."

The odds were better if he moved quickly, so Simon picked up the phone and began dialing from the list of numbers Angelica had given to him. "This is Mr. Obama, like the president," he said to the woman who answered the phone in the ER. He spoke carefully, enunciating each word, a far cry from the language he used on the streets. "I'm with Children and Youth Services. Have those children from the shooting scene arrived yet?"

He waited while she checked. A minute later she was back on the line, telling him they weren't there. The response was the same at two other hospitals, but on the fourth attempt he hit the jackpot. A very helpful woman told him the children had been brought in by the police and had already been evaluated by the doctor on duty. When he arrived they would be awaiting him in treatment room thirteen.

"Lucky thirteen!" Simon said. He grabbed a garbage bag from the kitchen and deposited the pile of clothes into it, everything from his shirt to his shoes. He couldn't take a chance that a single drop of Billy's blood had splattered onto him. Then he turned on the shower and climbed in, thinking of a plan.

# Chapter Seven
# Unrest

Nic couldn't sleep. She was exhausted and her eyes felt like sand, but as she lay in the darkness of her room, her mind wouldn't stop racing. She was nervous about the next day and irritated about her fight with Louis.

When Rae had finally left their apartment, Nic exploded, venting all of her fury at Louis. "Why did you ask me to dinner if you planned to spend the night talking to her?" she'd demanded.

"I wouldn't have spent the night talking to her if you hadn't spent the night sulking!"

"How could you forget the tickets?"

"I didn't forget them! They were sold out."

"How could you go to the Ritz without me?"

"Do you have any idea how ridiculous you sound? We're not married, for Christ's sake. We're friends. At least I thought we were."

"What the fuck does that mean?"

"What the fuck does it sound like?"

Nic took a deep breath and tried to let go of her anger. She was hurt, and she wanted Louis to know that. "Why did you have to invite her? This was supposed to be a special night for us. We haven't seen each other in months."

He was still angry, though. "Believe me, it wasn't my idea. As far as I'm concerned, she's much too nice for you. But she's been bugging me to introduce you ever since she saw your picture, and I didn't have a good excuse not to. I guess I should have just told her that you're a royal bitch and she'd be better off staying away from you."

Now Nic was mad again. Louis had drawn blood. "Maybe you should have!"

"I'm going to bed!" he said before he stormed off.

When she went into his room to offer an apology half an hour later she could hear the regular rhythm of his breaths and knew he was asleep. She closed the door behind her, returned to her own room. After studying the ceiling for half an hour she still couldn't sleep. She decided to work. It was always a good distraction.

This conference on emergency medicine held at the convention center featured examples of real-life drama, and Nic was presenting a case she'd managed. After thoroughly researching the topic and spending months following up on her patient, she knew the presentation inside and out. She'd prepared slides and a handout and practiced her delivery dozens of times. She'd presented cases many times before, during her residency. But this was different. She was a real doctor now, and all those other real doctors who'd paid hundreds of dollars to attend this conference expected her to know her topic. A well-received presentation would mean future invitations to present. If she screwed up, it would be the end of her speaking career and she'd look the fool in front of the men and women who'd trained her. She couldn't let that happen.

Sitting up, she switched on the lamp and squinted as her eyes adjusted to the light. She pulled her notes from her briefcase, glanced at them, then stood and began to pace, speaking in a muted voice so she wouldn't awaken Louis in the next room. She talked to her dresser, her lamp, her artwork, and they all listened attentively.

The patient she discussed was a woman in her mid-fifties who came into the ER in the middle of the day with pain in her wrist from a fall. Upon further questioning, she explained how her left leg had grown painful and numb after an extended time sitting at her desk. When she stood to walk it off, the leg seemed to collapse. She was uninjured except for her wrist, and her leg pain had completely resolved. When pressed for additional information, the woman admitted she'd been having problems with her leg for about a year. The symptoms of sciatica had been steadily getting worse, but she hadn't seen a doctor. Nothing could be done; she'd researched it on the Internet.

In addition to the broken wrist, Nic had discovered a golf-ball size mass in the left thigh, just below the buttock. The mass was firm, fixed in place, and not tender to touch. The strength and pulses in the foot and leg were fine. Subsequent outpatient testing proved the mass to be a malignant sarcoma, and after the patient had surgery to remove the tumor, her sciatica symptoms immediately improved.

Nic would proceed to talk about the sciatica and leg pain and weakness, throwing in interesting facts to keep the audience stimulated. She'd discuss the disease processes that caused it, the signs and symptoms, exam findings, lab tests, and finally the treatment. She'd wrap it up with the good news that her patient had made a full recovery. Nic would ask for audience input throughout her talk but also leave time for a questions and answers at the end. It was an interesting case study, and she hoped that alone would hold her peers' interest.

As she put her paperwork away and shut off the light, her mind wandered to Rae. Nic didn't often encounter women who stood up to her, but Rae had. If she didn't dislike her so much, she might have considered going out with her. That's what tonight had been all about, after all. She'd been paraded out and inspected to see if she was dating material. She could kill Louis. No, she thought. Forget it. Move on.

Grabbing the pack of cigarettes from the hidden compartment in her computer case, Nic headed for the balcony. Her bedroom had its own, a private but smaller version of the one off the living room. She took a seat in the lone chair, a deep, cushioned wicker rocker that swallowed her whole. Leaning back, she rested her feet against the matching table and wondered, not for the first time, what was wrong with her. Why wasn't she happy?

She wasn't unhappy. She'd read all about mood disorders and knew all the signs and symptoms of diseases such as depression and adjustment disorder, and she could never justify the use of an antidepressant medication in her particular case. She didn't have a loss of appetite, no change in sleep pattern (with the exclusion of this strange night), no loss of interest in sex (although she had a paucity of available partners at the moment), no loss of interest in the things she liked to do. No, it wasn't depression.

So what was it? Her job was stressful, but probably no better or worse than most people's. It had been her good fortune to be adopted by a family with plenty of money, and she had no worries there. Did she need to get laid?

She didn't think so. She'd never had anyone special in her life—ever, really, so she was used to being single. Her relationships tended to end quickly and badly, because she had no patience for other people's drama. Her vision didn't include the spectrum of color; things tended to be clear-cut: black or white. Choosing between extremes was much easier than separating shades of gray. Right or wrong, good or bad, attractive or unattractive. That's the way her mind seemed to compartmentalize. Either she liked someone or she didn't, and if she did, she wanted to spend time with them. If not, forget it.

While this way of thinking made much of life simple—it didn't work well in relationships, where compromise was key. Nic knew she was a failure in that department. She accepted it, and it didn't even bother her anymore. The idea that she'd probably spend much of her life alone, with occasional flings to spice up the flavor of her days, had occurred to her, and she was okay with it. She could do flings. She could enjoy a few weeks or a few months of dinners and movies followed by nights of passion. What she couldn't do was become comfortable with someone in her space, and that was what a relationship was, wasn't it? Allowing another human being into the most intimate recesses of your life. Into your thoughts and plans, into your home and your car, into everything that was neat and orderly, creating a big mess.

The ease with which others accepted the trivial infractions of privacy mystified Nic. It really bothered her that her girlfriend wore her socks, the ones with the black trim around the cuff, because she like to wear those with her black running shorts, and she couldn't if her girlfriend had worn them and left them in the pile of laundry. Her favorite mug was just that—hers. How frustrating to reach into a cabinet for something and not find it in the place it had always been—to find dirty dishes in the sink and a wet towel on the floor. All of these things overshadowed the joy of the dinners and the movies and the sex. So, inevitably, the relationship would end, and Nic would find herself alone again, but content in her neat and ordered universe. And she really, really was okay there. Wasn't she?

The thought of a relationship caused her to once again to envision Rae. What had Rae meant when she'd answered "fifty" to Nic's question about Jordan? She picked up her smokes, walked back into the bedroom, and slipped beneath her thick, soft comforter. Grabbing her smartphone from its charger on the nightstand, Nic connected to her search engine and typed. "How many countries are there in the world?"

"Wow," she said aloud. No one agreed, it seemed, whether to count Taiwan. She didn't care to read why. But if you did, the number was a hundred and ninety-six. Could Rae have seriously been talking about the world? Was it possible she'd been to a hundred and forty-five (or a hundred and forty-six) countries? "I'll never know," she said as she powered down the device and put it back in its place.

Her thoughts turned again to Louis. Why had he behaved like such a jerk with Rae? Or was he right—was she the jerk? It didn't matter. They'd been friends for too long for something like this to come between them. She needed to make this right or she'd never sleep.

Not bothering to be quiet, she slipped out of her own bed, crossed the hallway, and entered his room. She rolled onto the bed beside him. "Louis, wake up."

"What's wrong?" he demanded, fully awake as if just called to a code at work.

"I just wanted to tell you that I love you and forgive you for being unfaithful to me."

"What time is it?"

"After midnight."

"I accept your apology. Now go to sleep. I have surgery in like two hours, and I need to be awake for it."

"Can I sleep with you?"

Pulling the pillow over his head, he rolled away from her and groaned. Nic smiled and curled into her own little ball on the other side of the bed, asleep in minutes.

# CHAPTER EIGHT
# BEST ACTRESS

After assuring the street in front of the house was devoid of police activity, Katie and Nan quietly slipped through the door. Floorboards groaned a welcome greeting. To their fearful ears the noise was blasting, but no one else seemed to hear. They stopped for a moment to be sure before proceeding.

For several weeks, the streetlight in front of Nan's house had been burned out, leaving a section of the street in semi-darkness, and for once, Katie was happy for the city's ineptitude. A police car had blocked the entrance to the street at the corner, a hundred yards away, but no driver was to be seen. Thankfully, Nan's old Ford LTD faced in the other direction. She didn't want to execute a K-turn on the dark, narrow street.

As quietly as she could, Katie descended the stairs and walked to Nan's car. After placing the suitcase in the backseat, she turned the key in the lock and practically fell into the seat. A moment later, Nan sat beside her, smiling as the old engine roared to life. Katie knew Gerald had purchased the car before his death, and even though it was nearly as old as she was, it was still as reliable as the day he bought it.

Katie adjusted her mirror with one hand and turned the steering wheel with the other, and easily maneuvered the car on the deserted street. They both held their breath until they reached the stop sign at the end of the block, looking around to see who lurked in the shadows, watching. But no one confronted them. No porch lights came on in warning. The police didn't give chase. It appeared they'd made a successful escape.

As she steered the car, the women sat in silence and Katie tried to think about her mission rather than the evening's events. She couldn't afford to dwell on what had happened in her apartment—Billy's lifeless body lying in her living room or, perhaps by now, in the morgue. She couldn't think about Simon Simms and the gun he'd fired at her, or her frightened children waiting for her. She had to transform herself into someone else, and to do that she had to find the person she wanted to be in the vast video library of her mind.

Katie had always enjoyed playacting. In addition to music, her mother had loved musical theater, directing the church and school productions, and Katie had played bit parts from her earliest days. Becoming someone else had helped her during her darkest hours, when she was living in the streets, and still helped now when she had a difficult task to accomplish.

Thinking of people she'd known throughout her life, she conjured up images and voices and mannerisms. She needed to transform into someone who carried herself with a certain dignity and spoke proper English, so she remembered teachers who had taught her, nurses and doctors she worked with, and the pastor at the local church. She imagined herself as any one of them, and the script began to take shape in her mind. It was just like acting in one of her mother's musicals, only in this case there were no cuts and retakes. If she screwed up, her children would pay the price.

Less than ten minutes after leaving Nan's house, they pulled into the big deserted parking lot at the rear of the darkened medical clinic where Katie worked. The building was a stand-alone structure, 6,000 square feet of brick and glass, one story high. A very narrow drive separated it from the office suite next door, a five-story structure that blocked the moon from view.

Since Nan often watched her children, and Katie sometimes got stuck at the office, she'd given Nan a house key. And then Katie realized the intelligence of giving her an entire set, complete with car key and work keys. Since Nan could no longer drive, she rarely left home, and when she did, it was usually with Katie. It was a good bet that if she ever lost her keys, Nan would be home and she could retrieve the spare set. She'd never needed them before tonight.

"Do you wanna come in?" Katie asked. "I think you should." Even though this was a better neighborhood, she didn't want to invite trouble by leaving Nan in the car alone. A few cars passed on the street in front of the office, and the parking area was bordered by other businesses, all closed for the night. It wasn't likely anyone would accost Nan, but if they did, it wasn't likely anyone would come to her rescue, either.

Silently and slowly, Nan exited the car and followed her. The ground sloped gently back from the street, and three steps led to a landing and the back door of the building. She waited patiently as Nan navigated them. And then they were inside, adjusting to the glow from the security lights that lit the office, and Katie punched in the security code for the alarm system.

The clinic had been converted from an old appliance store, and in places, it showed. Large panes of glass across the front wall meant Katie had to avoid the lobby. Where she stood, near the rear door, office space was partitioned with half-walls. To the right, a kitchenette had been assembled with old furniture, mostly donated by the doctors who worked at the clinic. The central area comprised the doctors' space, housing the exam rooms and a common area in the center for the physicians and staff to chart notes and orders. Although the design allowed easy access to all ten exam rooms, it obstructed the traffic flow from the front to the back of the building. Now Katie was happy for that, because that workstation would obstruct the view of anyone looking in the front window.

Once their eyes adjusted, Katie sat Nan down in the kitchenette and began to gather the supplies she needed. Near the main entrance in front, the secretary's area overlooked the lobby and front door. That was Katie's first stop. She flipped a few switches and brought to life the sleeping electronic equipment that ran the office, mindful of the front window. While the computer went through its series of checks and balances and the photocopier warmed up, Katie kneeled behind the desk. After opening a few drawers, she found the file she needed and began to remove its contents. She pulled file folders from another cabinet and, using a Sharpie marker, began to label them. When she finished, she sat on them and then ran their edges along the carpeting to give them a worn appearance. Satisfied that she had the look she was seeking, she stood and scurried to the locker room.

In the event of a catastrophe where one of the employees was the target of a vomiting or bleeding patient, a shower had been installed. To her knowledge, it had never been used, and over time it had become a storage cubical for surgical scrubs. The resident doctors preferred to wear them rather than real clothing. She pulled a set from the clean piles and changed her clothing. From the coat rack, she removed several different lab coats and tried them on, deciding that Dr. Erin Donoghue's—a petite small—fit best. She ditched the ID. With her long black hair and dark skin she would never pass for the redheaded doctor. Dr. Mary Weeks's ID offered a more credible match, so she took a moment to attach it to the coat pocket in a way that made it difficult to read. Satisfied with her pickings, she went back into the outer office where the computer was asking for a password.

Katie entered the secret code and began typing, and after a few minutes of tapping on the keyboard, she produced a document that seemed credible. Turning the paper just a fraction of an inch, she made a photocopy, then photocopied the photocopy, and repeated the process until the paper had the telltale lines across indicating it had been copied many times. It looked genuinely awful.

Her next document contained just one word. Katie changed the paper in the printer and pressed a button and the machine came to life again, creating multiple copies.

She called Nan in to take her photo, and next she began printing ID badges. Since the resident physicians changed monthly, the clinic issued identification so the staff would be able to identify the doctors they worked with. Katie kept Dr. Weeks's name but changed her job description on each one, producing several badges with different information on each. When she was satisfied that they were acceptable, she shut down the computer and copy machine and straightened the work area. The secretary wasn't likely to know Katie was ever there.

Katie sat back and did a mental inventory. What else did she need? She pulled open the top drawer of the desk, just for some ideas. Plenty of pens were stuck in the lab-coat pocket, so she didn't need any more. She pocketed a pair of reading glasses and scissors. She might need to cut something, and if things went badly, they would serve as an excellent weapon. The glasses would add to her disguise. She pulled out several ID bands the clinic used for patients, the old-fashioned clear-plastic kind with a paper slipped inside. Anyone who needed any services more than an exam was required to wear one, to prevent miscues such as drawing blood on the wrong patient.

Back through the hall, she entered the office of the clinic's director, Dr. Jeannie Bennett. Jeannie had a bad hip and hated to haul her briefcase home, so it often sat beside her desk in an office she never bothered to lock. Katie took its presence as a good omen.

She sat at the desk and wrote a note to the doctor. She had to explain this pillaging—she didn't want Jeannie to believe what Katie knew she'd be hearing on the news. Dr. Bennett was one of the few people in the world who cared about Katie, and the feeling was mutual. It was important that she know the truth.

Dr. Bennett had been her first doctor, taking care of Katie since the day she was born. The doctor was always kind to her, no matter how stupid Katie was, but she was never afraid to speak her mind, either. She told Katie the facts—the risk of overdosing, the risk of contracting AIDS and other STDs—and showed graphic pictures to emphasize her point. Katie didn't always listen, but it made her feel good to know that Dr. Bennett cared. And eventually, her message sank in to Katie's somewhat thick skull.

She could still remember the day Dr. Bennett had saved her life by giving her a job as a nursing assistant here at the clinic. With her support she'd gotten clean and transformed into a respectable woman herself. She couldn't come in and rob the clinic without explaining. She at least owed Dr. Bennett that much.

Sitting at the desk, Katie composed a brief note, reassuring Dr. Bennett that she hadn't murdered Billy and promising to return everything she'd borrowed from the clinic. Satisfied, Katie made her way back through the hallway with the doctor's briefcase in hand.

Nan was seated at the table where Katie had left her. A nebulizer machine sat before her, connected correctly but not operational. "What is this thing?" Nan asked, fascinated. "Is this for delivering babies?"

Katie laughed once again. "No, silly, it's for treating asthma." How the little compressor with a tiny chamber and three feet of plastic tubing could aid in childbirth, she couldn't imagine, but once in the car, she planned to ask Nan her thoughts about that one. Relaxed from the light moment, Katie forgot to be scared. She forgot caution. After quickly punching in the alarm code, she opened the door and then, startled, jumped back.

"Hands up!" the police officer warned them. He stood in the doorway, his squad car behind him with a blinking light on top, casting him in a surreal glow that was sure to make Katie's migraine worse. Even though the light was blinding, though, she couldn't miss the gun pointed squarely at her chest. The shiny metal reflected the light in a beam that shot painfully into her eyes.

Katie raised her free right hand. Her briefcase was dangling from her left, and a set of spare scrubs was jammed into her armpit.

She recognized the officer from the neighborhood. He'd been in the clinic many times and was always friendly to the staff. He surely would remember her. Her mind raced, thinking of how she could use this to her advantage.

"Oh, hello, Officer!" Katie exclaimed with a calm she didn't feel. "Did we set off the alarm?"

He looked at her, and she could see the recognition register on his face. Conscious of the beeping alarm, Katie turned from him and punched in the code once again, and then once again faced him. "I'm so sorry!" she exclaimed.

Nan cleared her throat and, for the first time, the officer looked in her direction. He was unable to hide his surprise when he saw the tiny eighty-year-old would-be burglar. "I hope you aren't going to get my neighbor into any trouble, Officer," Nan pleaded, standing up and waddling toward him with a gait that resembled a penguin's. Nan struggled to breath as she walked, feigning shortness of breath so well she could have won an Academy Award. Pointing at the nebulizer machine on the table, she continued. "I had an asthma attack, and since she's such a nice doctor, I called her. She brought me here because we didn't want to be in the ER all night. She has to be in the clinic for nine a.m."

Katie, still wearing the lab coat and the ID tag of Dr. Weeks, tried what she thought was an apologetic stance. A grimace on her face, she slumped a bit and held up her hands in surrender. "I confess, I did it," she said, her tone light. "Mrs. Arlington watches my kids after school, and I can't afford for her to be sick. So here we are. Please don't turn me in."

He leaned back slightly, in a less aggressive posture, and looked from Katie to Nan, apparently thinking. Behind him that awful light continued to cast its schizophrenic pattern, and Katie began to feel sick. She did her best to hide it, but at this point vomiting was a serious possibility.

"What's your name, Doc?" he asked. Katie knew he'd seen her in the clinic, she had keys and the alarm code, and she was accompanied by a little gnome of a lady who was audibly wheezing. This was either one bizarre burglary or she was telling the truth. Katie hoped he'd lean toward the second possibility.

"Mary Weeks. My friends call me Mare." Katie extended her hand in greeting and he shook it.

"Jack Weaver." They shook, and then she immediately brought her small finger to her mouth and bit her cuticle. She silently chastised herself and dropped her hand to her side.

"Whatcha got there?" he asked, pointing to the scrubs tucked under her arm.

"Just some clean scrubs for tomorrow." She handed him the items. No surgical instruments were hidden in the folds, no needles or syringes or drugs. He handed them back and motioned to the briefcase, and when she handed it to him, he pulled his flashlight from his belt and shone it inside, finding only the paperwork she'd pilfered from the filing cabinet.

"I guess I can keep a lid on this." He winked at Nan and smiled at Katie, motioning them toward the door. "I'll wait while until you're on your way. You never know."

They thanked him profusely, both for his vigilance in guarding the clinic and his understanding of their delicate situation.

Nan discreetly winked at Katie, and while the policeman escorted her down the stairs, Katie carefully placed her briefcase and the scrubs on the backseat beside the blue suitcase.

"Holy cow," Nan exclaimed when they were back in the car. "This is more exciting than the television."

Katie chuckled. "Thank goodness for Gerald. You learned to lie like a champion, Nan."

Nan answered her laugh. "You ain't seen nothin' yet. We're gonna have to put on a good show at the hospital, you know."

Katie maneuvered the car onto the road and, after a moment of silence, she spoke. "That was supposed to be the easy part."

"And it was easy. We're doing fine. Just think of it as the dress rehearsal."

Katie fought the urge to bite her nail as she drove, wishing she could share Nan's confidence. A sense of urgency overtook her as she glanced at the dashboard. It was already after midnight; almost two hours had passed since the shooting. The clock was ticking. At any minute, someone could arrive at the hospital and take her children away. If she was going to pull this off, she needed to hurry. They couldn't afford another delay.

"You know the drill, right?" Katie still didn't have the whole plan together but had provisions for several different options. All of them involved Nan gaining access to the ER by feigning chest pain. Katie knew the lobby would be crowded with all kinds of people with all kinds of concerns, but none of them would have that kind of pain. It often meant a heart attack, and Medicare reimbursed hospitals and clinics based on performance in treating heart attacks. Nan would get the red-carpet treatment, no questions asked. She'd be taken right back, given oxygen, and placed on a monitor.

"I told you, Gerald Senior suffered from angina pectoris. I know all about it. Squeezing pain in his heart, shortness of the breath, sick to the stomach. You just leave it to me."

Katie pulled the car to the ER entrance and walked around to help Nan out. The area was so well lit a movie could have been filmed there, but fortunately, no one was hanging around. The less people who saw her at this point, the less likely she was to get caught later.

"What are you doing?" Nan asked. "Go park the car and meet me inside. I'll be fine."

Finding a parking place at the ER wouldn't be easy. If she took the risk and parked illegally, her car might be towed. And if she couldn't find a spot within a reasonable distance, the police would pick up her and the kids before they could make their getaway. Fortunately, she'd planned for that. She found the spot she was looking for and put the car into park. Pulling her briefcase from the back, she found four of the pages she'd printed. She opened the car door and, after making sure there were no witnesses, she circled it, placing one of the decals on each front door, the rear bumper, and the hood. She stood back and admired her work. The black letters stood out against the car's white paint. Satisfied, Katie grabbed the briefcase and the suitcase and walked just a few feet to the ER's main entrance. For the first time she could recall, she left her car unlocked.

Playing the role of the frantic relative, she ran up to the first hospital worker she saw and tearfully begged the security officer for directions to her grandmother, Mrs. Arlington. Katie ignored the cries of babies and the moans of people in pain, and an argument between a husband and wife. She ignored the dirty floor and the overflowing trash can, and the foul odor it emitted. She concentrated on the role she was playing—concerned granddaughter.

After the clerk verified that Nan could have a visitor, Katie was buzzed through the locked security doors and into the inner sanctum of the emergency department. Now, her night was really about to get interesting.

Just as she anticipated, she found even more chaos in the ER than in the lobby and hoped that could work to her advantage. She was counting on noise and action to help distract people from the fact that she was kidnapping two small children currently in the custody of the police.

Hospital personnel of all ranks hurried about, family members wandered to and fro, and stretchers lined the walls displaying a tragic parade of diseases. Monitors beeped. Phones rang. Human beings cursed and wailed and moaned. It was perfect.

Walking slowly, Katie reoriented herself to the layout of the emergency department. It was the closest one to her home, and with two small children she'd had occasion to visit half a dozen times for such issues as croup and vomiting and one small broken wrist. The nursing station was centrally located in the large rectangular space, and those rooms closest to that hub were in the direct line of sight of anyone who happened to be looking. They were equipped with monitors for a constant assessment of vital signs in the sickest patients. Beyond the nucleus, patient rooms were positioned every ten feet, and here a variety of workers skated about trying to provide care for the many patients seeking treatment on a busy Tuesday night. The ER was huge, with hallways leading to x-ray suites and supply areas and other departments jutting off the main area at irregular intervals. In spite of the fact that she'd been here before, if she took a wrong turn she feared she'd be lost.

No one noticed her presence as they scurried about in every direction, and Katie took advantage. The guard had given her a room number where she'd find Nan, but instead of heading directly there, she began a discreet reconnaissance mission. After all, she wasn't here to see Nan but to find Chloe and Andre.

The decision to wear scrubs had been wise. The majority of employees she noticed were similarly clothed so she blended in easily. Her ID badge indicated she was from the lab, and although it wouldn't unlock any doors to give her access, it helped create the shield of invisibility she needed to move about unencumbered.

Passing Nan's room, she paused outside the door to listen as Nan relayed the story she'd rehearsed. Once again, she was a convincing actress, and Katie smiled as she heard the nurse's sarcastic reply. "So this pain started at dinnertime and you waited until midnight to come in here? Don't you watch television? You're supposed to come right away."

Katie didn't linger long enough to hear Nan's retort. Rounding a corner, she walked the length of the hall quickly and then turned again. She was moving in a counter-clockwise direction and covered the entire perimeter in just a few minutes. She didn't find her children. She'd expected to find a nosy police officer loitering in the hall, but that hadn't been the case. Unless she went to the desk and inquired, she'd have to knock on every door to find them.

She began the task. A sign on the first door read CAUTION: RESPIRATORY ISOLATION. MASKS REQUIRED. Katie picked up a mask and tied it around her neck. It would help hide her face, and the disguise might buy her time if she needed it. She didn't enter the room but proceeded to the next room. There were thirty in all, and she planned to check every one of them if she needed to, but at the moment she didn't go into the quarantined room. Even in a crowded ER she knew they wouldn't house two small children and a police escort in a room with a contagious patient.

Pulling the mask over her face, she entered the next room. An elderly man was sleeping and didn't stir as the door opened and an arc of light filled the room, heralding Katie's presence. The next several rooms were the same. As she turned the corner and entered yet another closed door, Katie was startled to find a nurse seated at the bedside. When she looked up and saw Katie, she smiled.

"Thank God! I've stuck this poor woman three times and haven't gotten a drop of blood." Standing, she smiled at the patient, who looked as relieved as she did. Seeing the fear on Katie's face, the nurse smiled and whispered to her, "First night for you?"

Katie nodded.

"You've done this before, though, right?"

That Katie had. Thousands of times. Drawing blood was one of her many duties at the clinic. She nodded again.

"Well, get to it then. I need a rainbow," the nurse informed her, indicating one tube of every color.

Seeing no way out of this dilemma, Katie pulled gloves out of the basket at the bedside and applied a tourniquet to the woman's forearm. She draped the woman's arm from the bedside, allowing gravity to pool the blood in her extremity. Then, tapping the back of her hand, she watched as the vein there dilated. She easily drew four tubes of blood and handed them to the watching nurse, who applied identification stickers. "Good job," she said. "And thanks. By the way, I'm Liz. What's your name?"

Katie hesitated. What was her name? Then she remembered. "Mary."

"Well, Mary, welcome to night shift. I'm sure I'll be seeing you again before it's over."

She had to take a few deep breaths before she found the courage to leave the room. She hadn't counted on getting that close to any actual staff members. If Liz had paid closer attention to Katie's ID badge, her cover would have been blown. Finally, knowing she was racing the clock, Katie emerged from the room and continued her search. She was nearly back at Nan's room and losing hope when she saw a police officer, straddling the doorway and watching the commotion as a belligerent patient gave the nursing staff a hard time. He stood ready, hands on his hips, the left one dangerously close to the gun holstered there. Yet he didn't seem inclined to help the staff as they wrestled with the intoxicated man. Instead, he watched, smiling and shaking his head. No doubt he'd seen the same show many times before.

Her head down, Katie walked past him, moving quickly, with no opportunity to see inside the room and check if her children were hidden behind his large frame. Behind him, the door was open only a hair. But they had to be in there, unless Nan's intelligence was wrong and they'd been transported to another hospital. She had to find out, but how?

With a glance over her shoulder, Katie pulled back the curtain and disappeared into Nan's room. Their eyes met, and for the first time all evening, Nan had a concerned expression. "Any luck?" she asked.

"I'm not sure. I need your help."

Standing at the bedside, Katie explained the dilemma, and wordlessly, Nan sat up in the bed and began to disconnect the various wires attached to her body. Immediately, a monitor began beeping in protest, and Katie furiously pushed buttons to quiet them. She didn't relax until the last fell silent. When Nan was ready, Katie went to the edge of the curtain and pulled it back, checking the hallway for any problems. All was well.

"Remember to wait until I'm in position, okay?" Katie asked. "I just need one minute." Nan nodded in understanding.

Katie exited the room with her head down, walking purposefully to the right, Georgia's little blue suitcase in her hand. To her left, the scuffle with the belligerent patient was drawing to a close and the crowd was thinning. Perfect. She circled the corridor and, to her relief, the guard she'd noticed earlier was still at his post. Katie needed him there, for the moment.

Slipping into a restroom, Katie slipped the suitcase behind the trash can and was back in the hallway a few seconds later. A full minute had passed, but she still didn't see Nan. The officer was still at his post.

She hesitated outside a patient's room, bent her head, and pretended to read something she pulled from the pocket of her coat. Next, she stooped and tied her shoe, waiting. C'mon, Nan, she said to herself, counting the seconds by the pulse beating in her ear. Just when she thought she'd faint, Nan appeared. Always thinking, she'd had taken time to change out of her hospital gown and back into her clothing. After this, things might move fast.

Nan scanned the hallway, and after noting Katie in position, she embarked on her mission. Turning left, she took the route opposite of the one Katie had, approaching the police officer from the other direction. They now had him surrounded—two women, one old and one wanted by police. It wasn't ideal, but it would have to do. Katie didn't have any other options.

Holding on to the wall, Nan made slow progress, and Katie winced as she watched, keeping one eye on Nan and the other on her target. If he disappeared into that room again, Katie would have to resort to plan B. But luck was with them. Apparently he'd grown bored in the room and was enjoying the scenery in the hall, because he seemed planted now, watching the activity. When she reached a spot about twenty feet from him, Nan began to sway. Her knees started to buckle and she leaned into the wall for support.

The policeman might have stood and watched as the nurses suffered broken ribs in a scuffle with a drunken patient, but apparently he wouldn't allow an octogenarian to fall and break a hip. As soon as the officer saw Nan tottering on those old legs, he was off to the rescue. Before he even reached the woman's side, Katie slipped through the door he'd been guarding and into the semi-darkness of the room.

A forty-watt bulb above the bed provided the only light Katie needed. There, nesting in its glow, were the two loves of her life. Andre was snuggled in the arms of his big sister Chloe, sleeping. Just as the police officer had been guarding their doorway, so his big sister was guarding him. Tears of relief filled her eyes, but she immediately wiped them and steadied herself as she pushed forward into the room. She still had a job to do.

Chloe's eyes flew open and she sat up as she saw Katie. "Mommy!" She squealed in delight, a huge smile lighting her face. Her arms opened for a hug.

Katie brought her pointer finger to her lips to instruct Chloe to remain quiet. The shift in Chloe's position awakened her brother, but it took him a moment to come around fully. Katie took advantage of the delay and crawled next to them on the bed, pulling them both tight into her arms. "I'm here, now. Everything's fine," she said. Then she pulled back and looked at them.

"We're going to play a little game now. I want you to listen carefully while I tell you the rules."

# CHAPTER NINE
# TIMING IS EVERYTHING

Simon circled the perimeter of the hospital, again driving Angelica's Ford sedan. He owned another car—bigger and flashier—but was forced to leave it parked all too often. Big, flashy cars drew the attention of the police, and he didn't want or need that. He'd been able to operate his business right under their noses for years by blending in with the crowd instead of standing out among his peers.

Pulling his car to a halt in front of the large, brightly lit sign, he scanned the area. All was quiet, with the exception of a few people huddled in the smoking hut. At the moment, two ambulances were parked at the emergency entrance, their rear doors left open but lights and engines turned off. Not surprisingly, he couldn't find a vacant parking spot. He pulled his car next to the coroner's and sat, watching for a moment.

Katie would have to make her entrance here, through the emergency room. All other entrances were locked at this hour. Her escape route, though, was entirely unpredictable. She could easily slip through one of the dozens of emergency exits and be long gone before someone came to investigate the alarm her departure had triggered. His best shot of finding her was just as Angelica had suggested—to find the kids.

Katie was beyond his ability to comprehend. She was a beautiful girl, and smart. She could have had a decent life with Billy if she hadn't chosen to have those damn kids. Abortions were easy to arrange, but instead of opting for the simple solution, she'd gone and gotten a job and rented an apartment and played mommy to not one, but two little brats. And all his sources said she was happy. She never dated, just worked and took care of her kids.

Simon knew she'd been trying to make a better life for them, but where had it got her? The kids she loved so much were baiting the trap. In the end she was still going to die by the bullets she'd vowed to avoid. Coming clean hadn't done her or Billy any good, and Simon was willing to bet the kids would one day meet the same fate as their parents. There weren't many people who could climb their way from the bottom. Sure, he'd done it, but he was the exception, not the rule.

He'd made it out, and made a great life for himself—and he planned to keep it. He needed to silence Katie. Only a handful of people in the world could identify him, but he wasn't concerned about that. If he was ever arrested, he was prepared to leave the country on a moment's notice. A murder charge would be harder to dodge, though, and his avenues of escape could be cut off. Katie was the only witness who could link him to Billy's murder, and she had to be eliminated. Soon.

It was time to put this miserable night to an end. It'd been a disaster from the beginning. If it wasn't for the money, Simon would have had one of his associates do the shooting. But he couldn't trust any of them with the kind of money Billy was talking about, so he'd gone to the house himself. And of course, as soon as Simon demanded the cash, Billy had told him he didn't have the money yet. Simon had no choice but to silence Billy, which was relatively easy. He'd never seen it coming. Katie, though, continued to be a thorn in his side. First he'd had to jump off the roof, then shoot up the neighborhood, and the police had nearly stopped him as he was driving away. He'd be so happy when she was dead.

Dressed in a suit and shiny black shoes, Simon thought he looked like an official from Children and Youth Services. After showering and shaving, he could have been a teacher or a lawyer or even a social worker. He certainly didn't look the part of a gangster, unless he went back in time a century to the age of Dillinger and Capone. Those boys knew how to dress. The punks these days had no style.

His plan was twofold. He'd watch for Katie and shoot her on sight. The hospital had so many corridors and exits, he'd easily escape into the night. If she didn't show up, he'd monitor the children's movements and learn the address of the foster home where the children would be placed. It would be too risky to try to abduct them from the ER, with hospital security and the Philadelphia PD both a threat. He might be able to get out alone, but not with two little brats in tow. No, he'd let them get to the foster home, and once they were there, abducting them wouldn't be hard. When they were in his custody, Simon would put out the word on the street that he had them and force Katie out of hiding.

The waiting area was crowded with patients and family members, and Simon ignored them all as he walked past, trying to look professional and important. Too late, he realized he should have brought a briefcase or some papers. Weren't social workers always filling out paperwork?

The receptionist behind bulletproof glass was talking on the phone. He tried to appear nonchalant as he waited, staring at the clock. The longer he was there, he figured, the more likely the hospital staff would think he belonged. He wouldn't rush the woman, even though he'd just watched two minutes tick by on the clock on the wall over her head.

❖

Glancing from her kids' room into the hallway, Katie saw her opportunity and seized it. Nan was still on the floor, and in addition to the police officer, a nurse was now offering assistance. She slipped out of the room and walked briskly in the opposite direction. After looking around to confirm that no one was watching, she slipped back into the bathroom she'd reconnoitered earlier.

After locking the door, Katie retrieved the suitcase. Only a few minutes had passed since she deposited it there, but she was relieved to find it where she'd left it. Plans A, B, & C were in the suitcase. If someone had come along and stolen it, she'd have been forced to resort to plan D, which she hadn't written yet.

Stripping off her scrubs, she pulled Nan's old dress from the suitcase. It had weathered the journey well, with no wrinkles, and Katie easily slipped into it and raised the zipper in back. The dress was white and covered with large, colorful blossoms. A flower adorned the wide fuchsia belt attached at the waist, and blooms of all colors peeked out from flared pleats at the calf-length hem. Next, she pulled up her hair and fastened it with several pins, then placed the matching hat on her head. It was covered with flowers, a perfect match for the dress. A layer of bright-red lipstick, large, bold earrings, and tortoise-shell eyeglasses completed the picture.

Stepping back to inspect herself in the mirror, Katie was pleased with what she saw. The image that greeted her was so obnoxious and loud it was hard to see beyond the clothing to the woman who wore it. Even a close friend wouldn't have recognized her in this costume.

It had been Nan's idea.

*Hide right in front of them! Get in their face and make them notice your loud voice and what you're wearing, so they don't notice you. The police won't expect that and you'll catch them off guard.*

With her briefcase in one hand, Mary Weeks, MSW, used the other to open the door.

Both Nan and the police officer were now gone from the hallway, and Katie strode purposefully toward the door of the room where her children awaited, wondering what would happen, knowing it was too late to turn back. Would they jump up and call out to her, blowing her cover? Would the real social worker show up and expose her? Would the police officer recognize her? It was possible a photo of her had already been circulated. It would be an old photo, but she hadn't changed enough since her last mug shot to make her unrecognizable. Katie shook off the doubts; she just had to keep moving.

Feigning confidence and making as much noise as possible, Katie made her entrance. "Anybody here?" she demanded as she walked into the room. Her children were awake, expecting her. As she'd instructed them, they remained silent, and Katie was relieved.

The dim light was still the only light in the room, and that would work in her favor. The police officer, sitting in a corner chair, was less likely to recognize her in the shadows it cast.

He rose to meet her, and Katie made a conscious effort not to recoil. Police had been her enemy for so long, and every time an officer came into the clinic she nearly panicked. This night was no better. This one towered above her and outweighed her by a hundred pounds. On his left hip a long gun hung in a black plastic holster. A variety of weapons draped from his duty belt—pepper spray, a baton, a heavy flashlight—and for a fraction of a second Katie wondered which he'd use on her.

Looking to her children, she found her strength. She was armed with just her wits, but she was ready to fight for them.

Katie thrust a confident hand forward and went straight to business. She and Nan had decided that the personality of the woman wearing this dress was overbearing and demanding, and that's how she intended to play the part. "Mary Weeks, Social Services. I came as soon as I could," she announced with authority.

"Marty Edwards," he responded, assessing her as he did. He seemed to make an effort to hide the smirk on his face as he took in the obnoxious dress and matching hat. The plan worked, though. The disguise and aggressive posturing completely threw him off balance, and whatever questions he might have asked or protocols he might have followed were forgotten as Mary Weeks took over. He backed up into the chair he'd previously occupied.

"Well, Officer, I understand the doctor has checked the children and found them to be healthy. I just have a few papers for you to sign and I'll be on my way with them."

"Sounds good to me." He sat back in the chair and crossed his legs at the ankles.

Katie wished for a distraction so he'd look somewhere else but at her, but no such luck came her way. When he offered to turn on the light, she nearly screamed. "Don't disturb the children," she ordered him, and he retreated to his chair. He studied her in the shadows as she sorted through the paperwork she'd compiled at the clinic. When she'd pulled all the forms from the files she'd packed into the briefcase, she turned toward the bed.

Chloe and Andre stared at her, a mixture of fear and disbelief on their faces.

"Tell me your names," she instructed the children.

They looked at her and remained silent. Good! They were following their orders. Katie had feared that when they first saw her they'd welcome her just as Chloe had—with an exuberant greeting—and the game would be over. But sneaking into the room to prepare them for their role had worked. Just as her mother had produced the church theater productions when she was a kid, Katie did now, and her children were no strangers to role-playing. She'd told them she planned to return, dressed in a funny dress and hat, and they had to pretend they didn't know her. They weren't going to talk at all, until Katie said, "Simon Says!" It was a game they played often, and they would be able to follow her instructions.

"Tell me your names," she repeated, more firmly this time.

Andre began to speak, but his sister reprimanded him. "Be quiet. Don't talk."

"I got it here," the officer interjected, handing Katie a police report. He didn't even bother to read the paper. Katie hid her anger as she accepted his offering. He'd been with her children for nearly two hours and didn't even know their names.

"Thank you, Officer," she replied, feigning gratitude.

After copying her children's names onto the paperwork, she produced the ID bracelets and instructed Chloe and Andre to hold out their wrists. Katie nodded discreetly to her daughter and Chloe offered her arm. Andre followed, and Katie placed a band on each of them. "I don't like to take any chances with any kids getting misplaced."

"Yeah. That'd create a lot of paperwork."

Katie chuckled at the thought of the paperwork this jerk would have when his superiors found out she'd stolen her children from him.

"Sign here," she ordered Marty Edwards. Without looking at the paperwork she'd so carefully crafted, he did. "Now here." And that was it. Katie handed him his copy and turned to her children. "All right. It's time to go now."

Katie held out a hand to Andre and he accepted it, pulling himself out of the bed. Both kids wore their pajamas, with Crocs on their feet. "Simon says hold your brother's hand," Katie told Chloe.

"That was fast," Officer Edwards commented.

"It's late for these children, Officer. And they've been through a great trauma tonight. Best to get them settled as quickly as possible. Good night."

He nodded and walked in the other direction as Katie and her children began their escape.

❖

Seven minutes. The stupid bitch had been on the phone for seven fucking minutes. The urge to shoot the door lock and break into her secure booth and strangle her was becoming hard to ignore when suddenly she hung up the phone and stared at Simon. No smile, no apology, no explanation. “Can I help you?” she asked.

Forcing a smile, Simon played the part of charmer. “I’m Mr. Irving, from social services. I’m here about those two little children involved in the shooting.” Simon often used the name Irving when he needed an alias. Dr. J had been one of his childhood heroes, and it was a show of respect for him.

“Hold on. I’ll see if you can go back.”

Again he waited and watched the woman as she held the telephone receiver to her ear. Although she smiled into the receiver for the benefit of the person on the line, when she hung up, she had no smile for him. She pointed a finger toward a locked door next to the security booth. When he’d entered the waiting area, the booth had been empty. Now, a large, heavily tattooed man sat within. Simon approached him with the same confidence he’d shown the woman at the booth.

Reaching for his wallet, he took a proactive approach, hoping to avoid questions and scrutiny. His gun was safely tucked in a leg holster, but he didn’t want to take a chance and get frisked. Or shot. “Let me show you my ID, Officer,” Simon said. The driver’s license in Julius Irving’s name had come in handy over the years, and he always kept it hidden in his wallet for just such occasions.

“Oh, okay,” the man said, and looked at the ID. He was too young or too stupid to recognize the name, for he didn’t comment. “Let me buzz you through,” he said. “We’ve had a little commotion for a few minutes. Some old lady got dizzy and fell, but everything’s okay now.” At the push of his finger, the door buzzed loudly, and that easily, Simon was through the doors and in the emergency department.

❖

Forcing herself to walk slowly, Katie guided the children toward the door she’d come through just a few minutes before. Ahead of her and to the right, she saw Officer Edwards. He’d taken the long way around, but with two children beside her slowing her pace, he reached the exit first. As he reached for the wall button to open the door, it opened and Simon Simms walked through. Katie gasped and both kids hesitated, sensing her fear.

His attention was directed at the police officer, and Katie took advantage of the distraction and hurriedly changed direction, pushing the children before her into another patient room. She doubted Simon would recognize her in her costume, and he didn't know Chloe and Andre well enough to recognize them, but if the police officer spotted her, no doubt he'd point her out to Simon. The game would be over.

An elderly woman was asleep in the bed, with tubing feeding precious oxygen into her lungs and sustenance into her veins.

"Don't stare, it's rude!" Katie admonished her children when she caught them looking. At the moment she didn't care so much about manners as she did about terrifying the children. The woman looked to be near death. Katie felt the same way as she pushed back the curtain and saw the police officer chatting with Simon. Their voices were inaudible from this distance, but from their body language they appeared to be on friendly terms. She watched the officer motion down the hallway toward the room Katie and her children had just vacated. With a nod and a smile, Simon began walking that way.

Katie didn't know what to do. If the officer noticed her, he'd probably stop her, since Simon was obviously in search of Chloe and Andre. Maybe it would be best to hide in this room for a while, until they both left the ER. Then, just as she accepted that as her only option, the officer suddenly turned and followed Simon, clearing the path for Katie's escape. Without trying to hide her sense of urgency, she pulled the children into the hallway. "Let's go, quickly." Katie told herself to not look over her shoulder and forged forward, and they cruised through the first set of doors with no difficulty.

Nan was arguing with a nurse as Katie and the children passed her in the lobby. "I feel so much better, now," Katie heard her explain as they continued toward the car. Both children noticed her, but just as they'd been instructed, they remained silent.

Automatic doors opened for them as they approached the exit. "Open Sesame!" Katie whispered, and the children giggled but didn't say a word.

It was difficult to resist the urge to run through the hospital, but once they were through the doors, Katie became Mom again, and she couldn't control her fear a moment longer. "Simon says, run." Even wearing high heels, she strode briskly to the car. No one had towed it, and no one was blocking it in, although a black Ford sedan had parked illegally beside it. She pulled the stickers from the hood and door on her side as she made her way around but didn't waste time with the other two. As she climbed in the front, her kids jumped into the back. "Buckle up, guys," she told them.

Looking up, she saw the nurse heading back to the ER, shaking her head in frustration. Nan was halfway to her car, making slow progress. She and Nan had agreed to split up if anything happened, knowing that Nan would make her way home somehow. Katie would keep the car.

She was tempted to leave without Nan, but something told her to wait, and she did, with one eye on her children in the backseat and the other watching Nan's progress across the sidewalk. She diverted her gaze to the sliding-glass doors for signs of Simon. Just as Nan reached to car door, he materialized in the lobby. He was backlit, and she could clearly see him, but the car camouflaged her. In another few seconds, that would change. When he reached the sidewalk, he'd spot her.

"Get in, now!" Katie screamed.

And then a miracle happened. Marty Edwards ran through the ER doors and stopped Simon. He pointed over his shoulder toward the ER, and Katie watched Simon nod and begin walking back inside with the officer.

"Hello, everybody," Nan greeted them. Before she was even seated, Katie had the car in motion. "It looks like we got our babies back."

"Hi, Nan," Chloe and Andre said from the backseat.

Now that the silence had been broken, they were full of questions. "Why were you at the hospital, Nan? Are you sick?"

"Why did you have to go to work at night?"

"Why are you wearing that hat, Mommy?"

And then, the one she dreaded. "Why were the police at our house, Mommy?"

Katie made a series of turns to get them out of sight of the hospital. As she pulled to a stop at a traffic light, a thought suddenly occurred to her. "Oh, no," she exclaimed, a little too loudly.

Nan touched her arm. "What is it?"

"Where are we going? We can't go back to your house, and we certainly can't go back to mine." She'd been so preoccupied with recovering her children she hadn't even considered what she'd do once she had them back. Her house was a crime scene. The police would likely search Nan's after they reviewed the ER security videos and saw her leaving with Katie. She might have taken them to the clinic, but since her run-in with the police there earlier, she wasn't comfortable with that plan.

"I can always ask the reverend to take you in. But he's a tough one. I don't know how he'd feel about all this. Can't you think of anyone else? Anyone at all who'd help you?"

Katie was about to say no, a reflexive, defensive answer that reflected not only the state of her life for many years, but also her state of mind. She was used to taking care of herself. Then she reconsidered. She could call Jeannie Bennett. Jeannie would help her, without questions. But perhaps she had one other person to turn to. She made a left turn at the next traffic light and pointed the car toward Jet's house.

# CHAPTER TEN
# MIDNIGHT RENDEZVOUS

Janet Fox, addressed by all except her mother as Jet, sat on the top step of the stone stairs leading from the street to her apartment house. Scanning Wayne Avenue in both directions, she saw no light other than the streetlamps filtering through the leaves of huge oaks dating back to Creation. From her perch high above the street she could see the entire area, and on this early morning all was quiet. That wasn't unusual at this hour. What was unusual was the phone call she'd received minutes earlier from her friend Katie. Katie had asked if she could come over, explaining it was an emergency and promising to provide all the details when she arrived.

Lifting a bare foot from the cool stone beneath, Jet gracefully slipped her size twelve into a sneaker and tied the laces, then repeated the process on the other foot. Standing, adrenaline surging through her veins, she stretched and scanned the road again. Still no headlights. What the hell was going on? She'd been in dreamland when her cell phone rang, startling her back to reality. Katie's picture on the phone had filled her with dread.

She'd learned Katie's universal truth of motherhood on a trip to Jet's parents' vacation home at Lake Wallenpaupack—*No matter what time the mom goes to bed, the kids will still be up early.* The two of them had stayed up late, talking in front of the fire they'd lit to warm the cold mountain night. As the clock struck one, Katie stood and, groaning, predicted the kids would be awake in five or six hours. Sure enough, Jet found Chloe and Andre quietly watching a video when she went downstairs to put on a pot of coffee early the next morning. Katie had wandered down shortly after, and Jet heard her swearing to herself as she shook the sleep from her eyes.

"We need a curfew!" Katie had teased her as she squeezed her shoulder on her way across the kitchen to retrieve a coffee mug. "No talking after ten."

"Eleven."

Katie had just shaken her head and sipped the coffee Jet poured as a peace offering. Later, after a busy day chasing the kids through the woods, though, both Jet and Katie were exhausted and were unconscious by ten that night. Since then, they'd been very cognizant of the time as they talked on the phone each evening. If they weren't, they'd stay up all night talking and regret it in the morning.

The call from Katie was odd but not totally surprising. Jet knew something was going on with Katie, and she should have had the courage to ask her about it instead of tiptoeing around it. But she did what she always did with Katie—she kept quiet and allowed Katie to decide when and what to reveal. Still, the past few days since Katie's ex-boyfriend had reappeared had been awful for Jet as she tortured herself with thoughts of Billy filling the role she'd lately taken on.

Just what was that role, though? Were they destined to be friends? Or could they be more? Katie didn't allow many people to get close. Maybe she just looked at Jet as a best friend. Yet, they'd been slowly closing that narrow space between them, becoming more intimate in every way except a sexual one. They teased and talked and finished each other's sentences. Working together at the clinic and at home, side by side, they moved like one, anticipating each other's needs. They were perfect together, perfect for each other, with just one little problem. Katie had never slept with a woman.

The Saturday before, the four of them—Jet, Katie, Chloe, and Andre—had ventured to Rehoboth Beach, and that night, after the children were safely asleep in one of the rented hotel room's double beds, Jet and Katie fell beside each other in the other one. On their sides, they lay facing each other, talking for hours, studying each other in the glow of light escaping through the crack in the bathroom door—definitely violating Katie's rule. Yet neither wanted to stop talking, and Jet didn't want the intimacy of that night to ever end. A dozen times she suppressed the urge to pull Katie into her arms and kiss her. She'd never wanted to kiss anyone, to touch them and hold them and make love with them as much as she desired Katie. It was frustrating and wonderful at the same time, and Jet felt paralyzed to act. Paralyzed to even speak about what she felt. When a yawn escaped Jet's mouth, Katie had bridged the two-inch gap between them to kiss her gently, on the nose. Then, like the mother she was, she told Jet to go to sleep.

Inspired by the night they'd spent together, Jet fantasized of a room with just one bed and no children. She wanted more, and she sensed Katie did, too. Yet the next afternoon, on the ride home from the beach, Andre let it slip that his father was staying with them again. After that bomb dropped they spent the remainder of the drive in relative silence, with only the banter of the kids breaking the uneasy quiet. When they finally arrived back at Jet's apartment, Katie pulled her aside.

"I haven't slept with him in years, Jet, and I don't intend to now. Nothing, *absolutely nothing*, is going on between us."

Jet had started to ask more, but Katie silenced her. Still the questions lingered in her mind. Why the hell was he there? How long did he plan to stay? The bigger question in her mind also remained unasked—what was going on between Katie and her?

Jet had never practiced such chastity. Was she wasting her time on a straight woman? If so, why was Katie reassuring her? It could mean only one thing, right? Katie was interested in Jet. She hoped and prayed it wasn't just wishful thinking. Katie had touched her in a way no woman ever had, and Jet wanted more. Many women had made her laugh or made her think, but Katie truly made her *feel.* She was in love—with Chloe and Andre, and most especially with their mother. And before she went totally crazy, she needed to talk to Katie about her feelings.

Headlights drew Jet's attention to the road, and she watched the car approach and then stop in front of her house. Was this Katie? She'd been expecting Katie's silver Toyota Camry, but this car was a boxier older model. In the near darkness the car appeared white, and Jet could discern writing on the door, although she couldn't decipher the letters.

Hesitating a moment, she watched Katie hop out, wearing some sort of Kentucky Derby hat on her head. She briefly acknowledged Jet with a brief wave as she rushed to open the rear passenger's door.

Before Katie completed her task, Jet was halfway down the stairs. She was startled to see the word CORONER printed on the door. Without breaking stride, she met Katie on the sidewalk and took a sleeping Chloe from her arms. The passenger doors, front and back, opened in tandem, and Andre jumped from the car to the sidewalk. "Jet," he exclaimed, looking excited. From the front, an elderly African-American woman emerged, holding onto the car for support.

"Hey, pal," Jet said to Andre.

"Jet, this is Nan. Nan, my friend Jet." Katie quickly made the introductions and then without delay ordered Andre to follow Jet back up the stairs to her apartment. "I'll be back in ten minutes," Katie explained, then hopped into the car again. The sooner she had Nan home, the less likely she was to be caught taking her there.

She dropped her off at the end of her block, pulling to a stop where the street was dark. Both of them climbed out, but Katie rushed around to meet Nan on her side. "I'll call you as soon as I can, and I'll try to return the car in the morning. Please, please…" Katie was going to ask for Nan's protection if and when the police questioned her. Then she thought for a moment and smiled. After what they'd been through this night, she was sure Nan would do whatever necessary to protect her and the kids. "I guess I don't need to say any more, do I?"

"I've got your back," Nan said.

Katie laughed and hugged her. "Thank you. I'll call when I can, okay?"

"You make sure you do. I'll be worrying about all of you."

She turned to walk away, but before she'd taken a step, Katie spoke again. "Nan, there's something else."

Nan turned and looked at her, and though the light was poor, Katie thought she saw concern on her face. "What is it, honey?"

"I'm going to need your help about Billy. A funeral. I don't know what to do."

"Does he have a family?"

Katie shrugged. Billy had never known his father, and his mother had died of cancer when he was fifteen. Like Katie, he'd lived on the streets until Simon Simms took him under his wing. "None that I know of. Maybe a brother somewhere." Katie vaguely remembered Billy mentioning an older sibling who'd left town.

"I'll help you then. We'll use Marker's. They did a good job with Gerald, and you'll get a discount 'cuz the owner belongs to my church." Her reassuring smile suddenly replaced by a frown, she leaned closer to Katie, nearly whispering. "How are you going to afford this, Katie? Funerals aren't cheap."

Had it been only three hours ago that she'd told Billy she wouldn't give him a penny? Now she'd be spending her inheritance—some of it, anyway—on his funeral. "I have some money saved," she said, as she used her sleeve to wipe away fresh tears.

Nan nodded. "Okay. I'll find out if Mr. Marker's available." They hugged again and Nan patted Katie's back reassuringly, then turned and walked to the end of the block. Only when the porch light was extinguished did Katie finally pull away. She was parked in the space behind Jet's apartment ten minutes later.

Jet's door was ajar, and after crossing the threshold into the apartment, Katie turned and double-locked it. She checked to make sure the curtains were drawn, then kicked off her shoes and followed the sound of voices into Jet's kitchen. Andre was perched on the counter, with Jet standing guard beside him. Drinking a glass of milk out of a bending, curving, transparent straw, Andre said, "Look," pointing to the mixture of milk and bubbles moving through the hollow tube. This wonder of modern engineering totally amazed him, and he showed no fear or fatigue, just boundless joy.

"That's one amazing straw," Katie said.

Beaming, he answered her. "Jet bought it for me."

Katie prided herself on her independence, especially when it came to supporting her children. Yet for some reason, Jet's attentions didn't bother or threaten her. Her kindness wasn't calculated to gain Katie's affections; it was genuine. Jet loved her kids, and for that, Katie loved her even more. Gazing at Jet, who wore the cut-off sweatpants and soft cotton T-shirt Katie recognized as her pajamas, she smiled.

"Did you thank Jet?"

"Yes, he did." Jet ran her fingers through Andre's curly hair as she looked lovingly down at him.

"Well, drink up because it's way past your bedtime."

"I put Chloe in the spare bedroom. She never even stirred." Their eyes met and Jet said, "Nice outfit."

Katie ran her hand up the back of her neck and removed the hat. With a flick of her fingers, the hairpins came out, too, and her thick mane of hair tumbled down. She shook her head and looked at Jet. "Better?" she asked.

"Oh, I'm not sure. It's a pretty cool hat." Jet bit her lip to suppress her laughter, and suddenly Katie's spirits felt a little lighter.

Reaching up, she placed the floral hat on Jet's head and then brought her fingers to her chin as she appraised the look. "I'm not sure it goes with the outfit."

"I'm more of a Phillies cap kind of girl."

Katie nodded in agreement and removed the floral hat from Jet's head. She'd seen Jet in a baseball cap, and it was quite a sexy image. As much as she would have liked to linger on thoughts of Jet wearing nothing but a Phils cap, she knew they needed to get Andre to bed.

"Thanks for taking care of Chloe. She was exhausted," Katie said, rubbing her eyes and thinking of her daughter, guarding her brother as they lay waiting in the hospital bed. Andre had slept, but not Chloe. Now, though, with Katie to watch over Andre, Chloe could finally rest. It wouldn't surprise Katie if her children slept through the day.

Katie took the milk glass from Andre and, after rinsing both glass and straw, followed Jet and Andre toward the bedrooms. "Wait," Andre suddenly exclaimed. "I have to brush my teeth."

"It's okay. Sometimes in an emergency we're allowed to skip," Katie explained.

"I can't skip. If I don't brush twice a day all my teeth will fall out and I'll look like a zombie." He made a funny face, pulling his lips over his teeth and sucking in his cheeks.

Jet laughed. "I think I can save you, Buddy. I happen to have a spare toothbrush."

Katie winked at Jet, slumping a bit as fatigue began to set in. "Thank you." At this hour, after this night, she didn't have the strength to argue.

"Are we having an emergency?" he queried.

"What?" Katie watched Jet open a new pack of toothbrushes.

"You said we could skip if it was an emergency. Is that why the police were at our house? Are we having an emergency?"

Jet raised her head to look at Katie, the fear and confusion on her face evident, but Katie didn't explain. She just wrapped her arms around Andre and hugged him tight. "No emergencies. That's why you have to brush your teeth."

When they all finished brushing, Andre climbed on her back for the trip to the bedroom. "G'night, Jet," he said as he blew her a kiss.

After catching it, she blew one back to him. "Night."

"I'm going to lie with him," Katie told Jet.

Jet nodded, and they disappeared into her spare bedroom. Not sure what to do, she debated going back to bed. Although she assumed the kids would sleep in this day, she had to be up for work in five hours. As tempting as it would be to take a personal day, it would be difficult at the clinic if both she and Katie were out at the same time. Jet had taken over as nurse manager six months earlier, and Katie was second in command. A dozen daily crises demanded their attention, and Jet was fairly certain the place would cease functioning without them. And at this point, Jet was fairly certain Katie wasn't going to work in the morning.

Undecided, she glanced toward her bedroom. If Katie didn't fall asleep with Andre, and for some reason wanted to talk to her, she'd know where to find her. Jet could crawl back into her own bed and be comfortable. Then she looked at the couch and knew that's where she'd go. She wouldn't be able to sleep with all the questions and uncertainty racing through her mind, so she might as well wait for Katie. Even if Katie didn't come, Jet would still wait. She'd been doing it for months.

Less than ten minutes later, after Jet had produced a clean sheet and pillow for the couch, Katie reappeared. Springing to her feet, Jet met her across the living room and pulled her into her arms. She didn't know what was happening, but whatever it was couldn't be good. "Are you okay?" Jet whispered after a moment, never letting go. Katie was petite, just a fraction of an inch above five feet tall, and Jet was just that much shy of six feet. It seemed she could swallow Katie with her arms, and that was what she wanted to do, to protect her and take away all the sadness evident on Katie's face.

Tears began flowing silently down Katie's cheeks, the bright emerald eyes suddenly cloudy. Then the dam burst, and she was sobbing uncontrollably as Jet led her to the couch and sat beside her, managing to keep her arms around her the whole time. They fell back into the warm embrace of the couch, and Jet held her tighter, stroking her back gently and kissing the forehead that rested against her chin. When Katie's breathing slowed and the shaking subsided, Jet spoke again, keeping her voice soft and calm. "Can you tell me what's wrong?"

Clearing her throat, Katie sniffled, then wiped her nose on a tissue Jet provided. "Billy's dead."

Jet had prepared for bad news, but this was beyond her imagination. "Oh, no! Katie, I'm so sorry." Jet pulled her closer and held Katie's head, running her fingers through the luxurious thickness of her hair. Jet knew Katie was no longer in love with him, but Billy was the father of her children, so his loss was an awful blow for both Katie and the kids. The tears began again, and still Jet held her, comforting her, stroking her face and planting kisses of comfort. Again she waited for Katie's cue to probe further. Finally, when Katie's breathing once more sounded normal, Jet spoke again. "What happened? How did he die?"

Now Katie pulled back enough to look at Jet. She was so… gorgeous. Even with her black hair in a state of disarray, she was beautiful. Brown eyes flecked with gold watched her intently. Her broad cheekbones and angular jaw line, and her long straight nose suggested a strength Katie needed at the moment. And those full, red lips. They were so inviting that Katie shuddered.

She wanted so badly to kiss those lips. She'd spent hours—days, even—thinking about them. Could the fragile roots of the love growing between them sustain the awful pull of Katie's past? Their lives and their worlds were so different. Her life had been such a disaster, much of that of her own making. How could someone as amazing as Jet ever truly care for her?

She didn't know that she could. But if they were to have a chance, it had to be based on truth. She'd never lied to Jet and had shared more of her story with her than she'd ever told anyone. But she hadn't told it all.

"He was shot." Then before Jet could say anything and before Katie could lose her nerve, she said, "Jet, there's so much about me and my life you don't know. I came here tonight because I didn't have anywhere else to go. I'm alone. You're my friend, but I'll understand if you tell me to get out, because this is a lot to handle."

Shaking her head defiantly, Jet responded. "No, Katie. It's not that simple. I can't just walk away. I love you! I love the woman you are today. I don't know that person you were yesterday. Your past doesn't matter. I have a past, too. We all do. As long as you love me now, that's all that I care about. And whatever you're dealing with, I want to help you. We'll get through it together."

Katie cupped Jet's face. She'd never felt this before, this joy brought just by looking at someone. "I do love you," she confessed.

A smile spread across Jet's face. She wiped her tears with her sleeve, looked into Katie's eyes and brushed her fingers across her forehead. "I'm so relieved."

Katie couldn't help giggling at the theatrics. "Why?"

"Well…it's been slow going. I was afraid I'd lost my touch."

"Am I just another notch in a well-worn belt?" Katie kept her tone light, because she didn't have doubts about Jet or her intentions.

"No, I'm teasing you. I thought maybe you were just looking for a good friend. And I could have handled that…I think. But it certainly isn't what I want."

Katie nodded. "I didn't expect this, Jet. I've never…felt this way before. About anyone, man or woman. At first, I did think you were just my best friend, my favorite person in the whole world. But then I started thinking about…other things, like kissing you, and I realized that maybe my feelings meant something more. I was afraid that might be a problem, except I sensed you feeling them, too, which makes them completely, totally great. Does that make sense?"

Jet laughed, and in spite of everything, Katie felt blissfully happy.

"Perfect sense." Jet reached out and gently clasped Katie's chin in her fingertips. Love glowed in her eyes for a moment before they closed, and their lips met in the softest of kisses, and every part of Katie caught fire. They held each other for a few seconds—or hours—it was hard to tell, feeling each other tremble. Time and senses were suspended, every nerve fiber in Katie fired by the mere touch of their lips. When they pulled apart, she was shaking.

"I've never been with a woman, Jet."

"It's okay. It's really not that difficult." Jet's dark eyes held hers, and Katie felt all of her love. It was so pure, really, and sweet. Jet was sweet.

Katie laughed, pulling away and breaking the contact so she could look into the dark pools of Jet's eyes. What she saw there—love, tenderness, kindness—gave her the courage she needed to keep speaking.

"Is that why you've been taking this so slowly?" Jet asked.

In Jet's question Katie recognized the opening she needed. "Actually, no." Before she could have the kind of relationship with Jet they both wanted, Katie needed to bare her soul. "I'm sure I'll figure out the technical details," she said with a smile. "And my heart has been skipping beats at the thought of you since the night we met. But before anything happens, I have to tell you everything. I don't want you to ever be surprised by my past. If you know everything about me and still want me, then I'm all yours."

Katie looked to Jet for some sign—fear, hesitation, anger—but all she saw was the love in Jet's eyes.

Jet pulled Katie into her arms, kissing the top of her head once again. "So tell me."

# CHAPTER ELEVEN
# HAUNTED PASTS

Seeing no point in rehashing details they'd already discussed, Katie didn't talk of things like her mother's death or her father's neglect, the way her father's second wife had abused her. She'd shared many of those stories with Jet already, encouraged by Jet's kindness and the simple squeeze of her hand. Jet cared, and though the feelings were foreign, Katie felt safe enough to open up her heart.

Taking a big breath for courage, Katie slowly exhaled, staring at the wall, at nothing really, trying to sort her thoughts. She had so much to tell and wasn't sure where to begin the sordid tale. "Okay, let's start with the drugs. Heroin—check. Crack—check. LSD—check. Pot—check. Vics, Percs, fentanyl, methadone—check, check, check, check. Xanax, Valium, Ativan—check, check, check. Get the picture?"

With her face twisted into a frowning grimace, she looked to Jet for her reaction. Jet hesitated a moment, giving Katie time to go on if she wished. When she didn't, Jet replied. "What are you using now?"

Katie shrugged. "Ibuprofen and Maxalt for migraines. A multivitamin. Tums. That's it."

"When was the last time you did any of those other drugs?"

"When I found out I was pregnant with Chloe." She remembered that day in the clinic so well, Dr. Bennett's words sinking into her brain as no others had before. *You have to stop using. The drugs are going to hurt the baby.*

"So nine years, give or take?" Jet asked, and Katie nodded. "Sounds like you've got it kicked."

Katie shrugged again.

"Do you have cravings?" Jet's voice contained no accusation, only curiosity.

"Yeah, mostly for pot. It calms me." She frowned.

Jet laughed, then asked, "But you don't do it, right?"

She shook her head. "No. I have too much to lose." When she thought about it, she realized she really didn't really crave marijuana, just the peace it offered. She would have liked to take something stronger when a bad migraine hit, but the fear of slipping back into a pattern of habitual use frightened her. Never again would she live that kind of life. No headache pain was as awful as her life had been back then. "Too much to lose," she repeated.

Jet squeezed her hand but didn't say anything further, so once again Katie had the freedom to direct the conversation.

"Okay, so we've covered drugs," Katie said. "Let's talk about men. You've never slept with any, and let's just say I've got you beat." Katie didn't even want to think about the things she'd done, let alone find the words to describe them to Jet. She would if she needed to, but she hoped Jet's general animosity toward male anatomy would squash any desire for details. "Any questions?"

Jet nodded. "Are you healthy? No diseases?"

"Yes, healthy. I've been checked for everything and it's all good."

"You're lucky."

"Yes, I know." Her mood was suddenly somber as she remembered people she knew contracting incurable viruses like HIV and hepatitis.

"Okay, what else?"

Katie rubbed her temples as she thought about the laundry list of misdeeds she'd wanted to share. "Abortions. Two of them."

"How'd that go?"

"What do you mean?"

Jet raised her eyebrows. "Well, Katie. You're obviously a great mother and you adore your children. How did you feel about having an abortion? Two of them?"

"How did I feel? How do you feel?"

Jet shook her head. "You didn't do anything to me, Katie. You did that to you."

Katie leaned back into the couch and stared at the framed print on the wall opposite her. It was a copy of a Monet, one of the water lilies he'd done at Giverny, the soothing pastels intended to calm failing miserably at their task. It was one of her favorite prints, one that had hung in her childhood home, and she'd given a copy to Jet on her birthday. It seemed to have lost some of its magic.

How did she feel about that? She didn't typically feel anything, because she didn't allow herself to. That time of her life was filled with pain, and she'd chosen to bury those memories—the drugs, the men, and the consequences. The movie reel of her life held a huge gap where the teenage years had been edited, and keeping those clips on the cutting room floor was the secret to maintaining her sanity. Just telling Jet made a cold sweat cover her back and the polyester fabric of the dress cling to her with a sickening grip.

But it seemed Jet didn't want details, and Katie's relief was so powerful it made her weak. "Okay, then we don't need to talk about it," she murmured.

Seeming to sense Katie's angst, Jet squeezed her hand. "Katie, we don't need to do this."

But Jet's words, intended to rescue her, would only tighten the binds that shackled her. "Yes, we do," she said.

Their eyes met and held, and Katie could see the love there. Jet nodded. She understood, as always. "Okay."

Katie counted the beats of her heart, pounding in her chest, and when she reached twenty, she felt a little calmer. "All right, let me study my mental list. What's next? Police record. I've been arrested about a dozen times. So many times I've lost track."

Jet nodded. "Okay. For what?"

"Oh, let's see. Burglary—that was at my father's house. The pr…" Katie stopped and closed her eyes, letting out a deep breath to calm herself. Then she bit off a cuticle and nibbled on the nail. "That was bogus. When I moved in with Billy, I went to my dad's to get some personal things from the attic. Some were mine, some were my mother's. Pictures, a vase that had belonged to my grandmother—stuff like that. April called the police. Bullshit. Anyway, moving on. Drugs charges, most of them were drug charges. Prostitution, but that was dropped. I just got hauled in with some other girls. Theft. Drunk and disorderly. Assault. I think maybe that's it."

If any of this bothered Jet, she was good at hiding it. "Well, again, how long ago was all of this?"

"Most of it was on my juvenile record. I do have an adult record though, too. I think three arrests as an adult."

"All before Chloe?"

"Oh, yes. Of course."

"Okay, what else?"

Katie opened her mouth in mock surprise. "You want more? Haven't I told you enough?"

"No more than I can handle." She nailed Katie with a piercing gaze.

Katie locked eyes with her. "All right. You asked for it. Billy. He's next. Many, many, many arrests. Most of them drug related. Some violence, too, though. Assault, mostly." Katie looked at the question in Jet's eyes and answered it before she could ask. "He saved me, Jet. I was never murdered on the streets, I didn't die of an overdose, and I didn't get AIDS, because when I was sixteen, he took me in. I had a place to sleep at night, so I didn't have to sleep with strange men. I had food, so I didn't have to steal to eat. I didn't need drugs to help me cope, because suddenly, it wasn't so bad. He never hit me. He treated me well and gave me my freedom when I asked for it. He did the best he could for me." Katie wiped the tears that began falling again when she remembered Billy was dead.

Jet squeezed her hand, and Katie regained her composure. "He's only been out of jail since Friday. I don't know what he could have done in such a short time to piss Simon off enough to kill him!" Katie flashed back to her weekend at the beach, considering the possibility that Simon might be reacting to that. She'd seen him there, and he'd been surprised. Could that be why he'd shot Billy? It just didn't make any sense.

"Who's Simon?"

"The guy Billy works for."

"And he killed him?"

"Yeah."

"What happened?"

Katie told her about hearing the shots, about jumping from the roof and running for her life. She knew Jet well enough to recognize the concern on her face. She'd never seen Jet angry or scared, but when dealing with frustrated patients or arguing staff at the clinic, she assumed an even calmer demeanor that indicated to Katie she was on her A game. Her erect posture and neutral expression, the flexed wrists with tented fingers that barely touched all gave her away.

"Where's Simon now?"

Katie shrugged. "He took off when the police showed up. I thought he'd be lying low, but he showed up at the hospital."

Jet leaned forward and her eyes flew open wide in panic. "What were you doing at the hospital? Are you hurt?"

She shook her head. "No, no. I went there to get the kids." Seeing Jet's look of confusion, Katie remembered Jet hadn't heard all the details of the evening. She quickly filled her in, and again Jet sat silently as Katie talked. Her hands weren't quiet, though. They squeezed Katie's for encouragement and tenderly touched her knee, pushed a stray bang from Katie's eyes. And her eyes spoke volumes. Darkening to near black, they cried as they felt her pain and sorrow. Bright and clear, they showed strength and pride in Katie. Now, though, Katie saw something else there, a swirling darkness, and she didn't think she liked it. It was disapproval.

Jet ran her fingers through her own hair, making her bed-head stand nearly straight up. Clasping her hands at the top of her head, she asked, "Katie, what are you thinking? A killer with a gun is looking for you! You shouldn't be here. You should be under police guard."

Katie pulled back, reeling from the sting of Jet's words." I'm sorry, Jet. I shouldn't have come here. I've put you in danger, too. I'll go."

As Katie rose, Jet grabbed her arm and pulled her gently back to the couch. "Katie, Katie, calm down. It's not that I'm afraid for me—I'm afraid for you. And for your kids. You have to call the police."

Katie quivered with fear. She could outsmart Simon, and once she had the money from her trust fund, she'd find a place to live far away from Philadelphia where he'd never find her. He was a violent man, and in his little pond he was quite a big fish, but his power didn't extend into the ocean. Katie would get lost out there, simply disappear, and he'd never find her.

The Philadelphia police were another matter. Unlike some criminals who grew resistant to the fear of jail, hers had actually grown stronger over the years. Perhaps it was because she had so much more to live for now, more to lose than her freedom. She feared the police and the power they held over her more than she feared the killer who'd just gunned down the father of her children.

Shaking her head as she once again looked into the dark pools of Jet's eyes, she bit her lip. "You just don't understand, Jet. I have a record. A drug dealer was killed in my apartment. The cops won't care if they have the right killer for some poor dealer from a bad neighborhood. They'll throw me in jail for the rest of my life, and then they'll put my kids in foster care where God only knows what'll happen to them. Don't you see? There's no justice for people like me."

Jet turned to study Katie and saw nothing but goodness. She was an amazing human being who'd overcome tragedy and made a good life for her children. She saw a kind nurse, a hardworking woman as dedicated to her job as she was to her family. Obviously, Katie viewed herself in a light much different from the glowing one through which Jet saw her.

"Katie, what does that mean—'people like you'? People like you are great parents. They play with their children and give them piano lessons. They get out of bed every day and go to work. They have solid careers and pay taxes and earn the respect and admiration of their coworkers. They have people like me who love them."

Jet watched as Katie searched her face, looking for something undefined. Proof, perhaps? When a minute passed without a response from Katie, Jet closed her eyes, contemplating her own dark past. Did she dare dredge it up and lay her own soul bare as Katie had? Like Katie, she'd never shared her secrets, and for good reason. What she'd done was so awful, so unthinkable and unforgivable that she'd had no choice but to bury it. It surfaced, though, again and again, when she least expected it to. Now, though, the pain of her tragedy might serve some good. To help Katie, she'd take the risk.

"What do you think of me? About me?" Jet asked. "Am I a good person or a bad one?"

Katie didn't hesitate to reply. "Good, Jet. No, great. You're such a sweet woman. You have so much love in your heart. I see it and feel it every time you're with my family. And I see it every time you're taking care of a patient or rearranging the schedule to help the staff get a day off when they need it. You're good, good, good."

Jet ran her hand through her hair and looked at Katie as she sank into the couch. "Then let me tell you my sins, and we'll see what you think of me then."

"What are you talking about?"

Jet took Katie's hand and squeezed it. "Katie, do you think you're the only one with a past?" Jet shook her head at the eyes opened wide with wonder. "Well, you're not. A lot of people have made mistakes. A lot of them have regrets. I have regrets."

Katie's smile was sweet, her eyes soft. "You could never have done anything to change the way I feel about you."

Jet offered a weak smile. "Remember you asked be about that scar on my ankle? I blew you off. I didn't want to talk about it. And remember how I blew you off when you pressed for details about my college basketball career?"

Katie nodded and Jet said, "Well, Katie, if you want to talk about fucking things up, I'll tell you about that." Jet bit her lips, then moistened them with her tongue. "I need a drink. Do you want something?"

"Yes, water would be great."

Jet nearly jumped from the couch and ran to the kitchen, then returned with two glasses of water and sat next to Katie again. The long-buried pain had resurfaced. "I need a smoke," she said as she turned to Katie.

"That bad, huh?"

"Yeah, that bad."

"Be strong."

Jet studied the Monet for a moment and searched for her courage. "It was my junior year in college. Everything was going great—I had good grades, made the conference all-star team. It was all great." She paused and studied the ceiling for flaws for a moment. "I'd begged my parents to let me have a car at college, and, unfortunately, they caved in. We had a break at the end of December, and I decided to drive to Vermont. There was a girl. I lied to my parents, told them I had to stay at school over the holiday because of basketball. Anyway, I met up with this girl and her friends at a ski lodge, and we all went out to a New Year's Eve party at a rental house. Most of us were smashed, including me. One of the girls who wasn't drinking was afraid to drive in the snow. Did I mention it was snowing?" Now Jet laughed, the bitter taste of her memories tainting the sound with sadness.

She turned her gaze to Katie, who met her with compassion-filled eyes, seeming to understand this story wouldn't have a happy ending. "The other girl who wasn't drinking didn't wear her glasses to the party and couldn't see to drive. So, I drove us home. I tried to, anyway. We never made it. I hit another car, head-on."

Now Jet bit the inside of her cheek, a habit she reverted to in times of stress and deep contemplation. This was both. "Five of us were in the car, all of us hurt pretty badly. I was the worst. My ankle was shattered. I needed surgery. My season was done. My team was in first place when the accident happened. I was averaging more than twenty points a game and about ten rebounds. I was a leader. And then I was suspended for breaking a team rule. Not for drinking—they never proved that. I was out after one a.m."

Jet paused and wet her lips with a sip of water. "I couldn't play for the rest of the season. We lost the championship, didn't make the NCAA tournament. I let my team down. I let my parents down. I let myself down. After a lot of painful rehab, my ankle improved, but I couldn't play the way I could before. I didn't have any lift, I was slower, and it honestly hurt to run. For a couple of years it hurt, so my senior year was a bust. I was on track to be the school record holder for scoring and a bunch of other things. My team should have won, but they needed that all-star at center—and I wasn't her anymore."

"I'm sorry, Jet." Now Katie offered comfort with a hand placed gently on her knee.

"That's not all, folks." Again, she laughed, but it sounded haunted. "The other girls in my car were knocked around. Broken arms, broken legs, lacerations. They all healed, I suppose. But the kid in the other car—he died."

Katie gasped and her free hand flew to her mouth. "Oh, God, Jet."

"Five of us were in my car, all girls. None of us had ID. The hospital banded us without confirming identities and then drew alcohol levels. Three of us were drunk, two weren't. My parents hired a good lawyer who argued that they couldn't prove who was drunk and who wasn't. I got off on the DUI charges. The kid who died, unfortunately, had his wallet in his pocket and was as drunk as I was. Based on the skid marks in the snow, the police said he veered into my lane. So he took the whole blame for the accident, and I walked away. No jail time. Just a short suspension from basketball and a long recovery."

Katie offered an understanding smile of support along with a gentle squeeze of the knee. "So, this is why you don't drink, huh?"

"This is why I don't drink."

"And how do you feel about what happened? How do you deal with it?"

Jet scratched her forehead and then quoted Katie. "I don't think about it."

Katie scooted over and rested her head against Jet's shoulder. "I'm sorry, Jet. That's a terrible burden to have to carry."

"I think about it all the time."

"Would it help if I tell you to forgive yourself? You were young, and stupid, and you made a mistake."

Jet tilted her head so she could meet Katie's eyes. "Would it help if I told you those things?"

Swallowing, Katie shrugged. "Maybe. I don't know. But I suppose I could try. Could you?"

"I want to find his parents. To apologize. He was drunk, but so was I. And if I'd been sober, maybe I could have prevented the accident. Or perhaps it wouldn't have been so severe."

"If you need to do that, Jet, you should."

"I'm too scared."

"That you'll go to jail?"

"No, just to face them. I basically lied back then."

"Well, telling the truth can be healing. Maybe your wounds need a dose of that kind of medicine."

"Do you think I'm a jerk?"

Katie shook her head and turned the corners of her mouth up in a soft smile. "You were a kid, Jet."

"So were you, Katie. We both made mistakes. But if you can forgive me my past, I'll forgive yours."

"I can forgive you, Jet. I'm still trying to find a way to forgive myself."

"Yeah, me, too." Jet kissed her softly on the forehead, and Katie leaned into her, secure in the comfort of Jet's arms, her heart aching over the sins they'd confessed. They stayed that way, for a long time, silent, and clung to each other.

Finally, Jet said, "Do you think you're ready for bed, now? This trip down memory lane has exhausted me."

"That, and it's two a.m." Katie had been drifting off, like she knew Jet had.

Jet pulled back, once again finding Katie's gaze. "There's that, too." She pushed Katie from her lap, and then Katie reached down and pulled Jet to her full height. Jet looked down, the playful look replaced by a somber one. "In the morning, Katie, we're calling the police."

Katie looked up to meet her eyes. "We'll see."

# CHAPTER TWELVE
# MARRIED FOR MONEY

Simon wasn't sure what his next move was, but he *was* sure of something else—he had to go home. His wife had not been pleased at his decision to "work" tonight, and he'd been able to pacify her only with the promise that he'd conclude his business this evening at a reasonable hour. They'd been with her family at the beach for the weekend and gotten back so late on Sunday that he'd hardly had time to check on his various enterprises.

He feared losing the handle on his slippery, shadowy world. His employees were hardly trustworthy. Understanding his need to monitor things, she'd cut him some slack. He was, after all, a successful business owner, and if sacrificing time with him was the price she paid for the life of opulent luxury they shared, that seemed a reasonable request. For a few hours, anyway.

He'd planned to be home before midnight. Of course, that was before he'd gone to the bar and met Billy. That was before he'd killed him. That was before his trip to the hospital to kill Billy's girlfriend and kidnap their children. He'd planned to make the rounds, check in with a few of his distributors, then stop to see Angelica for a couple of hours of passion. None of it had gone his way, though, and he was feeling each tick of the clock like a needle in his spine. His wife would note the hour he arrived at home and find some trivial way to make him pay.

Marriage had seemed like a grand idea at the time he'd proposed it to Heather. It was an opportunity, an intelligent business move to breathe life into the plans that were then still distant dreams. It hadn't occurred to him there would be consequences—a woman who demanded explanations and children who demanded *everything*. With no model of comparison, having never known his own father and raised by a single mother, he'd had no idea the quagmire it would be, sucking from him the energy and time he wished to spend pursuing his own desires.

Yet his wife's money had enabled his lifestyle, at least in the beginning, when he'd married her. His father-in-law was so impressed with Simon's intelligence and abilities that he had, soon after the marriage, turned over total control of his enterprises to Simon, who hadn't disappointed him. His business had grown tenfold under Simon's hand, and they were all quite wealthy as a result—his father-in-law, who still owned half of the shares, and he and his wife, who controlled the other half.

His success allowed him the big house, the trips, the cars, the massages at the spa. He dined often at expensive restaurants, and had access to the best tickets to sporting events and concerts, too. He was living the dream, and it was almost as he'd always imagined. In his dreams he didn't have to answer to the woman who shared his name, or to the three children who ran noisily around their house, stealing from him any chance of the peace and quiet a man could hope for in his home. In his fantasies, the woman beside him was Angelica and there were no children, for she shared his idea that children were far more enjoyable as nieces and nephews than sons and daughters.

Lately he'd grown restless, tired of the charade of dinner parties with his wife and weekends at the beach with his in-laws. He was eager to sever the ties to his family and stay with his lover on a permanent basis. Perhaps that was partly why he'd brazenly shot Billy and fired at Katie without first carefully planning the attacks. Perhaps that was why he hadn't figured out that Billy was a snitch. Was his fatigue causing him to grow complacent and lose his edge? If that happened, he'd be a dead man. Better to get out now, while he still could.

He'd stashed away several million dollars, but he worried it wasn't enough. They planned to live in the islands, and houses there were expensive. They'd need a boat. They had to eat, and buy clothing, and pay a staff. It would require a fortune to maintain the lifestyle he wanted—and Angelica expected.

Navigating the streets of the neighborhood where he was raised, he came to a complete stop when indicated and used his turn signals as well. He had no drugs in his car and legitimate reasons to be out and about, but he still worried. Generally he tried to avoid the law, but tonight, after what had happened at Katie's apartment and at the hospital, he was even more concerned. He didn't want anyone to suspect that he'd been anywhere near the Northeast on this night.

Katie had outsmarted him at the hospital, and Simon was disappointed in himself for allowing it. Angelica was right, of course, that Katie would go to her children. His own wife would have done the same. But he had underestimated both her haste to reach them and her own aversion to the authorities. Of course she'd have wanted to keep them out of foster care. He suspected she'd had experiences of her own in the system, and she'd chosen the streets as a better option. And of course she wouldn't talk to the police. She had a record, and a man she was sleeping with was murdered in her house. She'd be the first one questioned. Had he thought about it more clearly, the drama of the evening would have had a much different ending.

She'd won this round, because of his haste and poor judgment. He wouldn't make those same mistakes again.

Simon pulled his Ford into the well-lit underground garage at his office, found a place next to a big Lexus sedan, and parked. After locking the Ford, he placed the key on the front bumper. No one would steal his car here. Opening the door of the Lexus, he bent his tall frame into the vehicle and turned it on with the fob he'd left in the cup holder. He then backed up and exited the garage the same way he'd entered it.

After a few more blocks, he signaled another turn and maneuvered the powerful vehicle onto the entrance ramp, picking up speed in preparation to merge into the fast-moving traffic on Interstate 95. Even at this hour, all three lanes were busy, and he was careful to keep control of the car, which naturally tended to drive itself much faster than the law allowed.

In thirty minutes, he'd be safely parked in the six-car garage sitting beside the 10,000-square-foot home on his estate in Bucks County. Once in his den, he'd pour himself a drink and try to forget the evening. Then, he'd try to rest. Fortunately, he required very little sleep, and he'd spend a few requisite hours in his own bed before heading back to Angelica's in the morning. He had no doubt he'd sort this mess out. He had no other choice.

# Chapter Thirteen
# Irresistible

Katie was exhausted, yet not a bit sleepy. The couch had been made up, and it would have been wise and appropriate for one of them to sleep on it, yet here they were, beside each other in Jet's bed. They'd been in this position before, a few times, in fact, but that was different. Because then, Katie could have pretended she was just getting to know her friend. She could claim it was all innocent.

Now, she knew better. They'd declared words of love, she'd thoroughly explored her feelings, and they'd made a sort of commitment when they confessed their sins on Jet's couch. They'd opened a door, and now all she had to do was walk through it. It didn't have to be tonight, but she couldn't sleep with the possibility lingering in the air.

She silently studied the room, cast in shadows by the bulb in the bathroom a dozen feet down the hall, trying to distract herself from the arousal that coursed through her. She lay on her side, with Jet behind her, enveloping her, igniting her with body heat, and suddenly the shirt that fit more like a dress seemed like too much clothing, for she was on fire.

Wiggling her toes to freedom, she escaped the sheet that covered her and kicked it aside. The cool air against her lower body did little to comfort her, though. The flow of Jet's breath across her neck was like a breath of life, awakening every cell. Her pulse pounded in her ears, in her chest, between her legs. Her mouth grew dry as her pussy grew very, very wet. Giving voice to her feelings earlier had freed them, and now they wouldn't go back into their box, where the tight lid of control had held them captive for months.

She should have been tired from nearly twenty-four hours without sleep, sad about the death of her children's father, frightened that a killer had her in his crosshairs. Yet she was none of those things. She was simply, completely, overwhelmingly aroused.

Unable to harness the restless energy any longer, Katie quietly eased her legs off the bed and stood. No destination beckoned her; she only knew that she needed to do something, to move away from Jet, because the desire to roll over and pull her into her arms seemed more reasonable as the minutes of this early morning ticked by.

Before she could take a step away from source of her unrest, Jet called to her softly. "It's going to be okay."

Perhaps she was referring to Simon's bullets, or to a life without Billy, or to a life with her. Or perhaps it was all of those things.

Katie turned and looked at her. Though the distant light was faded, Katie could still see her dark hair askew, the dark eyes fixed on her, the corners of her mouth turned up. As she dared to look further, Katie gasped to see the sight of Jet's breasts nearly spilling over the top of the shirt that had twisted around her as she slept.

For a moment, as she chose her future, Katie grew completely still. Then, finally making her decision—or accepting the one she'd already made in the past weeks—she let go of the control she'd kept for so long and, reaching over, turned on the lamp that sat dark on the nightstand. Its warm glow illuminated Jet's face, and Katie could see confusion there, replaced by delight as Katie crossed the room and locked the door.

Reaching for her hand, Jet pulled her back into bed, beside her. They lay facing each other, their noses an inch apart on the pillow as Katie stared into the darkness of Jet's eyes, slowly tracing the length of her nose with a finger, finally reaching her smiling mouth. They barely touched, yet Katie gasped, sucking in air like a weight had been lifted, and in a way it had. She could truly breathe for the first time in a very long time.

Her senses were spinning yet she somehow heard Jet breathing just as heavily as she was, sucking in precious oxygen from the heavy air. As that same wayward finger slid across Jet's lower lip, she kissed it, sucking it gently into her mouth. That invitation was all Katie needed, and she pulled the finger back, replacing it with her lips. This wasn't a chaste, tender kiss, but a hungry one, and Katie set the pace.

She'd never wanted someone before and so had never taken the lead. Now, though, she couldn't wait as she claimed Jet for her own.

Katie had never experienced the wonder of loving a woman. She hadn't witnessed two women together on television or read about it in a book. Guided only by her own wild imaginings, she slid her cheek across the softness of Jet's, dragged her lips along her neck, finding every touch electrifying and accompanied by murmurs of delight from the woman beneath her.

Pulling back, she paused to breathe and stared at Jet's beautiful face, flushed now with the heat of the passion Katie knew she'd ignited. It was an erotic transformation, and she wondered if she looked the same—eyes hooded, pupils dilated, nostrils flared. She certainly felt as excited as Jet appeared to be, and suddenly it seemed important to Katie that she let Jet know it.

"I love you," she said.

A smile exploded on Jet's face before she answered with a voice dripping with desire. "I love you, too."

"I've never felt this way before, Jet. I've never loved someone. I've never wanted someone."

Jet's smile grew. "It's okay to want me. It may even be legal soon."

Katie chuckled. The topic of gay marriage had been all over the news with the pending Supreme Court cases drawing national attention. They'd discussed it on more than one occasion, and it had been a hot topic at the clinic, where the fervor of one pious religious fanatic serving as both judge and jury had incited everyone to voice an opinion.

"It feels more than okay. It feels perfect. I just want you to know that."

Katie narrowed the gap between them and kissed her hungrily. Although she hadn't had enough, she found herself leaving Jet's mouth to venture down her neck, tasting the flesh as she went but not lingering, anxious now to complete this journey that had been so long in commencing. She reached Jet's breasts, still threatening escape, and pushed them free, up from the fabric and against her face. Caressing her skin against their softness, bathing them with kisses, she moaned, suddenly needing more. "Can I take this off?" she asked, pulling at the shirt.

Wordlessly, Jet sat up and helped Katie remove the garment, and then they worked together to free Katie of hers. They were left in just underwear, Jet in boxers of soft, worn cotton and Katie in bikinis that clung to her every curve. Katie wanted those off too, eventually, but she could wait a few more minutes. She planned to enjoy Jet's breasts first.

Even with both hands Katie couldn't fully cup them but instead kneaded them, kissing the tender flesh, pulling the hardened nipples between her lips, sucking hungrily on them until the sounds Jet uttered indicated she was enjoying this attention as much as Katie enjoyed giving it. Katie felt her excitement growing with each touch, each kiss, as her sex grew wetter and throbbed with need. She stopped for a moment and pulled back, the movement of Jet beneath her causing a pleasurable distraction. "Wow, Jet. That feels so good," Katie confessed.

She'd positioned her center against Katie's thigh, and Katie was now experiencing the pressure of Jet's hip against her as Jet rocked, pulling them closer together. She felt exquisite pleasure and forgot about the journey of exploration she'd been taking and she met Jet's eyes. The look of desire and joy on Jet's face encouraged her to let go, to take instead of giving, and she did, moving purposefully, grinding her hips against Jet's. Within seconds she closed her eyes and began to shudder in the seizures of orgasm. She cried out softly, mindful of her children in the next room, and opened her eyes to see Jet looking at her, still thrusting, but smiling and then moaning and laughing quietly as she, too, tumbled over the edge.

Katie joined her laughter for a moment but found, to her surprise, that her laughs quickly turned to tears. And as Jet pulled her closer and kissed her hair, murmuring words of comfort and love, she didn't know if they were tears of anguish or of joy.

# Chapter Fourteen
# Mistaken Identity

If you want to keep your job, put the phone in your pocket and keep it there," Nic said.

The young man dwarfed by the expansive marble desk in the Marjorie Place lobby jumped, lifting his dark eyes from the device in his hands.

Where do they get these people? Nic asked herself. With a few sparse whiskers sprouting from a weak chin and a frame barely able to fill the small-size shirt on his back, the man did little to inspire the sense of security his job description implied. He resembled a teenager at Halloween dressed as a security guard more than an actual working model. His lack of professionalism was even more appalling than his appearance, though, and she measured her words carefully, wishing to make her point without causing a scene.

Shoving the phone into his shirt pocket, he stammered, "I'm sorry. How can I help you, ma'am?"

Nic hid her irritation as she addressed him as she would a disobedient child. "It's *Doctor*. Dr. Coussart." With all the fees she paid for services in the building, was it too much to ask to have someone reliable at the lobby desk? Someone who knew her name? Although she no longer lived in the building, she expected the staff to know who she was—she was an owner, for God's sake. Yet seemingly every time she visited, a different face greeted her in the lobby, and none of them recognized her.

"I need you to hold my key," she said as she handed him a single key on a ring with a charm from the Louvre.

"Sorry, Doctor. I'd be glad to take care of that for you." He smiled as he reached for the key and revealed unevenly spaced, crooked teeth. After writing her name on a tag he attached to the key ring, he looked at her again. "Can I help you with anything else?"

"Not at the moment." Nic turned abruptly and glided across the marble floor toward the sheets of smoky glass that formed the vaulted lobby's wall, pushed open the door, and sprang into the muggy morning. With little traffic, this was as quiet as the day would be. Most of Philadelphia's citizens were still in bed, or at least still at home. But, because this was the city, a panhandler was already hard at work begging for change.

Lean and toned, Nic wore short nylon running shorts and a matching, ribbed tank top. Although she wasn't tall, her body was perfectly proportioned. She spent time in the gym, which showed in the swell of muscles from her shoulders all the way down to her calves. Resting one hand against the glass wall, she grabbed her ankle with the other and pulled it up toward her butt, stretching her quadriceps as she studied the vagrant.

He was a scary sight, unshaven, with long, stringy hair. His dark pants were torn, his shirt only partially buttoned. Even though he was a distance away, Nic could smell the putrid combination of alcohol and urine that stained his clothing. Or, at least, she imagined she could. She'd smelled it too many times to count during her residency in emergency medicine here in center city. So many times that the smell came back in nauseating detail and she involuntarily shuddered. She might not have pediatric-neurosurgery consultants at her fingertips in the ER in Wilkes-Barre, but the vagrants were scarce, too, and that was worth the trade. Well worth it. If she never had to lay her hands on another homeless person in this lifetime, it'd be too soon.

She'd heard the preaching of the social workers and psychologists, listened to their lectures linking mental illness and homelessness, but she just didn't buy it. Perhaps there was some connection, but she considered the numbers inflated and manipulated to improve funding in shelters and soup kitchens. People used any excuse they could for their laziness and ineptitude. They explained away their failures instead of finding ways to succeed.

That had never been the case with her. Even though both of her parents were physicians, she'd worked her tail off to earn the grades that got her through college and medical school. She'd pulled thirty-hour days and hundred-hour weeks and did what she had to do to get through. Colleagues in medicine and nursing had similar stories. They climbed their way out of poverty with hard work and determination, some of them leaving their native lands to come to America, searching for that fabled opportunity. They'd taken control of their destinies and made something of their lives, instead of making excuses for failing.

Nic turned and put the man behind her, hoping the police would have chased him away before she returned from her run. Then a better thought occurred to her. As soon as she saw a policeman, she'd report the derelict. She and Louis had put their apartment on the market, and the last thing a potential buyer needed to see was a homeless person on the doorstep.

At her home on a private lake in the suburbs of Wilkes-Barre, she didn't have to put up with this kind of nonsense.

She'd been born in Philadelphia nearly three decades earlier, when her parents were both residents at Temple University Hospital, but this city had never been her home. Just a newborn when they moved home to Wilkes-Barre, Nic had spent the first twenty-two years of her life in the northeast corner of the state. She'd come back to Philly for medical school and residency, and had spent seven years here before she fled back to the mountains at the first opportunity.

Even though she still owned her apartment here (or at least co-owned it), this was the first time she'd been back to Philly in the year since she'd left. And she didn't miss it one bit. Well, except for the food. Philly had many great restaurants, and that was perhaps its only redeeming feature. As soon as she finished with the conference that brought her here, she'd gladly head back up the Pennsylvania Turnpike to Wilkes-Barre.

Walking a few steps to the corner of Fifteenth Street, Nic turned north and began her morning run. She crossed a series of busy streets, all of them named after trees, and couldn't resist a glance over her shoulder at city hall. William Penn gazed down at her and the entire city of a million and a half souls. The pious Quaker would probably share her sentiments about modern Philadelphia, and she winked at him in solidarity.

At John F. Kennedy Boulevard, Nic turned into JKF Plaza, and after circling the fountain, she emerged onto the Benjamin Franklin Parkway. The parkway was a scenic and generally safe route to Kelly Drive, the tree-lined road along the Schuylkill River where Nic had been running since she first came to Philadelphia nearly a decade earlier. It was the perfect place—no traffic lights for miles, enough pedestrians to discourage crime, and as beautiful a scene as one could find anywhere. Her route across the city and out along the river and back was almost a perfect ten-mile trek, an ideal distance for her. Not too far to wipe her out and enough to keep her in racing form.

Jogging in place as she waited for the light to change, Nic wiped the sweat from her forehead. She loved wearing her hair down over her shoulders, but now it was pulled up in a ponytail. Her eyes were hidden behind sunglasses, ever present to ward off migraine headaches that the sun often triggered. She was alert and cautious, never at ease in the city, not even out here where this magnificent one-mile stretch of real estate boasted the Museum of Natural Sciences, the Franklin Institute, the Barnes Museum, and the Philadelphia Museum of Art. Priceless artifacts and a billion dollars in masterpieces lined the route she ran, and more cops probably roamed this area of town than at any other location, yet she still worried about random violence. She saw enough bad shit in the ER to know it happened, even to white, upper-middle-class physicians like her.

Sprinting cautiously across the intersection, Nic dodged a car speeding around the corner and then settled into a rhythm, her arms and heart pumping with each stride. She loved running. Something about the solitude beckoned her, and she pushed her body to reach very definable goals—one mile, two miles, ten minutes, eight minutes. She could set the bar and work to reach it, having to compromise with no one about the music she listened to or the route she took.

Some might call her self-centered, and she'd agree. How could she not be? Her parents, thrilled to have adopted her, had given her every privilege a child could want. She was the center of their world. Intellectual and scholarly, they both preferred an evening at home with a medical journal to a game show on television. Their board games were chess and Scrabble, their newspaper *The New York Times*. Their summer vacation was in London or Barcelona, not the beaches of New Jersey and Delaware.

She'd learned to read and keep herself amused as they did, in the words written on paper and in books, with occasional words spoken eloquently in conversation. She'd learned to become quite comfortable in her own mind. When she was very young, sharing was a foreign concept, and as a result, preschool was a near deadly experience for the other children who wanted to play with her toys.

Learning to socialize at school wasn't a painful experience, but it was trying, and Nicole always preferred to have one or two close friends rather than large squadrons of them. She preferred solitude most often and, with the exception of her closest friends, chose to limit the time she engaged with others. Running, pushing herself to joyful, breathless exhaustion, was one of her favorite activities.

Beneath the flags of a hundred and nine countries of the world, she broke free of the stress she'd felt just a few minutes earlier. She ran against the current of traffic bringing a wave of workers into the shops, hospitals, and office buildings of downtown Philadelphia, and set apart from the rest, she felt perfectly at home.

At the art museum, she slowed to cross the intersection and circled to the right onto Kelly Drive. Protected there from the relentless traffic by a wide sidewalk, the stretch was lined with trees that sheltered her from the bright sun. She instantly felt the temperature change, a drop of a few degrees in the shade, and looked forward to the mild breeze she'd find along the river. Timing her pace as she approached the entrance to the Water Works, Nic allowed a car into the parking area before once again pushing for her target pace. She glanced ahead to the iconic buildings that made up Boat House Row, paying no attention to the police car crossing the intersection in front of her. She was too far from Marjorie Place to report the vagrant.

Maybe she'd see boats on the water today. She loved to race them. The canopy of trees along Kelly Drive gave the air a fresh, clean scent, and she breathed deeply, giving her muscles the oxygen they needed. She didn't notice the police car slow down beside her, not until the flashing lights came on and the driver made a U-turn, pulling up beside her. An officer immediately jumped out of the vehicle, holding up a hand, signaling her to stop.

"Is some…thing…wrong?" she asked, sucking in breath as she continued to jog in place so her leg muscles wouldn't tighten.

"I need you to come with me, Kathleen." The policeman was short, not much taller than Nic, who was on the lower end of the growth charts. What he lacked in height, though, he made up in muscle and attitude. Huge pectoral and biceps muscles stretched his uniform, and he spoke with an authority she figured few people challenged.

She did, though. "I think you. Have me confused. With someone else," she said, and tried to step around him.

Before she could protest, his partner had flanked her and grabbed her right arm, jerking it behind her. As she turned to avoid him, the first officer pulled her left arm back, and the cold hard metal of handcuffs closed on her wrists.

"What are you doing?" she yelled. "Let me go!" She allowed her legs to relax and dropped her weight onto them, an old self-defense trick, but it was useless against two of them. It only served to put more tension on her shoulder joints. She quickly changed tactics and tried to wiggle out of their grasp.

Even as she protested, they dragged her backward. "Wait! What are you doing? Stop!" She begged, but they ignored her pleas. With one of them on either side of her and no arms for balance, Nic was helpless as they closed the ten-foot span to the police car. When they reached it, one officer opened the door as the other pushed her head down and forced her into the backseat. Although he wasn't unnecessarily rough, with no hands to stop her forward momentum, she crashed headfirst into the seat. Struggling to regain her balance, she grew more afraid than merely surprised, as she'd originally felt. What the fuck was going on?

Nic had heard stories about criminals impersonating police officers. What if she'd just been kidnapped? Or abducted by rapists? Since the *real* Philadelphia police had no feasible reason to subdue her like this, those seemed like plausible explanations.

She began screaming at the top of her lungs. "Help! Help me! I've been abducted!" In response, the driver put the car into gear and retraced the route she'd just traveled by foot. His partner in the passenger seat picked up a portable radio and spoke into it, and for the first time she wondered if they might be authentic police. After a drive of just a few blocks, Nic had her answer when the car pulled up at a police station on North Twenty-first Street.

"What's going on?" she demanded again as the officer opened the door and helped her out.

"We just need to ask you a few questions," he said.

"But why? About what?" She questioned one, then the other, as they escorted her into the Central Police Division.

The station was of newer construction, with a modern design that could have lent itself to any purpose. Once she was through the doors, though, a distinctly institutional feel prevailed, with gray plastic chairs that matched the paint on the walls and vinyl-tiled floors. A single police officer, a rather attractive woman with short dark hair and dark eyes, stood guard at the reception desk. Under other circumstances, Nic would have smiled at the woman and perhaps even started a conversation. But not today. She had nothing to smile about at the moment, and small talk was definitely not on her agenda.

The officers escorted her down a hallway and into an empty room, where they promptly unlocked her arms as they closed the door behind her. They'd never answered her questions. What the hell was going on?

Rubbing her wrists, Nic surveyed the room. It was a rather large rectangle, fifteen by twenty feet, and windowless, except for the two-way mirror on one wall. Four matching chairs surrounded a square metal table. The walls were painted a dull gray, the drab accentuated by the dim fluorescent lights flickering from the ceiling. She closed her eyes, concerned. Nothing guaranteed a migraine like flickering lights.

Walking around the table, Nic took some deep breaths, trying to soothe her frazzled nerves. She could really use a cigarette. Nicotine never failed to calm her. She'd done nothing wrong and had no idea why the police wanted her. That knowledge didn't help her though, and she trembled like a leaf floating on a gust of October wind. She was literally shaking.

At least, though, she was safe. This appeared to be a real police station.

Leaning against one wall, she looked at the two-way mirror and wondered who was watching her. She figured someone was. What were they looking for? How was she supposed to act? She couldn't have done much acting at the moment, even if she knew the lines. Her knees were weak, the trembling uncontrollable, and her voice would probably falter if she tried to speak.

Swallowing her tears, Nic closed her eyes and focused on her breathing. She imagined herself in yoga class and counted as she inhaled. *One. Two. Three. Four. Five.* She was breathing much too fast. Thinking only about her breathing, she exhaled but fared no better, making it only to four. After a few more tries, she was able to control the rate and depth of her breaths, and a few minutes later when she made her target count of eight, she felt much calmer.

Continuing to breathe slowly and deeply, Nic visualized herself on a sandy beach, with the crystal-clear turquoise waters of the Mediterranean lapping at her feet. Her parents hated the beach, but since college she'd been taking her own vacations. She still traveled to France with her family, but now instead of staying in the wine country with her parents, she'd escape to Nice or Cannes with her cousins. And when she had three or four days off, she'd often hop a flight to the Caribbean. Instead of the ten-hour trip to the south of France, she could be on the beach in Aruba in five.

She imagined it now. Above her, a cloudless blue sky reflected the rays of the sun, and they caressed her face, her breasts, and her belly, instantly warming her. She dug her toes into the sand, and the contrasting cool soothed her. Her hand rested on a tropical drink—was it a margarita? She tasted it, and the tangy flavor of lime confirmed her suspicion. Then, beside her, a woman moved, and she felt even more heat as the woman began to spread sunscreen over Nic's skin.

Breathing and fantasizing had the desired effect. A few minutes in paradise was all Nic needed. Opening her eyes, she felt awash with calm and was once again in control. Even though she was locked in a room in a police station, wearing skimpy running gear, with no identification and no idea what she'd done to deserve this fate, she felt completely relaxed.

She walked across the room to the two-way mirror, picturing the short police officer seated on the other side, watching. She hoped he could hear as well. Scanning the length of the six-foot long mirror, she began to speak. "My name is Dr. Nicole Coussart. I'm an ER doctor from Wilkes-Barre, and I'm scheduled to give a presentation at the medical conference at the convention center. I'm due to speak at eleven today, and as you can see, I'm going to need a shower. So I would appreciate it if you can do whatever is necessary to expedite my release. Thank you."

Instead of sitting, Nic walked across the room and began stretching. Dropping her head to her knees, she felt the pull in her hamstrings and allowed her arms to fall, feeling the stretch along her spine. After a minute she dropped her hands to the floor, ignoring the germs she imagined there, and stretched her Achilles tendons. After fifteen minutes of yoga, she sat down at the table, choosing the chair facing away from the mirror and those watching her. She continued her measured breathing, felt the chair where it touched the muscles and skin of her back and legs, cold against the thin fabric of the clothing that covered her. She was startled when she heard a door open and realized she must have dozed off. Arching her back, she reached overhead and stretched her arms, wondering how long she'd been asleep to have stiffened up so much.

"What time is it?" she asked the tall man wearing the tailored suit. It was hard to tell how long she'd been locked alone in this room, but his presence had to signal that her time was coming to an end. If only she could explain who she was, the police would be forced to release her. Offering a friendly smile, she waited for his reply.

"I ask the questions," he said, and the loud smack that echoed through the room as he dropped a thick file folder onto the metal table startled her. He didn't return her smile. Instead, he studied her as he removed his suit jacked and draped it over the back of his chair. Water stains soiled his shirt at the armpits, and Nic was happy to see him sweat. Wearing only her tank and shorts, she might have frozen to death if the air conditioning worked properly.

She frowned as she met his cool gaze. This wasn't the friendly encounter she'd hoped for after she'd given her soliloquy at the mirror, but before she could speak again, he did.

"I'm Detective Young. Philip Young. I need to ask you a few questions about the murder of Billy Wallace." Pushing back into his chair, he seemed to relax and settle in for what might be a lengthy conversation.

Bending forward, Nic placed both hands calmly on the table and stared into his eyes. "Are you serious?"

He cocked his head but otherwise didn't move as he studied her. "Very serious, Katie. Murder is a serious crime, and I take it personally when a police informant gets gunned down in his own home."

She shook her head and turned her palms up, shrugging. "I'm sorry about your informant, Detective, but you have the wrong suspect. My name is Nicole Coussart. I'm an ER doctor from Wilkes-Barre and I'm visiting for a conference. I know nothing about Mr. Wallace or his murder."

He leaned forward and barked. "Do you deny knowing William Wallace?"

"I know Braveheart."

"What?" The look of confusion on his face amused Nic. She'd clearly thrown him off balance.

"Braveheart. Hero of the Scots. Hanged by King Edward I at the Tower of London." She didn't mention that he'd been emasculated, eviscerated, and beheaded as well.

He studied her for another moment. "I saw the movie." And then Nic detected what she suspected was a flicker of doubt in his eyes, verified by his next question. "Do you have any ID, Doctor?"

Nic couldn't control her retort, and she wasn't certain, but she suspected she could be forgiven her bad manners in this one particular situation. "Are you fucking kidding me? Where would I put an ID in this outfit?" With her right hand she waved at the running clothes she wore. "I was out running."

"Not very nice language for a doctor. Do you talk to your patients that way?"

A sigh of exasperation escaped her lips. "You know what, Detective? I've had enough. I'd like to exercise whatever right it is that allows me to call my lawyer. And I'm going to sue you, and the two idiots who brought me in here, and the entire Philadelphia Police Department, and the mayor and whoever else I can think of, for harassing me. I need to be at a conference at eleven o'clock. It is vital to my career that I'm on time. Vital. So give me a phone and let me make my call."

Smacking his lips, he looked down his nose at her, seemingly ignoring her tirade. "You have a lawyer, do you? That's very convenient for a doctor from upstate to have a lawyer here in the city." He smiled, reached into the inside pocket of the suit jacket hanging on the chair, and retrieved a cell phone. After a delay of a moment, where they stared each other down, he slid it across the table to her.

"Who said my lawyer was in the city?"

"Well, if you wanna make that eleven o'clock conference, you better hope he's not in Wilkes-Barre. Would you like some privacy?"

She broke eye contact and shook her head as she dialed the phone. "I have nothing to hide. But I do have a concern. I'm going to dial my friend's pager, and he'll have to call me back. Is that a problem?" Once again, she stared him down.

Glaring right back at her, he responded. "Your personal lawyer has a pager, huh? How convenient."

"I'm actually calling my friend. A surgical resident at Temple. He'll know what to do. I don't actually know any lawyers here."

"I see," he said, nodding his head as he studied her. Then he waved his hand at the phone. "Be my guest."

Louis's pager number hadn't changed in the four years of his residency, and Nic had dialed it frequently enough to have memorized it. After she typed in the cell-phone number she wanted him to call, she added an additional three digits. Nine-one-two. Nine-one-one was a code often used by colleagues to convey the urgency of a page. Nine-one-two was a private code her group of friends used to identify themselves.

As she'd hoped, it took Louis less than a minute to return the call. She grabbed the phone and walked away from the table, away from the annoying man who was detaining her.

"Louis, it's me. I'm in trouble and I need your help."

"What's going on?" he asked, not sounding a bit alarmed.

"I've been arrested. Do you know any lawyers?"

"What? What the hell are you talking about?" Now, his voice rose to match his concern.

Nic spoke more slowly. "I've been arrested. I think. I'm not sure." Looking to the detective she shrugged and mouthed the question to him.

He responded by shaking his head.

"Actually, no, I haven't been arrested, but I'm in jail. I need a lawyer."

"Where are you? Do you want me to come?"

"Lou, I don't need surgery. I need a lawyer."

"I can call Rae."

Nic groaned at the mention of the annoying woman's name. She couldn't explain how she'd forgotten her, unless her subconscious was simply burying the painful memory. She'd hoped to never see her again, yet under the circumstances, Rae would be perfect. She was loud and obnoxious—exactly the kind of lawyer she wanted defending her.

"Okay. Call her."

"Give me the details. Where are you?"

Nic asked the detective for the particulars and she relayed them to Louis.

"I'll try my best to track her down. If I can't get her, I'm sure someone in her office can help."

"Louis, I love you. And one more thing."

"What?"

"Have her stop by the apartment and bring my wallet. They need me to show some identification." Louis had told her he'd given Rae a key to their shared apartment to keep for an emergency. This certainly qualified as one.

"I can't wait to hear this story, Nic. You never cease to amaze me."

Nic managed a smile. "I feel the same way about you." She disconnected the call, knowing she was forgiven for the bad behavior she'd displayed the night before. She was truly lucky to have Louis for a friend, and she promised herself to tell him that when she saw him later.

Pushing the phone back toward the detective, Nic met his glance once again. "Thank you. My friend's neighbor is a lawyer. He's going to call her." Nic laughed. "I actually had dinner with her last night, and I forgot all about her. I must be stressed. You don't happen to have a cigarette, do you?"

She watched him studying her and thought he seemed somehow more relaxed than before. Did he finally believe her?

"I don't smoke, and neither should you. Where'd you eat?" he asked.

"Excuse me?"

"Where did you go for dinner?"

"Domain," she said, then paused for a second. He was attempting to be cordial; she suddenly felt a reluctant obligation to do the same. It couldn't hurt, could it? Perhaps it could even help. "Do you know it?"

"I've heard of it," he said, raising his eyebrow at the mention of the pricey restaurant. "Good?"

Nic thought about the poor service and the unremarkable main course. "Actually, just okay. But maybe I was just tired. I worked all day, hopped in my car and drove two hours, then was stuck in traffic. By the time we ate last night I'd have been happy with a McDonald's cheeseburger."

The detective laughed. "There's nothing wrong with Mickey D's."

Never having been permitted to eat fast food during her formative years, Nic had developed an addiction to McDonald's when she lived away at college. Although she'd learned to control her cravings, they were ever-present. At times of stress, a fry dipped in a coating of milkshake could be quite a comfort. "There certainly isn't. But I was expecting something a little different."

"My daughter goes to college in Wilkes-Barre."

Nic smiled at the sudden change of topic. What was he up to? Was he trying to trick her? Was the mention of her hometown meant to throw her off balance? "Oh, really? Which school?"

"Misericordia."

"Oh, that's a great school. It's actually in Dallas, though." She looked at him suspiciously. "You know that though, don't you?"

He shrugged in response.

"Was that a test, Detective?" She was irked that she'd walked right into the trap he'd set and never even saw it coming. She'd been suspicious, and he'd still pulled that one, yet she felt a small measure of comfort that she had nothing to hide.

"Maybe."

She took a deep breath and exhaled loudly. Why not challenge him? It would pass the time, anyway. "Okay, then test away. The sooner you believe me, the sooner I'll be out of here."

Instead of asking, he told her about the mountains, about the house he and his wife had built next to a stream stocked with an ample supply of trout. Nic, in turn, told him her own fish tales. She'd spent much of her childhood on the lake, and one of her father's favorite pastimes was fishing.

"Do you really think fish lower your cholesterol?"

"That's what they say. Probably better to take fish-oil tablets, though. Too many contaminants in real fish."

"Tell me about cholesterol. Mine's too high."

"What does this look like? A free medical clinic?" Nic hated when people asked for medical advice. Why did they have doctors if they didn't talk to them?

"No, just making conversation. Since you *exercised* your right to call a lawyer, I can't talk to you about the case. So I'm just keeping you company, making conversation."

"Unfortunately, I don't know much about cholesterol. I just manage the aftereffects—heart attacks and strokes."

"I've already outlived both my parents. They didn't reach fifty."

Nic shook her head, frowning. "Choosing the right parents is very important, Detective."

"How do you do that?"

She slapped her hand to the table to emphasize her point. "Exactly! It's all luck. If you get the right parents, you've got it made. You inherit good looks, good health, and a good fortune."

It didn't hurt to be adopted by the right ones, either. Nic had the fortune, she didn't scare small children when she looked their way, and she was fairly intelligent. She could have used another inch or two on the yardstick, but other than that, she'd been blessed. The health risks coded into her DNA, though, were a big concern. All she knew about her biological mother was that she'd been a healthy college student. She knew nothing of her grandparents, and her biological father was a complete mystery as well. She'd had DNA testing, but the information it gave was limited and its meaning subject to interpretation.

He laughed and shook his head. "You aren't Katie Finan, are you?"

Nic blew him a kiss with both hands. "No! I'm not." Relief washed over her, and she realized how, under duress, she'd forgotten all the rules her parents had taught her. She'd lost her temper and used foul language. And she really didn't care.

For the first time since he'd entered the room, the detective smiled. "Well, Doctor, as soon as your lawyer gets here or you can show me an ID, I'll let you get outta here. And I'm sorry about this misunderstanding." He shook his head and reached into the file sitting before him on the table. After retrieving a picture from the inside cover, he handed it to her. "But you have to forgive us. There is a strong resemblance between you and Ms. Finan."

"Whoa!" Nic sucked in a breath of surprise as she studied the photo. The woman staring back at her was younger, with hair dyed a curious shade of pink, a large ring violating her nose, and a hardened look in her eyes that suggested to Nic that her life wasn't an easy one. But beneath all that were the green eyes that seemed familiar, the long nose, the high cheekbones, and the heart-shaped face that Nic had seen in the mirror a million times. "Yeah, you're right, Detective. She could be my twin."

He shook his head and frowned. "Be thankful this girl's not related," he said. "She's been in trouble her whole life, and now it seems the saga continues."

"What'd she do?"

"We're looking at her for murder. She shot the boyfriend while her two kids were asleep in the next room. Then she fled the scene so they could find his bloody body."

"How awful," Nic replied, before she fell into a stunned silence, staring at the photo and marveling at the resemblance.

A loud knock interrupted their conversation, and before either of them could respond the door opened and Rachael Rhodes walked through. Nic sucked in a breath and was grateful she was sitting, for the sight sent her head spinning. This was not the woman she'd met the night before.

The black hair that had been spiked was now worn down, falling softly across her forehead and framing her oval face. Her dark, almond-shaped eyes were sparkling with intensity. She wore a black suit tailored to hug her trim, lean body, with a pale-blue silk T-shirt beneath. The look of concern on her face was the only unattractive thing about her. She was absolutely stunning.

What the hell? Where had that reaction come from? The evening before, Nic couldn't think of a single thing she liked about Rae. Now, she was practically undressing her with her eyes. Shaking her head, she told herself she was just relieved to have Rae here. Not the woman, but the lawyer who'd hopefully put an end to this mess. But she suddenly forgot what it was about Rae that had irritated her so much. She couldn't, however, forget the rude way she'd treated her. Nic owed Rae an apology.

"Hey, are you okay?" Rae quickly asked, her eyes burrowing into Nicole's, their intensity once again a shock. As soon as Nic nodded, Rae handed her the much-needed wallet, which Nic accepted with relief. Although she'd always known this encounter with the police was a case of mistaken identity, she was still relieved to have it drawing to a close.

Rae patted Nic's back reassuringly as she walked to an empty place at the table. Placing her briefcase deliberately, as if it were a priceless piece of art rather than a sturdy bag of leather, she looked at the detective. "Do I need to open this? Or are we good here?"

"That depends on what her ID says."

Nic looked up, her driver's license in hand, and noticed the change in the detective's posture. He wore a hard, aggressive look once again, sitting erect, hands on the table and fingers flexing as if preparing to attack. He'd been relaxed, talking to her about McDonald's, and fishing, and College Misericordia, and now the two were facing off, ready to head into battle. Rae was a wall of steel, standing erect, unwavering, not intimidated by her surroundings and the man who danced in the opposite corner, awaiting the opening bell.

Nic suppressed a smile of amusement at their posturing. Such big egos at stake, she realized. But she was truly flattered that Rae would come to her rescue and felt a twinge of pride and some unfamiliar element fill her chest. She didn't question what it was. She also felt the need to step between them before one of the boxers drew blood.

She smiled at Rae and winked, silently telling her to stand down. Handing the ID across the table, she held Rae's gaze for a second and felt an explosion of heat in her belly. That annoying neighbor was suddenly sexy as hell as she played the role of lawyer.

Her thoughts interrupted by the detective's voice, Nic broke the eye contact and turned slightly to face him. "Well, are you satisfied?" she asked.

"I am, Dr. Coussart. Let me just make a copy of this and type up a statement for you to sign, and you can go."

"Can you make it snappy? I have to shower." Nic winced at her tone, not just because he had the power to hold her longer if he chose, but because she'd enjoyed their conversation. He'd actually been quite professional, even friendly toward her. And, in the end, he was only doing his job. Lord knows how often she was yelled at in the ER by irate patients and family members taking their frustrations out on her. Nic could empathize with the detective, yet she was behaving just as her patients often did. Shamefully. She tried belatedly to soften her remarks. "Please? This is an important event for me, and I don't want to be late."

He nodded slightly, accepting her unspoken apology. "I'll just be a few minutes."

"Thank you, Detective." Rae answered for them both and watched as the door opened and closed behind him. She finally sat down.

"So, what's new?" she asked, her expression blank but her dark eyes twinkling.

Laughing, Nic shook her head. "This is so bizarre." She quickly filled Rae in on the few details she knew about her involuntary trip to the police station.

"I heard about the shooting on the news," Rae said. "And I saw the girl's picture on the television. I didn't notice a resemblance. She had freaky pink hair."

Nic realized that aged photo must have been the only one the police had. "He showed me her mug shot, and aside from the hair, I do think there is one."

"Still, why would they bring in a jogger for questioning? Would you murder your boyfriend and then go for a jog along the Schuylkill?"

Nic couldn't help teasing Rae. She was so serious this morning. "I don't have boyfriends, remember?"

Rae blushed, a shade of pink that suddenly spread from the dark bangs covering her forehead all the way to her long, graceful neck.

"What? Shy now, are you?" The woman she'd met last night wasn't, and the one who'd walked into the room a few minutes earlier wasn't either.

"I don't know why, Nicole, but I like you." Rae leaned back into the stiff metal chair and crossed her arms.

Her remarks reminded Nicole of the less-than-delightful evening they'd spent together just a few hours before, erasing the playful mood Rae's teasing had created. "Well, I'll be happy to put this behind me. Thank you for coming so quickly."

"You're welcome."

Rae said it so quickly, Nic suspected it was an automatic reply. She wanted Rae to know she was sincere. "No, really, I appreciate it."

Rae met her eyes, and their coolness startled Nic. "I didn't come for you, Nic. I did it for Louis. He cares about you, and I care about him."

Nic nodded, understanding. She deserved the slap. And Rae deserved an apology. "I'm sorry I was such a bitch last night. There are many reasons I behaved the way I did, but there's no excuse."

Rae seemed to weigh Nic's words, deciding if she should accept the apology. After a moment, she said, "It's okay. No problem."

"Is there anything I can do to thank you for coming down here? Oh, you can bill me, you know."

"Not necessary."

"Free medical advice? Anything you want to know about? High blood pressure? Diabetes? Anything?" Nic couldn't believe she was stooping to this level, but something was pushing her to set things right with Rae.

Rae cocked her head and smiled, and the whole room seemed brighter. "You could have dinner with me."

Nic bit her lip and stifled a gasp. She'd planned on dinner with her godmother. But couldn't she take Rae along? Jeannie would most probably bring her partner. The idea of dinner with the stunning lawyer suddenly wasn't as repulsive as she would have previously thought, and she suspected this time would be much better than the last. It couldn't be worse! Jeannie wouldn't mind. Unlike Nic, she was the ultimate people-person.

Nic explained the situation, and Rae tried to back out when she heard about Nic's plans. "I don't want to intrude. Maybe another time."

Nic shook her head. Did she have to beg? She tried to keep her tone light, teasing, hoping to conceal her desire, for suddenly she was filled with an anxious anticipation that Rae would agree to the dinner plans. "Listen, hotshot. I'm in town for like fifty more hours. My apartment is on the market, and when it sells, you'll never see me again. If you want that date you were casing me for last night, let's get a move on. The clock's ticking."

Rae didn't have a chance to answer before Detective Young reappeared. He carried the large case-file folder tucked against the stain of his armpit and, in the other hand, a piece of plain white paper. "Here's your license," he said as he handed it to her. "And a statement. If you agree with it, sign it. You can cross out anything you don't like and add anything you want at the bottom."

Nic quickly read the synopsis of the morning's events, debated adding a few comments, and decided in the end it wasn't worth it. She was free, and she was going to put this morning behind her and get on with her day, and her life. She signed the paper on the indicated line and pushed it across the table to him.

She rose to her feet and smiled. "I wish I could say it's been a pleasure, Detective."

# CHAPTER FIFTEEN
# BAD NEWS

Dr. Jeannie Bennett's gaze followed the line of cars down Broad Street as she slid open the balcony door and stepped outside. The previous day's rain had moved on, and a hint of sun brightened the cloud-filled sky. Aircraft on approach to Philadelphia International Airport fell into formation, following the Delaware River, and she watched as they dropped below the clouds and flew over Citizens Bank Park and Lincoln Financial Field, the respective homes of the Phillies and Eagles. Below her, twenty stories down, the street was already crowded with cars and pedestrians hurrying to catch the early morning trains that ran directly below her building.

The morning was warm and Jeannie was happy to take her coffee and her newspaper and read on her balcony before she headed to her office for a busy schedule of patients. Curling her knees up beneath her, she put her weight on her right hip, protecting the left one that was predictably stiff in the morning, and opened the newspaper. The sports section always drew her attention in baseball season, and why she bothered to read it would require analysis to decipher. She already knew the Phils had lost. But the golf news was of interest. The men's PGA practice rounds were squeezed in between showers at the Merion Golf Club in nearby Haverford, and mud was likely to interfere with the 113th US Open, which was starting there the next day. She and Sandy had tickets for the weekend matches, and Jeannie was looking forward to watching the pros play.

Sandy had always been a great playmate, and since the two had been reunited, they'd been traveling as much as Jeannie's work schedule allowed and doing day trips whenever they could squeeze something in. Jeannie looked out over the city and realized that, for the first time in her life, she didn't look forward to work. She loved practicing medicine, running the clinic, interacting with people. Her passion had driven her for many years, after her children no longer needed her constant attention, and was a way to fill her days. Now, though, with Sandy in her life, occupying her thoughts and her time, work had lost some of its allure.

The few quiet feelers she'd put out hadn't turned up a suitable new medical director for the office, and she feared she'd have to make a more public search for a partner. She was hesitant to do so only because she feared scaring her staff. So many hospitals had closed and restructured, and offices and clinics were being absorbed left and right. Hers was still truly autonomous. She was the dictator, but a fair one, and her staff-retention levels were high, employee satisfaction higher. The staff joked that the only way to get a job at Jeannie's office was to inherit it when someone died.

With loyalty like that, Jeannie was understandably reluctant to retire and sell her practice. Yet she was constantly pulled by her desire to spend more time with Sandy. The solution was to take on a business partner, someone who'd share her passion and commitment, and her workload. It had to be an exceptional person, for she wouldn't subject her staff to abuse from someone lacking social skills, or her patients to someone who couldn't properly care for them. The search wouldn't be easy, and she needed to be patient until the right person came along.

A clicking behind her caught her attention, and she turned to see Sandy sliding the glass door open. They smiled as their eyes met. It'd been almost a year since they rekindled their old romance, and both still melted at the sight of the other.

"Hi, there, beautiful. How was your workout?"

Sandy bent and kissed Jeannie softly on the lips, then took a seat in the chair beside her. "I think it was an even exchange." Handing a coconut-crème Danish to Jeannie, she took a bite from a second one and swallowed it. "There's about three hundred calories in this, so I did three hundred calories' worth of exercise. I broke even."

Jeannie's eyes twinkled as she looked at the woman she loved, and her auburn hair shimmered in the morning light as she pushed it back behind her ear. "Yes, but the cardiovascular benefits go way beyond calories."

"That's my thinking, too." She grinned and took another bite, then sipped from Jeannie's coffee.

Jeannie took a bite of the pastry and moaned. "I think I'm in trouble living so close to all this good food. Unlike you, the only calories I've burned today have been on breathing. I'm only allowed about half a bite of this."

"I could help you burn some off," Sandy suggested.

Jeannie ran the big toe of her left foot along the inside of Sandy's leg, from the top of her sock to the bottom of her running shorts, and then teasingly rubbed it along the hem." I think I'll be in the mood for burning calories tonight."

Sandy groaned. "Don't we have dinner plans this evening?"

"Ah, yes, we do. But I have no plans for after dinner."

"Well, then, after dinner it is. Anything exciting happening in the world?" Sandy nodded toward the paper folded in Jeannie's lap.

Jeannie handed her the sports section. "We're going to need boots for our trek around Merion."

"As long as we don't need umbrellas, I'm game."

Scanning the front page, Jeannie nodded. Two female Swarthmore students were part of a fledgling campaign to change the way colleges across the country responded to reports of sexual assault. That was good news. The Justice Department was preparing to file charges against Edward Snowden for leaking confidential government information, Boeing had won a huge U.S. Army contract, and a drug dealer had been shot in the Northeast. As Jeannie scanned the article about the shooting, she gasped. "Oh, no!" she exclaimed.

"What?" Sandy sat forward, startled.

Jeannie looked up from the news and met her gaze. "Katie's in trouble." Handing the paper to Sandy, Jeannie reached for her cell phone and quickly dialed Katie's number.

"Holy shit," Sandy exclaimed as she read the details of Billy Wallace's shooting. The article mentioned that the police were looking for Katie Finan as a person of interest in the slaying.

Hopeful that Katie would answer her call, Jeannie listened helplessly as the phone rang unanswered and then diverted to voice mail. “Katie, it’s Jeannie. I heard the news and I’m just checking on you. You know my numbers if you need me. I’ll be at the clinic by nine. Call on the private line. Call no matter what. I want to know that you’re safe.”

“Wow!” Sandy said.

“Yeah. I didn’t even know he was out of jail.”

“Is she with him? I thought things were developing with Jet.”

Jeannie looked up and clasped her hands in relief. “Jet! She might be with Jet!” Jeannie dialed the number and this time was rewarded with an answer. It wasn’t the voice of the confident woman who ran her office, though. This voice sounded tired and strained. Obviously, she’d heard the news.

“Hey, Jeannie,” Jet said.

“Hi, Jet. Is Katie with you?” Jeannie tried to disguise her fear. If Katie wasn’t with Jet, she could be in real trouble. Otherwise, she’d have reached out to one of them.

After the briefest of pauses, Jet answered. “She’s right here.”

“Whew. Thank goodness. What’s going on?”

Jet stammered, “I think I’ll let Katie talk to you.”

Katie reached out for the phone. She should have anticipated this phone call. Jeannie Bennett wasn’t the kind of woman to ignore news like this. She’d always been there for Katie in the past, and she still was. “Hi,” Katie said.

“Hi, Katie. How are you? Are you okay? What’s going on?” Jeannie demanded in a rush of questions.

“Yeah, I’m okay,” Katie replied, choosing to answer the easiest of the questions.

“Then why are you running from the police?”

Katie squeezed the bridge of her nose, her migraine suddenly worse as she faced the one authority figure in the world whose opinion truly mattered to her. Jeannie wasn’t just her boss. She was a mother figure and a role model and a woman she truly respected and admired. Katie couldn’t stand to disappoint her.

As calmly as she could, she told Jeannie what had happened. “I wasn't running from the police. Not at first, anyway. A man with a gun was chasing me. But I don't think I can trust the police, either. What if they take my kids from me?"

"Katie, that's not going to happen. Everyone who knows you knows what a great mom you are, how much you love your kids. And we're also sure you'd never have killed Billy. I'll vouch for you, all the doctors at the office will vouch for you, all the nurses will vouch for you. Hey, even Judge Rabin will vouch for you. No one on this planet could say anything bad about you."

Katie walked across the living room to the long windows, draped to keep out the morning sun. Pushing the heavy curtain aside, she peered through the glass and was amazed at how normal the world seemed. Cars drove by, a squirrel ran through the grass, the sun shined down as if nothing had happened. She thought about Jeannie's words.

She knew she had Jeannie's unconditional love and support. Jeannie had taken a chance on her when she was still all screwed up with drugs. She'd helped her build a life. As for the other doctors she worked with, Katie thought she'd probably earned their respect as well. She worked hard and did a good job, never called in sick, and they all seemed to like her. She didn't rock the boat and got along with her coworkers. They were a tough group of women, mostly single moms and older women who'd earned their own keep and expected everyone else to earn theirs as well. And the judge—Katie had forgotten about the judge.

Murray Rabin was on the board of the clinic, and when his wife had been diagnosed with terminal cancer, he'd asked for Dr. Bennett's help with home-health services. Several of the nurses and techs had formed a team to provide virtually round-the-clock care for Mrs. Rabin. Katie and her kids had worked Friday evenings and Sundays for months, and Katie and the judge had developed a friendship of sorts. He'd sold the big house after his wife died two years ago and retired to Florida, but he still sent an occasional note and always remembered Chloe and Andre's birthdays. He'd surely put in a good word for her if she needed one.

Looking across the room at Jet, Katie felt her heart melt. She sat on the couch, with her hands clasped, her forearms resting on her thighs. She'd win the bed-head award again, with her dark hair sticking up in every direction. Even though she wore a wrinkled T-shirt and gym shorts, Katie thought her beautiful, and sexy.

She recalled the special moments they'd shared in the last few months and the incredible passion they'd shared in the last few hours, how those still hands had moved frantically over her skin, giving her more pleasure than she'd ever known. Jet loved her, and she loved Jet. This was a chance for her to have a happiness she hadn't known she even wanted, and she didn't want to screw it up. Was going to the police the answer? Might she, after all these years, count on them?

Jet had brought up some credible concerns during their talk in the early morning. Katie had thought of running, but how far would her inheritance check take her without some form of ID? She wouldn't even be able to cash it. And if she could, what kind of life would she and her children have if they were forced to hide from Simon and the police? She wouldn't be able to work, and the kids wouldn't be able to attend school.

Jet had told her she needed to talk to the police, and now Jeannie was telling her the same thing. The two smartest women she knew couldn't both be wrong. It was a scary prospect, knowing the police might not believe her, understanding that they could put her children in foster care when they threw her in jail, but she also understood she had to take a chance. The alternative wasn't so good, either.

"I guess I should talk to the police," Katie said at last. From across the room she saw Jet's shoulders relax in relief, and on the other end she heard Jeannie's supportive words.

"You have to, Katie. You can't hide from the police. It'll be okay, because you haven't done anything wrong."

"I hope you're right, Jeannie."

"I'm always right, Katie."

She laughed in response.

"I take it you won't be coming to work today, then?" Jeannie asked.

"I better take care of this first."

"Okay. Will Jet be coming in? Maybe she should stay with you. I can manage without you for a few hours." Jeannie's tone was teasing.

"I'd appreciate that."

"Okay. Tell her she can have the day off. I'll see you both tomorrow."

"Okay, Jeannie. Thanks."

"And Katie? If you need anything, call me."

Katie smiled as she walked across the room and sat beside Jet. If she wanted to spend her days and nights beside this woman—and she did—she'd need to find all of her courage. "I will."

Disconnecting the phone, Katie leaned against Jet's shoulder, and immediately Jet reached around and pulled her closer. Already, she felt better. She wished she could shake her doubts, though. Did Jet really know what she was getting herself into? Looking up into the dark eyes she loved, she asked.

"I'm sure."

"Well, then, what would you like to do today? Your boss gave you the day off."

"Uh…I think I'm going to take you to talk to the police."

"I want to talk to my lawyer first."

"You have a lawyer?" Jet asked, and Katie could hear the surprise in her voice. She supposed most people didn't; she supposed most people didn't need one.

"He was a friend of my mom. He's bailed me out of jail a dozen times…and he manages my trust fund."

Jet's jaw dropped. "Your what?"

"My trust fund." Katie told her about the lawsuit and the judge's decision to safeguard the money for her. "I'm an heiress of sorts." Katie laughed, although the memory still hurt. She often wondered if her father would have been kinder to her if he'd gotten the money from the lawsuit. What she never questioned, though, was the intentions of his second wife. April was evil, and whatever money her father had, the woman would have spent, and she would have been no kinder to Katie in the process.

Jet squeezed her arm. "Great, then. You can buy breakfast."

# Chapter Sixteen
# Police Work

Phil Young sat back in the hard metal chair and closed his eyes. He was getting too old for this job. His daughter really was a student at Misericordia University, and in two years, when she earned her degree, he hoped to retire. He hated to give up the security of a steady income and a few more dollars in his pension by taking a private-sector job until he fulfilled his responsibility for his youngest child. Then, though, he was gone.

He hated investigating murders. He hated seeing the battered and bullet-ridden bodies that had once been living souls. He hated the drugs that led to the violence. He hated the loss of family values that contributed to so many kids on the streets, taking drugs and committing a plethora of crimes. He hated that every murder caused him to question the security of his own family, who were just as vulnerable to random violence as any number of the victims for whom he tried to find justice.

And he really, really hated that so many murders happened late at night and forced him to leave the comfort of his bed and lose the sleep his body loved. Billy Wallace had been shot at ten in the evening, nearly twelve hours earlier, and Phil hadn't stopped running since he'd answered the call. He'd spent a few hours at the scene, talking to witnesses and waiting for the coroner to remove the body. He'd barely had a chance to begin digging into the victim's background when he'd had to rush over to the hospital and figure out that fiasco. He'd have that officer's badge if he could, just to make a point.

After heading back to his office, he'd had a chance to read about the victim and his common-law wife, Katie Finan, and had issued the alert for her before heading to the autopsy. He was there when the call came in that Katie Finan had been apprehended, and he'd rushed downtown, eager to talk to the woman.

According to the autopsy, Wallace would have died from either of the two bullets in his upper chest. The second, large-caliber round was literally overkill. The upper bullet ripped apart his aorta just as it exited the heart. The lower one entered the heart on the front side and exited on the back, then collapsed the lung. Death was instantaneous.

Wallace's bloody body had been found on the first floor of the small house, in the living room near the front entrance. The pattern of blood splattered there indicated that was the site of the shooting. He fell where he was shot, collapsing into the fetal position, with his legs bent, on his left side.

They hadn't found any bullets on the first floor but had retrieved two from Billy's corpse. They'd also pulled a bullet from the window frame of the bedroom one floor above, and another one had presumably shattered the window. At first light, officers at the scene had uncovered a few more. All seemed to be from the same large-caliber weapon. They'd recovered casings from the hall, the stairs, the bedroom, and the alley beside the house.

Witnesses, a total of seven of them, reported seeing a dark-colored SUV parked in the alley next to Wallace's apartment. They also reported seeing Katie Finan, or a woman resembling her, sitting on the roof over the first-floor porch when the first shots were fired. Three women saw Katie jump from the roof a minute later. One man reported seeing a man and a woman jump from the roof, but that witness couldn't remember who'd gone first in the bizarre game of follow-the-leader. The other witnesses had jumped for cover when the shooting started outside the house and couldn't offer any other information.

Some of the officers at the scene and neighbors outside speculated that Katie was the shooter. Phil already knew, without a doubt, that she was not. The evidence at the scene and the witness accounts told him that. If Finan had shot Wallace upstairs and missed, then chased him downstairs and killed him in the living room, why would she return to the bedroom and jump from the roof? She'd have fled through the front door, just a few feet away.

And why would she leave her kids in the house with their dead father's body there for them to discover? Everything he'd learned about her in the hours since she'd fled that house told him that Katie Finan lived for her children. Her criminal record—devoid of entry since her daughter's birth—clearly reflected that. Her neighbors described her as a doting mother. And of course, there was the incident at the hospital. If that didn't prove just how much she cared for her children, nothing did.

No, Finan wasn't the shooter. That meant the driver of the SUV had pulled the trigger. And Katie Finan knew who he was. He'd shot at her, too. If Phil could find her, she could finger the killer, and he could wrap up the case and get some sleep.

It seemed too good to be true when he'd heard that Finan had been picked up on Kelly Drive. But he'd rushed right over to Twenty-first Street, eager to question the woman. He'd missed her soliloquy to the two-way mirror but watched it on video several times before going into the room to question her.

From the moment he heard her speak, Phil was concerned that they'd picked up the wrong suspect. The woman they brought in looked a lot like Finan, but he was willing to bet they sounded nothing alike. The woman in custody spoke well, eloquently and with proper English. He'd be surprised if a woman living in Finan's neighborhood and with a drug dealer like Billy Wallace even knew the meaning of the word *expedite*. She wore expensive sunglasses and running sneakers, too, but that didn't persuade him one way or the other. They typically found expensive items like that in drug houses. But the way this suspect wore them—her entire demeanor, in fact—bespoke a confidence he rarely witnessed in this setting. This woman wasn't afraid and wasn't in the least bit intimidated by her surroundings. She was just biding her time, awaiting her release, and that wasn't at all what he'd have expected from Katie Finan. Katie had much to fear and even more to lose if their meeting didn't go her way, yet the woman talking into the mirror was more annoyed than afraid.

When he'd walked into the room to meet her, his suspicions were confirmed. The woman had an attitude, and gumption, but not the kind grown on the streets. She was just simply obnoxious, a spoiled brat, in his opinion. Used to having her way, but undeniably intelligent and articulate.

From that point, it was just a matter of time before she produced the proof of identity that won her freedom. He'd enjoyed their banter, matching barbs with her and of course talking about a part of the state he'd come to love. He and his wife had purchased a vacation home in the Poconos at Big Bass Lake, and they visited the mountains every chance they got. From the way she spoke, and the glimmer in her eyes, Dr. Coussart clearly loved that part of the commonwealth as much as he did.

So, his trip downtown had been for naught. And he wasn't happy. First of all, he still didn't have a suspect behind bars. And second, unless he found Katie before the killer did, he'd have another murder to solve.

Phil picked up his pen and applied it to the statement Nicole Coussart had signed, leaving his own signature below hers. Then he picked up the copy of Nicole's driver's license and studied it again. She certainly did resemble Katie. Then he noted with amusement that the doctor's thirtieth birthday was the next day. He was surprised she hadn't threatened to sue him for ruining her birthday festivities.

He opened the file on the Wallace murder, ready to put the information on Nicole into the back, in the section where the irreverent paperwork was filed. When he did, Katie Finan's profile slipped out. He picked it up and shook his head at the similarities between the two women. Even though the much-younger woman had pink hair and a nose ring, it was easy to understand how the patrolmen had confused them and accidentally hauled in the doctor.

He glanced at the information on Katie Finan, taking it in, wondering what his next move would be, and saw something that made him stop. He reread the information to be sure his eyes weren't deceiving him and then pulled the copy of Nicole's driver's license to recheck it.

"Whoa!" he whispered as he read the information below Katie's picture for the third time. She was also twenty-nine years old. And, like Nicole Coussart, she would turn thirty the next day.

# CHAPTER SEVENTEEN
# ART

Nic's presentation, and the subsequent minutes of the afternoon that followed (one hundred and sixty-five of them, at last count), had flown quickly by as Nic allowed herself the secret pleasure of daydreaming about her afternoon plans. Attempting to concentrate on conference topics had been futile as her thoughts wandered back to Rae, and so she'd left the conference early and headed home.

During the ride back to her apartment after her encounter at the police station, Rae had suggested that they spend a few hours before dinner at the Barnes. Nic was so excited about the prospect, and about seeing Rae again, she wasn't sure how she was able to focus on her presentation. She had though, and done well, but as soon as the opportunity presented itself, she bolted.

This was the birthday present she'd asked of Louis, the one thing she'd really wanted to do. How could she refuse the invitation? At the same time, it felt strange to be going to the Barnes with Rae, whom she barely knew. Stranger still to be looking forward to it. A bit of mystery lingered, too. The tickets had to be acquired well in advance, yet somehow Rae had managed to find a pair.

She told herself she was repaying a kindness, doing a favor for Louis's neighbor, who because of the abrasive nature of her personality most assuredly suffered from the lack of friendly companionship. And during the first moments after Nic's presentation, when she'd finished accepting the back pats and congratulations of friends and strangers, she believed that. As the minutes passed, though, she found herself thinking not so much of a particular Renoir she wished to see and more about what she would be wearing when she saw it.

Nic could easily have dismissed this thought as meaningless because she usually paid considerable attention to her appearance, applying gallons of toxic products to keep her hair perky and shiny, and spending a small fortune on her wardrobe. She would expertly apply her makeup, and then add the necessary pieces of jewelry to complement her outfit, without crossing the line into obnoxious. If she'd been going to the Barnes with Louis, as she'd planned and hoped, she would have devoted an equal allotment of time to the task. No, that wasn't unusual.

When she began wondering what Rae would wear, though, Nic had to face the fact that there was more to her mood, and to the lightness in her step, than a simple trip to an art museum. She was looking forward to seeing Rae.

Was she schizophrenic or what? The night before she'd thought slow torture too good a punishment for her, and she hadn't even been accused of any crime other than stealing Louis's attention. In her fury, Nic had been able to amass a half-dozen other charges, all of them equally offensive. The evening before, she'd have been happy to never see Rae again, and she was sure Rae's feelings didn't differ significantly from her own. Yet with the sunshine of a new day, and the peculiar situation in which Nic found herself, Rae was able to come to the rescue, revealing a new and much more appealing side that Nic couldn't so easily discount. Last night, the posturing and opinions had been overwhelming; this morning they'd been comforting and reassuring. Even though she'd never needed protection in her uneventful upper-class existence, Nic suddenly found the idea of a strong protector erotically appealing.

Even if said protector was on the bottom of the growth chart.

She was usually so decisive. What the hell was wrong with her? Her first impressions usually stuck—and even if she found out later that she'd been wrong, she had no reason to apologize or make amends. She'd simply move on. Not this time, though. Now, she was ready to forget the entire list of Rae's crimes and start over.

This, because the woman looked sexy as hell in a suit? Maybe she should consult the medical textbooks again. Perhaps medication would be helpful for her, after all.

Slipping her earring back through the dangling gold post in her ear, Nic hurried to the door as she heard the much anticipated bell ring. She was finally ready. As she passed the mirror she noted with approval the image that greeted her and smiled at herself as she raced by. She'd skipped out of the conference early for this trip, and she still found herself rushing. She'd showered, changed her outfit twice, and reapplied her makeup, all without cause, because she'd looked perfectly great before. "Okay, I'm ready," she said aloud as she reached for the door, then stopped with her hand on the knob.

Ready for what? How would she label this time with Rae? It was one thing to spend time with her, but did she want to call it a date? And what would Rae have to say about it? While she knew the evening before had been intended to put the two of them together in one of Louis's lab beakers, to see if a chemical reaction resulted, the mixture had caused a messy explosion. Rae might not want anything to do with her. This afternoon at the museum with dinner to follow could simply be an attempt at friendship, nothing more.

She frowned. Not only was she confused about what she wanted from this trip to the museum, she was frustrated by the knowledge that it might be Rae's call to make, not hers.

Nic opened the door to the woman of the hour and couldn't help appreciating the sight. Rae, too, had changed clothes, and this was the best look of the three Nic had seen so far. She didn't like the tough girl she'd met the night before, and although the lawyer in the suit she'd met earlier in the day was quite attractive, this casual Rae was outstanding. A bright-purple button-up over a black T-shirt was tucked into knee-length black pants. On her feet was a pair of funky black leather shoes, a hybrid between sneakers and loafers. "You look great!" she said before she realized her thoughts had morphed into words.

Rae's smile, and the twinkle in her black eyes, made Nic forget the slip of her tongue. She modestly appraised Nic, who wore a miniskirt and lightweight sweater, and returned the compliment.

"Our tickets are for three to three thirty, so we should make it with a few minutes to spare," Rae commented as they rode the elevator down to the lobby. They debated a taxi, but because they weren't completely sure of their dinner plans, Rae agreed to drive. Nic didn't mind conceding that control. She despised driving in the city.

As they left her apartment together, Nic couldn't hold back her smile and felt idiotic as she grinned broadly. But art was her first love, and if she hadn't grown up in a household with two doctors who talked shop nonstop, she'd have chosen a much less practical but satisfying career in art. She lacked the talent to make a living by painting, but she would have loved to do art restoration. Repairing damaged masterpieces at a large museum like the Barnes would qualify as her dream job.

She'd been to the Barnes before, as a medical student, when it was housed in the suburbs in the mansion built for the doctor's sizable collection. The new museum reproduced the rooms and displays Dr. Barnes had so painstakingly arranged, and she found that in itself amazing. Not to mention the Picassos, Cezannes, Renoirs, and van Goghs. That she was having this experience because of the woman she'd wanted to kill just a day before was equally amazing.

"How'd your presentation go?" Rae inquired politely as they awaited the elevator.

Nic's pulse pounded. The presentation had gone remarkably well. The audience was attentive, asked questions, and seemed intrigued. She was certain she'd be asked to speak again. "Really well, thanks," she said, and smiled, meeting Rae's dark eyes. She detected genuine interest there and was beginning to suspect that Rae took an interest in most things, and most people. They were polar opposites in that regard.

"Is this something you do often?" Rae asked as they stepped into the wood paneled elevator. Rae pressed the button on the wall and directed it to the parking garage.

"It's sort of standard to present cases during residency. Not so much now, though." She looked at Rae and realized that was precisely what she did for a living—present cases. "You do this every day, huh? Present your case?"

"Not every day," Rae said, smiling. "But enough."

"I guess it's hard to function as an attorney if you're shy, then, huh?"

"It helps to have a little cocky in you."

Nic burst out laughing. "Then I imagine you're fabulous at your job." Actually, she'd been impressed with how Rae had handled the morning and told her so again.

Rae shrugged off the praise. "It's what I do."

"Well, thanks again. And in case I'm too awed to speak when we get there—thanks for the Barnes." Their eyes again met and held for a moment, but before Rae could reply, the elevator door opened and they both averted their gaze. They exited and walked side by side in the direction Rae indicated.

"You're welcome," Rae said after a moment. "I'm happy to have an art lover to share it with."

"Have you been here before?" Nic asked after a minute.

They reached the car, an older-model Mercedes-Benz convertible, and Rae smiled slyly. "Yeah. I have a membership. That's how I got the tickets."

"Oh. I thought Louis said you hated art."

Rae laughed as she started the car. "You must have me confused with someone else. Is it okay if I put the top down?"

"Oh, yes, of course. And you like foreign films?"

"Is this a quiz show?"

"Yes. How many times have you been to the Barnes?"

"How many times?" Rae seemed to ponder the question. "I can't say. I usually go three or four times a week, just for an hour or so."

Nic's jaw dropped. "You have got to be kidding me."

"One of the benefits of living downtown."

"I guess I was busy working and sleeping when I lived here, because I didn't seem to make it to a museum more than once a month."

They were stopped as Rae waited for traffic to pass, and she turned to Nic. "That's really a shame."

Nic sank back in her seat, thinking. She was sure Louis had told her Rae hated art. Why would he lie? Unless—"Hey, Rae? Did Louis happen to make any suggestions to you about me?"

"I'm not sure what you mean," she casually replied, and a glance in her direction showed no evidence of deceit. Rae looked relaxed and, well, stunning behind the wheel.

"Did he suggest you wear cologne? Or state your opinion very firmly? Or talk very loudly?"

Rae glanced at her, the furrowed brows showing her confusion. "He did mention that you like the aggressive, take-charge type. And cologne, too. Why?"

Nic laughed and patted Rae's leg. "I'm not sure what our boy's up to, but he set us up to fail."

"You mean—?"

"Yes. I don't like to argue. And all scents trigger migraines, so I avoid them at all costs."

Rae frowned in thought. "I never would've thought Louis capable of such subterfuge. What's that about?"

Nic shook her head, baffled. "I have no idea. But last night he mentioned that you were too nice for me, so apparently he thinks we're not well suited for each other. Maybe he was just trying to help us come to the same conclusion."

"Hmm. I wonder," Rae said and then they were both silent.

"Why don't we start over, Rae? Would that be okay with you?"

Rae grinned from ear to ear in response.

"Do you know the whole story of the Barnes?"

"You mean about the controversy over moving it downtown?"

"Yeah."

"I have a feeling you know more."

Rae roared. "I am a know-it-all sometimes. But I'm a great partner to have in all trivia games."

"I'll keep that in mind. Tell me the whole story. About the Barnes." As they drove, and then as they walked, Rae related what she knew about the hostile takeover of the Barnes collection. From the legal point of view of trust funds and donor intentions, it was quite fascinating.

Dr. Barnes had amassed a fortune from his discovery of the treatment for gonorrhea, and used it to collect masterpieces of all kinds—paintings, statues, artifacts and more. He kept his treasures private, and upon his death a trust was set up to care for it. Barnes was eccentric, though, and his legacy was quite complicated by the terms of his will. He despised the way museums housed and displayed their works. He was a champion of the common man and wanted him, as well as poor students, to have access to these masterpieces. The Barnes Foundation, had it been financially stable, would have fulfilled all of the doctor's dreams. Inflation caused financial problems, though, and over time, Barnes's mission became harder to sustain. In an effort to protect and preserve forty billion dollars' worth of art, lawsuits were filed to move the pieces to a modern site. Opponents of the move argued that it was Dr. Barnes's right to have the art stay at his home in Lower Merion, even if staying there put the works at risk.

As they sat on a bench outside the museum, waiting for their assigned entrance time, Rae finished the tale. "So, what do you think?"

"About what?"

Rae shrugged. "C'mon, Nic. We don't have to argue, but can't we discuss? Debate? Something tells me you're not afraid to speak your mind, so pick a side. Were they right to move the Barnes downtown?"

"It's a difficult question to answer." She closed her eyes, feeling the sunshine on her face, and enjoyed the simple pleasure of its warmth. It was true that she spoke her mind, typically, but that didn't automatically translate into a desire to debate. In fact, the opposite was true. Debate required too much give-and-take, too much social energy. And she was having an absolutely wonderful time with Rae—why ruin it?

"You sound like a politician." Rae studied her, conscious of her own breath catching, of the slight elevation of her pulse rate as she studied Nic's body—from the features of her face, softened by this relaxed pose, to the lines of her neck and the swell of her breasts, rising and falling with each breath.

This was an erotic picture of a beautiful woman, as magnificent as anything painted on the canvases of the masters in the museum beyond the sidewalk. And this woman was alive, and vibrant, and destined to spend the next few hours with her.

Rae wasn't sure what had driven her impulse to ask Nic out today. Heaven knows it wasn't the overwhelming success of their first meeting. If that were the only issue in play, Rae would have been quite content to never see Nic again. Nic's behavior had been rude, and her arrogance had shone through the thin veil of social grace with which she'd attempted to conceal it. And if Nic had a sense of humor, she kept it well hidden.

Yet, to Rae's surprise and confusion, Nic appealed to her anyway. Nic was intelligent—that was evident from both the degrees hanging on her walls and from the conversation they'd shared. She was a beauty, possessing all the physical features Rae found attractive—long dark hair and vibrant eyes and a trim figure. She even met the height requirement. She was a patron of the arts and well traveled. Mostly, though, Rae thought there just had to be more to Nicole Coussart than she'd been allowed to see the evening before. Birds of a feather, she told herself.

Louis was one of the kindest, funniest, most genuine human beings she'd ever met. If she had any notion of attraction to the opposite sex—and she had exactly zero—Louis would have been the man for her. In fact, her parents, who held out hope that she would meet the right man one day, in spite of her gentle and persistent reminders otherwise, had suggested that very thing. That Rae marry Louis. This after they shared one dinner with him during a stop over in Philly en route to the beach.

As if having a very successful and wonderful friendship with a man could somehow be translated into the kind of passion that resulted in a lifetime commitment. It could not, of course, and Rae was pleased to have him for a friend, for she didn't have the same reservations about her sexuality that troubled her parents. Her attraction to girls had begun on the playground as a child and never wavered. It had only grown stronger as she began to understand it and embrace it. She never doubted that she wanted to make love with women, and only women, no matter how nice a friend she'd found in Louis.

Because of him, though, she supposed, she held out hope that Nicole might be more than she'd revealed at first glance. And because of him she was willing to take a closer look. It was just not possible that Nicole, being Louis's friend, could be *that* bad.

"Not a politician. Just an art lover, and I'm thrilled at the chance to see one of the greatest exhibits of the masters the world has ever known."

Nic smiled as she made her reply, knowing it would please her parents, but more so because she knew it would elicit further debate from Rae.

"I knew it. I knew you'd be in favor of the move." Rae slapped her thigh for emphasis.

Nicole dared to open one eye and kept her voice flat, unemotional. "You're very annoying, Rae."

"You shouldn't say that until after I've gotten you through the front door. Remember, I still have your ticket."

Nic bit her lip, suppressing a smile. It was difficult to believe how much she liked Rae, with her keen intelligence, sharp wit, and boundless energy. If she hadn't been in such a bad mood last night, the evening might not have been a total waste after all. "You're so very kind to bring me here, Rae," she said, with an excess of flattery. "I'm so grateful to you. You're a wonderful person."

Leaning back against the bench, Rae looked to the cloud-filled sky and laughed. Nic studied her in this pose. Gazing at the lines of her throat, the curve of her breasts beneath the double layer of shirts, the joy on Rae's face—the breath caught in her throat. There would be no paucity of debate between them on any subject, but no one could argue one simple point—Rae was a cutie. Blushing at the thought, she cleared a suddenly dry throat and looked away before Rae could notice her flush. No doubt she'd ask Nic what had caused it. Turning to the watch adorning her wrist, Nic said, "It's time."

Silently they walked to the entrance, side by side, and Nic didn't pull away when Rae gently placed her hand on the small of her back to guide her in the right direction.

"How would you like to do this?" Rae asked, and Nic understood the question immediately. They only had a few hours. No one could appreciate a museum of this size with a drive-by sort of approach. They'd have to skip total sections. Nic had to decide how to make the most of her time.

"Since it's my first visit, I think a walk-through would be great. Next time, after I know what I want to see…" She let the statement hang there, a carrot teasingly dangled in front of Rae, who pounced on it.

"I can get tickets for tomorrow, if you're nice to me."

"I find it very taxing to be nice."

"I got that impression."

It was playful banter, and both of them appreciated the change from their prior time together.

"I can be, though, if I'm sufficiently motivated."

"Well, if the Barnes can't motivate an art lover, nothing can."

They presented their tickets and walked through the entrance, and suddenly emotion overwhelmed Nic. Raising her head she saw lights so carefully positioned, heard the crisp, clear echoes of the voices around her, felt the dry, cool air across her forehead. And as she looked at Rae, she noticed, not for the first time, the magnificence of her smile.

Nic was pleasantly surprised to realize the emotion she was feeling was called happiness.

# CHAPTER EIGHTEEN
# IMPERSONATING A FUGITIVE

Attorney Chapman's office, how can I help you?"

Simon listened to the conversation on speaker, watching from a few feet away as Angelica recited her lines.

"Hi, this is Katie Finan. Can I talk to Mr. Chapman?"

"Who may I ask is calling?" the voice on the other end of the phone asked.

"Katie Finan," Angelica repeated, more slowly and deliberately this time.

"And what is this about?" the woman asked.

Angelica took a deep breath and spoke. "I'm a client of Mr. Chapman, and I need to talk to him about my trust fund."

"Hold on, please," she said.

Simon sat beside her on the couch and could hear classical music playing as Angelica was put on hold. Smothering the phone in her ample chest to dampen the sound, she whispered to him. "This could be the one. She sounds very uppity. Kind of like Katie."

In spite of his growing frustration, Simon laughed. Angelica had the ability to lighten his mood, and at this moment, it was quite dark. He needed to find Katie before she spoke to the police, and the clock was ticking. The longer it took to find her, the better the chance the police would find her first. Given enough time, she might even get scared enough to contact them. If that happened, he was in trouble. She not only knew his name and what he looked like, but she'd seen him at the beach. It wouldn't take her long to figure out his secret, if she hadn't already.

Simon was running out of ideas. Katie hadn't been home since the shooting; no one except the police had been in the house since they'd encircled it with yellow police crime-scene tape early that morning. A boy watching the house had been given a crisp fifty-dollar bill to watch the place, and Simon was confident that if Katie showed up there, he'd know it. Another hired hand had spent the day watching the clinic where she worked, and he too reported no signs of her. The police were there, though, staking out the place. Her kids hadn't gone to school, and they weren't in the church basement, where senior citizens helped working moms by babysitting a few hours each day. No one on the streets had seen her. It was if she'd disappeared. Not an easy task, with two kids in tow.

Now Simon was using his last lead, doing the methodical type of work that made him so dangerous. There was just a sliver of hope, just a possibility it would pan out, but he was nothing if not a dreamer. Dreams pulled him up and out of the ghetto and made him a success. Whenever someone told him he couldn't do something, it made him all the more determined to succeed. Now it seemed Katie was destined to escape him, and he rededicated himself to finding her. And he would.

Katie was due to collect her trust fund. Billy had told him it would be only two more days until he had the money, and after a few hours of sound sleep in his comfortable bed, Simon had awakened, showered, and traveled back to the city. His Lexus was safely parked in the garage, and his Ford sat in the driveway in front of the house he shared with Angelica.

During the drive, the idea had come to him. Since following the kids hadn't worked, he decided to follow the next best thing—the money. It always came down to money. Katie wouldn't walk away from that kind of cash. Staking out her lawyer's office was the best way to track Katie down.

Simon was now faced with another problem. He had a wonderful plan but no way to execute it. He had no idea who Katie used to manage her legal matters. She'd once mentioned the name of her high school, and he knew the lawyer who'd helped her in the past had an office somewhere in Katie's old neighborhood. So, he and Angelica had spent their morning driving around that area, looking for lawyers' offices in Northeast Philly, driving up streets and down alleys, into and out of strip malls, pulling up to marquees in front of office buildings to read the lists of tenants. They'd literally found the names of hundreds of lawyers but had no idea which one, if any, represented Katie.

Angelica had logged their names in a notebook, and after a few hours of driving they'd settled onto the couch at her house and began the tedious process of calling each name on the list. She made the calls, posing as Katie, while Simon sat nearby, listening on speakerphone, looking up numbers, and crossing names off the list. Between busy phone lines, time spent on hold, and lunch breaks at the offices, they'd made it through only three-quarters of the list, and it was already three in the afternoon. If Katie had panicked and gone to his office first thing in the morning, Simon was already too late. He was hoping she would have called to make an appointment, though, and he'd catch her in the afternoon or even the next day.

"Ms. Finan?" The voice returned to the line, interrupting the classical music.

"Yes?"

"Ms. Finan, we can't find a record of you having been our client. Are you sure you have the right office? Or could you have used another name, perhaps a maiden name?"

"No, no other name. I'm sorry. I must be mistaken," Angelica lied for the hundredth time that day and disconnected the phone. "Fuck, Simon. What if she has an alias?"

He studied the ceiling as if it held the answer he needed, ran his fingers through his hair, and massaged the back of his neck. "Shit," he answered after a moment. An alias hadn't occurred to him. Once again, Angelica amazed him. Was Katie Finan her real name, or one she'd taken on the streets? Lots of people had street names. Most people knew him as Simon Simms, and he had no idea who'd started calling him that, or why. Yet it had stuck.

Could Katie have taken Billy's name? Many women assumed the name of the man they lived with, often legally changing it without going through the wedding that usually accompanied such dramatic action. He thought of Katie, defiant and cocky, and doubted she would have. Hell, she hadn't even given Billy's kids his last name. She'd told Billy she wasn't giving them his name until he started acting like a father and earned the right. The little brats were named Finan, just like her. A smile appeared on his face and he explained his logic. "It's definitely Finan."

"Okay, then. Who's next?"

"Seven-four-two," he said, and rattled off the next numbers on the list without hesitation. He'd come this far, and he refused to stop until he'd contacted every lawyer they'd found. If they all turned out to be dead ends, he'd go back and hunt for more prospects. He wouldn't stop until he found the man, or found Katie, whichever came first. Instead of fatigue, Simon felt a renewed energy as he watched Angelica. They were going to find her, and when they did, Simon would take much pleasure in putting a bullet right between her eyes. And then, perhaps, he and Angelica could come back here and spend the afternoon in the big bed whose corner he could just see from his space on the couch.

He heard her begin her well-practiced recital and listened hopefully for the response of the woman who'd answered the phone.

"Oh, hello! You're not calling to cancel, are you? He just called me and said he's on his way. Court ended a little late today."

Simon used his hand in a slashing gesture across his throat, and Angelica disconnected the call. It was a lawyer on Fordham Street, a man named Bruce Smick. It would take them twenty minutes to get there, if they had the unreliable cooperation of commuter traffic.

"What's the plan?" she asked.

"We go there, and I shoot her."

Wearing a conservative blue suit with a white shirt and bright-blue tie, he certainly didn't look the part of a man on a mission to kill a woman. And that was exactly why he thought he'd get away with it.

Angelica's floral halter dress, pink sandals, and costume jewelry made her look presentable for just about anything that didn't require formal wear. "Okay, I'm ready," she said.

"Let's go." Simon stood, and Angelica was right beside him as they walked through the door.

❖

Phil Young leaned over a well-tended patch of garden and pulled an imaginary weed from the bed of petunias in which he was kneeling. The garden was in front of the house two doors down from the law offices of Bruce Smick, and Phil had been on his knees for a half an hour, patiently awaiting Katie's arrival. If someone was watching, his cover would be blown. Although he was dressed appropriately for yard work, wearing Bermuda shorts and a golf shirt, the apron he wore to conceal his gun made him look absolutely ridiculous. It hadn't taken him long to remember why he didn't do undercover work anymore. Not routinely, anyway. But Katie Finan and the Billy Wallace murder were anything but routine. Phil wanted to be on the scene, directing the action, making sure it went as planned.

Just to keep up appearances, he unwound the hose and stepped closer to the house's foundation, pretending to work on what would appear to be a leaky connection. It was bad luck that Mr. Smick had opened his office on this residential street, where they had absolutely no options for cover. He leaned against the duplex and removed his hat, wiping sweat from his brow. That action wasn't part of his act. He was sweating his ass off in the sun. More luck, that the front of the house had full afternoon sunshine. God, he hated undercover work. Another hour of this and they'd be taking him to the ER for heat stroke, and his investigation would be in ruins. Two more years, he told himself. Two more years until retirement.

After his meeting with Nicole at the station that morning, Phil had been quite intrigued to learn that she shared not only an astonishing resemblance to the fugitive Katie Finan, but her birthday as well. Reading through Katie's file, he hadn't been able to find much information about her family, but it was quite obvious that the women were twins. And after his conversation with the doctor, he knew she had no clue about it. How odd that they should come together under such strange circumstances. He'd done a little digging but came up empty. The house at the address Katie had listed on her most recent arrest record had burned a few years back and was now a crumbling mess awaiting the wrecking ball.

He tried another tactic. On each of the occasions she was arrested, the same attorney had come to her defense. Half an hour later, Phil was sitting across from him at his office on Fordham Street.

Like most lawyers, Bruce Smick wasn't very forthcoming with information about his client. When Phil told him he thought Katie was in danger, Smick offered to pass that warning along to her—if and when he talked to her. Phil had spent nearly a half hour learning absolutely nothing, and the man had practically thrown him out of the office so he could make it to court on time. Then, though, Phil's luck in the search for Katie Finan had changed.

Just as he had closed the door behind him and walked into the reception area, the office telephone rang. "Hold on, Ms. Finan," the receptionist said. "I'll see if he can talk to you."

Phil had wasted no time after that, and a large group of police officers was now scattered about the neighborhood awaiting Katie's arrival. They were jogging, pushing strollers, cleaning gutters, and painting a house across the street. In addition, four uniformed officers were inside the dentist's office in the other half of Smick's building. Fortunately for him, the dentist had taken this beautiful Wednesday afternoon off to play a round of golf.

The receiver in Phil's ear crackled to life as he fiddled with the hose. "This is Left Field to all players. Opposing pitcher just pulled into the back garage."

Phil glanced at his watch. It was half past three; Smick was back from court, where he'd been all day. Since they didn't know his schedule, they'd been on the scene since noon. Turning and leaning so he wouldn't be seen, Phil replied. "This is the Manager. All players be alert. Opposing Catcher should be along any minute now."

Stepping back onto the sidewalk, he began the slow process of rewinding the garden hose. Hyperaware, he noticed the black Ford slow down as it passed him heading toward Pennypack Park. A dozen officers noticed it as well, and his ear buzzed as they all reported in with descriptions of the female driver and her male companion. Phil pretended to stretch and watched as the car made a U-turn at the intersection and then came back and pulled to a stop in front of the lawyer's office. A man stepped out of the vehicle.

He was tall, dark, and well dressed in a business suit, carrying a briefcase. As Phil bent to tie an already double-knotted running sneaker, the man surveyed the street, then gracefully covered the length of sidewalk and disappeared through Mr. Smick's front door.

Everything about the guy was suspicious. The way he'd checked out Smick's office from the street. How he'd checked out the sidewalk as he exited the car. How the car was waiting for him at the end of the road, instead of in the parking area to the rear of the office. None of those things might mean anything, but the hair standing on the back of Phil's neck told him that wasn't the case.

This, he hadn't expected. He'd laid this trap to catch Katie, and it seemed another fish was swimming toward it. Who was this guy? Phil wasn't sure he had the time to figure it out before Katie arrived, and he sure as hell didn't want him in the office when they took her into custody. He suspected she was unarmed and harmless, but he'd learned the hard way not to take chances.

As Phil knelt with shoelaces in hand, debating his next move, his radio came alive again.

"This is Short Stop. A red Jeep in the alley looks like a match for Opposing Catcher. She's the passenger. An unidentified female's driving."

"Block the alley in both directions," Phil barked into his microphone as he stood, walking quickly along the sidewalk toward Bruce Smick's front door.

"This is Short Stop. The Jeep is parked. Both women are exiting the vehicle."

"Move in," Phil ordered. He hadn't planned to pounce on his prey like this, but with the unknown element added by the unidentified male in the office, he couldn't afford to wait.

# CHAPTER NINETEEN
# TRY, TRY AGAIN

It's cold in here," Katie observed as she led Jet through the basement of her attorney's office. They'd entered through the rear door, the same one Katie had used with her mother years before when visiting to settle her grandmother's estate. Parking was available in the rear that the front didn't offer.

Bruce Smick had been her mother's friend, a classmate from high school, and that should have made her more comfortable with him. Instead, she felt ashamed that he knew the troubles that Margaret Finan's daughter had gone through, as if Katie's behavior reflected badly on the memory of the woman he knew. For that reason, unless she needed his help to escape the confines of jail, she'd avoided him over the years. In fact, the last time she'd been in this office was to pick up the last of her college tuition money before Chloe was born.

"We're below ground. It'll be better on the first floor," Jet said, pulling Katie closer and rubbing her arm a vigorously as they headed up a flight of steps to the main level.

Katie paused on the landing and leaned into Jet for a hug. "I'll be so happy when this is over."

Jet offered an encouraging smile. "Just a little while longer."

After talking with Jeannie, Katie had placed a call to Bruce Smick's office early in the morning and kept on calling until his receptionist finally answered the phone two hours later. He'd heard the news of Billy's death and was relieved to know she was safe, and after advising her to keep out of trouble, he'd told her to come to his office at four that afternoon. He'd have seen her sooner, but he had an important matter before a judge that he couldn't postpone.

So Katie and Jet had killed time, spending their day in Ambler, a half-hour ride north on Route 309, at Jet's parents' house. To their surprise, they found her parents at home. The kids had spent the day in the pool, with Katie playing lifeguard on the sidelines and Jet and her father playfully tossing balls and children into the pool. They'd grilled hot dogs and slurped Popsicles, and everything had seemed perfectly normal.

It was hard for Katie to imagine that just hours earlier she'd been shot at, that she was wanted by the police, and that she'd made love with Jet. She'd experienced all the extremes of emotion in such a short time, she was completely off balance. Yet she knew Jet was there to help steady her, just as she would help Jet in any way she could. They'd put this tragedy behind them and work on building a life together. The thought gave her the strength to walk through Mr. Smick's door and face him and the police she knew he'd call.

Jet had already helped her so much today—by staying calm, and offering her refuge, and then by helping her to arrange a memorial for Billy. A service would be held at Katie's church, even though Billy hadn't seen the inside of a church since his baptism. The ritual would give Katie some measure of comfort, though, and one day she supposed Chloe and Andre would appreciate it, for they were learning the rites of Christianity and would understand the importance of a Christian burial for their father.

It was a short ride from the funeral home to her attorney's office, and they had made the drive in relative silence, broken only as Jet asked for or Katie gave directions. They'd allowed themselves enough time for traffic, but most of the cars were heading opposite them, taking commuters from their jobs in the city back to their homes in the suburbs, and so they were twenty minutes early when Jet parked behind the office. Katie hoped that meant they'd finish twenty minutes sooner and she could get back to her children.

"Let's get this over with so we can go home," she said to Jet. Jet's place, and her parents' place, felt like home to her.

At the top of the stairs, Katie made a left turn toward the front of the house, where the receptionist guarded the little office lobby. She caught Katie's eye and smiled, and suddenly Katie felt a sense of relief to be here. Mr. Smick had taken care of her through all her legal troubles, and he'd help her again. Reassurance from Jet and Jeannie had helped her build enough courage to face the law and make her case, but she'd need Mr. Smick's help.

She was halfway through the room when she heard a voice behind her, calling her name, and she turned to find the source. She didn't have time to register fear or surprise before a bullet hit her in the abdomen.

# Chapter Twenty
# A Stitch in Time

Standing before a mirror, a floss stick in hand, Louis tried and failed to remove a piece of chicken that had found a home between two of his mandibular molars. He'd learned early in his residency that the correct tools made every job easier, and he wondered what he might find in the OR to extract the offending sliver. It had to come out. He'd go mad otherwise.

Louis had grabbed dinner when he had a chance, and ate alone, thinking about the dinner date Rae and Nic would be enjoying this evening. He hadn't wanted them together, hadn't wanted his abrasive best friend to hurt the woman he'd come to respect and admire over the past year. Rae was a gem, and she deserved someone wonderful, and he didn't think that someone was Nic. He'd tried to prevent their meeting, and then had done what he could to make them both realize what a disaster they'd be together, but he failed. They'd figure it out eventually, though, and then Louis would forever find himself in an uncomfortable position between them. If he and Nic visited Philly, how would he manage to meet Rae for dinner without offending Nic? And if he met with Rae when she was home in the mountains, would Nic be jealous to learn of the plans? Probably.

No matter the details, Rae and Nic were a recipe for disaster. He only hoped they'd figure it out tonight and spare him any more worry.

The ever-present pager attached to his hip interrupted his thoughts with a loud beep. He glanced down and read the screen as he silenced it with the press of a button. *Trauma alert, five minutes.*

Throwing the floss stick into the garbage, he grabbed his lab coat from the hook on the door and slipped his arms through it, the chicken in his molars and his concerns over Nic and Rae already forgotten as he prepared for what lay ahead.

Most likely there would be one victim, but possibly two. Any other victims from a fight or a shooting or a car wreck would be sent to other hospitals. Each place had only a limited number of surgeons, so the OR cases were almost always spread out around the city, where they could all get the medical care they needed. Other than the knowledge that it wasn't a mass casualty (his beeper would have said so if it was) he had no idea what to expect. Young or old? Male or female? Blunt trauma or penetrating? The mystery of what would come through the ER doors was one of the most exciting and challenging aspects of his job. He skipped down the stairs to the ER, knowing he'd find out soon enough.

The ER was typically chaotic as the staff prepared for the arrival of the trauma patient. It was one victim, he'd heard, a female with a gunshot wound to the abdomen, and Louis joined the show, donning a gown to protect his scrubs and booties to protect his sneakers. They hadn't lied about their arrival time; he'd come directly from his call room, and already the ambulance crew was wheeling the stretcher through the doors of the trauma bay.

He approached and glanced at the portable monitor positioned between his patient's feet. The vital signs—rapid heart rate and low blood pressure—indicated blood loss and shock. He glanced at the head of the stretcher, looking for a breathing tube. That would be one of his first orders. Instead of an order, though, all that came from his mouth was a gasp, a sharp intake of air. Then he rushed to the side of the bed, no longer the surgeon but now the concerned friend.

"Nic! Nicole! Look at me!" he shouted, and turned her face toward him. She stared back with unseeing eyes, not seeming to recognize him, an indication that the shock was at a dangerous stage.

"Doc, hey, Doc. Easy." The medic pulled on his arm, and Louis turned to face him, ready to punch him for allowing this to happen to his best friend. "This isn't Dr. Coussart. This is the girl who shot her boyfriend last night. Her name is Kathleen Finan. I saw the resemblance to Dr. Coussart myself, but it's definitely not her. We had a positive ID on the scene from her people who know Finan."

It hit Louis, then—the phone call from Nic earlier that day, the case of mistaken identity that had landed her at the police station. Seeing this woman lying there, he quite understood the police's confusion. He'd known Nic for a dozen years and would have sworn this was her.

Sensing his anxiety, the chief resident stepped in, examined Katie, and began issuing the orders, preparing to take her to the operating room. Louis understood then every doctor's fear—to look down at that stretcher and see the face of someone you love. He stepped away, splashed cold water on his face, and took some deep breaths.

A few minutes later, when Louis had regained his composure, he gently tapped the chief on the arm. "I've got it. I'm good." It wouldn't do to give his surgical family the idea that he could be so easily shaken. He led his team to the operating room and, once there, was caught up in the rituals of surgery—scrubbing his hands, donning his gown, grasping his scalpel. With the calm, orderly efficiency that made him a great surgeon, he forgot the face of his patient and did what he was trained to do. He cut skin and tissue and blood vessels, placed sutures and tied knots, and removed the macerated spleen that would have caused his patient a fatal hemorrhage if left in place.

Every so often he glanced at the monitor that beeped in tandem with Katie's heart and saw that it was beating more slowly now, a good sign. Her blood pressure was higher, too, mostly because of all of those bags of blood that had been pumped under pressure into her circulatory system. The catheter in her bladder was draining urine, indicating that the kidneys were doing their job, that they were confident enough in Katie's stability to let go of a little fluid instead of keeping it in the bloodstream.

Louis inspected the abdominal cavity, confident that no tiny, leaking vessel would force him to bring his patient back to the OR later that night, and then began the process of closing it, one layer of tissue at a time.

When he was done, he stepped away from the table even as everyone else cleaned up and prepared the patient for transfer to the intensive-care unit. Reaching to his waist, with a sharp tug he ripped the string that held his blue disposable surgical gown closed. He gripped the thick paper at his chest and tugged the gown open and off his shoulders. As he peeled it down both arms with a practiced rhythm, both gloves slipped off as well, caught up in the elastic of the sleeves. He rolled the garment into a ball, holding it by the clean, interior surface, and deposited it into a hazardous-waste bag near the operating-room door. Using his back, he leaned into the door to open it and walked backward into the hall. The surgical mask was still in place; he pulled it below his chin and scratched the whiskers that were growing there, despite the razor he'd applied to them just that morning.

Relieved, he collapsed into a chair. He was glad to have finished the case. It wasn't a technically difficult one; the spleen had absorbed both bullets, which made his job easy. He didn't have to repair the stomach or resect the bowel; he'd simply detached the spleen from the connective tissue holding it in place and severed the blood vessels going into and out of the organ. All in all, the surgery had gone very well, and although he couldn't have guaranteed that Katie Finan would be alive tomorrow when she was wheeled through the ER doors ninety minutes earlier, he was relatively sure now that she would. He'd done a good job, but this patient's haunting resemblance to Nic made him want to walk away now and not come back.

Pulling an index card containing patient information from his breast pocket, Louis placed it on the desk before him and picked up the phone. He dialed the number that connected him to the dictation system, then followed with his personal ID code and began dictating his operative report. "This is Dr. Louis Pirro dictating an OR report on patient Kathleen Finan." He picked up the index card, which had been thoughtfully stamped and given to him by an attentive medical student, and spelled Katie's full name for the benefit of the transcriptionist who would put his words to paper. "Date of birth is six, fourteen…Oh, my God."

Louis dropped his hand to his lap, the phone still in it. June fourteenth was the next day. It was Nic's birthday. It was also Katie Finan's.

Katie Finan, lying on his OR table, hooked up to monitors and catheters and IVs, looked just like Nic. Identical, he could argue. She had the same birthday as Nic. Either Katie Finan was Nic and she was living some sort of sordid double life, or they were identical twins.

He dialed Nic's number instantly. "Shit," he said, when her voice clicked in. "Nic, this is an emergency. I need you to come to the hospital, now. Come to the SICU, they'll find me. Oh, and Nic, I love you."

# Chapter Twenty-one
# Meat and Potatoes

They'd managed to lose each other in the museum. As Nic searched for Rae, she clearly understood why Rae visited so often. Katie would come to the Barnes every day if she still lived in Philly. She'd be content to take her lunch break here, to just sit and be still, staring at the works of the greatest painters in history. She would need a year at the Barnes to view all the thousands of pieces to her satisfaction.

They'd split up upon entering the museum, allowing both of them to enjoy it as they preferred. Nic had been content to wander and get an overall feel for the place, while she knew Rae had wanted to look at a few specific pieces. She found her sitting in front of a Matisse, simply staring.

Even as Rae studied the picture, Nic studied her. The purple of her shirt was vibrant, reflecting all the red tones in her skin and Rae looked so alive wearing it. Her arms were behind her, supporting her weight, and her legs were crossed at the ankles. The pose was relaxed, and she couldn't have looked more comfortable had she been sitting in her own home.

Out of respect for the other patrons, Nic had turned her cell phone to the vibrate mode when they entered, and the frantic rattling in her purse told her she had a call. Slipping the phone from her bag, she saw the caller ID and headed to the ladies' lounge, but before she reached her destination, the call went to voice mail. Her return call to her godmother, Jeannie Bennett, went unanswered. Nic waited a minute and then checked her messages. Frowning as she listened to Jeannie's words, she paced the floor. Jeannie was canceling their dinner plans. She'd explain later.

That's odd, Nic thought as she returned the phone to her bag. She hoped nothing was wrong. While Jeannie's message was benign enough, her voice carried a noticeable strain. She'd spoken with Jeannie over the weekend, and they were both looking forward to their dinner. What would make her cancel at so late an hour, and without an explanation?

Returning to find Rae, she sat beside her and looked not at her, but at the painting, an oil on canvas of a nude woman. In greeting, Rae moved her hand slightly and gently scratched the outside of Nic's manicured finger with hers and then, just as suddenly, moved it back to where it had been.

"Dinner's canceled," Nic whispered.

"What? Why?" Rae looked puzzled.

"I'm not sure. Jeannie called and left a message. She can't make it."

"Oh." Rae frowned and then looked toward Nic. "Well, we can still get something, can't we?"

Nic smirked. "Well, I suppose I have to eat."

Rae sucked in a breath. Their playful banter had been fun, and at times flirtatious, but Rae knew that didn't mean a thing, that Nic had probably only spent the afternoon with her in gratitude for the free legal services Rae had provided. But she liked Nic, in spite of the numerous challenges she presented, and she wanted to know what Nic was thinking. It was time to find out. "But you don't have to eat with me." Rae stared at her, her eyes piercing, challenging, but allowing a hint of a smile at the corners of her mouth.

To her surprise, Nic neither backed down nor met her challenge, but rather presented one of her own. She held Rae's gaze, though. "That's true. So how about if we do this—let's each decide what we'd want to eat if we were eating alone, say top three choices. You don't have to be specific about what place. For instance, you can just say 'Italian.' And if we can agree on anything that would be palatable to both of us, we can continue our afternoon. If not, you can be on your way and I'll grab a cab."

After thinking over the suggestion for a moment, Rae responded. "That's a great idea. Do I have to write down my preferences?"

"Why, do you think you'll forget your answers?"

"No, no. It's not that. But how do I know you won't lie about what you want to eat just so you can go out to dinner with me?"

Nic erupted in laughter, drawing the stares of several museum patrons. When she was in control again, she patted Rae's hands. "Why don't we get out of here? Vocal cords don't like whispering."

They walked from the museum and out into the late-afternoon sunshine. The modest traffic on the parkway had quadrupled in volume, with a noise level to match.

"So, in response to your concerns. How about if I go first? I'll tell you my choices and then you can tell me yours."

"No. Not gonna work. We have to write them down."

Nic shook her head and reached into her purse. After a few seconds of digging her hand reappeared, clutching a notepad. "I'll go first," she said, and wasted no time in waiting for a reply. Rae watched as she scribbled, then pulled the sheet free of the binding and folded the paper before handing pen and paper to her.

Rae did the same and handed the supplies back to their owner. "Okay, let's have it," Nic demanded.

"We look together," Rae said, holding the folded scrap of paper tightly in her outstretched hand.

Nic rolled her eyes dramatically. "Fine."

Rae moved over on the bench so they were nearly touching and opened the palm that held her list, offering it to Nic. Nic gave her paper to Rae.

"On three. One, two, three."

"I can't believe this," Nic said as she read Rae's list. Dalessandro's. Nick's Roast Beef. Chickie and Pete's.

Rae looked down at the paper in her hand, at Nicole's nearly indecipherable scribble, and read the first choice on her list. Cheesesteak, preferably Dalessandro's. Cheesecake Factory. Nick's Roast Beef.

"This was a setup, right?" Nic asked, unable to believe they'd matched two of their three favorite choices of restaurants in a city that boasted thousands of eateries.

"I should be asking you that question. This was your idea, remember?"

Nic bit her bottom lip, still unable to believe what had just happened. "So it was. Umm, anyway, still feel like driving?"

Rae smiled and led Nic back to her car, and in a few minutes they were a part of the evening commute. She followed Kelly Drive into Manayunk and then made a few turns, bringing them around the football field next to their favorite cheesesteak shop. Luck was with them; they found a parking place in a relatively good spot on the street lined with duplexes and flower gardens. The luck ended there, though. The line of patrons stretched out the door.

"It'll move fast," Nic said reassuringly, as they took their place in line, behind men and women in business suits and construction workers in dirty pants and work boots. She tried to contain her excitement. This was her favorite place to eat in all the city, and she salivated as she smelled the scent wafting off the grill.

"Come here often?" Rae asked.

"As often as I can."

"You always lived downtown when you were here, right?"

"No, my first year, we lived out here." Nic shook her head at the memory. "It was a stupid decision. We spent half our time commuting."

"Well, you found this place."

"Oh, that's another story."

Rae raised an eyebrow and looked at Nic, who just shook her head. "You can't tease me like that. Tell."

Nic told her the story as they approached the counter. "I met this girl at the gym, at the end of my first year of med school. It was a really crazy time, with buying the apartment and getting everything ready to move. She didn't seem terribly horrific, so when she asked me out, I agreed. She brought me here, and I fell in love. With this place, not with her. My first impression of her was way off. She was a psycho. After a few dates I was ready to move on. And I did. Louis and I moved downtown and I never told her. We just left. No good-bye, no forwarding address."

"That's a really nice way to treat a lady."

Nic rolled her eyes. "She was no lady. But it gets better. Fast-forward six months. I met a really cute girl and asked her out. I brought her here, because, honestly, after the first bite I was smitten. So, guess who sits down next to us at the counter?"

"No!" Rae's mouth was open so wide an entire cheesesteak could have easily fit inside.

"I looked around. I thought there might be a hidden camera or something. Or that my date was in on it."

"So what happened?"

"She said, 'Hey, you moved.' And I said, 'Yeah.' And then I swiveled in my chair and turned my back on her and hoped she wouldn't stab me, and that she'd go away. She kept talking to me, anyway, practically leaning over my shoulder. Finally, my date leaned around me and said, 'Hey, we're having dinner. Would you please leave her alone?' Thankfully, she did. Not before asking me for my new phone number, though."

Rae was still chuckling as she placed her order, and Nic followed suit. A few minutes later they were carrying their baskets and drinks outside to the patio, where they shared a table with an older couple. They both attacked their food, although Nic could see the smile of amusement on Rae's face as she cut her foot-long sandwich into smaller, more manageable segments.

"So, let's talk about your list," Nic suggested as she wiped stray marinara from the corner of her mouth.

Rae seemed to be so absorbed in her food that she had difficulty following Nic. "Excuse me?" she said, and, like Nic, wiped her mouth and her hands.

"Your list. Chickie and Pete's? What's that about?"

Rae's look of shock was amusing. "Crab fries, of course."

"Ah, yes. I forgot about crab fries. I'll have to amend my list and add C & P." Their French fries, dusted with the spicy Old Bay seasoning used so commonly to add flavor to seafood, were unbelievably good.

"So what would you eliminate from the list?"

Nic rested her chin in her hand and thought. "Nothing. It's going to have to be a tie."

"You really are a diplomat, aren't you?"

"I wouldn't want to get banned from any of these places," she teased Rae. They talked about the other places they liked to eat in the city and found many common foods that pleased their palates.

"How'd someone from the other side of the tracks start eating Thai food?" Nic asked, playfully. "It's not like Thai restaurants are common in your neck of the woods."

"No, they aren't. It's interesting, though—for all the great food we like, our top three are basically some version of a cheeseburger and fries."

Nic thought of McDonald's and couldn't help laughing.

"But to answer your question—I've traveled a lot. My parents are both college professors, so you know that schedule. Summers off, extended winter and spring breaks. Basically, we've been all over the world. They told me if I ate my dinner, I'd grow up to be big and strong, and I believed them." Rae frowned. "Obviously, they lied."

"Height is overrated." Nic looked at Rae and offered a smile, but the frown didn't disappear. "Oh, have I touched a nerve?"

"No, not really. It only bothers me when I'm dating. I always date women shorter than I am."

Nic nearly drew blood biting her lower lip in an attempt to suppress her laughter. "That must be challenging, considering how *small* a dating pool you're dealing with. Get it? *Small*. Ha, ha!"

"If you weren't shorter than I am, I'd throw food at you."

"And I'd gladly eat it. But seriously, lesbians under five feet tall? What are there, like three of us in Philadelphia?"

Rae cleared her throat and stared. "I'll have you know, I'm almost five-three."

Nic reconsidered the sarcastic retort that came naturally to her tongue after seeing the lingering frown on Rae's beautiful face. Instead, she reached across and patted Rae's hand, even offered a gentle squeeze and allowed her fingers to linger there for just a moment before pulling them away.

At this moment, it was she who needed comfort, for the ease with which she found herself talking to Rae unsettled her. She, who so carefully guarded her thoughts and feelings, was discussing herself in a way she never had before. Not even Louis, who knew her best, had heard all the secrets of her heart.

When Nic focused her eyes, Rae was smiling at her, obviously expecting an answer to a question Nic hadn't heard as her mind wandered. And that smile, perfectly vivid, was a thing of beauty. The eyes, so intense as they listened to her, were captivating.

The world melted around them, the smudges on the periphery of Nic's vision the only evidence that cars drove down Henry Avenue, children played in the park, and other patrons ate at the restaurant. The only clear image was the face of the woman before her.

Nic wasn't familiar with this comfortable companionship she shared with Rae. They could tease and dance around the ring, occasionally throwing a punch, but with no underlying malice. The animosity had been there the previous night, but those feelings had dissipated, for both of them, and now Nic found it difficult to recall exactly why she'd felt like that. Now their sparring was playful, delightful. Rae's intelligence matched her humor. Her physical attraction matched the rest of the package.

"So that's why you've traveled all over the world? Except fifty countries? Because of your parents?" Nic was intrigued. She'd also traveled extensively, and her favorite magazines were the one that introduced her to new places.

"Yeah, they really love to travel."

"Hmm. So what are the fifty? I dare you to name them. All of them."

Rae cleared her throat. "The ones I've been to, or the ones I haven't?"

"You're serious, aren't you?"

Rae just nodded.

"Rae, that's impressive."

She shrugged, and Nic decided to save the topic of travel for another time. And she seriously hoped there would be another time.

"Did you save room for dessert?" Nic asked, arching her eyebrows suggestively.

"Hmm, shall we make a list?"

"No, that wouldn't work, because I'll eat anything that has chocolate or whipped cream. Those are in everybody's top three."

"Not mine." Rae shook her head.

"What? You're kidding me."

"Yes, I am."

They laughed on their way to the car and settled on ice cream, which they purchased in Manayunk but transported to a bench along the Schuylkill for eating. Between licks, they talked.

"Tell me about your job," Rae suggested.

"What would you like to know? The current recommendations for treatment of pneumonia or trauma protocols, or how to deliver a baby?"

"Hmm. I don't need that much detail. Why did you choose emergency medicine? How do you like it?"

"Well, the first question is easy. *ER*. The television show. It mesmerized me. The second question is more complicated."

Rae held up her ice-cream cone, now half the size it had been, eaten nearly down to the cone, and seemed to study it. "I'm thinking you have about three minutes."

"I could talk for three hours and not cover it all."

"That good, or that bad?"

"Both. Medicine—the art and science of medicine—they're great. It's wonderful to put the clues together to find out what's wrong with someone and then fix the problem. It's incredible to insert the tube into the lungs of someone who can't breathe or slide a needle into a vein and place a line that saves someone's life. To give someone just a little dose of medication to knock them out—and then pop their dislocated shoulder back in the socket. It's great. They wake up a few seconds later, their pain gone. It's a wonderful feeling."

Rae noticed that Nic had turned in her seat and was talking with her eyes and her hands, as well as her mouth. She could see Nic's passion and wondered for a moment what she'd look like in bed, about to orgasm under the influence of Rae's hands and mouth moving over her body. She sucked in a breath and adjusted in her seat, conscious of the sudden dampness in her boxers. Clearing her throat she replied, "That does sound wonderful."

"Yeah, but I have so much other stuff to deal with, it takes the joy out of it. Insurance, for instance. I can take care of your heart attack, spend half an hour at your bedside talking to you and examining you, I can insert your IV and inject your medications myself and read the EKGs, talk to the cardiologist. But if I fail to note on your chart that you appeared *anxious* as you were heading off to the cath lab to have a stent placed, if I fail to check that box, I get dinged, and I don't get paid. It's ridiculous, Rae. Doctors should be reimbursed for what we do, not what we write on the chart."

"So, standard fees?" Rae asked, burrowing her eyes into Nic's. Her perspective was interesting. The cost of health care was out of control, and the debate over health-care benefits for everyone was a political hot potato.

"We already have that, sort of. But payments are made based on documentation, not on the care provided. It should really be the opposite."

"Makes sense to me." Rae imagined this concept, wondering how it would affect patient care.

"We'd have more time to spend with patients. It would be great for patient care."

"I see. So would you climinate medical records?"

"Oh, no. I'd still have to keep notes, for when you lawyers want to sue me." She narrowed her eyes at Rae.

"Hey, I'm a public servant. Don't look at me like that."

Nic held her gaze as she patted Rae's knee. "Yes, you are. I'm sorry for carrying on like that. I'm sure this is boring you to tears."

Actually, it wasn't. Rae loved to learn about everyone and everything. Even if Nic never got to see her apartment, Rae would come away from their time together a richer person, armed with more knowledge and a better understanding of something outside her field of expertise.

"I would imagine you're never boring, Nicole."

Nic shrugged off the compliment. "Tell me about your job. How exactly are you serving the public?"

Rae had finished her cone and leaned back, gazing out at the river. It was quiet, with evening traffic now dissipated and the population of joggers and walkers dwindling as well. "My job's as frustrating as yours sounds, and as rewarding as well. I've had the chance to travel, which is great, and I'm doing something good, which makes me happy." She turned her head to face Nic and smiled.

"But what do you do?" Nic asked again, and she also turned, pulling her legs up beneath her on the bench as Rae explained her job as an attorney for the DEA and touched on the case she was working on now, putting together the prosecution for when they found their defendant.

"Prescription-drug abuse is a huge problem in the ER, too."

"You mean with staff?"

Nic laughed. "Well, you do hear stories now and then about nurses and doctors stealing meds for their own use. *Nurse Jackie* really does exist. But I was talking about the patients. People come in with all kinds of excuses for needing narcotics. Back pain, migraines, tooth aches, anything they can think of to get drugs."

"So how do you handle that?"

"I tell them to get lost."

Rae scowled. "But how do you do that? What about people with legitimate pain?"

Nic raised her voice an octave. "My job isn't to treat chronic pain. They should be getting those meds from their family doctors, not from the ER."

"So you let them suffer?"

Nic shrugged, softening her tone. "I don't suspect they have real pain, Rae. I suspect they have real addiction."

"So you don't think anyone deserves to be treated? What about someone with a broken leg?"

"Well, that's a new injury. Of course that should be treated. I'm talking about the chronic stuff—back pain and migraines and fibromyalgia—that sort of thing."

"Well, can't those people get worse some times?"

Nic rolled her eyes.

Rae was quiet for a moment before she responded. "Well, I guess if every doctor approached it that way, we wouldn't have such a prescription-drug problem in America." She allowed a flash of a smile before she turned away.

"Don't be mad at me," Nic said, and touched Rae's shoulder. Why did she care what this woman thought? She'd go home tomorrow and they'd probably never see each other again. Yet she found something appealing about Rae, something intangible that went beyond her looks and her intelligence and her humor. Some spark, some chemistry, a rare and elusive connection existed between them that she'd only once experienced before—with Louis. Never with a woman—although perhaps that wasn't completely true. Her best friend from high school had been very special, right up until the day Nic came out to her. It had certainly never happened with another lesbian.

Rae's smile was full this time, and genuine. "Oh, I'm not mad. I do find you challenging, though. Is there any topic we agree on?"

Nic held up her hands in offering. "Cheesesteaks."

Both of them laughed, and peace was made.

They sat quietly then, looking out at the river as the evidence mounted that this day was coming to an end. The sun was low in the sky, the mosquitoes making their appearance, and the temperature was beginning to drop just a little. Where had the time gone? Between the art and the company, Nic had had a lovely afternoon. But they couldn't sit on that park bench forever. She'd have liked to, though, and that realization was perhaps the most wonderful thing to happen to her in a very long time.

"Shall we go?" Rae asked as Nic rubbed the goose flesh on her arms.

"I think we should," Nic replied, disappointed. They walked to the car in silence, and as she opened the car door, her phone beeped to inform her of a message awaiting her. She'd spent the past two hours blissfully unaware that she'd forgotten to take her phone out of Rae's car.

"Do you mind if I check to see who called? I always worry when I'm away from home. My parents aren't getting any younger."

"No, I understand perfectly. Feel free."

"It's Louis," she said after scanning her messages.

"You can answer it."

"He probably called to warn me to bring you home in one piece." Nic typed in her password, listened to the message, and gasped. As she turned, she saw Rae watching her. "Can you take me to the hospital?" she asked.

"What's wrong?"

She looked at those brown eyes, now filled with concern, and knew her own probably matched them. "I don't know, but it can't be good."

# CHAPTER TWENTY-TWO
# CONFESSIONS

Jet sat with her face in her hands, appreciative of the comfort of Jeannie Bennett beside her. When the doctors had rushed Katie to the OR, her first inclination had been to call her parents. Then she realized they were doing a much greater service by watching Chloe and Andre. At the moment, the kids had to be their priority. So she'd called Jeannie, and within half an hour, her boss was there, worrying just as much as Jet but looking poised and together nonetheless.

It had been a great relief when the doctor entered the waiting room to inform them Katie had survived the surgery. He painted a grim picture and said Katie was extremely critical and still on a ventilator, but Jet understood the meaning of the vital signs and knew Katie was doing a lot better than she'd been on the floor of Bruce Smick's office.

A long night was in store for them, so Sandy, who'd come along with Jeannie, had gone for coffee and doughnuts and brought some back for the SICU nurses, a thoughtful gesture that Jet understood would gain her a favor with the staff when she needed one. Jet now sipped her coffee, but in spite of the fact that she hadn't had dinner, she didn't have any appetite for the doughnuts that sat on the table beside her chair.

It was approaching nine o'clock. Nearly five hours had passed since Katie was shot, three since her surgery ended, and ninety minutes since they'd been allowed to briefly see her. Katie was, of course, unconscious, with tubes inserted into her mouth and her bladder and veins, and complex machines were breathing for her and infusing fluids at a precisely calculated rate. Yet the sight of her was a comfort, watching her chest rise and fall reassuring, even if the ventilator was doing the work. Jet had groaned when the staff told them they'd have to leave and had checked the clock every few minutes, counting the time until she could see her lover again.

Jet looked at the other faces of anguish that surrounded her and knew she was probably more fortunate than most of them. Katie would live, in spite of the resident's dire words. She couldn't and wouldn't accept any alternative. Other people gathered here didn't have such optimism, nor did some of them have reason, and it showed on their faces.

The door to this private lounge opened, and Jet turned as Jeannie's words hit her ear just as hard as an imagined punch hit her gut, knocking the wind from her.

"Oh, shit," Jeannie said, to which Jet replied, "What the hell?"

Katie had just walked into the lounge, a dark-haired woman not much taller following closely behind. She wore a khaki miniskirt and a bright-green sleeveless sweater, with bright-green matching backless loafers. As always, she was phenomenally beautiful but seemed to have more confidence in her stride, like she was right at home in the hospital and on a mission. The contrast reminded Jet that this woman couldn't be Katie. Katie was unconscious, fighting for her life just a few yards away in the SICU.

She stood but Jeannie was quicker, a step ahead as they raced across the room.

The woman who held such a stunning resemblance to Katie noticed them then, and her face registered great confusion as she asked, "Aunt Jeannie, what are you doing here? What's going on?"

Jet caught up to her, and Jeannie looked at Jet, her expression clearly troubled. "Jet, I'd like you to meet my godchild, Nicole Coussart. Nic, this is the head nurse at my office, Jet Fox. And this woman, I've never seen before," she said as Rae pulled up beside Nic.

"Your godchild?" Jet asked, as if it were a complex concept.

At the same time, Nic offered an introduction to Rae.

"Jeannie, what's going on?" Jet demanded, still staring at Nic.

"That's what I want to know," Nic asked, but her tone wasn't as gentle as Jet's. She was staring intently at Jeannie.

"How did you find out?" Jeannie asked Nic.

"Find out what?" she replied.

At that moment the doors to the SICU opened, and a doctor emerged. He looked their way and then hurried toward them. "I'm so glad to see you," he said as he pulled Nic into a tight hug. "Something fucking strange is going on here."

"You've got that right," Jet said, still staring at Nic.

"Hey, Rae. Hey, Jeannie, how are you?" the doctor said, holding out his hand in greeting.

"I've had better days," Jeannie replied, and then she continued. "Oh, I see. Louis, you called Nic, huh?"

"Yeah. I had to see her. I have a patient back there who looks just like her and not only that—"

"Kathleen Finan? She's here?" Nic asked.

Louis nodded.

"What happened to her?"

"She was shot."

"Is that why you called me? You could have just told me on the phone."

"Nic, you're not going to believe—"

"Actually, Louis," Jeannie said, "can we go someplace a little more private? I think Nic needs to hear this from me."

"You know about this?" he demanded, taking a step forward, his posture both shocked and defensive.

"Yes."

"What's going on, Jeannie?" Jet was pleading now. Jeannie wrapped an arm around her waist.

"I'll explain it all in a moment," she said as they followed Louis into the surgical residents' lounge. Fortunately, it was empty.

They all sat and looked at Jeannie, who was studying the ceiling. After a moment she looked at Nic. "Nicole, you have a twin sister. An identical twin. Her name is Katie Finan."

After Jeannie's announcement, Nic spoke first. "What the fuck are you talking about?" She looked from the serious expression on Jeannie's face to the others in the room. They wore mixtures of confusion and concern as well, and Nic drew some small comfort in knowing she wasn't the only one who thought Jeannie had lost her mind.

"You have a twin," Jeannie repeated, nodding but saying nothing else.

Nic stared at her again and then at the others in the room. Rae put a hand on her back, and though Nic felt somewhat reassured by her presence, she still couldn't believe what she was hearing.

"Jeannie, how? What are you saying? That I was a twin and my parents adopted only one of us?"

"Yessss…no. It wasn't their choice, Nic. You were the second baby, and the other family didn't want both of you."

"What? That's absurd." All was quiet for a moment, and Nic silently studied the faces around her, looking for some reassurance, but none came. Her eyes once again found Jeannie. "Tell me what happened."

Jeannie cleared her throat. "I was working the night you were born. It was the last month of my residency—my OB rotation. Family docs delivered babies back in those days. Your mom—your biological mother, that is—came in. She was already in advanced labor when I examined her. Her mother was with her, and so was a priest. She was a college student, didn't tell her parents she was pregnant, apparently was planning to keep you. Her parents had other plans, though, and they arranged for an adoption, through the church. Before Katie was even born, the adoptive parents arrived. I delivered Katie and the placenta, and all seemed well. I went to check on the baby, talked to the adoptive parents, gave them my card, and offered to be the baby's doctor. A minute later one of the nurses came looking for me. Your mom was having contractions again. A few minutes later, you were born."

Jeannie took a sip of her coffee and, before she could swallow, Nic spoke. "Well, then what?"

"I went out to talk to the Finans and told them there was another baby. They were shocked, of course. Everyone was. We didn't use ultrasound routinely back then. No one knew there were twins. Marge Finan would have taken you both, but her husband would have no part of it. He told her no, and she couldn't convince him otherwise. After a few minutes, she asked if I could find another suitable family to take you."

Jeannie sipped her coffee and Nic once again spoke up. "So you called my parents."

Jeannie nodded and looked relieved that Nic seemed to understand. "Yes. First, I talked with your biological mom and told her about your folks. She thought they would be great for you. So then, I called them. Your dad tried to convince Jack Finan to keep you both, but he wouldn't waver. Then your dad offered to take both of you, and all that did was piss Jack off. He didn't just refuse to give up Katie. He also refused to allow any contact between your families. The Finans weren't planning to tell her she was adopted, and he didn't want her to think she'd got a bum deal by getting them, instead of rich doctors."

"Jeannie, this sounds like a bad movie," Nic told her. "You're kidding, me, right?"

"What's your birthday?" Jet asked.

Nic looked at her, wondering why Jet was here and what gave her the right to interrupt. Instead of telling her off, though, she answered the question. "It's tomorrow. Why?"

Jet shook her head, looking as confused as Nic felt. "Then she's not kidding. Katie's birthday is tomorrow, too."

"Just who the hell are you?" Nic demanded. What right did Jet have to be in this conversation? This was between her and Jeannie.

"I'm Katie's partner."

Nic noticed the look of surprise on Jeannie's face but didn't say anything to her. Instead, she continued to question Jet. "Did she know about me?"

Jet cleared her throat before answering and wiped away tears on the sleeve of her Phillies T-shirt. "She has no clue. She doesn't even know she was adopted."

"Jesus, this is unbelievable." Nic leaned back and felt Rae beside her, and never was she so grateful for the presence of another human being. Rae's hand moved in small circles on her back, the rhythm like a heartbeat, calm and soothing.

Jet turned to Louis and asked, "So are you Katie's doctor now?"

Louis nodded. "I did the surgery. I'm sorry I couldn't get out to talk to you earlier, but another trauma came in and I had to go back to the OR. Someone spoke to you, right?"

Jet nodded. "Yes, a woman. She told us the surgery went well but Katie was still critical."

Louis nodded again. "That's right. I had to remove her spleen, and she lost quite a bit of blood. But she's stable now. She's holding her own. You guys can go back to see her if you'd like."

"Jeannie, do you want to come with me or stay here?" Jet asked.

"Are you okay by yourself?"

Jet nodded. "I'll be fine. The initial shock is over."

"Okay, then you go. I'd like to talk to Nic."

Nic watched Jet's back disappear through the lounge door, uncomfortable in the silence. Finally, Jeannie spoke. "Nicole, listen to me. Your parents did nothing wrong. They've loved you—"

"Couldn't they have told me? When I think of all the times I said my prayers at night, begging God for a brother or sister, I…I…I could scream!"

"It was evident by the time you were two years old that reasoning with you would be a challenge. They couldn't have told you without breaking their promise to the Finans. You'd have hopped on your bike and ridden to Philly to try to find her."

Nic sniffed. "That's probably true. But when I got older, I wouldn't have done that."

"When you got older, Katie's life was a mess. I didn't even know where she was for about four years after she ran away."

"She ran away? Like seriously?"

"Oh, yeah. It hasn't been a picnic for her."

"So, is the news right? Did she shoot her boyfriend?"

"No, she didn't shoot him. Whoever shot him came back and got Katie tonight."

Nic rubbed away the tension that had formed at both temples, trying to ward off the migraine she felt coming. "Wow. I don't know what else to say."

Nic looked at Rae. All the while they'd been talking Rae had been beside her, silently supporting her with a hand on the back and a pat now and then. Nic offered her a little smile. "I guess you'll never forget this date, huh?"

Rae nodded. "This is going down in history, just like that time you met your ex at Dalessandro's."

Nic couldn't hold back a laugh, but it was bitter.

"Nic, do you want to see her?" Jeannie asked.

Nic rubbed her forehead as she pondered the question. "I don't know proper etiquette for a situation like this. But I suppose I should, huh?"

"It's up to you. No pressure here."

"Will you come with me?" she asked Jeannie, then looked to Louis. "You, too?"

When they both nodded, Nic turned to Rae. "Can you wait for me?"

"Of course."

Nic and Jeannie followed Louis through the doors into the sterile, cold environment of the SICU. It was like an anthill, bustling with activity, people hurrying in every direction. It was brightly lit, and the lights immediately caused Nic to cringe as the migraine began to take hold.

Louis took them to room three, where Jet sat at the bedside, holding a small hand in her large one. Nic took one step toward the bed and then stopped as she saw Katie's face, the mirror image of her own, but pale and sickly and penetrated by that awful endotracheal tube. Even though a glance at the monitor told her Katie's vital signs were normal, she was still a frightful sight, and one that Nic didn't want to see. She stepped back and turned, looking at Jeannie as she began walking back the way she came. "I have no business here, Jeannie. This isn't my sister. I'm an only child."

Not bothering to wait for a reply, Nic began running back toward the SICU doors, eager to get back into the real world and away from this madness. She found Rae in the lounge. "Can we please go?"

"Is everything okay?" Rae asked as she hurried to match Nic's pace.

"No, it's not. I need to get away from here. I have no obligations to that woman, Rae. The only thing we share is a common thread of DNA, and that's not enough to get me involved in her sordid life."

"Okay, okay," Rae said, patting Nic's back again.

"Just please take me home, Rae. Please?"

# CHAPTER TWENTY-THREE
# THE CANDY DISPENSER

Simon pulled his Ford into the underground parking garage beneath the headquarters of the Happy and Healthy Pharmacy, LLC, and parked it beside his Lexus. He'd returned the borrowed car he'd driven to the attorney's office and eliminated the garage attendant who'd lent it to him. Katie Finan was finally dead, and Simon now could go about his business without further distractions.

As he walked to the elevator, he had a bounce in his step and hummed as he used his key to call the elevator. Once inside, he again used his key to direct the elevator down, into the floor below ground that very few people knew existed.

The door opened into a corridor, a cube-shaped area only large enough to accommodate the elevator doors, two other tall, wide, solid doors that stood closed before him, and a hand truck that carried supplies. To his left was the narcotics storage area for the Happy and Healthy Pharmacies, all thirty of them in operation in the Philadelphia area. Twice weekly, shipments of controlled substances arrived and were stored in the vault behind that door until they were distributed to each of his stores.

He always kept a week's supply on hand, in the event of a hurricane or other emergency that shut down the avenues of supply that kept his business running. Depending on the day, between 750,000 and 3,000,000 tablets of controlled substances were stored here, with a potential street value of $15,000,000. Unfortunately, Simon wasn't selling those pills on the street. One day, when he was ready to skip town, he would consider raiding the narcotics vault, but only if the police were already suspicious. If they weren't, the simultaneous disappearance of him and all those drugs would definitely arouse their interest in him.

Simon turned away from the vault and keyed the lock of an even more secure area. After passing through the doorway, he then opened two more locks and entered the lab. It was here Simon made his money, where the legitimate pills that arrived in those bottles in the vault were smashed into powder, adulterated with other chemicals, and then pressed again into the tablets sold in the pharmacy and on the streets.

The concept was really simple—so basic he'd made his first narcotics tablets when he was in pharmacy school. He'd gained the trust of his father-in-law, who saw him for the bright and ambitious young man he was, and was given a tremendous amount of responsibility for the three stores he had then. Simon was only a twenty-year-old clerk, but even then he understood the value of the narcotics and set about finding a way to capitalize on his unique opportunity.

Simon knew about the manufacturing of pills—they all learned it in school. He began combining basic drugs with binding ingredients and fillers that he could get his hands on—diphenhydramine, glycerin, and cornstarch—and he carefully mixed his first batch of counterfeit cold medication. It was a paste, which he pressed into an empty lip-balm tube, and after it dried for several days, he held in his hands a solid roll of medication, which promptly shattered when he attempted to free it from the cylinder. It took more experimentation to figure out how to actually remove it and then how to cut the final product so it resembled a pill. In the end, though, he manufactured what would pass as a genuine tablet.

After playing around in his basement lab with other medications, he finally worked up the nerve to remove tablets of oxycodone from the pharmacy. He couldn't very well give a patient half a bottle of legitimate medicine and half counterfeit. Even the most trusting person, if they noticed the difference, would be concerned. So he took twelve tablets, which was the number doctors commonly prescribed, and crushed and adulterated and recast them into new tabs, each with slightly less oxycodone than the originals. When they were dry, he smuggled them back into the pharmacy in a Happy and Healthy Pharmacy bottle. He waited for the right opportunity, and when he saw it, he made the switch. A college student with a legitimate prescription, one whose wisdom teeth were no longer in their sockets, took home Simon's first batch of homemade oxycodone.

Simon couldn't sleep for days, worried that someone would discover his scam. But when three days went by and no one arrested or fired him, he decided to act again, this time creating twenty-four pills from twelve. Half left the Happy and Healthy Pharmacy in the hands of another dental patient, and he sold the remainder to a drug addict for fifty bucks.

When he calculated the total hours he'd labored to produce those twenty-four tablets, including those early fumbled attempts, he concluded the hourly wage for the production of his product was about five cents. This number wasn't discouraging, however. He'd already improved his process since his first trial, and he was constantly perfecting his operation. The twenty-four tablets, and the fifty dollars, were only the beginning.

Over the years, his operation expanded tremendously, to the current state overseen by a pharmacist, who wasn't likely to kill people by substituting dangerous chemicals when their stock ran low, as he'd known street dealers to do. His pharmacist worked three evenings a week, arriving at headquarters just after the staff of accountants and secretaries and computer people had left for the day. He'd descend into his subterranean lab, and, using additives like ibuprofen and diphenhydramine (to mimic some of the natural properties of the oxycodone) he'd transform 140,000 pills a week into a slightly larger number. Their margin was eight percent. The roughly 150,000 tablets his pharmacist created in the lab all contained ninety-two percent of the drug their labels claimed.

The originals were all replaced and sold to unsuspecting customers at the Happy and Healthy Pharmacies. The extra 11,000 tabs were Simon's, and he distributed them to a carefully chosen network of sales people throughout the area. His return was about $25,000 a week on these illegal drugs. He could increase his profits, he knew, by reducing the oxycodone content per tablet, but that would increase the risk of discovery. He could also pay his pharmacist and his distributors less. But he wasn't buying just their loyalty, but also their intelligence. They understood that they were well compensated, and, like him, they were cautious. None of them were greedy, and that was why they were still in business almost twenty years later. Other than Billy, they'd all done their jobs well.

He shook his head at the thought of Billy, forcing away the anger at his betrayal. Billy had been with him from the beginning, when he was just using a hand-turned candy machine to crank out pills. He'd taken bigger risks in those days—transforming a bottle of a thousand tablets into two thousand during long, sleepless nights. Billy had been his neighbor growing up, and he was the one Simon turned to when he needed someone to push the drugs. Billy did well, most of the time, and he'd never made much trouble. Until now, anyway, but that was over. Billy and Katie were both dead, and the secrets they knew would be kept forever.

Business had grown tremendously since that time. From the first candy press he'd purchased during his college days, he'd graduated to state-of-the-art machinery run by computers. Now, a large machine crushed the ingredients into a fine powder, precisely adding the fillers in the quantities the pharmacist specified. Another machine pressed the mixture into pills. They were air dried and sprayed with a coating and came out looking nearly identical to the original products, so much so that even Simon had a hard time distinguishing between the authentic and the counterfeit.

"How is everything?" he asked his pharmacist.

"No problems tonight."

"That's good to hear."

Simon reached into his pocket and removed a wad of cash, handing the man $5,000. Not bad for three days' work, considering he also drew a $100,000 salary for an imaginary job in the pharmacy up on the street level of this building. Not bad at all.

# CHAPTER TWENTY-FOUR
# COMFORT

Not even the combined powers of nicotine and alcohol could give Nic the gift of peace she desperately needed. The ride home from the hospital had been understandably quiet, that fateful moment at her front door even more awkward than the typical conclusion of a first date. What could have been a wonderful time with Rae had disintegrated into a disaster, and she saw no way to repair the damage of their evening. Who went on a first date to an art museum and ended up in the hospital because her date's long-lost sister (who happened to be a suspect in a homicide) had just been shot? Nic laughed as she thought about it, figuring at least Rae would have a good story to impress future dates. *"Worst date ever? No question about that one. We started out at the Barnes and ended up at the intensive-care unit..."*

Nic swirled her glass, noting with remorse that not much Ketel and tonic remained, mostly just ice. As much as she'd like another, she'd regret it tomorrow. All at once the alcohol would catch up with her, and she'd pass out and find herself in this same balcony chair in the morning, stiff and cold and with a pounding headache. Instead of another drink, she leaned back and thought about why she wanted one.

How was she feeling? Angry, confused, bitter, and perhaps even a bit frightened. With whom was she angry? The Finans, for sure. She presumed they were both dead, but she wished they were alive so she could enjoy a brief moment of pleasure by giving them a piece of her mind. Who in the world separated twins? Why hadn't they just given both children to the Coussarts if they couldn't afford to raise both of them? It wouldn't have been a sacrifice for her parents to have two girls. In fact, it probably would have made their life much easier, for Nic would have had a playmate and not have spent her childhood pestering them. And they'd offered to take both. Jeannie had told her that. How could the Finans be that selfish?

And to never tell Katie she was adopted was unbelievable as well. Nic could understand keeping that information from her as a child, but didn't they understand the medical consequences of genetics? What if their mother had breast cancer or some other treatable-if-detected disease? Nic had submitted to genetic testing when it became commercially available, to help ease some of her concerns, but she'd considered that option only because she knew she was adopted. Thankfully, her testing revealed no unwanted surprises and, instead of fear, filled her with relief.

Nic supposed the way Katie had turned out proved the Finans were awful parents, and each time she reviewed it in the courtroom of her mind she found more evidence to support her verdict. The Finans were jerks.

At the moment, she had to lump her own parents in the same category. They had no right to keep this information from her. Protecting her from disappointment as a child was understandable, but by the time she was a teenager she was certainly mature enough to handle the truth. It was her right to know, and in her opinion, their failure to tell her was a huge lie. The biggest. She couldn't fault them for adopting her—someone else would have taken her if they hadn't, because apparently the Finans weren't going to raise her. But they should have told her she had a sister. Period.

A sister was the only gift her parents couldn't give her, the only thing she'd ever asked of them that they didn't provide. They'd patiently explained that babies were gifts from God, and they didn't want to ask for too many blessings since they already were so lucky to have her.

So Nic had bypassed them and gone directly to the source, all of them, because she was never quite sure who the *real* God was. She'd knelt beside her bed, praying to the Jewish God of her father and the Catholic God her mother worshipped, and even talked to Buddha, because the family next door did, and what if they were the ones who had it right?

All she'd wanted in the world was a sister to keep her company. Someone to play with and talk to, someone to take the spotlight off her and give her parents another one to annoy once in a while. A confidante, who would share her secrets and keep them safe.

Nic remembered that strange time before the junior prom when all the girls were going soft in the head, their thoughts possessed by boys and dresses and flowers. "What's wrong with you?" her best friend had asked. "Everyone wants to go to the prom." She wanted to tell her, to share this secret that had been growing within her, watered by hormones and threatening every day to erupt. And with that opportunity she'd confided in her best friend that she liked girls. They were best friends no longer.

How differently that would have gone if she'd had Katie to talk to.

*"Katie, I don't want to go to the prom unless I can take a girl."*

*"Oh, really? You, too? Well, should we just host a big party and invite all the boycotters?"*

*"Great, let's make a guest list."*

She'd had a wonderful, privileged, lonely childhood. Had she sensed the loss of her twin, subconsciously aware that Katie was out there?

It was infuriating, and at the moment she wondered if she'd ever speak to her parents again. At the moment, it wasn't looking good for them.

And Jeannie was in on this, too. Jeannie, her practical, sensible, morbidly honest aunt, who was a voice of reason and giver of sound advice. Well, Jeannie clearly hadn't given this situation careful enough consideration. She knew about Katie and had kept quiet—hell, she was even her doctor! She had a relationship with her.

Couldn't Jeannie have said something, if not to Nic, then at least to Katie? Raised the hypothetical questions?

*"Suppose you were adopted, Katie. Now that your parents are dead, would you want to know? Would you like to perhaps be in touch with your biological siblings?"*

*"No, okay."*

*"Yes, well, in that case, do I have a story to tell you."*

Louis was right up there with everyone else, too. Just because he'd learned this troubling piece of information, why did he have to share it with her? It was another situation where some hypothetical questioning could have done some good.

*"Nic, suppose you had an identical twin? She's a drug dealer and wanted by the police for murdering her boyfriend, and she's quite possibly dying in the SICU. Would you like to see her? Say hello and bond?"*

*"No? Well, I don't blame you. Yes? Are you sure, because as your friend I have to tell you this could be a life-altering event. Still yes? Well, if you're sure..."*

This was a gigantic conspiracy, and all the people in her world whom she loved and trusted had betrayed her. She literally didn't have anyone to talk to about this. No one.

Nic sucked on an ice cube and closed her eyes. In the back of her mind lurked another issue as troubling as the others. It had popped up several times over the past few hours, but she'd pushed it back down as her anger and confusion consumed her instead. But there it was again, the nagging uncertainty of *what if*. What if the Finans had taken both of them? Or if they'd taken Nic instead of Katie? Would it be her in that SICU bed sucking on an ET tube?

Nic liked to take credit for her success. She'd studied and worked hard to get the grades and the volunteer hours she needed for medical school. She'd sacrificed extracurricular activities and ski-club trips to Vermont, skipped parties while other people were skipping classes. No one had handed her an admission slip just because her parents had medical degrees. She'd earned it.

But *what if*? What if her parents were dead and she didn't have their guidance? What if she didn't have their money and had to get a job on the weekends? Spending her time working instead of studying might have influenced her grades. She'd written the essay and submitted it to the chief of staff—the one that earned her a prized summer internship shadowing doctors, the one that was the basis of the essay she then wrote for her medical-school applications.

But even though she'd gotten the internship herself, she probably wouldn't even have known about the program if her parents weren't on staff at the hospital. She'd received privileges from the ER doctors there, who allowed her to wander into their sphere when she accompanied her parents to the hospital. She could literally just stop by for an hour and look at x-rays or watch procedures, coming and going as her schedule allowed. That experience was one she wouldn't have enjoyed without the connections her parents had made during their medical careers.

She shook her head, chasing away the thoughts. She was the master of her own destiny, and no one else. Louis came from a working-class family; no one in his family had even gone to college before him. And he'd made it. Katie Finan could have made different choices, and she didn't, and that's why she was in this dreadful state. It had nothing to do with Nic. Nothing.

The lights twinkling in the distance suddenly seemed comforting, or was that the alcohol taking effect? She thought of Rae and realized she was lucky to have met her. She wished it had been a different day, but she couldn't have done anything to change it. No use dwelling on it.

She ought to apologize to Rae. While she'd done nothing wrong, she couldn't help but feel badly for the mess she'd put upon her new friend. Rae had handled it so well. Offering quiet support, she'd sat next to Nic while they were talking with Jeannie, and then on the ride home, she'd allowed Nic the quiet she needed. Instead of forcing conversation she paid attention on the very important matter of getting them home safely.

It was certainly more than Nic would have done if Rae had been the one with all the drama this night. Nic would probably have fled about the time she dropped her date off at the hospital, running fast in the other direction. She didn't need chaos in her life, especially other people's. It was one of the most annoying parts of her job. All her coworkers loved to share the details of their marriages and their children's successes, but the divorces and failures were the topics that never died. Nic couldn't tolerate it, and she made avoiding trouble a habit.

Rae had done just the opposite. She'd been dragged into this, dragged away from the peaceful evening she'd been enjoying, and she'd barely even batted an eyelash when confronted with the peculiar circumstances of the first minutes of Nicole's life. Rae was a special person, just like Louis. And then Nic laughed as she realized she was ticked off at Louis for revealing the very same information she was blaming others for withholding.

Nic stood, opened the door, and entered the apartment. She rinsed the glass and set it out to dry, then took a hot shower, washing away the smoke and germs of the hospital, trying to talk herself out of the impulse that was gnawing at her. After she'd brushed her teeth and could no longer make an excuse not to, she went into the hallway and knocked on Rae's door.

"Hi," Rae said as soon as she opened the door.

Nic could no longer control the emotions she'd been fighting. Her parents would have disapproved, but at the moment, pleasing them wasn't important. Tears began falling just as Rae closed her arms around her, pushing the door shut in the process. Burying her face in Rae's neck, Nic clung to her and sobbed, comforted by the warmth of her and the strength that seemed to seep from Rae's pores. She longed to catch some, to soak it up and absorb it and let it become the glue that held her together.

It seemed an eternity later that Nic pulled back to see the sad smile on Rae's face. She'd held her silently, not bothering with meaningless words, but had stroked her back, occasionally running her fingers through Nic's hair. Nic understood there wasn't much to say, and she appreciated that, once again, Rae didn't give in to the temptation to fill the silence with unnecessary words.

Rae reached for the tissue box on the hall table, pulled one out and hesitated, then grabbed the box and handed it to Nic instead. "Do you want to come in and sit down?" she asked after Nic had dried her tears.

Nic nodded and followed Rae the few feet into the living room, where a plush leather couch beckoned. Suddenly, she felt exhausted.

She collapsed against the soft leather, but Rae remained standing. "Can I get you a drink? I have wine. And vodka."

Nic was touched that Rae had noticed her drink preference, but she shook her head. "I've already tried that, and it didn't work."

"How about some chocolate-chip cookie dough?"

Rae wore an expectant expression, and Nic was suddenly again reminded of how attractive she was. The soft-looking cotton Phillies boxers and a ribbed tank pushed her far over the top of sexy. "You're so cute," she said, before her brain could prevent her thoughts from morphing into words. What about Rae made her suddenly unable to control the expression of the thoughts she usually kept so closely guarded? It was so unlike her.

Rae winked and then disappeared toward her kitchen.

Perhaps the drink was finally doing its job, for when Nic closed her eyes and took a few deep breaths, she actually began to relax. Or perhaps fatigue was finally catching up with her. She'd been restless last night, and today was nearly twenty hours old. Her body's ability to pull all-nighters was clearly fading as she approached thirty.

Oh. She *was* thirty. This was her birthday. Opening her eyes, she sat up to see Rae emerging with two dessert cups in hand. As she offered one to Nic, Nic looked up at her. "It's my birthday, Rae. I'm thirty years old. I'm supposed to have it all together by now, but my life's a fucking mess!"

Rae sat down, studying Nic as she nibbled a spoonful of cookie dough. "Well, first of all, happy birthday. It seems sort of a strange thing to say under the circumstances, but it is good, Nic. You're alive. Your sister might not be. All those other people at the hospital—they have bigger problems than you do. So if you look at it from that perspective, you do have many reasons to be happy."

"It could always be worse," Nic said as she stared from the cookie dough to Rae. "One of the best fringe benefits of my job is a daily reminder that it could always be worse." Nic took a bite, chewed a chocolate chip, and licked her lips. "Got milk?"

Rae's eyes twinkled. "I was saving it for later, to serve with the cake…but since you asked…"

Rae disappeared into the kitchen, and Nic closed her eyes again. She didn't open them until the sound of footsteps told her the milk had arrived.

"Thank you," she said, and they sat silently as they ate and drank. When Nic finished her treat, she stood and took the cups and glasses into the kitchen, where she rinsed them and put them into the dishwasher.

"Did you really just wash the dishes?" Rae asked.

Nic shrugged. "Habit," she said.

"Well, thanks."

As Nic looked at Rae, her eyes filled with tears again, and as she sat, she felt Rae's arms around her once more. "I feel so betrayed, Rae. They all lied to me."

"Yes, they did," she said softly as she kissed the top of Nic's hair, still wet from her recent shower.

"And what about her? I have a twin! My whole fucking life I wanted a sister, and now I find out she's a life-long criminal and it probably doesn't matter, because she's probably dead already." Her words were punctuated by sobs and sniffles, and when she finished, she cried even harder.

"So you don't have any other siblings?" Rae asked, still holding Nic tight.

Nic sniffled. "No. How about you?"

Rae eased back on the couch and pulled Nic with her, so Nic's head was resting on her chest. She pulled a blanket over them, and Nic snuggled into her, marveling at how wonderful it felt to be held, how safe she felt with Rae.

"Yes, I have two. A sister about two years younger, and a brother seven years younger."

"What are their names?"

"Rhonda and Ricky."

Nic pulled back and looked at Rae, trying to control her laughter. When she saw the smile forming on Rae's face, she knew it was safe to tease her. "You've got to be kidding me. Rachael, Rhonda, and Ricky? What were they thinking?"

"I've been asking that since they were born."

Nic pushed herself off Rae and off the couch, then, after extinguishing the lights, resumed her position.

"You really make yourself at home, don't you?" Rae said.

The kitchen light was still on, and Nic could see the smile on Rae's face. "You look too comfortable to ask you to move. But don't change the subject. I have to know what kind of people would do this to their children. What are your parents' names?"

"You don't want to know."

"Oh, yes, I do."

"Rich and Ruth."

Nic burst into laughter, and Rae joined her. "You're making that up."

"I wish I was."

"Are all the towels monogrammed?"

"Yes, and so is the garage door, with a big R right in the middle of it."

"I'm sorry for laughing."

"No offense taken. I laugh at them, too."

"Are you close?"

"We are. Ricky is a computer geek and he moved to California, so we only see him on vacations. My family usually goes away together to someplace fun like Peru or China—it's a great time to bond. Rhonda is a teacher and lives in the house next to my parents, with her two kids and two dogs and a big, hairy husband."

Nic stifled a yawn. "What's your brother-in-law's name?"

"Ned."

"Oh, wow. How'd he slip through?"

"Ron was pregnant, so their hand was forced."

Nic wondered what it might be like at the Rhodes house, with a big R on the garage and a multitude of intelligent people debating things like liquor licenses in the state of Pennsylvania and a destination for their next exotic trip. It would probably be a bit more entertaining than a family meal at her parents'. As she drifted off to sleep, she imagined herself in the picture with them, she and Ned wearing monogrammed N sweaters, drifting in a sea of Rs.

# CHAPTER TWENTY-FIVE
# BEST PRESENT EVER

During her time in the hospital, and later when she was recovering from her ankle surgeries, Jet often dreamed of a day in court. She'd stand before the judge, who towered over her, and be pronounced guilty. In her dream his voice echoed. *Guilty, guilty, guilty.* With her heart pounding and her body drenched in sweat she'd awaken, the sweet relief of consciousness burying once again what she couldn't bear to face.

Her day in court had never come, and the nightmares had faded over time, but their memory was so powerful that just the thought of a courthouse triggered a panic like she'd never known. So, in addition to the fears she faced with Katie in the SICU and her shooter on the loose, Jet now faced the nightmare of a courtroom.

Sometime during a long night, after Katie's twin sister had fled the building and before the change of shift, a social worker had appeared at the hospital. The woman's concern was with Chloe and Andre, and she'd approached Jet and Jeannie for information. When neither of them gave her satisfaction, she announced a hearing, to be held in the morning, to determine the custody of Katie's minor children. Anyone with knowledge of their whereabouts was asked to come forth, as was anyone interested in taking custody of them.

Jet knew there was no one else, so while her body and mind begged for rest, she was forced to face the fears that had haunted her, knowing that having Chloe and Andre go into foster care was an even bigger nightmare than what she'd endured.

She sipped her coffee and waited for it to work, needing to get through this hearing and through the day. Her parents still had Katie's kids, and Jet didn't see a point in having them come to the courthouse. They were safe in a bubble of ignorance, protected by her parents and the innocence that gave credence to the excuses being made for their mother. They'd stay in Ambler, oblivious, until her parents told her that strategy was no longer working. Then she'd take them home, to her apartment, and care for them until Katie could.

In her heart of hearts Jet knew Katie would want Chloe and Andre to be with her, and she intended to do her best to prove herself worthy of Katie's trust. She could handle the kids. Hell, Katie did it every single day, and somehow she managed. Jet needed to just keep putting one foot in front of the other and keep them safe, and also let them know how very loved they were.

She'd stopped by her apartment for a quick shower and a change of clothes before heading to the hearing. She'd worn scrubs in the ER for years, and wore casual clothes to the clinic, but for this occasion she pulled her only suit from the dry cleaner's plastic. With a crisp white shirt and shiny black loafers, Jet thought she looked worthy. Although the hearing was a technicality—no one else in the world had a claim to Chloe and Andre—she wanted to make a good impression on the judge. Now as she waited in the hallway, sitting erect on a hard wooden bench, she felt the decision to present herself in a professional manner had been wise. All around her people shuffled about, some on their way to meet their own fates, others just doing their jobs, young and old, people of all races. They all had made the same effort as Jet, though, looking clean and wearing clothing appropriate to the occasion.

A few minutes before the appointed time, Jet noted with disdain the appearance of the social worker, dressed to kill and wearing a matching expression upon her face. A slight nod as she passed Jet was her only acknowledgment. Her demeanor the night before had been professional; nothing in her words or actions indicated she held any opinion in the matter of the guardianship of Katie's kids, yet Jet had a *feeling* the woman had passed judgment on Katie. She had another feeling now, and it was telling her something was amiss.

As soon as the woman entered into the courtroom, Jet followed. Unsure of protocol, she didn't want to miss the proceedings while she waited in the hallway for a summons. This woman knew the ropes, and Jet figured if she kept an eye on her and followed her, she'd be just where she needed to be.

The courtroom was unimpressive, with plain oak paneling on the walls and a white plaster ceiling shining light down onto six rows of gallery seating, and beyond the bar two small tables, the jury box, and above it all, at the very back, the bench. The seal of the Commonwealth of Pennsylvania adorned the wall behind the bench, and flags of the commonwealth and the country stood beside it.

Others were already seated in the first row on the left, and they turned to survey her skeptically as she walked in. Jet had a seat on the right. That section was all hers. In front of her, the social worker was speaking with a man in a suit, talking in an animated manner but with a hushed voice that didn't reach Jet's ears. A stenographer was seated to the left of the bench, talking with the bailiff. No one else was in the room.

Jet studied the four people across from her—an older man, who appeared to be in his eighties, with hunched posture and wearing an ill-fitting suit. A woman of fifty, probably his daughter, with bleached-blond hair and too generous a supply of cosmetics, no doubt to hide the wrinkles that had appeared in all the usual places. Her business suit was just a little too tight, and though once she'd probably had the figure to wear it, that day had passed. Two teenage girls accompanied them, also wearing too much makeup, also with hair a shade too light to be natural, and both wearing skirts that barely covered their ass cheeks.

As Jet watched them, she noted the two girls arguing in a hushed tone. She couldn't hear their words, but their gestures told Jet all she needed to know about them. They were trouble. The girls elbowed each other, made faces, and gave attitude to both their elders. The grandfather shook his head in a gesture of apparent disgust, and behind his back, their mother pointed her middle finger at them and told them, in a voice that resonated through the room, to shut their traps.

Jet tried not to make presumptions but sent a silent prayer that, if they were also before the court on a child-custody matter, His Honor wouldn't rule in favor of these unsavory people.

On cue, Judge Michael Rova entered, and the proceedings began. The social worker sat at the table to the right, and the man in the suit sat at the left. “Where are these children?” he inquired after the intent of the hearing was stated.

The suited man jumped from his seat at the table, eager to answer the judge. “Your Honor, that’s a great question. They haven’t been seen since their mother abducted them from police custody almost thirty-six hours ago.”

Jet wanted to jump up and defend Katie, but before she could, the social worker spoke. “We don’t know their present location. We hope to get to the bottom of that today.”

“Well, clearly, Your Honor, this matter must be resolved. Two small children are out there somewhere with no one looking out for their welfare.”

Who was this guy? How the hell did he know anything about Chloe and Andre and their welfare?

Jet stood and raised her hand, as if back in school. How else did you get the attention of a judge if you weren’t seated at the attorney’s tables? He noticed her and nodded in her direction as he addressed her. “You, do you know something about this matter?”

“Actually, I do. My name is Janet Fox, and my parents are watching Chloe and Andre. They were babysitting for them when their mother was shot. Since she couldn’t come to get them, they’re still there.”

“Well, why aren’t they here?” he demanded in a booming voice that echoed through the empty hall.

“No one told me to bring them.” Jet shrugged and held out her palms.

The attorney glared at her before turning to face the judge again. “Well, Your Honor, now that we know where they are, can we proceed with the temporary custody hearing?” he asked.

The judge nodded again and looked toward the social worker. “I think that would be appropriate. Miss Landry, who, in your opinion, should be made guardian of these children?”

Jet wanted to raise her hand again. Miss Landry didn’t even know her name—

how could she make a recommendation?

Before she could try, Miss Landry replied to the judge’s question. “Your Honor, it has come to my attention that the children’s maternal grandparents, Mr. and Mrs. Jack Finan, would like to care for them until their mother is able to resume her parental duties."

Jet sucked in her breath and looked suspiciously at the bunch in the front row behind the lawyer. Shit! This had to be Katie's father and his second family. Why the hell would they show up now, after all these years, when they hadn't seen Katie since she ran away? They didn't even know Chloe and Andre.

Before she could object, the man in the suit addressed the judge. "Your Honor, I represent Mr. Finan, and he would indeed like to assume custody of his grandchildren."

The judge nodded still again. "It always makes it easier when family helps out in a situation like this."

Jet couldn't contain herself any longer. If she didn't interrupt, he'd swing his gavel and close this case and Katie's kids would be in the clutches of that horrific family. "Your Honor!" she shouted, and as he looked at her, everyone in the room turned to glare at her.

"What is it?"

"Your Honor, I am…" Jet thought for a moment. Who was she to Katie? She certainly couldn't claim the title of partner. Although she had no doubt that was the next step for them, they didn't currently share a residence. "Friend" didn't seem to adequately describe the nature of their relationship or the depth of their feelings. Was "lover" too strong a word to use in court? Fuck, it was the truth. "I'm Katie Finan's lover. I came here today expecting to get custody of her children, because I know them, and I love them, and they love me. They sleep at my house and I know their routines…I'm the best person to take care of them, sir."

"I'll be the judge of that, miss."

"But your honor, Katie ran away from them." Jet pointed at her father and his family. "They were neglectful and abusive toward her and—"

Before she could utter another word, the Finans' attorney was on his feet, waving his arms, objecting to her inflammatory remarks. The lot of them had turned in her direction as she spoke and were glaring at her, shooting daggers with their eyes, and one of the teenagers aimed the middle finger of her right hand in Jet's direction.

"Counselor, let the woman speak, please." The judge's voice was loud and commanding and they all heeded its silent warning.

"Thank you, sir," Jet said, and once again waved a hand in the Finan family's direction. "They may have good intentions, Your Honor, but they don't know these children. It would frighten the kids and disrupt their lives to have to go live with strangers."

"Your Honor." The lawyer objected loudly. "These are not strangers. They are flesh and blood."

The judge stared directly at Jet, and she couldn't help feeling small beneath his gaze, suddenly exposed and vulnerable beneath the microscope of the courts. It was her nightmare all over again, yet very real this time. "I tend to agree with him, Miss Fox. I am strongly inclined to assign guardianship to their grandfather. No matter how you may feel about them, and how they feel about you in return, there is no stronger bond than blood."

Jet felt flushed and anxious and her knees suddenly threatened to give way. Reaching out, she managed to grab the back of the pew in front of her, maintaining her balance and, in turn, her composure. She couldn't lose the children to those people. Even for one day. She took a deep breath and hoped this idea that had spontaneously popped into her mind wasn't total foolishness, that she could pull it off.

"Actually, Your Honor, Mr. Finan and his family are not Katie's blood relatives. Katie was adopted. But if blood is what you want, would you consider granting custody to Katie's twin sister?"

The suit erupted in objections once again, but the moans and shouts from the Finan family drowned out his cries.

"That's a lie!" Mrs. Finan said, but Jet noted that Mr. Finan was still seated and very quiet.

"Miss Fox, these are very strong accusations."

"Yes, Your Honor, but they're easy enough to prove." Jet turned slightly and faced Katie's dad. She wanted to punch him, but he was so pathetic she didn't think he was worth the effort. "Mr. Finan, you know hospital records are easy enough to locate. Tell the judge the truth."

"Tell me the truth, Mr. Finan, or be held accountable to the court."

His voice was rough and weak, the result of too much tobacco and booze and not enough breath. "She was adopted. But I don't see what that matters. I'm the only family she has."

"No, not true, Mr. Finan. You know Katie has a twin. Remember the other girl—the one you wouldn't adopt because your house was too small? She and Katie are like this." Jet crossed her fingers to show him their sisterly bond and to hope lying before the judge wouldn't get her into trouble. "She'll take the kids."

"Well, why isn't she here now?" the judge demanded.

Jet apologized to the court, explaining her surprise at the sudden reappearance of Katie's family in the court this morning. She hadn't even considered that they would want Chloe and Andre, since they'd never even met them. It had never occurred to Jet to ask for Nicole Coussart's help, and she only hoped that if she had to, Nic would be willing. So far, Katie's sister didn't seem very friendly.

"One hour, Miss Fox. You have one hour to get the sister here. And bring the children as well."

The suit jumped to his feet. "Your Honor, before we recess, I'd like to request that the court freeze Kathleen Finan's assets. You never know who might try to take advantage of her while she's incapacitated."

"That is not within the jurisdiction of this court," the judge barked back.

Jet was stunned, but at least now she understood. Katie's father was here for Katie's money, not for Chloe and Andre. The thought sickened Jet, who became more determined than before to keep them away from Jack Finan and his family.

Jet would have protested to the judge that an hour wasn't nearly enough time to find Nic and bring her to the courthouse, but he'd already risen and had turned his back to her.

"Fuck," she whispered, and sat back in her seat, thinking. She didn't have any idea how to begin. But Jeannie would know how to reach Nicole and help persuade her to help Jet. She dialed her phone even as she was walking from the courtroom. "Fuck!" she said, when the call went to voice mail. Jeannie had stayed with Jet most of the night, sitting beside her in the waiting room and at Katie's bedside. She'd gone home in the middle of the night to shower and change and sleep for a few hours, and had gone back to the SICU so Jet could leave for court. If she wasn't answering her phone, it was going to be very difficult to reach her.

What now? And then it occurred to her. Rachael Rhodes would know how to reach Nic. Rae had given Jet her business card, and she murmured a prayer of thanks as she fished it from the pocket of her backpack, where she'd carelessly dropped it the night before. She dialed the number and held her breath, waiting. Rae was her last hope.

❖

Rae sat at her desk, staring out the window at the park across the street instead of the papers she'd spent the morning shuffling about her desk. She was tired and distracted, and it would have been evident to anyone who saw her that she hadn't slept well. Fortunately, she didn't have any meetings or conference calls this morning that demanded the attention she was having so much difficulty keeping focused.

The day before had been one of the most bizarre of her life. Her time with Nic at the Barnes and at dinner was wonderful. Nic was all the things she hoped for in a woman—attractive, intelligent, tough, cultured. They had so much in common. At the moment they'd climbed into her car at the river, Rae would have ranked her time with Nic as the best date ever. And then that message from Louis had beckoned them to the hospital, and Nic's life was suddenly in chaos.

Rae had tried to show Nic her support, but she feared she'd failed miserably. Perhaps no one could have said or done anything to comfort Nic, but Rae wished *she* could have offered Nic sage words of advice to guide her through her difficult time. Instead, she'd offered her fucking cookie dough.

She'd been surprised when the doorbell rang shortly after midnight, but not at all surprised to see Nic through the peephole. Rae had held her on the couch until her tears were all cried out and then lay beside her until the rhythmic cycle of her breathing told her Nic was asleep. She'd kissed her softly on the forehead before slipping from beneath Nic's firm body. After Rae had covered her with a blanket and once again crawled into her own bed, she'd reflected on the fact that she'd finally gotten a woman into her apartment, a very attractive woman, and all she'd done was cry.

It could have been worse, Rae thought. At least she hadn't caused all the tears. When she'd left for work this morning, with Nic still sleeping on her couch, she'd hoped it wouldn't be the last time she saw her.

The ringing of her cell phone was a welcome distraction, and even though she didn't recognize the number, she answered anyway. "Hello."

"Is this Rae?" a woman's deep voice asked.

"Yes."

"This is Jet Fox calling. I met you last night at the hospital."

Rae's heart went to her throat as she realized the call couldn't be bringing good news. And when she heard Jet's tale, she knew she was right. "So I have an hour to get her there?"

"Actually, we're down to fifty-seven minutes."

Rae looked at her watch, setting the stopwatch feature as she replied, "I'll do my best."

Only half a dozen blocks separated the DEA offices from the convention center on Arch Street, but in a business suit and loafers, Rae's best effort was a modestly paced jog. When she stopped in front of the building, she glanced at her wrist. Forty-four minutes left.

Signs everywhere announced the medical convention and directed her upstairs to the meeting rooms. Rooms. Three topics were currently being presented, and Rae had no idea which one Dr. Coussart would have preferred, which door held the grand prize. Was she a spinal-cord-injury enthusiast or would she prefer EKGs to Remember? Or, perhaps The Difficult Airway interested her. Rae looked around and spotted two women seated at a table, beneath a banner welcoming her to the conference. She jogged over to them and looked at both as she spoke.

"Hi. I have a minor family emergency and need to find someone at the conference. Can you tell me which room Nicole Coussart's in?"

"Oh, my. I'm sorry to hear that. Let me check," one of the women said.

Rae glanced at her watch while the woman flipped through pages in a binder. Thirty-nine minutes left. She looked up, awaiting the woman's response, wanting to rip the binder from her hands and find the information herself. "Oh, dear. This isn't good."

"What?" Rae asked. "Isn't she here?"

"No, it's not that. She originally signed up for Updates in Arrhythmia Management, but that was rescheduled because the speaker couldn't make it until this afternoon. Dr. Coussart had a choice of the other three lectures, but the change wasn't marked on her registration form."

"So she can be in any one of those rooms?"

"I'm afraid so."

"Is it possible to have her paged?"

The woman frowned and looked to her colleague for advice. It didn't seem like a difficult concept, but apparently they weren't accustomed to this sort of request.

"Let me check with Dr. Scialla. He's in charge."

"Where is he?"

"I'm not sure."

"Okay, I'll tell you what. I'll look for her, and you go look for him."

Without waiting for a reply, Rae turned and headed into the lecture called The Latest in the Management of Spinal Cord Injuries. The room was darkened, and some sort of scary-looking image of the human body was displayed on monitors conveniently located throughout the auditorium, as well as on a giant screen at the front of the room. After allowing her eyes to adjust, Rae began to walk slowly along the wall toward the speaker. Nic had told her she always sat in the front, so she could see, and sure enough, that's right where Rae found her. Quietly, she leaned down and whispered in Katie's ear. "Bring your things, we have to go."

The intrusion startled Nic, yet she'd never been so happy to see anyone. It was her birthday, and she should have been happy, but she'd just been stressed—about her parents' betrayal, Katie's situation, and because those two factors had combined to ruin a wonderful night with a really wonderful woman. Nic thought she might never see Rae again, yet here she was. The trepidation she felt at wondering why she was there was overshadowed by the thrill of seeing her.

She followed Rae, holding her questions until they were in the hallway. "What's going on?"

Rae held her by the elbow, walking her toward the exit on Arch Street. "We have a little emergency."

"Oh, no. Did she…die?" Nic whispered.

"No, no. Not as bad as that, thankfully. But your sister needs your help."

"She's not my sister, Rae." A chill swept through her as she said it, but it was true. Katie meant nothing to her. Nothing but trouble.

"She's still your flesh and blood, Nic. She's in trouble, and she needs your help."

"No. No, Rae. I can't get involved. This is just too screwed up for me."

Rae stopped, gripping Nic's biceps so she couldn't turn away. "I know this is an awful situation for you, but there's more than yourself to worry about now, Nic. You're a doctor, for Christ's sake. You're supposed to give a shit about human beings, even if they're not perfect like you."

"Ouch."

Letting go of Nic, Rae turned and ran her fingers through her dark hair, looking out into a beautiful spring day with a sadness on her face that touched Nic's heart. It wasn't just that she liked Rae, but that Rae seemed so strong—so untouchable. That she was worried now worried Nic.

"How? What do you want me to do?" Nic eyed her suspiciously and Rae leaped into her arms, hugging her tight, then pulling back to plant a perfectly electrifying but brief kiss on her lips. Nic was speechless as they resumed walking.

Rae relayed the scant details Jet had given her. "Katie's mom died when she was a kid. Her father remarried. Imagine Cinderella and you get the picture. Anyway, Jet went to court today to appeal for custody of Katie's kids, and Katie's dad was there, with the evil stepmother in tow. They want the kids. What they really want is Katie's money, but they'll use the kids to get it. The judge wants a family member to have the kids. You're Katie's only known relative, Nic. You have to do this. You have to ask for custody."

Nic shook her head and stopped in her tracks, looking at her. "Are you out of your mind? I don't even know this woman."

"It doesn't matter."

"It does matter. I didn't even know she has kids. I know nothing about her, except she's into drugs and guns."

"What matters is that children—your nieces and or nephews—are in a lot of trouble. You can help them. You're the only one who can help them." Rae was pleading with her, as if she knew these children, as if she cared.

Nic closed her eyes and thought about the facts, wondering if it was really as serious as Rae seemed to think it was. And then she thought of her own perfectly prim-and-proper parents and her perfectly normal life. How had Katie gotten so screwed up? Probably because of her parents. Nic didn't know that she could help in the long run—that was Katie's job. But might she prevent them from getting into the wrong hands while their mother recovered from her wounds? Did she dare take on this massive responsibility? "How many children?"

Seeming to sense progress in her argument, Rae gently grabbed an arm and pulled Katie toward a waiting taxi. "I'm not quite sure."

Opening the door, Rae gently pushed Nic inside and gave the driver the address they needed.

Suddenly frightened, Nic clutched Rae's arm. "Rae, it doesn't even matter, really, how many. I'm allergic to children. They're messy and write on the walls with crayons and break stuff. And I'm irresponsible. I can't even keep a damn plant alive."

Rae laughed and placed her hand on Nic's thigh. "Kids are easier than plants. They know when to ask for food and water."

"You're out of your mind. I can't take her kids. Besides, I don't even know them."

"Neither does her father. Will you please just meet them? They could be really great kids."

"And they could be little drug dealers like their parents."

"Jet's crazy about them."

"Yeah, well, I think she needs her head examined. What's a respectable nurse who works for my aunt doing hanging around with drug dealers?"

Rae turned, giving Nic her full attention. "Nic, do you suppose it's possible there may be more to this story than you've heard on the news?"

Nic looked down her nose at Rae and scowled.

"From what Jet said at the hospital last night, it sounds like Katie was in the wrong place at the wrong time. You read about it every day in the newspapers and see it on TV. Can't you give Katie the benefit of the doubt until you know the whole story?"

Nic leaned back and rested her head against the taxi's warn seat, still staring at Rae. "Why? Why should I? This is not my problem, Rae."

"Because, Nic, whether you like it or not, or whether you acknowledge it or not, Katie Finan is your sister."

Nic didn't respond, but instead turned again and stared out the window, not seeing anything but the image in her mind of Katie's still form in the ICU bed. She digested Rae's words as she replayed the scene from the hospital. Katie and her children meant nothing to her. She had no obligation. So why was she sitting in the cab on her way to court? Was it curiosity? Or some deeper need, that childhood desire for a sister beginning to ooze from the depths of her, where it'd been buried for so long? Or did she just want to be with Rae?

After a few minutes of silence, Rae squeezed her thigh. "I'm sorry about last night," she whispered.

"What?" Nic turned and met Rae's eyes.

"I'm sorry."

"Whatever for?"

"For not doing anything to help you."

Nic swallowed. Rae had done so much the night before just by being there. She'd sat beside her in the hospital and in the car, and then later, she'd fed her cookie dough, and listened to her, and then held her and made her feel safe, in spite of all the turmoil. Nic couldn't remember ever falling asleep in a woman's arms before this early morning with Rae. She smiled at the memory. "Rae, you were perfect last night."

"Really?"

Nic gave her a hint of a smile. "Yes, perfect. Thank you for being there for me. I…I really didn't know who else to talk to."

Rae squeezed Nic's hand. "I'm here with you now, Nic. And I'm on vacation next week, so I'm available to baby sit if you need me."

"Me or them?"

Rae chuckled. "Whatever you need."

The cab pulled to the curb, and Rae paid the driver and glanced at her watch. There was little traffic at this hour and they'd made it with twenty minutes to spare. Following signs to the designated courtroom, Nic noticed a group of people huddled just outside the doors. Jet was among them, with an older couple and two children. She stopped.

"Oh, my God. They're black."

Rae followed Nic's gaze and saw the children, a girl of about nine and boy of six or so. Their skin was the color of coffee with extra crème, their hair suggestive of African ancestry. "Yep, it looks like they are."

"Oh, wow. I wasn't expecting this."

"Is it a problem?"

Nic looked at Rae. She still hadn't decided whether to take them, but their skin color wasn't the issue. They could have been green or purple. She was just shocked, having assumed they would be as fair skinned as she was. Nic was concerned only that they were young enough to have needs she likely couldn't satisfy and that they'd require her time and attention. "No, I suppose it isn't," she said softly as she looked at them, and realized that for only the second time in her life she was looking at someone who was her flesh and blood.

And then they were spotted, and before Jet could stop him, the boy sprinted across the hallway and threw himself around her. "Mommy! I've been missing you so much," he mumbled into her stomach.

"Andre. Hey, buddy, take it easy," Jet said as she caught up with him.

Nic knelt, peeling him away from her, and looked him in the eyes. She searched his face for a resemblance, but she could find none. And then she pulled herself back to reality and wondered what the hell was she supposed to say to him? She took a deep breath. "Hi, Andre. My name is Nicole. I know I look a lot like your mommy. Do you want to know why?"

Pulling back, he looked confused and afraid as he turned to Jet for comfort. She kneeled down as well and he backed into her arms. She kissed him on the cheek. "It's okay, buddy."

"Who are you?" This question came from the girl.

Nic stayed down at Andre's level but looked up at her and smiled. In her, she saw the resemblance of family. The hair was wrong, as was the eye color, but the shape of her face, the nose and mouth, and the serious look she gave Nic, reminded Nic of herself at that age. "My name is Nicole. What's yours?"

"Chloe. Why do you look like my mom?" Her voice was strong, her posture challenging.

Nicole leaned back an inch to give her more space. "Well, Chloe, that's a great question. She's my sister."

Chloe shook her head and jutted her hip, full of nine-year-old attitude. "My mom doesn't have a sister."

"It's kind of amazing, isn't it? We've never known each other, but we're sisters."

"I don't believe you."

"Would you like to see my driver's license? It has my birthday on it. My birthday is…today. Just like your mom's." It was hard to believe this was her birthday. She'd celebrated some unusual birthdays in her thirty years. Because school was usually dismissed for the summer by the time June fourteenth came, she'd spent her birthdays on many different vacations. She'd been all over Europe, hiking in Colorado, and white water rafting in Idaho. Because medical school doesn't allow for summer holidays, once, as a student, she delivered a baby on her birthday. But just like that memorable date at Dalessandro's, this day would forever be remembered.

Nic reached into her purse and retrieved her wallet and the ID she was looking for. She handed it to Chloe.

Chloe took the card from Nic, eyeing it suspiciously before she glanced up, looking not at Nic but at Jet.

"Is this true? Does my mom really have a sister?"

"Yeah, isn't that great?"

"Why can't we see Mommy?" Andre interjected.

"You will, in a couple of days. Until then, though, the judge is going to ask Nic to take care of you. Just until your mom is out of the hospital."

"I don't wanna go with her. Why can't we stay with you?"

Jet hugged him tighter for a second, then opened her arms to

Chloe and included her in the hug. "I want to be with you guys, but your mom needs me, too. So when I'm with your mom, Nic is going to watch you."

Nic wanted to point out to Jet that she hadn't agreed to do this, and Jet seemed to sense her hesitation. "Now guys, I need to talk to Nic for a minute. Can you go back over there with my mom and dad?"

They nodded, and she pushed them in the direction of her parents before turning to look at Nicole. "First of all, thanks for coming." Jet glanced at her watch, and noted they only had a few minutes to spare. "My parents and the kids just got here a minute before you. Fortunately, they don't live too far away."

"Yeah, it was pretty lucky that Rae knew how to find me," Nic offered.

"Well, I can see the fear all over your face, and I know this is sort of out of left field, but you're my only chance of getting the kids."

"What do you mean? You want them?"

"Well, yeah. Of course. I just need you to talk the judge into giving you custody, and then you're free. I'll take total responsibility for them."

Nic looked up at Jet, who seemed to be about three feet taller than her, and took a step forward, challenging her. "Wait a minute, here. You want me to lie to the judge?"

"Lie is a strong word."

"No, it's an accurate word."

Jet leaned against the wall and closed her eyes for a moment. Nic thought she looked tired and realized she'd probably been at the hospital all night. "I'm sorry for putting you in this position, Nicole. I really, really wish it hadn't turned out this way, but it did. And this was all I could think of. If you have another idea, I'd be happy to listen. I just don't know what else to do. I can't let those people have these kids. They turned Katie into the street when she was fifteen years old. They abused her and abandoned her. They're unfit to care for a gerbil. These are sweet, innocent kids caught up in this nightmare, and I just want to protect them."

"I can't lie to a judge, Jet. I just can't." Nic shook her head, feeling like she was shaking all over, about to jump off a cliff. "But I'll take the kids, if he'll give them to me. They can stay with me."

Jet closed her eyes, clearly fighting tears, then ran her fingers through her hair. "I'll help as much as I can."

"Me, too." Rae winked at her, and suddenly Nic felt a little bit better.

"Okay, let's do this."

In the courtroom, Nic saw the Finan family and immediately understood Jet's fears. When the older woman saw her, she eyed her suspiciously, as if inspecting her to see if she was an imposter wearing a Katie Finan mask. Nic turned her back to them and gave her attention to Katie's kids. Her niece and nephew.

"So are you guys hungry? I'm famished. I had to skip lunch to come get you."

"We had pancakes for breakfast," Andre volunteered, suddenly quite friendly. "At Denny's."

Chloe was silent while Andre was a chatterbox. Apparently, he wasn't going to stonewall her, but Nic could see she'd have a tough job breaking through Chloe's armor. Before she could speak again, the judge was announced and they all turned their attention in his direction.

"Do you want me to represent you?" Rae asked.

"Can you do that?" Nic asked.

"I'm a lawyer. Of course I can."

Rae approached the bench and made her introduction to the judge.

"Well, let's get this over with, then." The judge apparently wanted his lunch, too.

Nic came forward and stood at the table beside Rae. She introduced herself to Judge Rova, and the Finans' attorney immediately asked for ID. For the second time in ten minutes she produced it.

"Do you dispute this woman's claim that she's Miss Finan's sister?" He was addressing the Finans' lawyer.

"No, Your Honor."

"Thank you. Miss Coussart, do you wish to serve as the guardian for these children?"

Nic wondered if it was appropriate to remind the judge that she was a doctor. Would it help her cause? It was her cause now. She'd decided to help Jet, to help these kids, and now it was important that she do her best for them. Using her title never hurt. "Your honor, it's Dr. Coussart, and yes, I do. I do wish to serve as their guardian."

"Well, Doctor," he said, stressing the word, "then you shall have your wish."

The Finans' lawyer objected, and the judge told him to stand down, and the Finans began shouting and cursing until they were threatened with arrest. Nic was too scared to celebrate, but Rae smiled and then hugged her.

"That was easy," Nic said, when the judge rose from the bench and left the courtroom. She had a terrible fear in her heart that she wouldn't have too many more easy moments in the coming days.

Rae shrugged and held up her hands. "I'm a great lawyer, Nic. What can I say?"

Nic tried to suppress her smile, but somehow it emerged anyway, as it had been tending to do when she was in Rae's company. "You're just lucky there are no diapers to change."

"Well, it was my pleasure. And Nic—happy birthday."

Nic looked at her niece and nephew. Andre was talking to Jet, his face animated as he relayed something of vital importance. Chloe stood behind and to the side, her arms wrapped around Jet, her eyes piercing Nic with a threatening stare.

Nic swallowed and forced a smile. "Best. Present. Ever."

# CHAPTER TWENTY-SIX
# SHOPPING SPREE

Much to her surprise, Nic learned her car was equipped with a LATCH system to hold Andre's car seat in place. After watching Jet struggle to secure it, she hoped for the sake of her manicure that she never had to do it herself.

After taking inventory of the kids' clothing, supplied in a duffel bag by Mr. and Mrs. Fox, Nic decided they needed to shop. They couldn't possibly function with one bathing suit, one pair of shorts, and one T-shirt each. Her heart raced at the thought of a few hours at the King of Prussia mall; she'd seen a new purse in a magazine and was sure they'd have it at Bloomingdale's or Nordstrom. Her mouth watered at the thought of the delectable lunch they'd have at The Cheesecake Factory. She could hardly wait.

"So where do you guys normally shop?" she asked after they were all buckled up and heading toward the mall. "Bloomie's? Lord and Taylor?"

"Target!" Andre continued to speak for both of them, and Nic was unsure if his sister was shy or skeptical of Nic's ability to function as their caregiver. Or perhaps she sensed something more was happening than she'd been told. They knew their mother needed surgery, but not why. They didn't know their father was dead. And they didn't know the circumstances of their mother's birth and why this strange woman named Nicole Coussart was suddenly in charge of their welfare.

Nic looked in the mirror, but she couldn't see Andre's eyes. "They sell clothes at Target?" She'd been there for a hair dryer and a toaster, but never clothing.

"Yeah. They have superhero underwear."

"And Hello Kitty," Chloe added shyly.

"You like Hello Kitty?" Nic was thrilled to hear Chloe's voice. "I loved her when I was little. I even had a Hello Kitty lunch box in second grade."

Suddenly, Chloe came to life, her voice enthusiastic. "Really? That's cool. I just have a shirt, and pencils, and a backpack. And pajamas."

Nic smiled to herself as she remembered the little girl she'd been on her first day of second grade, with that pink lunch box clutched tightly in her hands. "Well, I guess it's Target then. But do you want to eat first? I'm kind of hungry." She tried to recall if there was a Target near the mall but couldn't remember seeing one there.

"Yes, please," Andre said.

"How's The Cheesecake Factory sound to you guys?"

After a moment's silence, Chloe answered quietly. "No, thank you."

"What? You're not hungry?"

"We don't like cheesecake, Aunt Nicole."

"Oh, don't worry. You don't have to eat cheesecake. They have other things there."

"Why can't we just go to McDonald's?" Andre asked.

Nic groaned in ecstasy as the image of a cheeseburger came to mind. "You guys like McDonald's?"

"Yes," they shouted in unison.

"Me, too." Maybe kids weren't so bad after all.

She drove to City Avenue and exited the expressway, and in a few minutes they were walking into the restaurant.

"What will you guys have?" she asked.

"Can we get Happy Meals?" Andre asked.

"Of course. What kind?"

Andre chose chicken nuggets, with barbeque sauce and a Hot Wheels toy, while Nic and Chloe had cheeseburgers, with Twinkle Toes toys. Nic allowed each of them to carry their boxes to the table, and then they filled their own drinks from the beverage fountains.

"My mommy likes cheeseburgers, too," Andre informed Nic.

"Well, she's a smart lady." Nic was more than a little curious about his mother but had been hesitant to interrogate the kids. Since Andre had opened the door, though, she decided to walk through it. "What else does your mommy like?"

Chloe chewed, swallowed, and then frowned. "Vegetables."

Nic chuckled. Obviously Chloe didn't share her mother's taste. "Is she a good cook?"

"She doesn't like to cook too much," Andre said.

"Me either," Nic said, wondering if this was a genetic flaw they'd inherited.

"She cooks sometimes," Chloe said, sounding defensive.

"What's your favorite thing your mom cooks for you?"

"Hot dogs," Andre replied, very seriously, and Nic was quite relieved. She, too, could manage hot dogs.

"How about you, Chloe? What do you like to eat?"

"I like it when we have breakfast for dinner. My mom makes good pancakes."

"I like pancakes, too." As they ate their lunch, Nic asked more questions about their mother, and the obvious joy they felt in talking about her assuaged any guilt Nic may have felt about pumping Katie's children for information.

"You guys are so lucky," she said after a while. "When I was little, my parents never let me eat at fast-food restaurants."

At first she thought she imagined the look that passed between them, but when they suddenly both became very interested in their French fries, she knew she'd been conned. "Wait a minute, you two. You aren't allowed to eat here, are you?"

Chloe looked up first, guilt and remorse all over her beautiful face. "Only on special occasions."

Nic looked from her to her brother and took a deep breath. "Well, I think this is sort of special, don't you? I mean, us meeting each other?"

"Yes!" Andre screamed, and Chloe smiled.

"Aunt Nicole," he asked, "how come you never came to see us before?"

Nic sat back and thought about an answer, then decided it was best to deflect it. "I'm going to let your mom tell you that story. But I've been thinking, Andre, and I don't think I like being called *Aunt*. It makes me feel old. How about if you call me AJ instead?"

"What's AJ stand for?" Chloe asked.

"It's an acronym. A for Aunt, J is for my middle name, Jeanne. AJ. Sound good?" Nic's suddenly thought about Jeannie and had a clearer understanding of her mom's loyalty to her dear friend. There was certainly a good story behind her middle name. Too bad it'd taken thirty years for her to hear it.

"Yeah, and I can be AF," Andre said conspiratorially, bringing Nic's thoughts back to the table.

"What can I be?" Chloe asked. "I want an acronym, too."

"Okay, you can be CF. How's that?"

"I don't like it." She frowned and shook her head, then bit into her cheeseburger.

"Why don't we think about it for a little while, okay?"

Nic could tell by the frown on her face that Chloe wasn't thrilled to be cheated out of an acceptable nickname. Nic looked at the toy in her food box, then reached in and handed it to her. A smile instantly replaced the frown. All was blissful for exactly half a second.

"Hey, how come she gets two toys and I only get one?"

Nic wasn't prepared for this parenting psychology and frowned in frustration. She'd warned both Jet and Rae that they shouldn't trust her with small children, but they'd insisted anyway. She looked at her watch. It was approaching one o'clock. She'd had custody of them for less than an hour and already faced her first conflict. But if she could just hold out for seven more hours, Jet would come to the rescue. She sat taller, fortifying her conviction. She could do this.

Nic looked at his adorable face and tried not to laugh. "Well, I'm sorry about that, Andre. Would you like a Twinkle Toes toy, too?"

"Ewww!"

"Well, then why are you complaining?"

He had no answer, but Chloe seemed to like the way Nic had handled that and was a little friendlier as they headed to the store.

"I don't like shopping," Andre whined as they unbuckled their seat belts.

Nic turned in her seat and faced him. "Okay, you can stay in the car while we shop. When you need a clean shirt, you can wear one of your sister's."

"Ewww! I'm not wearing *girl* clothes."

"Well, then I guess you have to shop with us."

To keep their interest, they stopped first in the toy department, where Andre picked out a dozen things. Nic made him narrow it down to two, and he held his Legos triumphantly while Chloe browsed the aisles slowly and carefully. Finally, she settled on a board game and shyly asked if she could get a book instead of another toy.

Her hesitancy nearly melted Nic. "Of course you can," she said as she patted her shoulder. Nic picked out her own toys—a Frisbee and a plastic ball and bat. They had a lot of time to kill, and she figured they'd stop at the park next.

They picked up the necessary toiletries to sustain them and then made good time through the clothing sections, picking out a variety of items in a sufficient quantity to allow Nic to avoid washing laundry for at least a few days. Andre found superheroes and Chloe found princesses and Hello Kitty, and when they left the store several hundred dollars later, both children wore broad smiles on their beautiful faces.

Nic looked at the clock on her dashboard as she buckled her seat belt. It was 2:15. What the hell could she do for another six hours? Counting perhaps another hour for dinner, she still had almost five hours to fill with fun and exciting activity. She didn't possess the endurance to throw a Frisbee for that long. Then she had an idea. She could take them to see a movie. Whipping out her smartphone, she searched for movies playing locally. To her dismay, she found none with a rating appropriate for her niece and nephew, who she'd learned were eight and six years old. Then another idea occurred to her. She was just around the corner from the zoo, and she knew they could easily spend the afternoon there. She zigzagged through gardens and ghettos and finally found her way to Girard Avenue. From their backseat views they recognized the zoo's entrance as they approached. "Did you ever go to the zoo, AJ?" Andre asked as she rounded the corner toward the parking area.

"Oh, once or twice. How about you? Did you ever go?"

"We went last year. But they didn't have an elephant." His voice was heavy with disappointment.

"Oh, that's too bad. I guess we shouldn't go today then, if they don't have an elephant."

"It was still fun," Chloe exclaimed.

"Yeah, they still have snakes and giraffes." Now Andre was excited, too, and as she pulled the car into a parking space, he shrieked. "Are we really going to the zoo?"

Nic turned in her seat to face them, trying hard not to smile at his enthusiasm. "If we go to the zoo, we need rules. Are you guys okay with that?" They both nodded. "First, no running. Second, you always have to keep me in sight. If you can see me, I can see you, right? That way, we won't get lost. Third, Andre, you have to pee in the girl's bathroom."

"Ewww, why?"

"I think they have a family bathroom, AJ. We can go together," Chloe informed Nic, her excitement overriding the hesitancy she'd displayed earlier.

"Okay, that's fair. So do you guys agree to my terms?"

"Your what?" Chloe asked.

"The rules."

They both nodded, and Nic smiled as they reached the sidewalk and Chloe took her brother's hand. It surprised her that Andre allowed it; he was rather feisty. Yet he seemed to like the attention she paid him—at McDonald's she'd wiped the ketchup from his face, and at the store she'd helped him to pick out a toothbrush and found the right size clothes for him. Her affection for him was obvious, and as Nic took a closer look, it was just as obvious that he loved her, too.

They reached the gate and Nic pulled out her credit card as she requested the tickets. The attendant informed her it was only a few dollars more for a season pass, good for an entire year from the date of purchase. Nic calculated the math in her head and reasoned that they only needed to make one return trip to the zoo to make it a worthwhile investment. As far as she was concerned, they could come to the zoo every day if it kept them occupied.

"You mean we can come here all the time?" Chloe asked, seeming bewildered.

"Whenever you want."

"AJ, this is the best present ever. Thank you!" Before she knew what was happening, Chloe's arms were wrapped around her waist, and then Andre joined her.

The sudden display of affection surprised her, and she had to admit that these children had as well. Although she'd never met them, she'd pre-formed her opinions of them based on what she'd learned about their mother, and Katie didn't sound like the kind of person capable of caring for herself, let alone her kids. She'd truly anticipated meeting juvenile delinquents and had been fully prepared to tell Jet and Rae to go to hell. Then the look of delight on Andre's face when he first saw her had melted her heart, and the hug he'd given her weakened her knees. She was smitten.

In the two hours they'd been together, Nic had seen that Chloe and Andre were two intelligent, well-mannered kids. The unsavory details Detective Young had shared and the news accounts she'd heard about Katie just didn't jibe with what she was seeing. Something was off here, and knowing that made Nic even more confused about her feelings for their mother. It would be easy to walk away and avoid Katie if she were truly the woman who'd been described to her. Could Jet and Jeannie's version be closer to the truth than she wanted to admit?

It was all so overwhelming Nic was truly grateful that Katie was in the SICU and she didn't have to worry about it just yet. Things had a way of sorting themselves out, and she hoped that with time they would.

"You're welcome, guys," she said, clearing her throat of the tears forming there.

Their first stop was at the snake habitat, followed by polar bears, giraffes, monkeys, and a variety of big cats. They saw the city from a hundred feet up in a replica hot-air balloon and then ate ice cream in the shade of a giant oak tree. They saw a lemur exploring the new Treetop Trail, a walkway for animals suspended above them, winding its way around the entire zoo. Nic was exhausted by the time they left and wondered, not for the first time, how parents kept up with their children. But they had been polite and well behaved, inquisitive and enthusiastic. In spite of her fatigue, Nic knew as they walked through the gate on the way to the car that she would bring them back to the zoo anytime.

After making sure everyone was buckled in, Nic leaned back and took a deep breath. She was fucking exhausted. The dashboard clock now read 5:05. How could it be only 5:05? "Are you guys hungry?" she asked. It had only been a few hours since lunch, but they'd hopped around the zoo like kangaroos and certainly worked up an appetite.

They answered yes and no simultaneously, and Nic was amazed at how many times they'd wanted to go in separate directions in their short time together. Keeping them on the same page was a challenge.

"Well, we're going to have to eat tonight. How's pizza sound?"

When they agreed, she pulled out of the zoo parking lot and into the rush-hour traffic. The roads were crowded even heading into the city, and it was forty minutes before they were seated at the restaurant. She'd texted Louis and asked him to join them, but he was understandably tired after his night on call and asked only that Nic be kind enough to bring leftovers for his dinner, because he wasn't up to the challenge of cooking.

Chloe and Andre showed no signs that the eventful forty-eight hours was affecting them. Chloe continued to mother him, and they remained pleasant in spite of the occasional flash of sibling rivalry. Andre tended to whine, and Chloe's tactic of ignoring him seemed to be the perfect remedy.

"Do you ever make pizza?" Nic asked as they sat waiting for theirs, playing with straw wrappers to see who could create the best design out of the long strip of thin paper.

"I'm a great pizza chef," Andre said. "And I don't make a mess."

"That's probably the most important thing," Nic replied. "What do you like to put on your pizza?"

"My favorite thing is chicken," Chloe said.

"I like meatballs," Andre added.

"Get out. You guys are really creative. I usually just do pepperoni."

"Boring," Chloe commented.

"Tell me about the chicken pizza."

"Well, you cook the chicken in the oven, cut it in little pieces, sprinkle it on the pizza, and then put cheese and sauce on top."

"Oh," Nic said, "so it's kind of like chicken Parmesan."

"Yeah, that's what my mom calls it. Chicken-Parmesan pizza."

"And I guess Andre's is called spaghetti-and-meatball pizza."

He giggled at her clear display of ignorance, shaking his head. "No, there's no spaghetti, just meatballs. It's meatball pizza."

"And you're telling me that tastes good?"

"Really good," Chloe said.

"Great," Andre added.

"Well, guys, I hope you aren't too disappointed with this plain old cheese-and-pepperoni pizza I ordered for us."

"Pizza is still good, even without meatballs."

Just a little while later, the server brought their pizza to the table and Andre's prediction proved accurate; the pizza was good, even without meatballs. The busy day had stimulated all of their appetites, and Nic was worried there wouldn't be any left over for Louis. There was, though, and when she paid the check and walked back to her car, she was happy to see it was close to seven. The finish line was in sight, and she was going to cross it in one piece.

With full bellies and tired legs they crossed the threshold into Nic's apartment, each of them hauling bags filled with the treasures they'd collected at the store. They were greeted by Louis, who, in spite of the fatigue Nic knew he must be feeling, jumped from the couch to help with their load of packages. "Where were you in the parking lot?" Nic teased him.

"Just hand over the food and be quiet," he ordered, then turned his attention to Chloe and Andre, whose ceaseless chattering suddenly halted. "Hi, guys. I'm Louis," he said, and shook their hands. "And you must be Chloe," he said as he pointed to Andre.

This drew a smile as Andre shook his head. "I'm Andre. That's Chloe," he said, and pointed toward his sister.

"Well, I've heard all about you guys and it's nice to meet you. Did you buy me anything?" he asked as he pointed to the shopping bags.

Both children shook their heads apologetically.

"Yes, we did," Nic replied. "Close your eyes."

As Louis closed his eyes, Nic removed a tube of toothpaste and a can of air freshener from one of the bags and gave them to the children, who began giggling at the absurd gifts they were about to present. "Okay, you can open them now."

His laughter was as genuine as theirs as he accepted his presents.

"I really needed these. Thanks. Do you want to show me what you guys bought?"

As the kids began pulling things out of bags, Nic looked at Louis. "How is she?" She silently mouthed the words so Chloe and Andre wouldn't hear.

"Extubated."

Nic didn't know why she felt such relief to know that someone she'd never even met was breathing on her own, but she was. Removing the ventilator was a great sign that Katie was stabilized and would survive. He didn't need to tell her anything else, and she simply nodded, but inside, her heart was pounding at the news.

He smiled and winked at Nic. "Why don't you get a shower or something? I can handle them for a little while."

Nic raised both hands to her lips and blew him a kiss. "I love you so, so much," she said as she ran the other way, not giving him the opportunity to change his mind.

As the warm water spread over her, Nic didn't feel revived but exhausted. A million questions raced through her mind. How could she do this again tomorrow? Or the next day? How did Katie do this every day? How long would Katie be in the hospital? Who was Katie, really—the drug addict, dealer, and murderer the news had described or the woman who was raising two delightful children? What would Nic do about work? She worked part-time, twenty hours a week, which in her ER schedule equated to five shifts every two weeks. She wasn't due back until Monday, for an evening shift. It would be a royal pain in the ass to switch, so in the next few days she had to figure out a plan.

Maybe she should take the kids to the lake. The weather was warm. What better way for kids to spend their summer days than jumping off the dock and splashing each other in the water? It was how she'd spent her childhood, and those were some of her fondest memories. She only had two kayaks, but they could paddle them around the dock while she watched, and if they were really good, she'd take them on the Jet Ski. They could run around in the yard without fear of abduction and climb a tree and hike in the woods. She might even take them to Ricketts Glen, the state park just a short drive from her house. They had trails that followed magnificent waterfalls through the mountainside, and some were short enough for the kids to endure. It would be good for them to go to the mountains. Mostly, though, it would be good for her to be home.

The past day and a half had been more stressful than any ER shift she'd ever worked, and she felt like she could climb into bed and sleep for twenty-four hours. The city stressed her, with its noise and traffic and Katie Finan lying in a hospital bed just a few miles away. She'd talk to Jet, and as long as she didn't object, Katie would take the kids home.

And why would Jet object? She clearly felt the need to be at Katie's side, and as good as her intentions were about Chloe and Andre, she couldn't be in both places at once. Jet needed help. And besides, the judge had put her in charge of the kids, so she felt a responsibility to take care of them. Even if Jet told her she didn't have to, she couldn't escape the burden she had, for better or worse, agreed to carry.

As she toweled off and donned her pajamas, the sound of laughter filtered in from the living room. She ran a brush through her long wet hair and went to investigate. They were all gathered around the television, Wii remotes in their hands as they guided Mario and Luigi through a maze of deadly turtles and Venus flytraps. To her delight, Rae was with them. She smiled as Nic met her gaze, and Nic couldn't control the butterflies that fluttered in her stomach. Rae had told her she'd stop by later, but in the chaos, she'd completely forgotten. What a perfect ending to her day.

"So you're still alive," she said. The remote cast aside, she stood and walked toward Nic. "How bad was it?" she whispered.

"I'm fucking exhausted, thanks for asking." But Nic smiled, and Rae did, too. "Would you like a drink? I'm sticking to water tonight or I'll pass out, but I'd be happy to get something for you. I still have that Shiraz you liked, the one from Jordan."

Rae teased her. "I've never been to Jordan."

"So I've heard." Nic teased her back. Suddenly, she wanted nothing more than to visit the Middle East and drink wine with Rae. That would have to wait, though. She had children to think about. "What would you like? To drink."

"Just water for me, too."

Nic noticed Rae discreetly assessing her pajamas. The loose

silky tank and Capri-length pants were made more for comfort than to impress, and she was suddenly self-conscious about her attire and the wet mop of hair that must have looked dreadful. "Please excuse my appearance, Rae. I'm ready for bed."

Rae smiled. "I kind of like the wet look."

Nic sucked in a breath and their eyes locked, the pounding in her ears deafening. They held, until Andre tugged frantically at Nic's arm, breaking the spell.

"We have a surprise!" he announced.

"Andre, hush!" Chloe said.

"What are you guys up to?" Nic asked, squinting at them.

"Hold on, hold on," Louis told Nic and Rae, and then he addressed the kids. "Come on, guys."

Rae arched a questioning brow in Nic's direction, and they both looked toward the kitchen, listening to the muted voices that seemed to be plotting some larcenous activity. And then Andre dimmed the lights and the three of them emerged, their faces glowing in the flickering light of thirty birthday candles.

Nic bit her lip and held back tears of joy. The day had been unlike any other, filled with so much excitement she'd forgotten it was her birthday. Had she fielded calls from anyone at all, they might have reminded her, but she'd been too busy playing the role of AJ and had avoided everyone.

It took three blows to extinguish the inferno, even with Andre and Chloe's assistance, and then the five of them sat on the floor around the coffee table and devoured an ice-cream cake. When they were done, Rae helped with the cleanup.

She and Rae talked for a few minutes in the privacy of the kitchen before returning to the living room to watch the action. Both Chloe and Andre seemed to know their way around all the worlds of the Mario Brothers and were thrilled to be playing. Nic was startled when the house phone rang, and she saw it was after eight. The lobby guard was calling to announce Jet's arrival, and Nic gave permission for her to come up to the apartment.

Jet proved a more powerful lure than the Mario Brothers, and Chloe and Andre abandoned their remotes as they rushed into her arms. Louis took the opportunity to excuse himself; after forty hours of consciousness he was ready to sleep. Jet helped the kids with their baths while Nic and Rae removed the tags from their clothing and folded them into neat stacks, which she then placed in piles on the chaise lounge in her room. She supposed she'd give the children her bed and sleep with Louis; she doubted she could separate them.

"I'm going to lie down with them," Jet said when they were both done showing off their new pajamas.

"Night, AJ," Andre said as he waved to her.

"Night," Chloe said.

Nic smiled at them both. "Good night."

Rae poked her as they walked back to the couch. "AJ?"

"Yeah." Nic explained the logic.

Rae tried not to laugh. "That's RS."

Nic frowned. "What's RS?"

"Really sweet."

Nic took the pillow beside her and hit Rae with it before resting back with her feet on the ottoman. She looked at Rae and frowned. "I'll be more careful in the future. I don't want to ruin my reputation as a shark." After their laughter died down, Nic told her the plan to take the kids to the lake.

"It's a great idea. It'll probably be a few days before they can get into their house, and this is no place for kids." She waved her arms around.

"I'm just nervous. What if I can't handle them?"

Rae looked into her lap before she spoke. "You know, I'm on vacation starting tomorrow and will be in West Nanticoke for the week. I can help out a little."

Nic grunted. "What, no trip to Jordan planned?"

Rae's face saddened as she shook her head. "No, no trips." She cleared her throat and found Nic's eyes. "My dad was diagnosed with cancer a few months ago. He's still getting his treatments, so I've been trying to go home as much as I can."

Nic closed her eyes. "I'm such a jerk. I'm sorry."

"No, not your fault."

"What kind of cancer?"

"Colon. He's got a great prognosis, and he's doing well, so no need to be glum. I'm just trying to spend more time with them, you know?

We take our parents for granted, and then something like this happens and you say, 'Holy shit. They're not going to be around forever.'"

Nic nodded and covered Rae's hand with her own. "I'm so mad at my parents. But I know you're right. I still love them. And, they're all I have other an aunt and an uncle and a few scattered cousins. When my parents die, I'll be alone, Rae."

"Do you think you want kids?"

"Honestly, I've never even thought I'd be in a relationship." She didn't add *until now*, although that was how she felt. Rae made her feel, and that in itself was amazing, such a change from her typical reaction to new people. "I spent so much time alone as a kid I never really learned how to play well with others. I have friends, don't get me wrong. I'm not antisocial. I just feel most comfortable with myself." She laughed. "Except for Louis. He got under my skin and grew there, kind of like a fungus."

"He has that ability."

"He does. If only he didn't have a dick, he'd be perfect for me."

Rae laughed and rested back against the couch. "I feel the same way about him. But for the record, I don't have one."

"Is that supposed to be a sales pitch?"

Rae faced Nic and put her hand over hers. The look on her face displayed the fear she felt at making this confession. "I'd like to see you again, Nic. You're a pain in the ass, but I like you anyway."

"Your pitch is improving."

"I've been rehearsing all day. So, do you want to get together some time this week?"

"Like a date? Are you asking me on a real date?"

"Yeah, I am."

"I don't know, Rae. I have kids to think about now." Her tone was teasing but she kept a straight face, the whole time thinking about the pleasant shock she'd had earlier when Rae had kissed her.

"Well, this would be a first for me, dating a woman with kids. But I'm willing to try it. I have two nieces, and I've never allowed either of them to starve or break a bone under my watch."

"Any concussions or communicable diseases?"

"Well…"

Nic laughed and then smiled at her, deciding to admit what she was feeling. "I'd like to see you, too, Rae. And help with the kids would be a bonus. If Jet agrees, I'll take them home tomorrow. When are you heading back?"

"Saturday morning. I'll catch up on some things at the office before I leave, because otherwise they'll haunt me while I'm gone."

"How about Sunday, then? Have you ever hiked Ricketts Glen?"

Rae's face lit up. "I love it there."

"Perfect." She nodded her head toward her bedroom door. "Let's check with Jet."

Nic walked across the room and into the foyer that led to her bedroom, and quietly opened the door. The light was off, but the light behind her lit the room enough for her to see within. Jet was fast asleep, her feet hanging off the bottom of Nic's queen-size bed. In each arm she held a child, both of them asleep as well.

Closing the door behind her, she walked back into the living room. "You can always sleep at my place again," Rae offered when she told her about the slumber party in her bed.

Nic sat and turned, looking at her. She'd had an unbelievable forty-eight hours, starting with the awful time the two of them had spent on the evening they'd met. So much had happened since then, and something in Nic had changed. It was hard to describe, but suddenly she understood her discontent. Her life, with all of its wonders and blessings, lacked laughter. Louis had made her laugh, had truly enriched her life, and that was why she loved him so much. Now he wasn't a part of her world anymore, not on a regular basis, and she missed him and the joy he brought. Chloe and Andre made her laugh, and the feeling was wonderful. And Rae, with her sarcasm and insight and tremendous wit, made her laugh as well. Nic wanted to keep laughing. She wanted to see Rae again, to explore what might happen if she let down her guard and allowed someone to get close.

"If I sleep at your place again, Rae, I won't be spending the night on the couch."

Rae's jaw dropped, and she didn't say a word before Nic spoke again. "Now, I think you should go. I need my sleep. I'm exhausted, and I fear my niece and nephew will be up before the roosters."

She walked Rae to the door, and this time when they reached the threshold, it wasn't awkward at all. Nic reached up and gently stroked

Rae's cheek, then placed a soft kiss on her lips. It wasn't frantic like the earlier one, just a soft brush of her lips against Rae's, with no tongues probing or arms encircling, but it was electrifying just the same. It wasn't passionate, but it was full of promise and left her hopeful about what the coming days would bring.

# CHAPTER TWENTY-SEVEN
# MOUNTAIN AIR

Footsteps in the house caused Nic to sit up, and in the dim light of the lamp she saw Andre approaching her as she rested on the couch. It had been another exhausting day, and, even though it was only ten at night, she was tired.

Jet had wholeheartedly agreed with Nic's plan to take the kids to the mountains. Katie was making progress, taking liquids now and getting out of bed, but Jet was still stressed. She'd have to go back to work Monday, and afterward she'd want to spend time with Katie at the hospital. Even if the kids stayed in Philadelphia, she'd probably only see them at bedtime. And after spending the night at Nic's fifteenth-floor apartment, blocks away from the nearest park and with no place to ride bikes or throw balls, they needed to do something. Katie's house was still off-limits. Jeannie had offered them her house in Mount Airy, and Nic would have loved to spend time with Jeannie's kids Sandy and Bobby, who rented the house from their mom, but she would still have had to come up with an agenda for them. At the lake, they didn't need one. The kids would never be bored.

Jet had also suggested a marvelous though intimidating option—that Nan go to the mountains with the kids. They knew her, and she knew them, and it would make it easier on everyone to have her along. It also meant another person in Nic's well-protected personal space, but in the end she decided the benefits outweighed the inconveniences. Besides, Katie was making such progress, it was likely she'd be heading to the mountains herself by the middle of the week, and Nic would no longer have to worry.

She'd picked up Nan at nine, and even after a stop at the grocery store, they were settling in at Nic's place by noon. Nic nearly had a heart attack when she saw Andre sit at the bench of her piano—it was *her* piano—but before she could stop him, he played the opening notes of Beethoven's Fifth Symphony. While Nan put away groceries, Katie stood in stunned silence as he flawlessly performed the piece from memory. Chloe followed his performance with her own piece, and Nic had to once again pinch herself to make sure she wasn't dreaming.

The weather had cooperated for a day on the water, and the kids had loved every minute of it. They'd done cannonballs off the dock, slid on the slide, and paddled around in the kayaks. The fire pit was lit at dinnertime, and they'd cooked hot dogs over the open flame and then roasted marshmallows. At dusk the kids ran around with jars catching fireflies, while Nic and Nan enjoyed the fire. Fatigue spared none of them, and they'd all fallen asleep soon after showering and changing for bed. Nan was in one guest room, while Chloe and Andre were sharing another.

All in all, it had been an absolutely fabulous day.

"AJ, I think I broke my toe," Andre said as he limped toward her.

"How'd you do that?"

"I don't know, but it hurts."

Nic turned up the wattage on the lamp. Laying him on the couch, with his foot in her hands, she examined the toe. It wasn't red or swollen, and wasn't tender when she compressed the bone. But when she looked on the plantar surface, she found a large sliver. "I see the culprit, pal. It's a sliver, probably from the deck. Stay here. I'll be right back."

Nic hunted in her medical kit for the proper gear and then retrieved a roll of plastic wrap from the kitchen. Squeezing a dollop of a numbing cream from the tube, she smeared it on the toe and wrapped it up tight. She sat back on the couch and tickled his other foot while they waited for the medication to provide adequate anesthesia for a painless surgical procedure.

"Tell me a story, AJ," he suggested.

"Hmm, let's see. What kind?"

"You get to pick."

To her surprise, he swiveled on the couch and climbed into her arms, resting his head against her chest. She cradled him, surprised at the softness of his hair and the familiarity of his scent. He'd used her verbena shower gel instead of the baby wash she'd purchased for him. Oh, well, she thought, it's only thirty bucks a bottle. He smelled wonderful.

Nic squeezed him, thinking about the past few days and all the wondrous things that had happened to her. "Once upon a time, there was a princess who—"

"What was her name?"

Nic hadn't thought of that. What was her name? Her friends on the tennis team had called her Jersey, because her initials were NJC, and sometimes she used that when she met women at bars or other large social gatherings. "Jersey, her name was Jersey. An evil sorcerer cast a spell on her, a spell that made her sad. And—"

"Why did he do that?"

Nic pulled back and looked into his brown eyes, wide with wonder. "He's an evil sorcerer, Andre. It's his job."

"Oh."

"So, she was sad. Even though she lived in a beautiful castle—"

"Was there a moat?"

Nic thought of the lake. "Yes, a large moat, and she had a Jet Ski to ride across it. And she had everything she wanted—a nice car—"

"I thought princesses had horses."

"This is a modern princess. She also has a job. But she wasn't happy, because of the evil spell. Then one day, she met a little prince. He was very little," she said.

"Did an evil sorcerer cast a spell and make him little?"

"No, he was little because he was only six years old."

"Just like me. I'm six years old."

"Yep. Do you want to hear more?"

"Yeah, what was his name?"

"His name was Andre."

"I can't believe this. What happened then?"

"The prince was very happy. He loved to play and run and swim and eat hot dogs and play the piano, and just watching him made the princess feel better."

"So was the spell broken?"

"No, not yet. But then, one day, he gave the princess the biggest hug ever, and she could feel all of his joy coming out through his fingers and his hair and his smile, and all of the joy shattered the spell, and then the princess was happy."

"Did they get married?"

"Andre, the prince was only six years old. And the princess didn't really want to get married, anyway. Now let's see that toe."

Nic carried him to her kitchen and let him sit on the island, where the lighting was best. After testing the toe to ensure it was numb, she used diamond-tipped tweezers to open the skin and grasp the splinter. After removing it in one piece, Nic scrubbed the wound with antibacterial soap and studied it under magnification, looking for smaller fragments that might lead to infection. When she was satisfied that none remained, she put a bandage on the toe and carried him back to his bed.

"How does it end, AJ?"

"The prince came to see the princess often, and they ate hot dogs and rode the Jet Ski and played video games, and they were both happy and lived happily ever after."

"That's a great story, AJ."

Their eyes were just about level with him sitting on her hip as she carried him. His were full of wonder and excitement, even at the late hour, when they should have been clouded with fatigue. "I love you, AJ," he said as he wrapped his arms around her in one of those magical hugs that broke spells of sadness.

"I love you, too. Now go to sleep, or you may turn into a frog."

Carefully, she deposited him on the bed beside his sleeping sister and pulled the blanket up to his chin, then kissed him on the nose. As she closed his bedroom door, her phone began to ring.

A smile formed when she saw the caller ID. Rae. "Hi," she said.

"Can I see you?" Rae asked.

"What? Where are you?"

"On the turnpike, a few miles from the Wilkes-Barre exit, and as I get closer and closer to home I've forced myself to admit the truth. I told myself I should leave tonight so I wouldn't have to drive in the morning—I could just get up and relax. But I really wanted to be nearer to you. So since I've come all this way, can I see you?"

"Are you out of your mind?" she asked. Or am I out of mine? It was late, she was tired and ready for bed, and she'd like nothing more than to see Rae.

"I think perhaps I am. Yes. I am."

She smiled the sincerity in Rae's voice, understanding Rae's need—she felt it, too. "Well, I'm a doctor, you know. I spent a month in the outpatient psych clinic. Perhaps I can offer some therapy." Her tone was teasing, and Rae sounded relieved.

"Well, Doc, there's this girl. And she's beautiful, and smart, and funny, but she's tough as nails, too, so I'm not quite sure how she feels about me."

"How do you feel about her?"

"I like her, Doc."

"Then I'd say you should call her. If she invites you over, she probably likes you, too."

"Okay, thanks for the advice. Send me a bill. No, don't. This makes us even. I'll talk to you later. Bye."

Nic heard silence on the other end as Rae disconnected. "What the hell?" she said, staring at her phone in confusion. It rang as she was looking at it, and Rae's face appeared on the screen. "Did you just hang up on me?"

"Can I come over?"

"What?"

"My shrink said that if you invite me over, it means that you like me."

"Rae, you're inviting yourself over. I don't think it's the same."

There was no reply, just silence.

"Rae? Did I lose you?"

"No, I'm here, waiting for you to invite me over."

Nic cleared her throat and laughed. "Rae, would you like to come over tonight?"

"Okay!"

"Do you know where I live?"

"Lake Silkworth?"

"Yep. Do you know where that is?"

"As a matter of fact, I do. I just don't know which house belongs to you."

Nic gave her the details. "I should go now. I have to put some clothes on."

"Oh, you don't have to get dressed on my account."

"Behave."

"See you soon."

"Drive safely," Nic said before turning off the phone.

To her amazement, despite the fact that she'd awakened this day with the responsibility of two small children, added a frail senior citizen to the party, and then drove two and a half hours home, she hadn't had a cigarette all day. A few times she'd wanted one, but she'd suppressed the urge, and with the constant chatter and activity, she'd practically forgotten about smoking. She'd been busy getting everyone settled into their rooms, then chasing the kids off the dock and teaching them to swim.

As she smelled her hair, for the first time in as long as she could remember, she didn't need to wash away the lingering stench of smoke. She would brush her teeth, just in case her lips found the occasion to brush across Rae's, a possibility she sincerely hoped for. With her teeth clean, she slipped into a pair of shorts and her favorite Scranton shirt and then surveyed the house. It gave no hint that two small children had spent the day here. They were as neat as Nic, picking up after themselves and putting things in their proper places. The same went for Nan. As far as houseguests went, she couldn't have found a neater group.

She turned on the landscaping lights in the front of her house, then walked out and sat on the porch steps. The night was warm, the sky was clear, and the stars were out in full force. Even if Rae wasn't coming, she should have been outside enjoying this. But she was tired. These kids were wearing her out, and without the adrenaline rush fueled by Rae's call, she'd probably have been asleep by now.

Headlights weren't a rare sight on a Friday night in the summer at the lake, but the slow pace of the set approaching her told her they likely belonged to Rae's car. She stood and waved as the car approached, and Rae stopped, rolling down her window.

"Hi, there. Did someone here order a pizza?"

"Pepperoni?"

"Nope. Meatball."

Nic laughed. She'd shared that story with Rae the night before. "You've got the right place."

Rae smiled and pulled into the driveway, parking just at the edge of the walkway where Nic was approaching. She hopped out of the car and encircled Nic in her arms, and before Nic had a chance to say a word, Rae's mouth was on hers. Just as quickly, Rae pulled back, leaving Nic breathless and wanting more.

"Well, hello to you, too," Nic said.

"It's good to see you. I know it's only been twenty-four hours, but I've forgotten what you look like."

"You could have gone next door and stolen a picture."

"I did."

Nic was mortified. "Did you really?"

Rae chuckled. "No. I'm not that desperate."

"I won't comment. But would you like to come inside? Have a drink? Go out on my deck? I was just stargazing at this wonderful sky."

"The deck sounds great, and maybe some water."

"Just water? I have a few bottles of wine and some hard stuff, too."

"No, just water. Do you have lemon?"

"I happen to have some limes. Would that do?"

They walked into the kitchen, and Nic poured water over ice for both of them and garnished both glasses with lime wedges.

"Where are the kids?" Rae asked.

"Snoozing. Would you like to peek in on them?"

Nic guided Rae up the stairs and to the bedroom where Chloe and Andre were sleeping. Boards creaked in the old stairs, echoing through the silent house, threatening to wake them, but when Nic opened the door, the hall light creeping in revealed them both to still be asleep. Chloe was spooning Andre, her arms lovingly wrapped around him.

"Oh, look at them. It's so sweet," Nic whispered.

"She's really protective of him, isn't she?" Rae asked as they closed the door once again.

"Yes. She watches him like a hawk."

"Is she getting comfortable with you?" Rae asked as she followed Nic back down the stairs.

"She's tolerating me. Having Nan helps—Chloe seems to adore her. But Andre is my new best friend. I can't go to the bathroom without him."

"A shadow, huh?"

"Yep."

"How's their mother?"

"A little better. Sipping liquids, getting out of bed, sitting in the chair. We're going to do a video chat tomorrow if she's out of ICU."

"Does she know about you yet?"

"No. Jet didn't want to stress her any more, and I don't blame her. As long as Katie knows her kids are safe, she doesn't need to know who they're with." Nic slid open the door to the deck and stepped out, leaving it open an inch so she could hear her guests if they awakened. She seated herself on one of the chairs, and Rae was about to follow suit when she noticed Nic's hammock.

"May I?" she asked.

"Be my guest."

Rae handed over her glass of water and then eased herself into the hammock. Once settled, she could enjoy an unobstructed view of about a million stars. "Wow," she said softly. "What a view."

Nic leaned back in her chair to share the sight. "Yeah, it's pretty amazing, isn't it?"

They were quiet then, enjoying the night, with only the soundtrack of nature filling the silence.

"How was your day?" Nic asked, not just curious, but concerned. Rae had been sacrificing sleep and time for her, and there had to be a price to pay for it.

"Work was productive. It seems this drug ring in Philly may be imploding. The bullets that hit Katie and killed Wallace are probably from the same gun used to kill a parking attendant in a garage downtown. He was a known dealer, too."

"So three of them? Any others?"

"It doesn't look like it. But three shootings in less than a day is sort of a crisis."

"Is this a good time for you to take off?"

"It's up to the police for now. I'll come in later."

"It sounds dreadful."

"It is, Nic. So many lives are destroyed—people like Katie who seem to be caught in the crossfire—"

"Do you know that for sure? Is she really innocent?"

"Nic, Katie has had her share of troubles, but it seems that she really got herself together when she was pregnant with Chloe. She's been squeaky clean since then."

"Hmm."

After a while, Rae spoke. "So, anyway, about Katie. I think that's a good idea, to not tell her about you right now. She's dealing with enough."

"Yeah, she sure is."

"How are you doing?"

"I'm just going with the flow. They're actually really easy. They swam the day away, and when I made them get out of the water, they chased each other around the yard. Tomorrow we're going to some yard sales to see if we can find used bikes, and then we'll ride around the lake. Simple stuff. No stress."

"That's great, Nic."

"AJ, the name is AJ."

"Sorry, AJ."

"Their mother has raised them well, Rae. They're great kids."

"That's good to know, huh? She can't be all bad if she has good kids."

"I suppose not."

"Speaking of mothers, have you spoken to yours?"

Nic groaned and closed her eyes. "No. Jeannie must have called them before I left the hospital that night, because I had my first message when I got home, and about fifty since then, from both my parents. And a few from Jeannie, too. I don't want to talk to any of them. I don't know what I feel. I don't know what to feel. Until I do, I'd rather just not deal with it."

"I'm guessing they all love you. You'll work it out. Maybe you just need more time."

"Of course they love me. I know that. That doesn't make this okay, though."

"When you have kids, you'll probably do things that piss them off. I think it's part of the parent-child relationship."

"Hmm."

"Do you want to hear the story of how I learned about my dad's cancer?"

"If you want to tell me."

"Okay, I'll share. It was a Monday night, and I'd just gotten home from the office. I sat down to watch the news—I was still wearing my suit, just put my feet up, and my phone rang. I looked at the caller ID. It was my friend Mary Jane—one of my closest childhood friends. She still lives in West Nanticoke and she's an OR nurse in Wilkes-Barre. She doesn't call me often, so I figured something was up, and I answered.

"Shc started talking as soon as she heard my voice. 'How come you didn't tell me about your dad? I saw his name on the OR schedule for tomorrow and changed room assignments so I can be in on his case.'

"So I took a deep breath and leaned back, thinking. I didn't want her to know I had no idea what she was talking about, so I just pretended I did. I was hoping he was having some minor wart removal or something, but the fact that she was calling was a concern. 'How long do you think the surgery will take?' I asked.

"'Oh, it could be anywhere from two to four hours, depending on if the tumor is stuck to stuff.'" Rae turned to Nic. "I'm using layman's terms here, of course.

"'Are you on your way home yet?' she asked.

"'I'm packing now,' I said, and I was by that time. I called my brother in California and he had no idea. Then my sister who lives in the house next door, and neither did she. Two hours later, I was sitting in their living room, crying, and they were mad at me for taking the day off from work to come home. They told me they planned to tell us after the surgery, when they had more information. They were trying to protect us."

"Have you forgiven them?"

"Of course. They're my parents. What choice do I have? I'm never getting any more so I have to make it work with them."

"Good point."

"So you should call your parents, Nic."

"I'll think about it," she said, stifling a yawn.

"Do you want to lie in my hammock with me? It's very cozy."

"Actually, I think I should go to bed. I can't keep my eyes open."

Rae sat up and hung her legs over the side. "Any big plans for tomorrow?" she asked.

"Yard sales in the morning, biking and swimming in the afternoon. I'd invite you to join us, but I know you want to catch up with your parents."

Rae made a funny sound. "Tsk. They're not home. My mom called last night and told me they were going to the Finger Lakes for wine-tasting this weekend. Someone invited them on a bus trip and off they went."

"You poor baby," Nic said. "Stood up by your parents is pathetic."

Rae nodded in agreement. "Tell me about it."

Nic looked across at her—black hair melting into the night around her, eyes dark shadows on her beautiful face, mouth upturned at the corners in a hint of a smile—and her heart skipped a beat. "You can always stay here, you know."

Rae's smile was so bright it was evident even in the darkness. "I happen to have my jammies in the car."

"Well go get 'em."

Nic rinsed their glasses and put them into the dishwasher, and that quickly Rae was back, a duffel bag dangling from her hand. "Ready?" she asked, and when Rae nodded, she steered her up the stairs to her bedroom. While Rae sorted through her bag, Nic slipped into the bathroom and changed back into the pajamas she'd been wearing before Rae had called. Then she brushed her teeth, turned off the light, and walked back into her bedroom.

The sight of Rae there, standing beside her bed, wearing only cotton boxers and a tank top, caused Nic to stop moving. Rae turned slowly, a smile lighting her face. It lit up Nic's heart, too. She'd never felt this sort of attraction before, and the force of it upset her equilibrium. She was tempted to push Rae back onto the bed and climb in with her, to take off her clothes and spend what was left of this day making love and to bring in the new day that way as well. Yet something inexplicable held her back, and so she simply smiled back and then pushed Rae—not onto the bed, but away from it.

"This is my side," she said as she pulled back the sheets and slipped beneath them. But a few minutes later, when Rae finished in the bathroom and lay next to her on the other side of the bed, Nic closed the gap between them and rested her head on Rae's chest, and the last thing she heard as she drifted to sleep was the comforting sound of Rae's breathing.

# CHAPTER TWENTY-EIGHT
# FORGIVENESS

Nic carefully wrapped potatoes in aluminum foil and carried them to the fire pit at the edge of her patio. It was late afternoon on a beautiful late-spring day, and this was her version of Sunday dinner. A small fire was blazing, and she placed the potatoes on its perimeter, where they'd slowly bake to perfection. Salad and barbeque chicken would complete the meal.

She could hear the sounds of laughter and splashing, and as she looked up, she saw the source. Rae, who'd been standing on the edge of the dock a minute earlier, was now in the water with Chloe and Andre. They were playing football with a waterproof ball, the kids jumping off the dock and catching passes from Rae in midair, holding tight to them to prevent fumbling as they landed in the water. Apparently, Rae had bent over a little too far in an effort to catch a return pass and had paid the penalty.

Pausing for a moment to watch them, Nic could hardly believe the turn her life had taken in just a few days. She'd gone from living alone to having an instant family, complete with the two kids, a beautiful woman, and a nanny. This was a scene of blissful domestication, and Nic figured they'd covered most things a typical family did together over the course of a lifetime in just four days. They'd suffered a tragedy, taken a trip, gone shopping, ridden bikes, eaten at McDonald's, removed a sliver, and were now preparing a cookout. Chloe had slowly come out of her shell, and now both kids were having a great time with Rae, and had been since they'd first awakened the day before.

Nic's Saturday morning had been wonderful, too. She'd awakened early to find Rae still asleep beside her, curled up on her side, the first hints of sunshine lighting her face. Nic could get used to seeing Rae in the mornings. That wasn't such a strange idea—having a woman in her bed. It wasn't expected, but it wasn't altogether out of the realm of possibilities. The family, though—that was a strange one. And what was even stranger was how good it felt to have them around.

Nic had spent more than two days as sole caregiver of her niece and nephew, and rather than finding herself anxious to return them to their rightful owner, she was savoring every minute of their time together. They'd video-chatted with their mother, and Nic knew Katie was recovering and would be discharged from the hospital soon, removing Chloe and Andre from this scene of domestic bliss. The thought was as unimaginable as taking custody had been a few days earlier.

She wasn't sure who'd be more devastated at their departure—her or Rae. Rae was a natural with them. They'd found a bike for her, too, and she'd raced around the lake with them. Rae had spent so much time in the water Nic feared she'd prune. And they'd matched her step for step on their hike past the falls at the state park. It had been a wonderful few days, and Nic tried not to think about how soon it might end.

A sound behind her startled her, and she turned to see a familiar pair walking down the stairs toward her patio. Her avoidance tactics had worked for a few days, but apparently, the game was over. Her heart raced and her breath caught, but Nic refused to let her tension show. She was ready to face them. Her parents were opinionated, overeducated, highly successfully people, though, and disagreements were rarely easy. She braced for the worst.

"Hi, Mom, hi, Dad," Nic said, and stood tall, meeting their gaze.

"How are you?" her mom asked.

Nic shrugged.

"I think your phone's broken," her dad teased her. "I've left you several messages, but you apparently haven't gotten any of them."

Her mother continued the atypical, lighthearted banter. "Mrs. Bloom wants to know what time the chicken will be ready."

Nic's jaw dropped at the mention of her nosy neighbor. Mrs. Bloom had been spying at the lake for about three hundred years, and nothing escaped her notice, but this was unbelievable. "How does she know it's chicken?"

"Someone saw you at the store. With *black* children. Buying chicken." Her mother whispered the word *black* for effect.

"I'm surprised the police haven't been here yet."

"I think they were, but you were out."

"Oh. My. God."

"I'm just teasing," Ann Coussart said, and then her voice softened, and so did her expression. "We came to apologize, Nicole. We should have told you about Katie. We're sorry. We thought we were protecting you—but we were wrong."

Nic closed her eyes, summoning the will to hold back her tears. She hadn't thought about this moment, but if she had, she would never have imagined it like this. Debate, yes. Reprimands, yes. Admission of guilt? Never. And then her parents did something else unprecedented—they hugged her, in broad daylight, on the lawn in plain view of a dozen boaters on the lake and Mrs. Bloom's binoculars. Her mom's arms wrapped around her, thin but strong, her frame just a few inches taller than Nic's, and her father engulfed them both, wrapping his long arms around their shoulders as he kissed the top of Nic's head. She wasn't sure what made her happier—the hug or the fact that they were giving it to her. "We love you, Nic," her father said.

"I know, Dad. I'm just having a hard time with all this. The… betrayal and the fact that my twin is in the SICU recovering from bullet wounds." Nic sniffled, no longer able to hold back the tears. "I always wanted a sister, you know?"

To their credit, they offered no further excuses; they simply acknowledged her feelings and validated them.

"Perhaps you always missed her, honey. Maybe on some subconscious plane you knew she was out there," her mom offered.

"Or maybe I was just a lonely only child."

"We did our best, Nic," her father whispered, not defensive, but perhaps sad that he'd let her down.

It saddened her to hear the defeat in the strong voice of the man whom she loved so much, and she was ashamed to have done that to him. She hadn't intended to hurt them, any more than they'd wanted to hurt her, and the irony was difficult to ignore. She couldn't do anything to change what they did, but she could control how she responded now.

They'd raised her well. "And you did a great job. Especially compared to the Finans."

"We would have taken both of you if we could have," her dad told her.

"I know. Jeannie told me the whole story. It's okay, really." Nic couldn't bear to see them so upset, and suddenly her anger faded as she realized how much she loved them and how lucky she was that such wonderful people had adopted her. No, the Coussarts weren't perfect parents, but they had always done what they thought was best for her. They'd tried her whole life to give her everything she needed, and most of what she wanted, and to guide her in the right direction. They provided her with love and opportunity and the tools to make something of her life. And she had. She might not have found personal happiness, but she'd done something good with her life, and it was in fact a wonderful life.

As she looked across the yard to the lake, where Rae and Chloe and Andre were playing, she thought that perhaps happiness might be in her grasp as well.

"Okay, knock it off, you two. You're going to confuse Mrs. Bloom. She's probably got binoculars trained on us. Come down to the lake. I want you to meet my niece and nephew."

"And how about the young lady? Who is she?" her father asked, his tone teasing once again.

Nic had been out to her parents since college, when she grew tired of their questions about boyfriends and decided to tell them about her girlfriend. Since then, she'd had many dates, and never had she brought a single one home to meet her parents. In fact, it was a rare occasion that a woman even came to her apartment in Philly. She preferred to meet people on their turf, so she was free to escape when she felt the need.

Her parents had politely inquired and occasionally kidded her, but had never pressured her about the women she was dating. Nic knew they were curious, but she suspected they were also concerned. They wanted her to settle down so they could die happy, and so far she wasn't cooperating.

"She's my lawyer," Nic said.

"Oh, no, what have you done?" her mother asked.

"Don't worry, Mom. It's all good."

"Hey, guys," she called to them from the edge of the lake, "come meet my parents."

They emerged from the water with skin the texture of raisins, and Rae rubbed a towel over a shivering Chloe as Nic gave Andre the same treatment.

"Are you going to be our grandparents?" he asked.

"Why not?" Ann replied, shocking Nic yet again.

She looked at her mom skeptically, wondering just how much her parents would do to get back into her good graces. They really didn't need to do anything—she'd already forgiven them—but it seemed they were going to make the effort anyway.

After chatting for a few minutes, Rae took the children into the house to bathe and change while her father prepared cocktails, and Nic talked to her mom.

"You seem to be adapting," she observed.

"It's been exciting. And exhausting. How do parents do this?"

"I suppose you're treating them with a little more attention than their mother does. She has to concentrate on things like homework and housework. You can just have fun."

"Well, all of this fun is wearing me out."

"When do you work?"

"Tomorrow afternoon."

"Who'll watch them?"

"Oh," Nic said, surprised. "You haven't met Nan. She's their sitter."

"Well, that's convenient."

"Yeah, it is. She's great."

"What about Rae?" Ann asked. She looked up at the sky and then flecked imaginary lint from her shorts, and her obvious disinterest told Nic just exactly how interested she was in the answer to her question.

"She'll help, too. The kids love her."

Her mother smiled at her. "I can see why. I like her very much, Nic."

"Me, too." That was about as much information as Nic had ever revealed to her mom about a date, and for the moment, it was all she was prepared to say. Each hour she spent with Rae seemed to strengthen the bond forming between them, and she was growing more comfortable with Rae and the idea of them together. The attraction between them was undeniable, but Nic had learned all too well that attraction faded quickly when there was no substance to support it.

For most of her life, that would have been fine. A brief affair with Rae would be passionate and fun, but now for the first time, Nic wanted more. She'd glimpsed what it might be like to be in a relationship with Rae, and she loved the pictures—Rae's strength in the face of adversity, the gentleness with which she'd held her, the sound words of advice she'd shared. For the first time since high school, when Virginia Yoon had broken her heart, she didn't feel alone.

All of the signs indicated that Rae was interested in more, too. She'd asked her to the Barnes and then for dinner. She'd comforted her after the disaster at the hospital. She came to find her, coerced her into taking Katie's kids, and had been helping her with them ever since. She had no obligation to be with Nic, and so Nic reasoned Rae was with her because she wanted to be.

Taking baby steps now seemed prudent as she waded into these unfamiliar waters. Yet the current of attraction was powerful, and for two nights she lay beside Rae and fought its pull, fought the impulse to scooch over beside her and kiss her senseless. And run her fingers through Rae's shiny black hair. Was it as soft as it looked? The brief kisses they'd shared had been teasers, but Nic could still feel her lips burning with their heat, and her stomach did flips anticipating a *real* kiss.

Disappointment filled her as she realized it probably wouldn't happen any time soon. Although they hadn't discussed it, Rae would probably be leaving tonight to go to her parents', and Nic knew she wanted to spend some quality time there. Perhaps later in the week, when the kids were gone, they might meet for lunch. Nic would be traveling back to Philly in a few weeks to help Louis pack for his move, and they might get together then. After that—who could tell?

Suddenly the idea of a long-distance relationship occurred to her. Was that really something she wanted to do? It had never been an option before, but with Rae, it might work. Perhaps it was the perfect solution to her dating troubles—a lover who she could see on a regular but limited basis, who gave her space and freedom but all the benefits—sex, a traveling companion, and a date for parties.

She looked to the early evening sky, avoiding her mother's gaze. That scenario suddenly didn't sound so great. She feared she wanted what she'd had for this wonderful weekend. A partner. And perhaps a couple of kids, too.

Her father handed her a cocktail, calling her out of her daydream, and she talked with her parents about Katie and the children. Jeannie had kept them up to date through the years, so they had an idea of her troubles, but they were as shocked as anyone to hear about her run-in with the bullets. Then Rae, Chloe, and Andre came scampering down to the patio, and all talk of their mother ceased. Nan followed them and was introduced to the Coussarts, and they all got to know each other while Nic put the chicken in a grill basket over the fire.

Their group of seven sat on the patio, enjoying Nic's efforts, and Nic realized it was the most animated dinner she'd ever shared with them. Her parents were much more reserved than the two children and friends who'd joined her family. Nic decided she preferred the current setting over the one she was used to, and she realized how much she'd changed in just a few days. When the cleanup was finished, she was sorry to see her parents leave.

"I guess you've forgiven them?" Rae asked after they'd put Chloe and Andre to bed. Nan retired before all of them, claiming exhaustion from exposure to clean mountain air, and so they were alone as they walked out onto the deck.

"It was good advice that you gave, Rae. I'm never going to have any other parents. I have to make it work."

"Have you ever thought of finding your biological mom?"

"All the time."

"So why didn't you?"

"I'm afraid of what I might find." Nic had read horror stories on the Internet about bad reunions with birth parents, and she was understandably cautious about initiating a search.

Rae was silent for a moment. "I guess I never thought of it that way, but I imagine it is a scary prospect."

Nic digested Rae's words. "Maybe someday. What I am looking forward to…don't laugh…is talking to Katie."

"Really?"

"Well, I have to try to make friends with her so I can see my niece and nephew from time to time." Nic didn't say that she was curious about Katie, too. She already knew they shared a love of cheeseburgers and women, but what other interests did they share? The idea of a sister was growing on her, and thanks to Rae, she might have an opportunity to actually meet Katie, and get to know her. Who could tell? They might actually share some common threads beyond DNA.

"That's a good enough reason for me. But you might actually like her."

"Maybe. How about you?" Nic asked, trying to divert the conversation away from the topic she wasn't quite ready to discuss. "Any plans to see your family on your trip to their house?"

Rae chuckled. "My parents won't be home till midnight. They're squeezing every last drop of wine out of those grapes."

"So I guess you'll be leaving soon."

"I suppose I should."

"I don't want you to go." Nic looked up and their eyes met, a gaze filled with heat and longing.

"Do you want to come in the hammock with me?" Rae asked.

Shaking her head, Nic stood and reached for Rae's hand. "Let's skip the hammock and go to my room."

Rae stood, and before Nic could blink, Rae's lips were on hers, singeing her with their heat, and Rae's tongue was in her mouth, gliding over Nic's with an ease that suggested they'd been doing this for years. Nic led her through the house and to her room, where she locked the door behind them. "I don't think I've ever locked this before. We're lucky it works," she said.

"I would have just shoved the bed against the door," Rae said, and then pushed Nic, gently, toward that bed.

Nic reached out to her, tugging Rae's shirt from her shorts, feeling the silkiness of her skin as she ran her fingers across the planes of her back and then her abdomen. Up and over she lifted the shirt, and then she softly kissed the place between her breasts, where her bra pushed them together in a tantalizing display of cleavage.

Nic moaned as she felt their softness, and again as Rae ran her fingers across Nic's shoulders and down her back and gently tugged on her shirt, pulling it up, forcing Nic to pull away. Their eyes met, pools of desire bubbling with heat, and then their lips found each other, too. The kiss was deep, but tender, as they cautiously explored each other's mouths. In seconds Nic's bra fell away, and she felt fire in the places Rae's hands touched her, along her flanks, and then her belly, and finally, her breasts. Tongues slid in slow, lazy circles around each other, and then Rae's hands dropped as she pulled her closer, allowing their breasts to graze each other. Her mouth never left Nic's, even as she grasped the waistband of her shorts and began sliding them down.

Nic stopped her by holding her hands and then pushing them away, and then, she stepped back and sensually slid them down over her hips, as Rae stood watching, anticipating. Rae took the hint and slid her own shorts down, then dropped to her knees before Nic, burying her face in the triangle of fabric that covered her. Rae reached up, cupped Nic's ass, and slowly pulled the underwear down, kissing the flesh as it was exposed, following the path until she had Nic on the bed, with no underwear to impede her, her mouth buried in the soft curls between her legs.

# Chapter Twenty-nine
# Going Out of Business

Simon sat at his desk, trying his best to follow the conversation between the computer wizards who kept Happy and Healthy Pharmacies running. It wasn't even eight a.m., and already he was bombarded with the problems that came with running a multimillion-dollar corporation. In their attempt to explain the most cost-effective remedy for a problem with one of their computer servers, they'd just confused him. He wouldn't admit that, though. He was the boss; therefore he was always right and always understood every facet of his business, no matter how complex the issues. To admit otherwise would have been a sign of weakness. Weakness would make him a target, and that would never do. He was the hunter, not the prey.

The men before him had no idea of the thoughts running through his head, and if they did, they themselves would have been running. None of the fifty employees in the building understood, and neither did the three hundred other people who worked at his pharmacies. His wife and children were clueless. The only one who understood was Angelica, and that was why at this moment she was preparing them to leave the country.

That Katie had survived his efforts to kill her not once, but twice, was reason enough for him to flee. That he'd shot a cop—even one wearing a bulletproof vest—was an even bigger incentive. One of his top distributors had been hauled in for questioning. He too was a parking attendant, and after the police linked the bullets in the shootings at the lawyer's office with the killing at the parking garage, things began to really get interesting. Simon assumed the man would talk to the police, which was yet another reason to hasten his retirement plans. The temperature in the kitchen was suddenly getting way too hot for comfort.

The risk really wasn't the parking attendant—although he could become a nuisance. The problem was Katie. On the streets he was known only as Simon, a person of his own creation, and only Angelica knew his real identity, until Katie had stumbled upon the truth, resulting in a ton of problems.

Her discovery was totally random, unpredictable, and unpreventable. He'd been in Rehoboth Beach with his family, strolling along the boardwalk like thousands of other tourists. When his son, Justin, asked for an ice cream, he didn't hesitate to queue behind the others at the vendor's window. Just as Katie turned around with her cones in hand, his wife had touched his arm. "Marc, we'll meet you at Funland," she'd said.

Katie had looked from his startled face to hers, offered a generic smile, then walked across the boardwalk to her own children.

Marc Simonson didn't resemble his alter ego Simon Simms in the slightest. Of course, he couldn't change his height, but the way Simon carried himself made him seem larger than he was. Bulky clothing helped in that regard as well. Other than the physical attributes, the two had few similarities. Their language, personalities, and manner of dress were all radically different. Simon was a street thug and acted the part. Marc was a nerdy but highly successful businessman. If he hadn't met Katie face-to-face, hadn't been so startled by seeing her in that setting, she probably wouldn't have guessed it was him. She would have gone home wondering about the similarities but ultimately would have dismissed them as simply too improbable. But instead of a calm, cool, reaction, he noticeably flinched when their eyes met, and he knew that she recognized him.

From the moment she walked away, cones in hand, he was left wondering how to handle the situation. A part of him had hoped he wouldn't have to kill her, but in the back of his mind he knew it would ultimately come to that. He couldn't rest with her knowing his secret. He'd been sitting at the bar, nursing a beer, when Billy walked in that fateful night. "Katie said she saw you at the beach. You workin' on your tan?"

Simon knew then that he had to act quickly. Who else would Katie talk to while he was trying to figure out what to do? He'd shot Billy and tried to kill her, yet she seemed impervious to his bullets. Now, he'd have to try again. No, he thought. He'd have to do it right this time. She was the only witness that any crime was committed, and eventually, she'd tell someone what she knew. The police might be able to trace him to the islands, and they might not, but it wasn't a chance he wanted to take. He'd worked too hard to allow a little detail like Katie Finan fuck up his plans. When he disappeared, there'd be no reason for anyone to look for him.

He'd already shut down his factory. His pharmacist had left with a severance package of $25,000 and no explanation. They'd wiped down the place, and the next day he'd begin moving the machinery, so all evidence of their illegal activity would be gone.

And tonight, he'd tell Heather that he wanted a divorce. Simple and clean was his goal. The money he had in his safe was enough to sustain him, if he could get it to the islands undetected. If not—well, he didn't want to think about that possibility.

Hopefully, Heather would his accept his reasons and allow him to walk away. He planned to offer his shares of the pharmacy as lifetime child and spousal support. She could have it all—more than a million dollars a year, and several million in equity, in exchange for his freedom.

"Just fix it!" he told the computer experts. "Cost isn't an issue." The bottom line of the Happy and Healthy Pharmacies no longer concerned him.

# CHAPTER THIRTY
# THE PIECES COME TOGETHER

Sunrays, filtered through the sheer fabric of her bedroom curtains, bathed Nic's face, and although the warmth was delightful, the brightness of the light blinded her. She pulled the down comforter up higher, shielding her face, and breathed deeply, intoxicated by the wonderful smell of…sex.

Even as her eyes flew open, she was rolling over in her bed, searching for Rae. Before disappointment could dampen her mood, someone knocked on the door and opened it. Rae, Chloe, and Andre entered. Rae was carrying a tray, Andre the newspaper, and Chloe a flower.

A chorus of "good mornings" greeted her.

She smiled at both kids, their faces glowing with happiness, and ran her hand across her chest to ensure she was properly dressed for this party. Fortunately, she was. Somewhere in the night, her pajamas had found their way onto her body, and she was relieved. Although, knowing Rae, she wouldn't have brought the kids into the room unless she was aware of that.

This was the day they'd be reunited with their mother. As happy as she was for them, Nic was a little sad for herself. Even though she'd known this day was coming, she hadn't been prepared for the feelings she now had to deal with.

After a busy evening in the ER, Nic arrived home in the early morning to find Rae in her bed and was overwhelmed with emotion. The little fantasy they'd been living was over.

As she cuddled with Rae, and made love with her, she'd thought about how great it would be to come to bed in the middle of the day, or to make love in the hammock, without fear of young eyes discovering them. Telling herself she was free to hike the long trails at Ricketts Glen, instead of the modified version they'd climbed with the kids, she tried to coerce herself into feeling happy. She'd eat what she wanted and do what she wanted, take a nap because she was exhausted, and she should be relieved that they'd be gone.

She wasn't, though. And long after Rae had succumbed to her fatigue and drifted off to sleep, Nic had stared into the darkness thinking about her niece and nephew, and their mother, and what she might do to keep them in her life.

Katie would arrive at Lake Wallenpaupack in the early afternoon. Jet had spoken to Rae and offered to pick the kids up, but since Katie was still weak, and her house was out of the intended travel route, Rae had offered to drop them off. Nic, of course, would go with her. Not only did she want to prolong her time with Chloe and Andre, but she also wanted to meet Katie.

Jet had told Katie that she had a twin, and apparently she'd handled that information with a whole lot more class than Nic had. Katie was shocked, of course, but after that initial surprise wore off, she was full of questions. Jet had warned Rae that Nic should be prepared for a thorough interrogation.

"This is for you," Chloe said, a huge smile on her face as she offered Nic a daisy, no doubt freshly picked from the garden in front of the house.

Nic smiled, brought it to her nose, and pronounced it beautiful, thrilled at the change she'd seen in her niece during the six days they'd been together. She opened her arms for a hug, and Andre pounced on her as well, followed by Rae. They formed a huge giggling ball of arms and legs bouncing on her bed. As she tickled Andre, Nic thought that bed had never been such a fun place as it was since these three people had entered her life.

"Okay, sleepyhead," Rae said, "it's time to get up. You're going to have a little breakfast and then a shower. We're going to my parents' for lunch."

"What time is it?"

"Ten."

"Wow, I must have been tired."

Rae grinned mischievously, and Nic blushed at the thought of what they'd done to cause such fatigue and how late they'd been up doing it.

Nic peeled the banana she'd received and ate her yogurt, complimenting the chefs on the meal they'd created. After a shower, she tried very hard not to cry as she helped Chloe and Andre pack their things. Rae loaded their bikes onto the rack on Nic's SUV, and by noon, Nic was following Rae to her parents' house, her car stuffed with children and a nanny and the ton of stuff they'd accumulated in just a few days.

Her sadness and the effort to hide it occupied her mind to such a degree that it wasn't until they approached West Nanticoke that she thought to be nervous about meeting Rae's parents. Mr. and Mrs. Rhodes knew their daughter had been spending her nights, and most of her days, with Nic, and from their intimate talks Nic knew that Rae wasn't in the habit of taking women home to meet her folks. Had it been her choice, Nic would have delayed this encounter for a few more days, or weeks, or months, but Rae had been so enchanted by Chloe and Andre that she wanted them to meet her parents, and circumstances dictated that the meeting be this day.

The Rhodes home was on a corner lot, and from a block away, Nic could see the huge R on the garage well, just as Rae had described. She couldn't suppress her laughter, and if Rae had been beside her they wouldn't have been fit to meet her parents. They'd have been rolling around in the grass giggling. Nan and Chloe and Andre didn't get the joke, though, and so the laughter died before she pulled into the driveway beside Rae.

The Craftsman Cottage she called home was immaculately maintained, with a pristine lawn and flower gardens, and a row of towering pines lining the perimeter near the road. Nic guessed the yard work was a chore for Rae's parents, especially since her father's illness, and wondered how they managed to keep the place looking so good during their travels.

She didn't have time to ponder the question further, as an Old English sheepdog came running toward the driveway and nearly knocked Rae onto her butt. Everyone in her car witnessed the attack, and the kids quickly joined Rae in chasing the big ball of fur around the yard. A man and a woman, looking much too young to be the parents of a thirty-five-year-old daughter, stood on the sidewalk enjoying the show. Nic helped Nan from the car, walked over to them, and introduced herself.

Rae looked just like her mom—same eyes, same hair, same coloring, same height. Her father wasn't much taller, but with lighter hair and skin. Nic could detect no resemblance until he began talking, and then Nic could see where Rae's energy and intelligence came from. He showed no signs that a cancerous tumor was trying to take over his body and every sign that he was determined not to let it.

After the introductions, Rich Rhodes led them around the house to his backyard, where a play set drew the kids' attention. After asking permission, they raced each other to the swings. Rae helped her mom with refreshments while Nan and Nic relaxed on a bench swing. Rae's sister joined them, and her two daughters scampered into the yard after Chloe and Andre.

Mrs. Rhodes had prepared tea sandwiches for the group, and when she and Rae emerged carrying trays of food, Nic had to coerce the children from their play. They ate hungrily, though, and, when they'd finished, ran straight back to the play set. An hour later, when Rae told them they'd have to leave, only the knowledge that they'd be meeting their mom made the separation from the sliding board tolerable.

They took Nic's SUV, and everyone was unusually quiet during the drive to Lake Wallenpaupack. Nic looked over to see Nan snoozing in the passenger seat, and in her rearview mirror she saw both kids staring out their windows. Rae was busy checking emails on her smartphone, leaving Nic alone with her thoughts.

Meeting Rae's parents had been a delight, and Nic had been made to feel welcome. Rae didn't say or do anything to indicate to her family that they were a couple, but she guessed that the information must have already been passed along, for they treated her with a reverence that was truly flattering. Their love for Rae was evident and Nic felt it spilling over to her, as if by mere association she must be worthy of all their kindnesses. It felt good. Rae felt so good.

Their night of romance had opened previously locked doors within their hearts. That connection had triggered an explosion that knocked down walls, and suddenly they were standing with nothing between them and with a decision to make about the direction their lives would take. They'd chosen love, and although it was a foreign concept for Nic and a scary one for Rae, they recognized something good in each other and in what they became when they were together. They had details to work out, for sure, but they'd be able to overcome whatever they faced.

Having Rae's love made the fear of the next hours easier for Nic. It was time to meet Katie, to come face-to-face with the only adult on the planet she knew who was her flesh and blood. It was time to examine herself, and the life she'd lived, and take credit where it was due, and give some back as well. It was time to accept the blame for her mistakes. Katie had started out with the same raw potential, and Nic couldn't help but feeling that Katie had done so much more with it than she had.

There was another thought plaguing her as well. Money. She had plenty of it, but what she'd learned about Katie suggested she didn't. Jet had mentioned a trust fund during one of their talks, but she'd also mentioned other details that suggested that her sister didn't enjoy the same privileges she had. And she bought clothes at Target, of all places. How would Nic respond if her sister asked her for money? She knew she'd do just about anything for Chloe and Andre, but she feared being put into that position. It was the main reason she'd never contacted her birth mother.

Scenarios flashed through her mind as she imagined how this would go, with feelings ranging from happy to sad to angry to curious. It would take all her strength to meet Katie, and much work to build a relationship with someone who was seemingly so different from her. But she'd try anyway. She'd always wanted a sister.

"Hey, big news," Rae said from the backseat.

"What's that?"

"I have an email from one of my colleagues about a break in the narcotics case. I have to call to get the details."

"How's your pain?" Jet asked Katie, removing her hand from the steering wheel to stroke Katie's knee.

Katie had turned off the morphine pump as soon as she understood what it was and had adamantly refused the pills offered to help ease her pain. Pain was tolerable, no matter how bad it was. Addiction was not.

Grinding her teeth, she sucked in air through closed lips. She'd underestimated what the drive to the mountains would do to her. The Jeep's front seat was fully reclined, and her body was cushioned with pillows and blankets, but she still felt every pothole the car hit. All the Motrin in the world wouldn't ease this torture. But once they settled in, Katie knew the lake house would be the best place for her to recover. She knew they needed to get out of the city, at least until the police apprehended Simon. He'd clearly painted a bull's-eye on her back, and the mountains seemed like a safe place to hide out until he was apprehended. It would be good for her recovery, too—breathing in the fresh air and watching her kids running and playing, safe from harm. Jeannie had given Jet two weeks' vacation, and they'd make the most of it.

"It'll be better when we get to the lake," Katie replied. "How much longer?"

"Twenty minutes."

"I'll make it," she said, and she knew she would. She'd been through worse.

"Hang in there."

"When will I get to see my kids? And my sister?" Katie was so excited she thought she'd burst. She'd spent much of the drive dozing and daydreaming about the mysterious twin she'd just discovered and couldn't wait to meet Nic. She was exhausted, though, from the combined effects of pain and surgery, and she'd need to take a nap. Jet wanted to get her settled, buy some groceries, and unpack before she had the kids to deal with.

"They'll be here in a couple of hours. Relax." Another squeeze of the knee followed Jet's gentle admonishment.

"You know what I've been thinking about?"

"Hmm?" Jet asked.

"I've always wanted a sister, and now I have one. It's sort of a miracle, you know? And the fact that I'm adopted means I have a mother out there somewhere, and a father, and maybe even a few more siblings."

"Do you want to find them?"

"Of course."

"Well, it's possible Nic has already made those connections. She's always known she's adopted."

"I'll ask her."

"What else are you going to ask her?"

"A million things. Like her favorite color and her favorite book and her favorite music. If she gags when she eats mushy foods, the way I do. If she chews her nails or smokes. I could go on and on."

"Well, you'll have the chance. You can talk to her today, and since you'll be here recovering most of the summer, I'd imagine you'll have an opportunity to see her again. She's fallen in love with Chloe and Andre."

The mention of their names filled Katie's eyes with tears. She was so fortunate they hadn't been harmed. They still didn't know their father was dead, and that would be a hardship for them, but they'd get through it. They had her, and Jet, and Nan to help them. And now, perhaps, their aunt Nicole.

The memorial service for Billy had been that morning—that was why she'd insisted on being released from the hospital. It was a private affair, with only a few friends and the minister there to pray, but it had been a touching sermon, and Katie hoped that a merciful God would find compassion for Billy's soul. This world hadn't been kind to him; she hoped the next one would be better.

"But they are irresistible," Jet said when Katie didn't respond.

"I hope I'll have the chance to get to know her," Katie said. "It was nice of her to take care of my kids."

Jet laughed. "I can tell you she wasn't eager. The thought of little kids seemed to spook her."

"I can imagine."

"Andre charmed her, though."

Katie smiled. Her son was definitely a ladies' man. "I can't believe my father showed up and tried to get them. He's such a fuck. I'm sort of happy to know I'm not his flesh and blood."

"Nic saved the day in court, that's for sure."

"Something else to thank her for."

Jet turned off the main road and onto a narrow lane that led down toward the water, then pulled her Jeep into the garage of her parents' lake house.

"Thank God," Katie said as she gingerly pulled herself up using the overhead strap. The act exhausted her, so she waited for Jet to help her out of the car. Her energy was tapped out.

With Jet's help, Katie was quickly tucked in to the big bed in the master bedroom on the first floor. Jet was out the door a minute later, off to the grocery store. When the phone rang shortly after that, Katie was sure it was Jet, but the caller ID showed it was a Philadelphia number she didn't recognize. With all that had happened lately, she figured she'd better answer it.

❖

Simon had always considered himself a lucky man, and he wasn't about to contemplate the possibility that his luck might be running out. The series of coincidences, all misfortunate, were just that—random events.

His request for a divorce had gone worse than he could have imagined, with Heather crying and pleading with him until he was forced to tell her the harsh truth—he was in love with someone else. He'd hoped to spare her that indignity, but she'd forced him to say it. Then, after hours of fighting, she'd simply walked away and allowed him to leave. Somehow, he didn't feel good about the way they'd left things. Instead of feeling free, he feared the fury of the proverbial scorned woman.

His instincts had been dead-on. His father-in-law was waiting for him at the office in the morning. Unlike Heather, he didn't plead with Simon but simply met him in the garage and handed him a large box filled with personal effects, all from his office, and told him to get off his property. Simon didn't argue; in fact he wanted nothing more.

There was still the matter of the equipment in the basement. Simon had planned to remove it, but that plan was thwarted. It didn't matter, though. There was nothing wrong with a compounding pharmacy having such machinery, and his father-in-law was so out of touch with the times Simon doubted he'd even understand the significance of his find. If he did, Simon was sure the man would conclude that Happy and Healthy Pharmacies was planning to begin compounding medications. It was a great idea, and if Simon was sticking around, he might have implemented it.

Determined to finish his task, he arrived at the hospital in good spirits. Wearing a tailored suit and loafers, and carrying a briefcase that held a syringe with enough potassium to stop an elephant's heart, he found Katie's room and, before entering, took a deep breath to calm his nerves. He opened the door to find a cleaning lady disinfecting the space. She didn't know if the former inhabitant of the room had died, been transferred, or been discharged. Inquiring about Katie was the last thing he could do. When she was found dead someone might remember he'd been looking for her. Simon was forced to do some clever detective work, but he was successful in the end. He was too smart for the morons who surrounded him.

A secluded corner of the surgical waiting room offered him privacy. "Hello, this is the pharmacist," he said to the woman who answered the phone. "I have medication for Katie Finan, but she isn't in her room."

"She was discharged," the nurse informed him.

Thinking quickly, Simon showed some of the cunning that made him such a success in the drug business. "Yes, I know. She dropped off the prescriptions, but the number we have on file for her has been disconnected. Is there any chance you have one for her?"

The very helpful women who'd answered his call quickly read to him the ten digits that comprised Katie's cell-phone number. When he disconnected the call, he immediately dialed them.

Using the voice of Marc Simonson, he knew Katie would never recognize him. "This is Ted from the surgery team. I'm looking for Katie Finan," he said when she answered.

"This is she," Katie replied.

Simon thought she sounded tired. Good. She'd put up less of a fight when he finally put that needle in her arm. "How are you feeling?" he asked.

"Tired," she admitted.

"Well, you did rush out of here somewhat unexpectedly," he gently chastised her.

"Yes, I did. But I needed to get to a funeral."

Ah, that explained it. If he hadn't been so preoccupied with the police and Heather and his father-in-law, he might have attended the funeral himself. And it would all be over now. Instead…it was too frustrating to think about. But it was good that he was going out of business, getting out of town. So much was getting past him lately he'd be lucky to stay alive on the streets if he stayed. He remembered the purpose of his call.

"Katie, the reason I'm calling is we forgot to schedule the nurse to come out and check on you."

"Oh, that won't be necessary. I'm staying with my friend, and she's a nurse. She can check me."

Simon frowned and slapped his hand against his forehead in frustration. Remain calm, he told himself. You can't lose her now. You may not have another opportunity. He looked around the drab waiting room, the sparse furnishings worn and the magazines dated, the walls in need of paint and a light bulb in need of changing, and thought about the Caribbean. In a few days, he and Angelica would be there, in the warm sunshine, in a brightly painted, modern, elegant suite befitting them. He was inspired.

"Can I say anything to change your mind? The doctors prefer to have someone impartial evaluate you. Family members and friends are often overly concerned about trivial things, or not concerned enough about real problems. We've found more complications in patients who are followed by family members."

"Is there a charge for this? Does my insurance cover it?"

"Yes and yes. No charges to you."

"Okay, I suppose there's no harm in getting checked."

Simon fought the urge to leap for joy. Instead, he brought his pen to the paper. "If you could please tell me the address where you're staying, I'll make all the arrangements."

Thirty minutes later, Simon picked up Angelica, a few suitcases filled with essentials, and eight million dollars. He programmed the address Katie had given him into the Lexus's GPS and headed for the mountains.

# CHAPTER THIRTY-ONE
# IDENTICAL

Nic followed the instructions given by the robotic voice on her GPS, exiting Interstate 84 at Lake Wallenpaupack, and only then did she begin to feel panic setting in. Her destination was just a few miles ahead. Her final destination, though, was so much farther than the address on the computer in her car. She wished she knew where the roads were leading, but she just didn't. She was scared.

Taking Katie's children had been the right and decent thing to do. It had always been a temporary remedy, though, and Nic had never felt any sense of permanence about it. Eventually, Katie would recover from her wounds and resume caring for her children. She'd gone into this knowing the outcome, thinking she could and would walk away when her duty was done. She had no obligation to have a relationship with them, and no one would judge her if she didn't.

She hadn't anticipated the impact they'd had on her life, though, and how in such a short time she would come to love them so much. It was now crucial that she meet the woman she'd hadn't intended to meet, for Katie was the key to Nic's relationship with Chloe and Andre. And she feared Katie—the judgments Katie could and would make about her, from her hairstyle to her manners to her career choice. What if Katie didn't like her? The thought was devastating.

"Left turn ahead," the GPS voice instructed, but Nic couldn't see any place to turn. To the left she saw only trees and, as had been the case for the past mile, the glint of sunshine reflecting off the lake in those odd places with a break in the thick spring foliage. And then she saw it, a gravel road squeezed in between a pair of towering evergreens, and turned sharply before the chance escaped her.

The road was in need of repair, and the combination of abrupt deceleration and uneven terrain awoke Nan from the nap she'd been enjoying, and also captured the attention of her backseat passengers.

"Are we there?" Andre asked. "I can't wait to see Mommy."

"I think we're here," Nic answered, although the lack of clear signage allowed for some doubt. Then she saw a red Jeep and an extraordinarily tall woman unloading packages from its hatch, and she knew she'd found the right place. "Yep, there's Jet. We're here."

"Jet," Chloe exclaimed, forgetting that the windows were still up.

Jet heard their car, though, and looked up, a smile on her face when she recognized them. Dropping her packages, she took a few steps toward the car and opened the passenger door behind Nic before the car was even fully stopped. Chloe jumped into her arms, and Andre ran around the car to join her. Nic opened her door, intending to walk around and help Nan, but the sight of the woman on the porch stopped her cold.

Katie's eyes were on her children, the smile across her face almost hiding the strain of the past week. She was pale, and her hair, though wavy like Nic's, hung limply over her shoulders. Her right hand held the porch rail for support, and the way her body was leaning into it told Nic she needed all the help it provided. Her peripheral vision must have caught Nic's movement, and her eyes shifted, capturing Nic where she stood, paralyzed. Katie held her gaze. There was none of the appraisal Nic had anticipated, no judgment in her eyes, just a reverence that surprised and touched Nic. Then a slow smile spread across the corners of Katie's face, tightening the hold she had on Nic and pulling her closer.

Nic could hear the commotion around her, but it blurred to insignificance as she slowly covered the dozen feet separating them. When she reached the bottom porch step, Katie began to laugh. "Is this the twilight zone, or what?"

Nic nodded, laughing as well. "That about sums it up." She bridged the gap between them, mounting half the stairs that separated them without ever averting her eyes. "I'm Nicole Coussart," she said, offering her hand.

Katie wouldn't accept it. "Don't make me move, Nicole. It hurts too much."

And so Nic climbed those last two stairs, and when they were eye to eye, like lovers contemplating their first kiss, Katie removed the hand that held her steady and reached toward Nic, not to shake her hand but to embrace her.

Nic looked down for a moment at the arm resting on her shoulders. It seemed as foreign as a third arm sprouting from her own body, an alien from the twilight zone Katie had referenced. But then her eyes rose and Katie was suddenly as familiar as a glance in the mirror. The pink hair of the mug shot had grown out and was now the same dark color of Nicole's. The eyes were a cloudy green, and deep, holding a million secrets. The lips were full and sensual, and Nic didn't wonder if Katie used them to kiss boys or girls, for she already knew about Jet and only wondered at how beautiful her sister looked at that moment—weakened, recovering from near-mortal wounds, worried about the man who'd shot her, lonely for the company of her children—yet with a calm about her that Nic could only envy.

Her arms moved to pull Katie gently closer, for she wanted some of that peace. She'd found it in the last week, in the arms of Rae and Chloe and Andre, and she no longer feared what her sister might think of her or want from her. In a startling moment of clarity she realized Katie had everything that Nic could ever want.

The sobbing was spontaneous and mutual, and in spite of her wounds, Katie fell into Nic, and Nic resisted the urge to pull her closer, fearing the injury she might cause. No words came and none were needed—both understood the other's isolation and frustration, a lifetime of need satisfied with this one gesture of affection. A flashback came to Nic's mind, of her mother's suggestion that she might have remembered on some unrecognized plane the existence of this woman who was her mirror image, and Nic knew her mother had been right. She'd always known about Katie, and she'd spent the past thirty years mourning her loss.

Neither could have pulled back at that moment except if guided by some external force, and it arrived in the shape of Andre.

"Why are you two crying?" he asked as he wrapped himself around their legs. Another flashback came to Nic then, of the moment in the courthouse when she'd first met him. Of when she fell in love with him and her life changed forever.

"Allergies," Katie replied, her tone sedate.

"Did you take your medicine, Mom?" he asked, hands on hips, expression stern.

"I'll have to do that."

"Mom, can you make AJ some meatball pizza? She never had it. And she bought me a scooter."

Nic frowned, hoping no parental admonishment about spoiling her child or endangering life or limb would be forthcoming. Instead, Katie's face lit up, sharing the obvious joy her son felt about his new toy. "Did you get a helmet, too?"

He beamed. "Monsters, Inc."

"Which monster?" Katie asked.

"Mike. I'll show you." He scampered off the porch to Nic's BMW, where everyone had gathered to empty the car. Even Nan was carrying something.

"I guess I should help," Nic said, taking the opportunity to escape for a moment, needing to regroup, and walked toward the car as Andre ran in the other direction, carrying the green bicycle helmet with the large eyeball on the front. After bikes and such were deposited in the garage, they made their way into the house, and Nic helped Chloe and Andre unpack their things in the upstairs bedroom, while Rae helped Jet with the food and Nan went to work on a pitcher of lemonade.

When the kids were changed into bathing suits, Nic followed them down the stairs and onto the porch, where Katie and Nan were catching up. She stopped but continued to watch her niece and nephew, who'd run through the yard to the water's edge before she could tell them to stop.

Katie's conversational voice was soft, and Nic suspected it was irritated by the tube that had been forced into her lungs and by the weakness she must be feeling. But it rose to a booming level as she reminded both kids about life vests. "You need eyes in the back of your head," Katie told Nan and Nic.

"I don't know about that. Maybe just younger eyes than I have,"

Nan said. "I'll go watch them, Katie, but if one of them falls in, you'll be rescuing me, too."

"They'll be fine, Nan. You stay here and rest."

"No, no. I'll go down there. You and your sister have some catchin' up to do."

The quiet was peaceful as they watched Nan make her way to the edge of the lake. "Do you like the water?" Nic finally asked, breaking the silence.

Katie's face lit up. "Oh, yes. My family vacationed every year at the Jersey shore, and I never got out of the water. At home, my best friend had a pool, and we swam every day. How about you?"

"Yeah, me, too. I practically lived at the lake in the summer. My mom's mom lived there, and I spent my summers with her."

"You got good parents in the raffle?"

"Great, actually. How about you?" Nic had met the father—well, seen him anyway, and couldn't help but think Katie had drawn the short straw.

"My mom was great. My dad…he wasn't too bad, until she died. I think he must have needed her strength, and without her, he just sort of crumbled."

"That's really sad."

Katie shrugged.

"Jeannie says you didn't know."

"No. This has been quite a shock." After a moment of silence, Katie continued. "But in a good way. I went from being an orphan to possibly still having parents and having a twin."

"So you want to contact them? Our DNA donors?"

Katie chuckled at Nic's choice of words. "You've never tried?"

Nic looked at her sister—beautiful, sweet, articulate, smart—and she knew their parents had the raw potential to be amazing people. What had they done with those gifts, though? What circumstances in life had caused them to make bad choices and screw things up? Or had they been fortunate and done well? Nothing would have been surprised Nic at this point. Finding out her mother was a Nobel Prize winner would be no more surprising than learning their father was in prison. It was a rabbit hole, and she wasn't even a little bit curious.

"No. I think I'll leave that up to you. If you give them the thumbs-up, then…maybe."

Katie nodded. "Well, no matter what happens with that, I'm glad I found you. I want to know everything about you."

"Everything?"

"Everything. Start with your first memory and end with getting arrested for looking like me." There was a twinkle in Katie's eye, excitement shining through all the turmoil.

Nic leaned back and looked out at the lake, seeing her own young self at a different lake as she watched Chloe and Andre splashing in the water. That was just one of the memories that came to mind as she searched the colorful files of her brain. Which was the first? She had so many good ones, great ones, in fact. "I suppose my first memory is at the lake. I was about four, and my dad was teaching me to swim. I'd jump off the dock into his arms, and then he'd hold me while I swam back to shore."

"That's a good memory."

"What's yours?" Nic asked.

"Praying. My mom and I prayed a lot. My cat was lost, and I remember praying with my mom that he'd come home."

"Did he?"

Katie shook her head. "No."

"I'm sorry."

Katie smiled. "It's okay. We can't always get what we want."

Nic thought about how true that statement was. "Do you still pray?" Nic asked, knowing how far from spiritual her own feelings ran.

Their eyes met, and the excitement Nic saw in Katie's startled her. "Oh, yes. How else could I have survived?"

Nic wanted to ask more, to understand the kind of unquestioning faith that could pull Katie through so much torment. In time she would. For the moment she followed Katie's gaze to the lake, where her children were making memories of their own. Her expression revealed a love and contentment that, before recently, Nic had only dreamed of. Katie had certainly managed to make the most of that short straw.

Nic watched them for a moment and felt such joy she thought she might cry. Again. What in the world had become of the tough woman she'd been a week ago? She swallowed, knowing that Chloe and Andre were no longer going to be a part of her life, at least not on an everyday basis. Could she maintain the happiness they'd brought to her life, or would she go back to her lonely existence?

Just then, Rae and Jet emerged from the house, wearing bathing suits and carrying a small cooler and a key on a floating key chain. "We're going skiing," Jet announced.

Nic looked at Rae, so handsomely beautiful, so fit and healthy and happy, and thought that perhaps she could.

# Chapter Thirty-two
# The Powers of Observation

What a great day," Nic said as Rae hopped into the front seat beside her. Her sister had been a quite pleasant surprise—feisty and witty and intelligent, even while in obvious pain. The time they'd spent talking was amazing, their connection immediate and strong, and Nic knew she'd found a friend.

The dinner had been super, and Nic was quite pleased to have found another friend—Jet—who could cook. She'd be happy to supply the food and provide the cleanup, as long as someone else did the cooking, and that arrangement seemed to work well for Jet. The steaks were succulent, and the veggies grilled to crispy perfection.

Andre and Chloe continued to delight, and she'd had a great afternoon chasing them off the dock and helping with those first painful efforts to hold their bodies erect while their feet were anchored to water skis.

Another unexpected surprise of the afternoon and evening was the discovery that Jet and Rae got along famously. Nic could imagine going out on double dates and traveling with them, with the kids along, too. Before they even finished the cleanup from dinner, Katie had inquired about Nic and Rae's next visit, and plans were made. The day, and its ending, were perfect.

"It was a great day," Rae said. "And now that we don't have any kids, we can make it a great night, too."

"Hmm, I like that idea," Nic said as she ran her hand slowly down Rae's arm until it rested on her hand and then held it.

"Can you control yourself until we get to your place? Or should we find a room? I saw a vacancy sign at the motel up the road."

"It'll be hard, but I think I can wait."

Her tone was flat and sarcastic, and Rae laughed. "Would you mind if I check my voice mail? I have quite a few of them."

"Anything important?" Nic knew Rae had the feature that allowed her to see a list of voice mails so she could prioritize her responses, and she knew her dad was always on her mind.

"My friend Art called. He's with the DEA, too. I should check that one."

"Be my guest."

"Wow," she said as she listened. When she finished, she hung up. "He says they've identified the source of the counterfeit narcotics. The owner of Happy and Healthy Pharmacy turned in his son-in-law, and they found a lab and a bunch of pills. Would you mind if I call him back?"

"No, not at all. If it's not confidential, put it on the Bluetooth so I can hear, too."

In seconds Rae had her phone connected, and she dialed her friend's number. After making sure nothing confidential was to be discussed, Rae asked Art for the story. Mr. Green, the founder of the pharmacy, became suspicious because his son-in-law had asked his daughter for a divorce and had turned over all of his assets to her. Green figured no one was that nice—he had to have money hidden somewhere, so he began searching the office. He found a lab with pill-manufacturing equipment in the basement of his office and became suspicious because the place had been completely wiped down. He searched the Dumpster behind the building and found thousands of tablets in the trash. Fortunately, the garbage hadn't been collected. The police were searching for the son-in-law, Marc Simonson. He was last seen earlier that morning driving a white Lexus SUV.

"Art," Rae asked. "Is this guy connected to the recent murders? Is he dangerous?"

"Well, if he's been distributing these oxys on the street—not just at the pharmacy—he might have known the people who were shot. And if he thinks one of them can finger him, he'd have a reason to get violent. There's enough evidence already to send him to jail for a long time. Add in murder, though—and he's going to get very desperate to avoid the law. He's probably got a fortune stashed away somewhere, and if he's dreaming of retiring to the islands, he might get angry if someone interferes with his plans."

"Stop the car, Nic," Rae ordered her.

"What?" both Nic and Art asked.

"A white Lexus SUV was parked in the driveway of the house next to Jet's."

❖

They'd arrived at the lake in the mid-afternoon and immediately found the house where Katie was staying. Simon considered multiple options to get to her, including renting a boat, but after several passes by the house, he'd determined that the property next door was vacant and he'd use that fact to his advantage. He and Angelica had enjoyed a lovely dinner at a restaurant overlooking the water and afterward still had all but a hundred dollars of the eight million he had on hand.

As darkness descended upon the lake, he pulled the Lexus into the driveway next door and left Angelica to guard the car. It wouldn't do to have the homeowners calling the police if they turned up unexpectedly. Simon circled the house, grateful no dogs were milling about, and even climbed into a tree house to have a better look. He watched as Katie hugged the women sitting on the back porch and then walked through sliding-glass doors into what had to be a bedroom. The light in the room was briefly illuminated before the room once again went dark. Not long after, two of the three women left, walking directly under him on the sidewalk before driving away in an SUV. The porch light went off, and then an upstairs light went on and off again.

Simon weighed his options. Katie was clearly in that room off the deck, alone, and even though the tall woman—the one who'd been with Katie at the lawyer's office—was still wandering around the house, what were the odds she'd check on Katie? Katie was recovering from surgery; she needed her rest. He could wait until the house was dark, but that could be hours. Or he could sneak into that room now, while the tall woman was occupied, and get this over with.

Silently, he descended the rungs that had been nailed into the tree, walked across the yard, and climbed the steps to the back porch. The screen door didn't squeak as he opened it. Neither did the sliding-glass door to Katie's room.

When his eyes adjusted to the darkness, Simon found a lamp and turned the switch. A halo of light spread across one corner of the room; the rest was still in shadow. There, though, on the bed, he saw all he needed to see. Katie was asleep, her eyes closed and hair fanning out across the pillow. He watched her carefully, but she showed no sign that the light had disturbed her.

Darkness would have been better, but he couldn't do what he needed to without some light. He readied the syringe that had been taped to his chest and then placed one hand over Katie's mouth and his gun at her temple. Her eyes flew open at the contact and she started to move beside him. Fear filled her eyes as they met his, and he couldn't help laughing. Then he whispered to her.

"Don't move, or I'll shoot."

When she settled, he spoke again. "It's over, now, Katie. I'm going to inject you with potassium—it'll be painless. Your heart will stop, and the coroner will say you died of a blood clot from your surgery. I'll leave your kids alone. But if you fight me—he tapped the gun against her forehead for effect—I'll kill them, too. Nod if you understand."

Katie carefully nodded.

"Pull down your shorts," he ordered her, and when he saw the startled look on her face, he frowned. "Don't flatter yourself. I need the femoral vein."

Carefully, as tears flowed down her cheeks, she did as instructed.

"Surely there are thousands of white Lexus SUVs," Nic said, but she turned the car around, doubt and fear causing her voice to crack.

"Art, call the police and send them to this address." She read Jet's address from the GPS. "I'm going to call Katie Finan and warn her. Someone's already tried to kill her twice, and I'm not taking any chances."

"Let me know what happens. I'll call the locals for you."

"Rae, you don't really think—"

"Nic, I'd never have thought anything about it if I hadn't talked to Art. But that car wasn't there when we arrived today, and the house was dark all night. So why is a car in the driveway if no one's in the house?"

She'd already dialed Jet's number and was relieved when she answered. "I don't want to alarm you, but we're coming back, and I just sent the police over. It may be nothing, but I have a bad feeling. Do you know how to use those guns in the cabinet?"

"I sure do. Would you mind telling me why?" Jet asked as she unlocked the gun cabinet and began loading bullets into the Remington revolver she'd learned to shoot as a teenager. She fought to keep her hands from trembling and nearly dropped several of the bullets. Though she'd fired the weapon hundreds of times, it was always at still targets. Never at anything that might shoot back. And never with so much at stake.

"Wow," Jet said after Rae relayed what she'd learned from her friend. "It's probably coincidence, right?"

"Probably, but let's not take any chances."

"How far away are you?"

"Two minutes."

"Maybe I should check on Katie," she said, suddenly anxious for her company.

"Good idea. Wait in her room with her, so the two of you are together."

Jet held the phone with her chin, the gun in her right hand while she turned the doorknob with her left. The sight before her caused her to jump back, and the phone hit the floor.

The man on top of Katie flinched, too, causing him to drop the syringe he'd held in his right hand. The gun in his left hand was pointed at Katie's temple. Jet had never seen his picture before, but she knew this had to be Simon Simms. He seemed smaller than Jet imagined him, and wearing a golf shirt, linen pants, loafers, and glasses, he looked more like a college professor than a drug-dealing killer.

"Drop your gun, lady, or I'm going to put a bullet in Katie's brain."

"You're going to do it anyway, so why should I drop my gun? Then you'll shoot me, too."

He began easing off the bed, still holding the gun. "I'm going to back out of here, with Katie, and you're going to stay where you are," he said.

"No, Simon, you're not taking her anywhere," Jet said, taking a step closer, angry. This man had caused so much harm to Katie already, there was no way she could allow him the opportunity for any more. Jet was a decent shot; maybe she should try taking him down. She knew her first words to him were true—he was here to kill Katie. What did Jet have to lose?

"Come on, Katie. You don't want me to hurt your kids, do you?" Simon spoke to Katie but his eyes didn't leave Jets.

He crouched beside the bed, out of her view, leaving only his head and shoulders as a potential target. Jet kept her gun trained on him, even as his was pointed at Katie.

"Jet, back off! I'll go with him." Katie looked at her with pleading eyes and began to ease from the bed. It was a slow process.

"C'mon, Katie. Don't fuck with me. Let's go."

"I'm trying," she cried, and gave herself another push. It took another minute, but as soon as she was upright, Simon pulled her close to him, using her as a shield, and began pulling her backward toward the door."

"Katie, he's going to kill you," Jet said.

"I don't care! Just take care of Chloe and Andre."

Simon pulled Katie with him as he took a tentative step back, his eyes trained on Jet as he held his gun fast at Katie's temple. Jet's chance was slipping away. Another few steps, and he'd be out the door, and Katie would be dead. She had to act quickly!

Before she had the chance for further debate, the curtain behind Simon moved. Jet couldn't keep her eyes from darting in that direction, and Simon must have felt something, too, because he jerked his head in perfect time to meet the butt of Rae's gun.

Jet's breath caught for a moment as she saw him collapse, pulling Katie down, too, and only when they hit the floor with a thud and groan and no hint of gunfire did she allow herself to breathe again. And then another sound filled the air, a siren heralding the arrival of the lake police, and as she cradled Katie in her arms, she could finally, honestly tell her it was over.

# Epilogue
# One Year Later

At precisely six a.m., the radio on Rae's nightstand came on, awakening her. Instead of turning it off, though, she stretched and listened to the news. She liked to know what was happening in the world before she went out to face it.

A moment later, the warmth of Nic's hand on her abdomen turned her attention from the announcer's voice, and she rolled over to face her lover. "Good morning," she said.

Nic slid closer, into Rae's arms, and sleepily kissed the flesh at her collarbone, causing Rae to quiver. It had been a year since they met, and Nic's hands and lips still held the power to elicit an instantaneous response from Rae. More amazing, they managed to have a good relationship, despite their different views on many things and their potentially fatal propensity to express them.

"TGIF," Nic said.

"Yes, TGIF. TGIFBV."

Nic pulled Rae closer and thought about the letters. This was one of the many challenges Rae presented to her, something as simple as an acronym that would give her brain fits until she finally solved it. They didn't agree on everything, and they never would, but they respected each other enough not to hit below the belt when they disagreed and were sensible enough to back off when it was appropriate.

Nic had never thought she'd want to share her life with someone; the sacrifice of her space and time was never easy. Yet with Rae, she didn't find it a sacrifice at all. She longed to see her at the end of each day, smiled at the sight of her toothbrush beside hers in the bathroom and her shoes beside hers in the closet. This, she'd realized a while back, was love.

While Nic's conscious mind had been wandering, her subconscious had been processing, and suddenly the answer came to her. "That was easy."

"What?"

"Thank God it's Friday before Vacation."

Rae tickled her. "You're too smart for me."

"No, just the right amount of smart, I think. So how's your day look? Will you be home at a decent hour?" Nic asked.

"Unless something disastrous happens, we'll be on the road on time." Rae's office was as busy as ever. She'd spent months putting together a prosecution for Marc Simonson for illegally manufacturing and distributing controlled substances. They never found any money, and the white Lexus that had alerted her to his presence at the lake disappeared, but they had enough evidence to convict if the case went to trial. If. Simonson had already been convicted of murdering Billy Wallace and two garage attendants, and unless those cases were overthrown on appeal, she didn't think the drug charges would be attested in court. Why waste taxpayer money to convict a man on death row for another crime?

It had been a great outcome, and Rae was happy to put the Simonson case behind her, but there was always a new fire to extinguish, and with the drug problems facing the country, they were usually infernos.

"Well, that'll make about a million cars heading to the mountains for the weekend." Nic hated the traffic in the city, and on this Friday before the July Fourth holiday it would stretch all the way to the Pocono exit of the PA Turnpike, some eighty miles of speeding, swerving cars challenging death at every curve of the road.

"Ah, but we'll be staying for the week." Rae sounded pleased by the thought.

Nic liked the idea, too. Since she'd moved back to Philly nine months earlier, she hadn't made it home as often as she'd have liked. She and Rae made the two-hour trip at least once a month, but by the time they unpacked and cleaned up the house, it seemed it was time to turn around and head back to Philly. Nic always left with a heavy heart, disappointed that she couldn't spend more time with her parents or relaxing at the lake before coming back to the chaos of every day life and the apartment they now shared.

They'd put Rae's apartment on the market. After six months of living next to each other, during which time they spent very little time apart, they'd decided to move in together. Nic's place was the logical choice, since it was roomier. Nic secretly hoped to sell her place as well and move to the Northeast, where she could be closer to her sister.

Getting to know Katie over the past twelve months had been one of the greatest experiences of Nic's life. It amazed her to see the power of their common thread of DNA. Of course, they looked alike. The behaviors they shared were startling, though—from compulsive habits like nail biting and their common addiction to nicotine to their preference for classical music and their love of art. That they were both amateur artists who paid the bills with their careers in the medical field was too improbable to be a coincidence.

Every day, Nic seemed to discover something else about Katie that fascinated her, and every night she said a prayer of thanks—to all the gods—for the gift of her sister. They were friends, too, not just linked by some familial obligation, and Katie made Nic smile and laugh and think. She wasn't afraid to give Nic a piece of her mind, and that was one of the things she liked most about Katie. A genetic factor had definitely determined this feisty component of her personality.

Chloe and Andre were the big bonus in this lottery she'd won. They were full of energy and optimism and love, and being in their company was wonderfully exhausting. She and Rae had been keeping them overnight on Fridays, to give Jet and Katie a date night. And Nic saw them every Tuesday, because she was off from work. With Katie and Jet both working, and Nan getting too blind to use the stove, Nic spent her Tuesday mornings preparing dinner for the Four Fs (Finan, Finan, Finan, and Fox) and Nan, who'd moved with them when they bought a house. Nic cooked very little but could make basic meals like lasagna and pot roast, which she delivered to the Four Fs once a week. She'd spend an hour playing cards with Nan before the kids arrived home from school, and then she'd help them with their homework before she headed home to feed Rae her dinner. It was nauseatingly domestic, and wonderful.

Nic showered and read the paper and kissed Rae before heading out the door to work. Friday was one of her three days at the clinic, Jeannie worked the other two, and they rotated Mondays, so every other week they could have a three-day weekend. The arrangement worked perfectly for them. Jeannie had time with Sandy, and Nic could cover for her so she could travel, but she still had control and the peace of mind of knowing the clinic was in good hands.

In the end leaving the ER had been easy. Since Jeannie's clinic offered walk-in services, Nic still had some excitement in her practice. At least once a day she had to suture a wound or drain an abscess, and about once a week she saw someone truly sick, with heart disease or uncontrolled diabetes, and put her skills to use. It wasn't as exciting as the ER, but the trade-off was a good one—she didn't have to work overnight, she didn't have to work weekends, and she didn't have to work holidays. She could have gotten a job in a Philly ER if things hadn't worked out at the clinic, but they were turning out just fine, and everyone was happy.

It was only a fifteen-minute ride to work, and Nic parked right behind the building and let herself in the back door. She started at seven, taking the early patients with a skeleton staff of one nurse and a receptionist. Later the residents and other doctors would arrive, and the place would be hopping.

"Hey, Jet," Nic said.

"Morning, Nic."

"Anyone here yet?" Although their scheduled appointments didn't begin until nine, they left the first two hours of the morning open for walk-ins and encouraged their patients to use that time for any minor emergencies. It kept them out of the ER and helped provide a continuity of care.

"Mr. Danbury is in the treatment room."

Nic turned and frowned. "Again? Wasn't he just here like a week ago?"

"Yep."

"Argh," Nic replied.

She deposited her lunch bag in the kitchen and her purse in her locker, donned her lab coat, and made her way to the treatment room. She could smell Mr. Danbury's foul body odor even in the hallway.

He was curled up on the stretcher in the darkness, quietly awaiting her arrival.

Nic didn't turn on the light. "Good morning, Mr. Danbury," she said as she found a seat in the chair beside the stretcher. "What's going on today?"

"It's another sick headache."

"Did you try your medicine at home?"

"Yes, I did. It don't seem to help much."

Nic inquired about recent head trauma and fever, but nothing was unusual about his headache other than it was a bad one.

She rose to examine him. "You smell awful," she teased him.

"Sorry about that. I lost my water."

He smelled like he'd lost his water, that was for sure, but when he continued Nic realized she'd misunderstood his words. "I lost my electric, too. Fell behind on the payments."

"So you have no water at your house, and no electricity?"

"That's right."

"How are you eating?"

"My neighbors have been helping me."

Nic completed her exam and told him that all seemed well. "I'm going to have the nurse start an IV and give you some medicine for your headache."

"I appreciate that, Doctor."

Nic found Jet in the hallway. "Can you please start an IV and give Mr. Danbury a liter of saline? And thirty of Toradol and four of Zofran."

"Sure."

"Oh, and Jet? Call the social worker. The man is diabetic and had a bypass. I'm sure those are good enough reasons to have his power and water turned back on."

Jet smiled at her. "I'll take care of it."

Nic handed her the chart and walked back down the hall to the staff kitchen. She opened her lunch box, which was packed with food, and removed a few items. When she was done, she headed down the hall to Mr. Danbury's room.

"I brought you some breakfast. When you have migraines, it's important not to skip meals. That goes for your diabetes, too. Your sugar can drop too low and you can die. Do you understand what I'm saying?"

"Don't skip meals."

"Exactly."

Nic opened the bottle of organic, sugar-free orange juice and handed it to him, then peeled a banana. She placed both on a paper hand towel, then removed the wrap from a blueberry muffin and added that to his makeshift plate.

"Doctor, could you find me a cup of coffee in this office?"

Nic tilted her head slightly and scowled. "Don't push your luck, Mr. Danbury."

Then he smiled, a wide grin that revealed mostly open space in the places that God had intended for teeth.

Nic smiled back, a genuine smile filled with warmth and affection. "Do you want cream and sugar?" she asked.

# About the Author

Jaime Maddox grew up on the banks of the Susquehanna River in northeastern Pennsylvania. As the baby in a family of many children, she was part adored and part ignored, forcing her to find creative ways to fill her time. Her childhood was idyllic, spent hiking, rafting, biking, climbing, and otherwise skinning knees and knuckles. Reading and writing became passions. Although she left home for a brief stint in the big cities of Philadelphia and Newark, as soon as she acquired the required paperwork—a medical degree and residency certificate—she came running back.

She fills her hours with a bustling medical practice, two precocious sons, a disobedient dog, and an extraordinary woman who helps her to keep it all together. In her abundant spare time, she reads, writes, twists her body into punishing yoga poses, and whacks golf balls deep into forests. She detests airplanes, snakes, and people who aren't nice. Her loves are the foods of the world, Broadway musicals, traveling, sandy beaches, massages and pedicures, and the Philadelphia Phillies.

On the bucket list: Publishing a novel, publishing a children's book, recording a song, creating a board game, obtaining a patent, exploring Alaska.

# Books Available From Bold Strokes Books

**Rest Home Runaways** by Clifford Henderson. Baby boomer Morgan Ronzio's troubled marriage is the least of her worries when she gets the call that her addled, eighty-six-year-old, half-blind dad has escaped the rest home. (978-1-62639-169-7)

**Charm City** by Mason Dixon. Raq Overstreet's loyalty to her drug kingpin boss is put to the test when she begins to fall for Bathsheba Morris, the undercover cop assigned to bring him down. (978-1-62639-198-7)

**Edge of Awareness** by C.A. Popovich. When Marija, a woman in the middle of her third divorce, meets Dana, an out lesbian, awareness of her feelings bring up reservations about the teachings of her church. (978-1-62639-188-8)

**Taken by Storm** by Kim Baldwin. Lives depend on two women when a train derails high in the remote Alps, but an unforgiving mountain, avalanches, crevasses, and other perils stand between them and safety. (978-1-62639-189-5)

**The Common Thread** by Jaime Maddox. Dr. Nicole Coussart's life is falling apart, but fortunately, DEA Attorney Rae Rhodes is there to pick up the pieces and help Nic put them back together. (978-1-62639-190-1)

**Jolt** by Kris Bryant. Mystery writer Bethany Lange wasn't prepared for the twisting emotions that left her breathless the moment she laid eyes on folk singer sensation Ali Hart. (978-1-62639-191-8)

**Searching For Forever** by Emily Smith. Dr. Natalie Jenner's life has always been about saving others, until young paramedic Charlie Thompson comes along and shows her maybe she's the one who needs saving. (978-1-62639-186-4)

**Blue Water Dreams** by Dena Hankins. Lania Marchiol keeps her wary sailor's gaze trained on the horizon until Oly Rassmussen, a wickedly handsome trans man, sends her trusty compass spinning off course. (978-1-62639-192-5)

**Let the Lover Be** by Sheree Greer. Kiana Lewis, a functional alcoholic on the verge of destruction, finally faces the demons of her past while finding love and earning redemption in New Orleans. (978-1-62639-077-5)

**Blindsided** by Karis Walsh. Blindsided by love, guide dog trainer Lenae McIntyre and media personality Cara Bradley learn to trust what they see with their hearts. (978-1-62639-078-2)

**About Face** by VK Powell. Forensic artist Macy Sheridan and Detective Leigh Monroe work on a case that has troubled them both for years, but they're hampered by the past and their unlikely yet undeniable attraction. (978-1-62639-079-9)

**Blackstone** by Shea Godfrey. For Darry and Jessa, the chance at a life of freedom is stolen by the arrival of war and an ancient prophecy that just might destroy their love. (978-1-62639-080-5)

**Out of This World** by Maggie Morton. Iris decided to cross an ocean to get over her ex. But instead, she ends up traveling much farther, all the way to another world. Once she's there, only a mysterious, sexy, and magical woman can help her return home. (978-1-62639-083-6)

**Kiss The Girl** by Melissa Brayden. Sleeping with the enemy has never been so complicated. Brooklyn Campbell and Jessica Lennox face off in love and advertising in fast-paced New York City. (978-1-62639-071-3)

**Taking Fire: A First Responders Novel** by Radclyffe. Hunted by extremists and under siege by nature's most virulent weapons, Navy medic Max de Milles and Red Cross worker Rachel Winslow join forces to survive and discover something far more lasting. (978-1-62639-072-0)

**First Tango in Paris** by Shelley Thrasher. When French law student Eva Laroche meets American call girl Brigitte Green in 1970s Paris, they have no idea how their pasts and futures will intersect. (978-1-62639-073-7)

**The War Within** by Yolanda Wallace. Army nurse Meredith Moser went to Vietnam in 1967 looking to help those in need; she didn't expect to meet the love of her life along the way. (978-1-62639-074-4)

**Desire at Dawn** by Fiona Zedde. For Kylie, love had always come armed with sharp teeth and claws. But with the human, Olivia, she bares her vampire heart for the very first time, sharing passion, lust, and a tenderness she'd never dared dreamed of before. (978-1-62639-064-5)

**Visions** by Larkin Rose. Sometimes the mysteries of love reveal themselves when you least expect it. Other times they hide behind a black satin mask. Can Paige unveil her masked stranger this time? (978-1-62639-065-2)

**All In** by Nell Stark. Internet poker champion Annie Navarro loses everything when the Feds shut down online gambling, and she turns to experienced casino host Vesper Blake for advice—but can Nova convince Vesper to take a gamble on romance? (978-1-62639-066-9)

**Vermillion Justice** by Sheri Lewis Wohl. What's a vampire to do when Dracula is no longer just a character in a novel? (978-1-62639-067-6)

**Switchblade** by Carsen Taite. Lines were meant to be crossed. Third in the Luca Bennett Bounty Hunter Series. (978-1-62639-058-4)

**Nightingale** by Andrea Bramhall. Culture, faith, and duty conspire to tear two young lovers apart, yet fate seems to have different plans for them both. (978-1-62639-059-1)

**No Boundaries** by Donna K. Ford. A chance meeting and a nightmare from the past threaten more than Andi Massey's solitude as she and Gwen Palmer struggle to understand the complexity of love without boundaries. (978-1-62639-060-7)

**Timeless** by Rachel Spangler. When Stevie Geller returns to her hometown, will she do things differently the second time around or will she be in such a hurry to leave her past that she misses out on a better future? (978-1-62639-050-8)

**Second to None** by L.T. Marie. Can a physical therapist and a custom motorcycle designer conquer their pasts and build a future with one another? (978-1-62639-051-5)

**Seneca Falls** by Jesse Thoma. Together, two women discover love truly can conquer all evil. (978-1-62639-052-2)